Praise for *Company Town*

"The skill with which Ashby introduces her various SF elements is worthy of the best Heinlein. . . . *Company Town* never falters in its pacing. It's a terrific ride."
—*Locus*

"This is brave, bold, crazy storytelling at the edge and doesn't read like anything else I've seen up or down the pike. I don't even know where she gets these ideas, but I hope she keeps getting them and writing the stories that result."
—Chuck Wendig, *New York Times* bestselling author of *Aftermath*

"A brilliant and chilling look at our post-oil future. I haven't been this hooked by an SF novel for ages."
—Charles Stross, author of the Laundry Files series

"Loved *Company Town,* Madeline Ashby's wonderfully imaginative new sci-fi mystery with a fascinating female protagonist."
—*Feminist Frequency*

"The world is an updated version of Raymond Chandler's, with gray morals and broken characters, and Hwa's internal monologue has just the right balance of introspection and wit. . . . A very solid page-turner."
—*Publishers Weekly*

"A fascinating mix of detective noir and near-future SF with cinematic world-building and a broken, but resilient, unquestionably badass heroine."
—*Booklist*

COMPANY TOWN

MADELINE ASHBY

TOR

A TOM DOHERTY ASSOCIATES BOOK
NEW YORK

COMPANY TOWN

Copyright © 2016 by Madeline Ashby

Edited by Miriam Weinberg

A Tor Book
Published by Tom Doherty Associates
175 Fifth Avenue
New York, NY 10010

www.tor-forge.com

Tor® is a registered trademark of Macmillan Publishing Group, LLC.

The Library of Congress Cataloging-in-Publication Data
is available upon request.

ISBN 978-0-7653-9887-1 (Canadian edition)

Our books may be purchased in bulk for promotional, educational, or business use. Please contact your local bookseller or the Macmillan Corporate and Premium Sales Department at 1-800-221-7945, extension 5442, or by e-mail at MacmillanSpecialMarkets@macmillan.com.

Printed in the United States of America

0 9 8 7 6 5 4 3 2 1

This book is dedicated to Richard Kedward,
the teacher who taught me about the past
and changed my future.

And it is written in memory of the missing
and murdered indigenous women of Canada.
Rest in power.

PART ONE

SEPTEMBER

1

Broken Nose

Hwa wondered if today was the day she would finally get to finish that sorry son of a bitch once and for all. She checked her watch. Eileen was officially late. She pinged. Waited. No answer. The client had paid for another tier of service, one where a bodyguard would keep a discreet distance. That tier was only for clients with trusted status. In Hwa's experience, that trust could be a mistake. If the tower had recognized her face, Belle du Jour would have pinged the client and told him to finish up because she was on her way. But the towers never saw her face. And neither did some of the clients' filters. That was part of her value to the organization. They simply didn't see her coming until it was too late.

She checked the hallway. Just a few stragglers: kids on their way to school, jostling each other at the elevators. No big guys. No roughnecks. No riggers. Nobody who would give her trouble if she was already in the process of making it for Eileen's client. Ideal conditions.

Hwa spoke into her watch: "Belle, my safecall is late; proceeding to contact."

There was a pause. *"Keep us posted! Good luck!"*

Hwa stood up, checked the hall again, and knocked on the door. Inside there was giggling and a muffled, "I *told you* so!" Hwa rolled her eyes. The hallway was almost empty, now.

"It's okay, Mr. Moliter," she said to the door. "Nobody's gonna see you."

The door jerked open so fast he had to have been waiting for her. All these years later, he was still a pallid, fishlike man, with a weird gawping mouth and almost colourless eyes. He was short, and he acted like it. This morning was no exception.

"How *dare* you say my name out here?" he hissed. "What if somebody's parents heard you? What if—" He blinked. She watched the filters fall away from his eyes. He saw the stain. He recognized Hwa. He shut up.

Hwa plastered a smile across her face. "Hi, Mr. Moliter," she said in her cheeriest cute-half-Korean-girl voice. "How's the eye?"

The old scar across his right eyebrow twitched. He swallowed. Then he gathered some dignity by closing his robe and standing a little straighter. "It's fine," he said. "Doesn't bother me at all."

"That's real good to hear. So they reattached the retina and everything, huh?"

Moliter licked his thin, raw lips. The man was dumb as a pike and twice as mean. He watched Hwa with one side of his face as he directed his voice into the apartment. "Eileen! Time to go!"

Eileen was still giggling. She bounced out of the apartment and made an *I'm sorry* face at Hwa. She looked fine: rich red hair in place, eyeliner expertly winged, no bruises, no funny walking, no tears in her stockings. She even squeezed Moliter's hand.

"I had a great time," Eileen said.

"Yeah. Great. Bye."

"The United Sex Workers of Canada thank you for your business, Mr. Moliter."

He slammed the door in her face.

Eileen turned to say something, but Hwa was already talking to her watch. "Belle, my safecall is accounted for. I'm taking her home, now."

"Good job!" the watch said. *"Have a nice day!"*

"Thank you for knocking." Eileen threaded one perfumed arm through Hwa's. "Can we mug up? I'd dies for a real coffee."

"Teachers can't afford the good stuff, eh?"

"I have fucked teachers with *much* nicer coffee. Hell, I've fucked *tutors* with better taste." Eileen squeezed her arm. "Please? Can we stop? There's a good spot on my floor."

"Sure."

Eileen cocked her head to the side and closed her eyes. There was an audible crunch in her neck. "Ugh. I've had that all night."

They hustled into the elevator, and Eileen leaned against the glass. The massive blades of the windmill whirling outside cast her in shadow briefly, and then revealed her again. On and on, dark and light, as the blades of the mill cut and cut and cut through the veil of morning mist.

"Busy night?" Eileen asked.

Hwa shrugged. "Not too."

"People are just saving their money," Eileen said. "New sheriff in town, and all that."

"It'll be fine."

Hwa hoped she sounded more certain than she felt. She honestly had no idea what the Lynch family would decide once they took ownership of New Arcadia. They could invite another agency in to encourage competition and bring down the hourly rates, or change up the fee-for-service model. Or they could be uptight about it and fire the agency, send all the sex workers scurrying back into massage parlours or whatever it was they used to pretend they did for money. And, of course, they could just shut the whole rig down, and watch the bottom fall out of every other business in the city once the roughnecks left. Lynch was still a privately held corporation. They didn't have to release any policy statements on the subject of their sexual broad-mindedness or their employment strategy or anything else that might concern the town they had just bought. Not until they chose to bring the hammer down.

She tried to smile. "Hey, if we have to move, at least you won't have to fuck that fish-faced asshole again."

Eileen rolled her eyes. "Sacred Heart of Christ, Hwa, he's not *that* bad."

Most of the other people in the elevator were pretending not to overhear them. A mother took her children out of the elevator on the next floor. Only a rigger was left. He stared openly at Eileen, blinking only when she adjusted her dress. Hwa watched him do this three different times before the doors chimed for Eileen's floor.

"Hold it."

Eileen pressed the hold button. She stood at the open doors. "What's the problem?"

"This guy's the problem." Hwa jammed her thumb and all her fingers into the salivary glands under the rigger's greasy jaw. He swung for her and missed badly. She was probably nothing but a blur in his vision. "He's got a staring problem, and I don't like it."

"Fuck you," the rigger managed to choke out.

"No, fuck you, creepshot. She didn't give you permission to take those pictures. Eileen, take his face and send it to Belle."

Eileen nodded. "Done."

Hwa pressed his throat so hard she held his Adam's apple in her fingers. "Good. Now we know your face. So we'll know if you ever make a date. Which means that if I ever catch you acting up with one of our workers, I'll shave your balls with a cheese grater."

He spat in her face. Hwa let him go. She ushered Eileen out of the elevator. When the doors closed, they watched each other for a moment. Eileen laughed first. Then they were laughing together. Eileen wiped Hwa's face and hooked her arm into Hwa's again. "Itching for a fight, were you?"

"Always am, when I see that asshole." Hwa flexed her fingers. "Moliter, I mean."

"You know, you could go back to school. I asked him."

Hwa pulled up short in the middle of the elevator court. "What?"

"Moliter. I asked him. I asked if you could go back and finish. I know it was a few years ago, but he said you—"

"You talked about me? During your appointment?"

"Well, not *during*. . . . But after."

Hwa's wrist squeezed. She checked it. The message was marked urgent. It was from her union rep's personal account. Her immediate presence was requested.

"No time for coffee," she said.

. . .

Underneath all the bird shit and salt scars, the architecture of the docking platform was still grand: huge arches left over from some other investor's future, all straight and white and minimalist. Now they were a dingy grey, like most everything else on the rig. People stretched a long way down the catwalks leading up to the platform. Most of them were young. They had the uniform builds of state-sponsored genetic tailoring. Nothing fancy, just the bare minimum Ottawa had finally guaranteed. They were recent hires, Hwa guessed, angry about the sale of the town and their sudden uncertainty within it. They looked like they'd stayed up all night. Thin grease filmed their foreheads, and they were all sharing droppers with each other.

"You want?" one of them asked. She was a very pale girl with a bald head and a huge mandala spanning her gleaming skull. It glowed and pulsed along with her heartbeat, barely visible. The whole bioluminescent inkjob trend really didn't work for white people. Not enough contrast.

"I'm fine."

"Going to the handoff?"

"Hadn't planned on it." Hwa watched the other girl's eyes carefully. No nervous flickering gaze. She obviously couldn't see Hwa's true face. But her friends could. Their gazes kept landing on it and then flicking away, as though to make sure that the stain was still there, that it wasn't a trick. It made sense. The bald girl had the inkjob. She obviously liked herself better augmented.

"I just don't think Lynch is the best solution for this community," the bald girl said. "You know they're just gonna flip it. Just take this whole town apart and sell it for scrap. That's what they've been doing with every other rig-burg they buy."

"They might." Hwa leaned over the rail. The early September sun was already hot at this early hour. She yearned for winter, when no one would look twice at her long sleeves.

"Doesn't that, like, *concern* you?"

"They wouldn't have bought this place if they didn't think of it as an asset." Hwa watched the maglev slide into place above them. It, too, came from somebody else's future: a smooth fibreglass one where every machine looked a bit like a dolphin. "I'll worry about it more when they make some kind of announcement."

"But we have a chance to influence them right *now!*" the girl said. She blinked furiously in Hwa's direction. Then she did it again. Four times, with an earnest stare at the end.

"She doesn't have any eyes," one of the girl's friends said. He winced just looking at Hwa. "You have to show her something . . . real."

"What? Really? No way." The girl closed her eyes tightly, waited a beat, and then opened them again. When she did, her mouth fell open. Her hand raised to cover it. She had seen Hwa's true face, without any Mind Your Manners filters. Now she couldn't help but stare. "Oh," she said, finally.

She knew Hwa was poor, now. She knew that whatever test might have warned Sunny about the baby she was carrying had been either ignored or unfinished. She knew that Sunny hadn't thrown her embryo in the CRISPR drawer and looked at what came out. What she didn't know was that the only reason she could see Hwa's face at all was that Sunny had missed the province's new twelve-week cutoff and had to keep her. That Sunny had even talked about giving her up, until the girl behind the desk at the agency's adoption arm talked her out of it. Because nobody would want Hwa. Not unedited. Not with a face like that. Not with Sturge-Weber, and its associated potential for blindness and seizures and Christ knew what else. Not when they could just buy a better baby somewhere else, one that came pre-edited and perfect. So Sunny should just try and be a good mother. After all, she obviously loved her little boy—the one she'd brought out to this city, this tower of flame and poison floating on a dead ocean—so very much. She just needed to try harder with Hwa. Really. The love would come. Eventually. Maybe.

"Does it . . . ?"

"No," Hwa said. "It doesn't hurt."

• • •

Nail stood waiting for her in the elevator court at the base of Tower Three.

"Morning," she said, as he guided her to the private elevator that would take them to her union rep's headquarters. Nail didn't answer. He had given his voice to Mistress Séverine; he spoke only when allowed to. It took a bit of getting used to. The first few times they'd met it was awkward. Now Hwa just considered him a good listener.

Nail had to duck his head as they entered the elevator. As they descended, so did the temperature. Hwa kept her eyes averted from the numbers above the door as they changed. She hated to think of all that water pressing in above them. Finally the elevator came to a stop, and the red light in the ceiling turned vibrantly green.

Nail spun the winch on the door. When it swung open, the smell of burnt sugar and saddle soap wafted through. They entered a circular space walled almost entirely in glass save for the door behind them. The space was completely underwater. Through the glass, the black waters of the Atlantic and whatever inhabited them were plainly visible. Right now, what inhabited them was a man in a breathesuit. He stood chained inside a shark cage.

"Oh, good, Hwa." Mistress Séverine stood up. She wore a white silk robe that gleamed and rippled as she crossed the room to shake Hwa's hand. Her grip was as ferociously strong as ever. Hwa could still feel the power in her hands through Séverine's leather gloves.

"Ma'am."

"Please sit. Nail, please bring another place setting. You will eat, won't you?"

Nail disappeared into another room before Hwa could protest.

She almost called out to him that he didn't have to go to any extra trouble for her, but the kitchen door clanged shut behind him and she swallowed her words.

"Hwa, do sit. Please. And ignore the man in the cage. One of his neural implants started malfunctioning during his third tour of duty. He has asked me to help him reexperience fear. The process requires our complete disregard."

Hwa found her seat on a low white sofa. Mistress Séverine resumed her club chair, which sat quite a bit higher. Hwa understood that the arrangement of the furniture was meant to make clients feel like supplicants, but it was annoying for everyday business. She hunched forward.

"Don't slouch, Hwa."

She sat up straighter. "Yes, ma'am."

"And take that hair out of your face. I like seeing people when I speak to them."

Hwa tried to secure the left parting of her hair behind her ear. When she met Séverine's gaze, the older woman smiled. "That's better." She turned her gaze to the kitchen door, and out walked Nail and Rusty, bearing a silver tea set and a tower of pastries on their respective trays. The men set each tray down silently and stood, staring at Séverine.

"Rusty, please tell Hwa about her breakfast."

Rusty was Nail's opposite: short where the other man was tall, talkative and not silent, gingery blond and not dark. He gestured at each item as he described it. "Good morning. For breakfast you have Earl Grey tea, steamed egg custard with smoked salmon, laminated croissants with bakeapple filling, and goat's milk yogurt topped with blueberry-verbena compote."

Séverine began removing her gloves. "Thank you, Rusty. The two of you may leave. I'll ring for you when we're finished here."

Both men bowed, and took their leave. Hwa reached for the teapot, but Séverine shooed her hand away. "I'll pour. You may begin assembling your plate. The tongs are just there."

The china Séverine favoured was so thin Hwa could perceive light through it. The sight of her own grubby fingers on it made her wince. She grabbed one of everything and waited for Séverine to finish pouring. Then she waited as the other woman took her time putting together her plate, unrolling her napkin, and choosing her cutlery. She weighed her spoon in her hand thoughtfully, as though evaluating a weapon.

"I have work for you today, Hwa." Her spoon slid into the custard and along the edge of the ramekin to bring up a steaming lump of yellow flecked with pink. "Rusty and Nail are going to the handoff, and I want you to escort them."

Hwa swallowed her yogurt. She had never been to the new platform. After the Old Rig exploded, the town had voted to build another. But it hadn't come cheap. It was part of why all the other companies were pulling out, and how Lynch could buy the town so cheap. What remained of the old platform waved halfheartedly from beneath the water like a veteran waggling an accusatory stump at passersby. Whenever her train swerved over it, she made sure not to look. If the dead caught you looking, they might start looking back.

"I understand if it's difficult for you."

"It's not difficult." Hwa plunged her spoon into the savoury custard with a bit too much force.

"And for this job, it will be necessary for you to escort the boys at a distance. Be as unobtrusive as possible."

Hwa frowned. "Wait a second." She hunched over her knees, slouching be damned. "You want me to *spy*—"

"Oh, hush. I'm not asking you to do anything untoward. Just follow them and make sure they're safe, as with any other job." Séverine watched Hwa over the rim of her teacup. "This town is changing, Hwa. My boys want to see that change happen. But I've already watched my share of train wrecks."

• • •

The new platform afforded good views of the other towers and their windmills. There was her tower, Tower One, the oldest and most decrepit with grimy capsule windows jutting out at pixel intervals, and Tower Two, all glass bubbles and greenery piled like a stack of river rocks, and Tower Three, made of biocrete and healing polymers, Tower Four, gleaming black with solar paint, and Tower Five, so far out on the ocean that it was easy to forget it was even there. It had been designed by algorithm, and its louvers shifted constantly, like a bird fluffing its feathers up against the cold. Occasionally this meant getting a sudden blinding flash of glare when the train zipped past it, or when a water taxi approached its base. Hwa's old Municipal History teacher said the designers referred to the towers by their respective inspirations: Metabolist, Viridian, Synth, Bentham, and Emergent. There was an extra credit test question on it, once. Mr. Ballard wrote her a nice note with a smiley face in the margin when she got it right. Now she couldn't seem to get rid of that little factoid.

She watched Rusty and Nail milling through the crowd. Rusty kept shading his eyes. Nail stood stoically, eyes narrowed to the sun, seemingly unperturbed. He'd remembered to turn his eyes on, apparently.

From the sky, she heard the guttural churn of a chopper homing in on the platform. It bore the Lynch logo. As one, the crowd surged closer to the stage. Rusty and Nail must have moved with them, because she saw no sign of them at the edges of the crowd.

Then the explosions started.

They began as a high whistle. Then a bang. Firecrackers, maybe. Acid green smoke rose above the crowd. Some people fell to the ground. Others ran. Someone ran past Hwa and knocked her down. She rolled over into a crouch and called out: *"Rusty!"*

Maybe Rusty and Nail had fallen down, too. She couldn't see through the rush of legs and green smoke. The smoke itself was thickening, spreading, moving as if by design. A group of people stood under the centre of the cloud, moving their hands like old people doing tai chi, shaping the smoke. It wasn't smoke at all, then. Nano-mist. Hwa zipped the collar of her jacket over her mouth. In the shadow cast by the mist, Hwa saw the pulsing glow of a man-dala tattoo.

The kids from the platform. They had done this. From her crouch-ing position, Hwa saw them deploy a swarm of flies that projected words against the mist: TAKE BACK YOUR TOWN. LYNCH THE LYNCHES.

"Oh, for Christ's sake," Hwa muttered. "Talk about low-hanging fruit. *Rusty! Rusty, can you hear me?*"

She stood up. Maybe they had run away. She hoped they had run away. Far away. Already, she heard sirens. NAPS saucers buzzed low across the sky. What was she going to tell Séverine? She had to find them. She needed higher ground. Through the veil of green fog, she caught a glimpse of the caution-yellow stairways she knew led up toward the refinery.

She ran.

She ran as though she were running away, far to the edge of the crowd, keeping her head down, ducking behind a waste bin as the first wave of NAPS officers in riot gear washed across the plat-form. After they passed, she made for the gate to the staircase. It was locked with only a rusting sign and a corroded chain. She kicked it open and started climbing.

From the first tier of the catwalks, she saw only the fog. It was rising, now, and she pushed on and up another tier. From that sec-ond tier, she saw the fringes of crowd. NAPS kettling the crowd. People already squid-tied to each other. She looked for Rusty's hair next to Nail's tall body. Nothing. She kept running.

On the stairs to the third tier, she saw the man with the rifle.

He paced the refinery catwalks high above the fray. As Hwa watched, he paused and began examining the rifle. Hefting it in his hands. Peering down the scope. The gun was illegal on the platform; since the fall of the Old Rig there were laws against projectiles and explosives and all the other things that could cause a pillar of fire to vaporize a crew of roughnecks like tobacco leaves. Not that that mat-tered, in this long and terrible moment. What mattered was that he

could shoot into the crowd. What mattered was her promise to protect two men in that crowd.

The chopper was louder, now. Closer. Who was he with? The riot
cops? The protesters? Was he going to shoot the Lynches, or was he
going to shoot into the crowd? Maybe he'd had his eyes done. Probably. He would be sharper than she was. Faster. The only thing she
had going for her was the ability to surprise him.

She felt the air *whump*ing on her sternum as the chopper hovered, seemingly unwilling to land. It was hard to swallow. From
behind a girder, she watched as the man rested his rifle on the railing. His eyes remained on the chopper. He snapped open a shoulder rest on the rifle. She gauged the length of the catwalk. She had
fifteen feet by three, with a four-foot clearance on the railing. All
her kicks would have to be three- and four-pointers aimed at the
head. Steel grate, no purchase for her feet. The man was six feet tall
or just under it. She would have to jump to make up the difference.

Well, that was one way of surprising him.

When he reached into his pocket, she rushed him. He must have
felt or heard her feet clanging across the steel, because he looked up:
blue eyes, ginger hair, deep lines, mouth open. He gripped the rifle
and swung it toward her; it was the opening she needed. She batted
the business end of the weapon and pushed it down and away, then
turned around as though to run. Her navel met her spine, her right
knee met her chest, and her left foot pivoted to rise. Her body became a pendulum. Her eyes met his just before her heel crunched
into his nose: he looked oddly hurt, as though he were confused at
this sudden imposition of violence, at the rudeness of it. And then
he was really and truly hurt, and bleeding everywhere.

"Fuck!"

Hwa grabbed for the gun. He wouldn't let it go. Well-trained; he
didn't grab for his broken nose. Blind and bleeding, he gripped the
gun crosswise with both hands and shoved it at her face. She had to
bounce backward. His head jerked; he was listening for her feet on

the steel. Hwa yanked the gun toward herself anyway. He refused to let go.

"I don't want to hurt you," he said through the blood.

"You won't," Hwa said, and ducked under the gun to plant her right leg behind his left and throw her weight at his thighs. He tumbled backward and then she was on him, locking her ankles behind his waist and squeezing her thighs together hard. She heard the air leave him in a rush.

"Jesus," he hissed.

"Give up." She stared hard into his eyes and slowly curled the gun up to her. His shoulders rose with it. Her arms were trembling, but so were his. They shook and rattled together over the gun. She breathed through her teeth. "Let go."

His hands fell away. Suddenly she was a million pounds lighter. Her body snapped up, towered over him, the gun absurdly huge and awkward against her chest. Hwa watched his gaze flick over her shoulder. She turned. Above them, against the hazy blue of the sky, was a thin silver disc. A flying saucer. As she watched, a single laser painted her skin.

Beneath her, the man shouted: "No, wait, stop, don't—"

Then the pain started.

2

Broken Arm

The holding cell was unlike any Hwa had ever seen. It was a small room. Hwa had a hard time estimating just how small, because the edges of it had a tricky way of blurring away just at the periphery of her vision. Tower Five, then. Five had all the bells and whistles. At least, it had most of the programmable matter in Newfoundland and Labrador. Lynch, then. Not the NAPS. They were wasting no time taking control of things.

Carefully, Hwa stood up. Both her ankles and hands were gelled together. She knelt down and then sat. The floor beneath her was oddly warm, like skin. It moulded up around her the longer she stayed in place. Raising her legs parallel to her chest, she rocked back and forth until she could fall back on her shoulder blades with her legs and core straight up in the air. Slowly, she slid her legs through the loop of her bound arms. Now, at least, they were in front of her. Where she could use them.

A seam opened in the wall. It was the man from the platform. And he was carrying a big knife.

"Back for more?" Hwa asked.

"What? Oh." He looked down at the knife. It looked so incongruous in his hand. He'd cleaned up and changed into a blue Lynch polo shirt and cargo khakis. The knife trembled a little in his right hand, until he gripped it more tightly. "Hold your hands out, please."

Hwa held them out. He cut the bonds in one quick motion. Experienced, then. He knelt at her feet. Looked up at her for a moment cautiously. He was afraid she would kick him again, she realized. She stood straighter and looked away. He cut the ties, and flicked the knife back into its handle and put the whole thing in a back pocket as he rose.

"Sorry about that. How are you feeling?"

Her mouth worked. It was painfully dry. This had to be some sort of game. It certainly didn't feel real. He was being too nice. Then she remembered her script: "My name is Go Jung-hwa and I want to speak to my union representative. Séverine Japrisot, USWC 314. I won't answer any questions until she sends an attorney for me. Also I want to see a doctor. I have a seizure disorder. It can be triggered by things like pain lasers or whatever the fuck was on that saucer."

"But . . ." His eyes flicked back and forth rapidly, like he was reading up on the keywords in their conversation. "The saucer should have picked up your stimplant, or your subscription—"

"I don't have a stimplant. Or any subscriptions. At all. I take drugs, not machines. That's what my plan covers." She gestured at herself. "All of this is completely organic."

"Organic?" His gaze refocused sharply on her. "Completely?"

"Are you asking about my IUD or my diet?"

To her satisfaction, he went red to the roots of his hair. Apparently that much of him was still organic, too. "Neither," he muttered. He held his hand out. "Daniel Síofra. I'm with Lynch."

Hwa nodded pointedly at the logo on his shirt. "No shit?"

He snorted. "And I'm not pressing any charges."

His hand was still out. She flexed her fingers before shaking it. He had a good handshake. Right-handed. Long-fingered. Skin too smooth for the strength she knew was there. She watched his eyes and his smile widen as she intensified her grip.

"You just don't quit, do you?" he murmured.

She relaxed her grip and slid her hand away. They had already been talking too long. "Am I free to go?"

"Aren't you going to apologize for breaking my nose?"

Now he was just being ridiculous. Hwa squinted. His nose was straight. His eyes were clear, no puddles of purple beneath. "Your nose looks fine. You had it reset. And drained. Or . . ." She watched his eyes. He was not staring at her skin. He was not watching the left side of her face, or trying hard to avoid looking at it. Filters, then. Like the bald girl on the platform. Hwa wondered where she was, now. She decided she didn't want to know. "You have programmable tissues."

He blinked. "Something like that."

Augmented people were so uptight about their augmentations. As though everyone around them actually gave a damn. As though learning about what they'd fixed could really tell you anything about the places they were broken.

"How did you do it?" he asked.

"Kick you? With my feet."

"Surprised me. I didn't even see you coming." He tilted his head. Tapped his temple. "For some reason your face doesn't show up on the camera. It's just a blur."

It's because my face is a natural dazzle pattern, Hwa thought of saying. But she didn't. Let him keep whatever vision of her face his eyes were feeding him. Let the cataract of data growing over his vision blind him completely.

"Oh, sorry. No wonder you don't feel like talking." From another pocket, he produced a flask. "You did so much screaming, your throat must be raw."

Hwa took the flask. She opened it up and sniffed.

"It's just water," he said. "I promise."

Hwa sipped. Seemingly just water. And it did feel nice on her throat. "Screaming?"

"The pain ray. You just went rigid, and . . ." He swallowed. "I didn't want them to. So you know. I don't like those things."

"But you're cool with pointing rifles at crowds of people."

He sighed. "It wasn't a rifle. It was a long-range microphone. The company doesn't have access to all the networks in the city, yet. So I was using the scope to pinpoint the sources of the conversations I was listening to. You probably didn't notice, what with all the karate—"

"Tae kwon do."

"Tae kwon do?"

"Karate is Japanese. I'm Korean. Half Korean."

His brows rose. "And clearly very proud of it."

"I'll learn karate when the Empress apologizes for the comfort women." She folded her arms. "Anyway. Guns are bullshit."

"It was a ricochet that set off the chain reaction that blew up the Old Rig, wasn't it?"

Hwa nodded.

"You knew someone in the blast?"

Hwa levelled her gaze with his. Made sure he could see her eyes, if not her true face. That was the nice thing about anger. It could burn away any hint of embarrassment. "It's a small town, Mr. Síofra. Everybody knew somebody."

She tipped the flask high before he could say anything, but left some water sloshing at the bottom. He gestured for her to finish it. He was back to being the version of himself he'd introduced himself as. "You're the escorts' escort?"

Hwa swallowed and shook her head. "Just one of them. There are more."

"Is it a good job?"

"There's a pension. Flexible hours. Nice people."

"Nice people who won't cover a machine subscription that could improve your quality of life."

"It'll come up next bargaining session. I talked to my rep about it." Hwa tried not to sound defensive. It wasn't like it was any of his business, anyway. He was just trotting out the usual multinational rhetoric about how much better he had it as a corporate drone.

"Would you ever consider leaving? For a job with Lynch? I work in our Urban Tactics department."

"The fuck's that?"

"I change the moods of cities."

Hwa gave him the look she gave clients who refused to pay overtime.

"It's applying a design thinking sensibility to urban engineering, on a day-to-day basis. Changing light levels in a building so its

inhabitants sleep more easily. Raising the tempo of music in the refinery to increase production." He gestured as he spoke, and Hwa
immediately understood that this was part of his work, that he or-
chestrated cities like a symphony conductor. "I have a certain knack
for it. A sensitivity. Or so I'm told."

Hwa looked at the dead gel ties on the floor. She toed one of them
and flipped it up into her waiting hands. She twisted its length in
her fingers. It twitched back to life like bait on the end of a hook.
"You start every job interview in handcuffs? Because if you're hurting for talent, that might be why."

"You have skills we need," he said, seemingly undeterred. "You
got the jump on me. Literally. That's not easy to do. It hasn't happened in years. Also literally."

Hwa grinned. "There's plenty of muscle in this town. You don't
need mine."

"I don't need it. I want it." He thrust his hands into his pockets.
"And I'm willing to pay for it. Handsomely."

The laughter bubbled up out of Hwa before she could stop it. Maybe
it was the pain ray, still playing with her nerves. *Handsomely.* Jesus
wept. Men always sounded the same, when they tried to buy women.

"I'm sorry." She got herself together. "It's a very kind offer. But
the answer's no. I like me own job just fine."

He opened his mouth to answer. Then his head jerked to one
side. He scowled, and then nodded. "Mm. Mm-hmm. I'll let her
know." He refocused on Hwa. "Someone's come to collect you. She
says she's your mother."

Hwa winced. "You sure you can't just arrest me?"

• • •

Sunny stood in the halo of green light cast by an EXIT sign. She wore
a sleeveless red dress and a black scarf of smart silk that adjusted
itself over her blond tease-out as she turned her head this way and
that. For those that had the eyes to see it, Sunny's profile would be
popping up along with her contact info and relevant testimonials.
Stuff like how she still knew all the steps from all her old routines,

how she still spoke perfect Korean in perfect baby talk, how she'd call you "big brother" and punch you in the arm when you teased her just the littlest bit, how her blow jobs made you see stars. Hwa knew. Sunny made her do a spell-check on the whole profile, once, back when she was still in school.

Behind her, Síofra pulled up short. "That's your mother?"

Of course, he could see Sunny's profile, too. Hwa felt only the tiniest tingle of embarrassment. Not because of Sunny's job. Nothing to be ashamed of, there. She kept more money fucking than she ever had singing or dancing. But the profile itself, the old songs, the duck lips, the overwhelming pink tide of cuteness currently washing across Síofra's vision: that was fucking embarrassing.

"That's her."

Síofra said nothing. He was staring at Hwa, now. Making the comparison, probably. Between her wasp-waisted mother with the delicate limbs and perfect skin and the titless wonder in the black running tights and rash guard. He couldn't see her face, but he could see everything else: the empty space around her, the lack of outputs and lack of profile, the lack of connections and lack of status.

Sunny spoke in cheerful Korean with a radiant smile: <<*Hwa-jeon!* Hurry up! You're making me late!>>

"I have to go." Hwa passed Síofra his flask. "Thanks for the water."

Síofra nodded. "It's no trouble." He sized up Sunny and looked back at Hwa. "Is she taking you to your doctor? To check you over?"

Hwa almost laughed. Strangers were adorable. "Right. Sure. My doctor."

Hwa hurried down the hall. Sunny held her arms open again. Those arms took hold of Hwa gently, pressing her close but not too close, as though Hwa had just told her she had something contagious.

"You were so brave!" Sunny said in loud, bubbly English.

And with that Sunny ushered her down the hall. Sunny kept her smile as tight as her grip until they hit the elevator.

When the doors closed, her hand left Hwa's elbow. Then it

smacked hard into Hwa's left ear. And then again, across her face, so hard her head *clunked* against the side of the elevator.

<<You half-breed half-wit. What were you thinking? Don't even think about coming home tonight.>>

. . .

She could have slept on Eileen's couch. Or maybe Mistress Séverine's. Or even her own squat, on the condemned floor of Tower One. But there was a paying gig in her messages, off-book, and she offered the client a discount on the service if she got to crash for the night. She offered an even deeper discount if the contract offered dinner and breakfast, which he did. She just had to be gone before his parents came back from their shift.

"Wait! Stop! Is this gonna hurt?"

Hwa's fist stopped an inch from Wade's nose. For a moment she saw him as the kid she remembered from grade three, the one who gave her sorry eyes when the other kids made fun of her face and her name and her English. He'd been cute then, too. Over twenty-two years he'd grown into his good looks in a very pretty way: bright blue eyes, blond hair in a persistent state of bed-head, broad shoulders with solid definition, a body like an inverted triangle on two strong swimmer's legs. He had good clear skin that tanned just right, and he got dimples when he smiled. Back when she actually went to school, almost all the other girls had crushes on him, even the girls who didn't like the same guys that all the other girls liked.

Now he was asking her to break his nose.

"What's the procedure?" she had asked, after he slid her a coffee.

"My abs." He had pulled up his shirt and showed her. "See that line down the middle? That's good, but the doc says he can get me real definition on the sides. The *tendinous inscription,* it's called. And down here," he gestured at the line where his torso ended and his thigh began, "that's the *inguinal ligament*. He's going to define that, too. Just make it pop, visually. So I can wear my jeans lower."

Hwa had considered showing him her own stomach, which had

some good cuts, but then he'd have to see the stain and nobody wanted to see the stain. Besides, she doubted he wanted to try her diet.

"Bio or nano?" she asked.

"I'm not sure," Wade said. "He asked for a fat sample, 'cause it's a custom job. That's why it costs so much."

"What's the subscription fee? For the maintenance, I mean."

He shrugged. "He says he'll take a percentage of whatever I earn, after."

"And you get a discount if there's something else to fix?"

"Three jobs." Wade reached inside his mouth and plucked out a tooth. "See? I need another one. A better fit. They printed this one when I was, like, eleven."

Hwa nodded. "Why the abs?"

Wade pinked. It started at his ears and marched across his face, as though his blush were on a quest to embarrass him. "The oil's drying up. Most everybody's already left. All the other companies, I mean. That's why they're selling it. There aren't any jobs. I want to get off the rig, while I still can."

"Doesn't everybody?"

"Well, yeah, but . . ." His lips pursed. "I want to go to *university*."

Hwa winced. "Sounds expensive."

"Exactly. There's no way my parents will help pay for it. I already asked. They flat-out told me no. They think it's a waste, when there's still some money to be made right here. So I have to get a job. And I *can*, I just have to get some work done first." The pink had become magenta. "I got an offer to do some modelling," he said. "Online."

Hwa willed her eyebrows to remain in a neutral, nonjudgmental position. "Do your folks know?"

He shrugged his shoulders and looked down. "You have to spend money to make money, I guess," he said.

Well, he had that right, at least. He was probably getting naked for somebody, but if it paid enough to get the hell off this floating asylum, that wouldn't be so bad. Besides, he'd look like a hard case once the doc was finished. Nobody would ever hit him again, after today. Not unless they paid Wade for the privilege.

"Okay," Hwa said.

"Great!" Wade dabbed at the corners of his mouth with a napkin. He rolled his shoulders, bounced on his toes, and clapped his hands. "Let's do this."

Hwa pulled her right arm back. She pivoted her hips to give her maximum follow-through on the strike. One pop, and it would be done. She twisted forward, and Wade's hands flew up. And that was how her fist got to be there, hovering in front of his glistening mouth, tension climbing up her arm as she held it in place.

"Yes. It's going to hurt. Of course it's going to fucking hurt."

He frowned. "There's no need to be *mean* about it. God. Why do you have to be such a bitch?"

Her fist connected with his face. It was a short, sharp strike. Wade fell to his knees immediately. He dragged the placemat with him, and his plate landed facedown on his back, streaking his shirt in beans and hot sauce. He knelt on the floor, hissing and rocking. He reached for his wallet.

"Keep your money," Hwa said. "Thanks for the eggs."

• • •

On the train to Tower Three, someone played "This Train Is Bound for Glory" on a conch shell ukulele. She found the students in her self-defence class sitting in the hallway outside the door to their studio at the gym there. Eileen gave her a little wave and Hwa nodded at her. She addressed the rest of the class. "What's going on? Why aren't you warming up? Is Destiny not done with Astral Yoga, yet?"

"There's other people in there," Sabrina said. Sabrina was one of Hwa's best students. She was a big girl, but agile, and always had a ready smile, even when her face was glowing red with exertion and the sweat had completely soaked through her shirt. Her reserve in Ontario didn't much take to the genetic editing; the tribe held the position that the province should expect the nearby chemical companies to clean up their act, rather than expecting the Chippewa to clean up their genes. Like Hwa, Sabrina was mostly organic. She was very popular among a certain set of clients. "One guy was really big. The other one looked just like a kid."

"Nothing creepy, though," said Calliope, from the floor. She didn't look good. Her black hair was greasy and she hadn't even bothered with eyeliner. Without a pronounced cat-eye, she looked like an entirely different person.

"Are you okay?" Hwa asked. "You look kinda sick."

"Gee, thanks, Coach. Not like my whole career depends on my looks, or anything."

Sabrina reached over and patted her arm. "This job isn't just about looks, and you know it."

Calliope gave Sabrina's wide, soft body a long, shady look. "Keep telling yourself that."

"Hey!" Eileen leaned over to catch Calliope's eye. "Don't be a bitch. So what if you look like shit? We're here to work out, not make dates." She squared her shoulders and stared at the other two women. "And besides. We should all be supporting each other as best we can. Times being what they are."

"Sorry I'm late!"

They turned, and Layne stumbled into the hallway. The door caught the hem of her shorts, and she had to turn around and tug it back to herself. For some reason, Layne always treated these classes like they were make-up days in some long-ago gym period. Like Hwa, she'd quit high school years ago. Her parents figured it was for the best, after her second suicide attempt. They sent her to an in-patient hacklab in Toronto run by the Centre for Addiction and Mental Health, instead. In the city, she'd had her gender confirmed. Now she ran tech support on the Belle du Jour system.

"How come we're not in class?" Layne asked.

Hwa looked at the door. "That's a good fucking question."

Calliope heaved a massive sigh that caused the huge Greek cross tattooed across her ponderous cleavage to stretch and bounce.

"I knew I should have scheduled my tattoo appointment for today, and not next week."

From behind the door, Hwa heard a heavy thud and a high, surprised yelp. The other women all froze. Hwa held up a hand. "Get someone," she said, in a low voice.

She pulled open the door quietly and slipped inside. Inside the studio at the far end of the room, a well-built man stood with his back to her. Before him stood a skinny teenaged boy. The boy was white. The man wasn't. The wing tattoo across his broad shoulders fluttered slightly. Hwa recognized it, and him. His name was Angel.

Angel had thrown her through a glass coffee table, once, when the choking game he was playing with Connor Donnelly got too rough. Connor tapped out—made the emergency call—and Hwa burst in. She'd jumped on Angel and he'd thrown her off. The moment the glass shattered, he'd come back to himself. But by that time, it was already too late. The union blacklisted him. His money was no good in the New Arcadia sex trade.

Apparently, Angel still liked hurting men who looked like boys.

"Get up!" He bounced on his toes. Moved his fists. "Come on. No rest for the wicked, son."

The kid shot him a mutinous look from his position on the floor. Then his gaze fell. He saw Hwa. Hwa saw him seeing her; he quickly checked the mirrored wall behind Angel and then she knew he saw her face, too. In the mirror, she lifted a finger to her lips. Slowly, awkwardly, the boy got to his feet. His movements were messy. Loose. Gangly. He focused on the man in front of him. On his face, not his shoulders. Beginner mistake.

"Now, you come at me this time," Angel said.

"You're supposed to be teaching me self-defence," the kid said, wheedling. He was playing for time. Hwa took off her shoes. "Shouldn't you be teaching me blocks and stuff?"

No, Hwa thought. *Survival and escape techniques first. Then posture and breathing.*

Angel brought up his fists and exposed his forearms. His right arm was heavier than his left. The grip in the fingers a little softer. He'd had the nerves cut and sewn, then. Probably by a poor tailor. Good. "This is a block."

The kid jabbed out at a weak angle. He drove from the elbow, not the torso, with no pivot in the toes or hips. Terrible form. No power. Angel slapped his little fist away with his left arm and pulled a punch with the right. His fist hovered just above the kid's left ear. The boy didn't flinch. He just stared at Angel's fist like he was waiting for it to tell him something. Like they were playing a game whose rules he didn't understand.

"Gotcha," Angel said, and Hwa didn't need to check the mirror to see his shit-eating grin.

Hwa padded up behind him swiftly and silently. "Hi, Angel," she said, just to be nice, and drove a back kick straight into his right knee from behind. He fell down and twisted to the right, left arm up, right arm reaching for her legs. She quickly swung a leg over him and trapped the right arm between her knees at the elbow.

"You fucking crazy bitch!" His left fist hammered her in the thigh and the stomach. "Get the fuck out of here, this is my gig—"

"It's my class time, Angel." She pivoted away from his swinging left fist, grabbing his right hand and stretching his right arm and feeling it twitch between her legs. Squeezing it, she could feel the machinery at work. Off-brand, she decided. Maybe secondhand. So to speak. "And that means it's my studio. And I don't like it when people use my studio to pick on people smaller than them."

"I'm gonna fuck up the other side of your face, you useless cunt," Angel said.

"And I'm gonna break this arm," Hwa said. "I'd turn it off, if I were you."

"Fuck you," he spat.

It didn't take much. She kept pulling on the right fist until the arm hyperextended, and then she twisted her knees. It was just the gentlest motion. The snap wasn't even properly audible. And he had turned off the arm—he didn't howl, didn't cry, didn't throw up, just stood and spat on her.

"I'm gonna sue the shit out of you," Angel told the boy. The boy said nothing. He just kept watching the scene play out. "Fuck you both," Angel added, turning to Hwa. "Especially you, freak. Watch your back. Karma's a bigger bitch than you are."

He stalked away. Hwa watched him the whole time, and let her breath out when he was gone.

The boy held out a hand. Hwa could stand on her own, but she took it anyway. "Wow," he said. "Weren't you scared?"

"Not really. He's just an asshole. Were you scared?"

He shook his head. "I don't get scared, really. Not anymore. They fixed that part of me."

Hwa snorted. She thought of the man in the shark cage outside Mistress Séverine's studio. She decided that telling the kid about him would mean explaining too much. "Right. Well. That part of *me* is still broken. And I like it that way, because fear is useful. Fear tells us when to run. And running is what stops a fight before it starts. You want to defend yourself, you have to learn that, first."

His head tilted. "So you still get scared?"

"Sometimes." Hwa looked the kid over. A nice welt was already building on his shoulder. Angel had knocked him down but good. "But I have a trick for being scared."

The kid brightened. "What's the trick?"

"I imagine the master control room."

"What's that?"

"It's a rumour my brother—my half-brother—heard once. About a room that controls the entire city. Water, power, cameras, the whole thing. We spent a whole summer looking for it. So when I'm scared, I pretend I'm there. In control of things."

The boy seemed to consider the possibility. He nodded. "That sounds like it could exist. Did you ever find it?"

"No, but we found other cool places. A whole abandoned floor. A secret way into an elevator shaft. Stuff like that." Hwa rolled her neck until it popped. "Who hired that guy?"

"My dad. Sort of."

"Your dad doesn't know much about this town, eh?"

The kid's smile broadened. "Not really. We're new." He pointed at himself. "My name's Joel Lynch."

Behind her, Hwa heard the gym door creak open. She knew who would be standing there before she turned around. She wasn't quite sure how, but she knew.

"Oh, hi, Daniel," Joel Lynch said. "This is, um . . . I don't know her name."

"Go Jung-hwa," Daniel Síofra said. He sounded like he'd rehearsed the Korean pronunciation.

"Just Hwa," she said. "My full name was too much for the kindergarten teacher."

"She broke that guy's arm," Joel said. "She says he's an asshole."

A smile touched Síofra's eyes but not his mouth. "Does she? What a shame. I suppose you'll need a new self-defence teacher. And a new bodyguard, as well."

Hwa looked at her class, standing outside the door. She glanced at the studio, and the kid standing expectantly under the cold lights. "You should spray down those mats on the floor and put them away, since you're done here," she said, nodding at the rack of crash pads and mats on the opposite wall. He got right to work.

"You must really want me for this job," she said, when the kid was out of earshot. "Changing the gym schedule around like that, on such short notice. Just so I'd come here and see all this. It's pretty manipulative, if you ask me."

"I prefer to think of it as enterprising," Síofra said. "Creative. Strategic. That's the Lynch way."

She watched the kid awkwardly move mats from one corner of the room to the other.

"You *change the moods of cities*?"

"It's in the job description. Much of it is urban planning and design. But some of it is also communications. Optics."

"Seems a long way off from personal security."

"Hiring you, and not a skullcap or someone like Mr. Ramirez, sets a tone. I'm in charge of that tone."

"So it's just good PR." Now she was certain he'd never seen her true face.

"It's establishing a relationship. Between the company and the city. We promised to bring better jobs. This is one of them."

He had an answer for everything. Hwa watched the infinite reflection of the two of them in the mirrors on either side of the studio. Every version of him looked wrong for the place, his gleaming blue silk suit too soft and too pretty for all the sweat and blood the cork floors had soaked up over the years. She gestured at the bare bones of the space, and a thousand of her made the same movement. "You couldn't just have the bots in HR send me a nice note telling me all this? You had to come all this way yourself?"

"The company prefers us to follow up with prospects on a personal level. We're a large corporation, but not a faceless one."

Hwa didn't believe that for a second. "And what if I still say no? What will you do next?"

He smiled. "I'll find something you want, and give it to you."

Hwa cocked her head. "You know what I want, b'y?"

"You want what everyone in this town wants. You want a way out." His eyes lit on her, and for the first time she saw how very blue they were. It was an unnatural blue. Edited in. He spoke in a low tone, so low she had to step closer just to hear him. "Give us a year. Enough time for Joel to finish school here. And after that you can go wherever you like. Do whatever you want. Save the money, spend the money. But the choice would be yours. Your fate would be your own."

Hwa licked her lips. "I get by just fine," she lied.

His gaze flicked across the gym. "You could be doing more than this."

"Like what? Catching a bullet for the heir apparent over there?"

Softly, Síofra shook his head. "No. You see, Miss Go, I don't want someone who will die for Joel. I want someone who will *kill* for him. And I believe that someone is you."

3

Polio

They were inside a diamond. That was the only way she could think of it. It felt like the top of the tower—the sudden needling pain in her sinuses said it was the top—but Hwa didn't remember Tower Five wearing this glittering crown on its head.

"Do you like it?" Síofra strode ahead of them and gestured at the walls. The gleaming facets moved with her, angling gently so multiple reflections of her appeared to follow along behind her, each more hesitantly than the last. "We had it programmed in months ago. The crystal only just, well, *crystallized* last week."

"Your boss have a thing for *Enter the Dragon*?" Hwa asked. "The old one, I mean, not the reboot?"

"Indeed I do," said a voice behind her.

Hwa turned. The facets louvered shut behind a very old man. His appearance alone made it difficult to place his age: the skin had the vellum smoothness of a good chemical peel, and he'd clearly never spent too much time in the sun. You might never have guessed he was the sole survivor of a primitive commune based somewhere outside Palo Alto, where they didn't believe in shots or pills or dentistry. But it was there in his joints, in the places where the polio had ravaged his body and where stem cells and print-jobs had provided scaffold for the repair work. He moved like an old toy. During his media appearances as CEO, he was still charming: a huge smile, a ready handshake. Looking at him now, though, Hwa understood his desire to protect his heir. At a hundred and five, he didn't have much hope for training up another one.

"Zachariah Lynch," he said, lifting one gloved hand. It was incredibly warm in Hwa's. Gold thread, she realized. A semiconductor in the palm. Something to give him the tactile feedback that age had taken away.

"Go Jung-hwa."

He nodded. "I know."

Of course. She could only guess at the file they'd developed on her; by now he'd probably read every text she'd ever sent. His gaze shifted over to the kid. "Joel," he said. "This is your choice?"

Shyly, the kid stepped forward. "Yes, Father," he said. "Mine and Daniel's. I really like her accent."

"Oh, please." The facets of the room flipped open to admit a man in a suit. He looked a lot like Joel, only his posture was perfect and his hair was cut too short to be curly. Hwa felt Joel take a step back as he entered. "Joel. Come on. You can't be serious. Look at her—"

"We're very serious, Silas," Síofra said, and Joel's lookalike stopped in his tracks. Now that he was standing still, Hwa realized he was probably a lot older than he looked: the skin around his eyes was too plump, his forehead no longer moved, and his eyebrows were a shade darker than his hair. Also, he was far too tanned. His skin was burnished darker than either his father's or his brother's, but it was a hell of a lot more *orange* than that of the men who worked the container ships. Nothing screamed *"I'm terrified of aging!"* louder than a mela-nano infusion.

Silas folded his arms and gave Síofra a long look. If pumpkins could glare, it would have looked about the same.

"We've already budgeted for additional security personnel," Silas said, finally. "And if Joel and Father would let go of this frankly moronic notion of sending Joel to public school, none of this would be an issue."

Zachariah held up a single finger. Hwa practically heard it creak as the joints bent. "Silas, Joel is the future of this company. He's also the face of it, for young people. It's important that he get to know the people whose lives we're responsible for. Especially given our plans."

"What plans?" Hwa asked.

Lynch smiled. It was like watching the wax seal on a very dusty bottle of vinegar crack open. "I would be happy to describe them to you, after you have signed a nondisclosure agreement."

Silas eyed Hwa up and down. "This is what you're looking for in an assistant? She's epileptic. Or something. I don't know. And her mother is a prostitute. A prostitute who pays union dues, but still a prostitute."

Behind them, Joel gasped. "Silas!"

"It's okay," Hwa said. "My mom *is* a whore."

"See?" Silas smiled. His teeth were huge and perfect and white. "I was just saying what everybody was thinking."

"Yeah, having her raise me really introduced me to a lot of assholes," Hwa said. "Professional assholes that pay their taxes and everything, but still assholes."

Silence. Hwa directed a grin at Silas. It was more like a baring of her teeth.

"But, you know, as we say in the business: the bigger the asshole, the smaller the cock."

Silas opened his mouth to say something, when another set of facets opened up and allowed a woman in. She had Joel's dark hair and eyes, but an entirely different nose and jaw.

"Dad, we need you to sign off on the—who's that?" Lynch's daughter stared at Hwa's face. *That*, she had said. Like Hwa wasn't even in the room. Like only her stain was there.

"Katherine, this is Joel's new bodyguard," Síofra said.

"I'm really not," Hwa said. She made for the elevator. "I haven't agreed to anything. And it was lovely meeting you and all, but—"

"She can't be hacked." Síofra said the words a little too loudly. He stared at the elder Lynch as he spoke. "She has no augments. So there's no recognition algorithm in her eyes that can be rewritten. There's nothing in her pancreas that can foul up and send her into diabetic shock. She has no neural implants. She can't hear voices or see visions or be made into someone's puppet. She doesn't have legacy code floating around under her skin, waiting to be exploited. She's . . ." He trailed off. "Pure."

There was an awkward pause. Everyone was staring at Síofra, even Joel. The air started feeling heavier and heavier. A terrible sinking feeling opened up in Hwa's stomach. He had stuck his neck out. She'd kicked him in the face and he'd stuck his neck out. Shit. Even if she didn't want the job, she didn't particularly want him to look bad in front of his boss. At least, no worse than she'd made him look by mouthing off to someone he clearly didn't have much respect for anyway. She cleared her throat to say as much—maybe make an excuse about how he clearly still had a concussion from the force of her kick—but the elder Lynch held up a single finger, forestalling her.

"Once again, Daniel, you have found exactly what I need." His gaze shifted to Hwa, and his lips pulled back to expose false, perfect teeth. "Let's see how pure you really are."

. . .

The walls closed in on her. Literally. The facets of the room shifted once more, and it was just the two of them in a tiny space: Hwa and Lynch. As Hwa stared, the walls shimmered and clips swam across their surfaces. They were of Lynch in younger years. Lynch at state functions. Lynch shaking hands. Lynch with his competitors, arguing silently over some talking point or another.

"I'm a powerful man," he said, "but you already knew that."

He waved a hand. The clips changed to static scans. Notes. Packages. Texts. Mutilated animals.

"For men like me, death threats are a sign of success."

"Yeah?" Hwa winced as blood filled the mirror. "Maybe you should quit while you're ahead."

Lynch coughed a laugh. He waved all the images away, then picked something out of his pocket. It looked like a Christmas ornament. At least, what Hwa had seen of Christmas ornaments. Sunny could never be bothered with anything seasonal, unless you counted bikinis. Holidays reminded her of the passage of time.

"What's that?" Hwa asked.

"It's a crystal ball. Do you know what that is? It's something that shows you the future."

"Why are you showing me this?"

"You have to hold it, for it to work. With your bare hands. Hold them out."

Something inside told her not to do it. She was about to pull her hands away when he dropped the ball into them. It was cool on her cupped palms. No, not cool. Cold. Very cold. Like she'd grabbed a causeway rail on a winter morning after a long and brutal run. She wanted to let go. Couldn't. The cold stiffened her hands and then her wrists and then her arms.

In the crystal, she saw her brother.

In the crystal, Tae-kyung was the same age Hwa was now. He was running beside her. It was a nice day. Blue skies. Summer. She remembered those sneakers. The lucky red laces. She remembered because he was pausing to tie them, again, and she was running ahead, completely unaware, and he yelled something as she got further away, about how

"You shouldn't run where I can't see you!"

She runs backward. Cocky. But the summer is in her lungs and her blood and drying on her skin. The promise of it. A whole three months without school. "Stop yelling! It's not like anybody's going to molest me in broad daylight." She turns and jogs forward. "That only happens to the girls people actually want."

For a moment, Tae-kyung looks like she's slapped him. But he keeps running. His stride is so graceful he manages to trip her up without even breaking his rhythm. He just pushes forward and kicks back, landing a foot on her shin and bringing her toppling to the street. She feels the concrete biting into the heels of her palms. She looks up and he's still running, back straight, knees high. He is not pleased.

<<Idiot!>> he calls in his first language, and now she knows just how very angry he is. <<Never say something stupid like that again. You're in just as much danger as all the girls in this town. The animals on this rig don't give a shit what you look like.>>

"Stop." Hwa's face hurt. Her throat hurt. "Please stop."

The image shifted. The crystal grew hot. She tried to let it go.

Drop it. But it was fused to her hands. It was melting into her flesh. She felt the skin of her fingers webbing together. In the crystal, there was fire. And in her ears

The alarm is howling an endless banshee wail. She is standing in the green level above the school. It's a farm day. Gather the eggs, monitor the bees, deadhead some blossoms. Dessicated flowers fall from her hands as she runs to a window with open louvers. Even this far away, the heat is so intense the windows are throwing up warning sigils. The rig is on fire. Smoke plumes from it thick and black and wide, so wide there is no longer any blue, no sky or sea, just billowing black and licking orange. Her teacher's hands are on her shoulders, pulling her back, but Hwa can't leave, has to stay there, right there, watching, because oh Jesus, oh Christ, Tae-kyung is in there, on fire, burning—

"This isn't the future." It took everything she had to make the words and push them out. "Show me the future."

She is standing at the prow of a boat. They are behind schedule, and making up the time with speed. Spray in her face. Breeze on her skin. Her hands curl around the railing and they're stronger than they've ever been. She looks down at them, at her strong new hands, and the left hand is still clean, still clear, and the arm is stainless, and when she turns and sees herself in the porthole, the stain is still gone—

The crystal dropped from her hands. It dropped only a few inches, because she was kneeling. She was crying. Weeping. Silently. From her good eye. She had a moment to feel shame before anger boiled up from her belly to replace it. It surged up into her face, and she felt the pulse of her blood in the skin of her cheeks like she'd been running for hours. When she looked up, Lynch was smiling.

"What the fuck was that?" Hwa pushed herself to her feet. She thought seriously about stomping on Lynch's little crystal ball. Or maybe just lobbing it through one of the mirrors and out into the ocean. She pointed at it, instead, without looking at it. "What the hell is that thing?"

"It's an artifact from beyond the Singularity," Lynch said. "I received it the day Joel was born. I believe it contains high-resolution digitized memories. Raw files from our uploaded future. And every time I look into it, Joel dies."

Hwa blinked. "What?"

"Every year, on his birthday, I receive one of these." From his other pocket, Lynch withdrew an empty fist. He opened it. As he did, something glowed. A small white square. Not white like the colour, but white like brightness itself. Like light. Like lightning. Hwa smelled ozone as it crackled into being. Something hummed in her teeth, and there it was: HAPPY BIRTHDAY, JOEL. YOU HAVE ONE MORE YEAR TO LIVE.

"That's from his last birthday," Lynch said, and pocketed the . . . whatever it was. "His birthday is in June. If I do not act, his final year of secondary school will also be his final year of life."

Hwa swallowed. She wanted desperately to sit down. Or throw up. She took deep gulping breaths instead. In: two, three, four. Hold: two, three, four. Exhale. And again. And again. How had the thing accessed her memories like that? How had it played them back so accurately? It was like her memories were already squirrelled away somewhere, for other people to watch.

"Beyond the Singularity?" she asked.

"Yes. I believe that these artifacts have been engineered to appear here and now by an artificial superintelligence, or group of super-intelligences, to tell me about Joel's death."

Hwa wished she'd eaten something. Then she'd have something to vomit all over Lynch's shoes. That would have been nice.

"You believe that?" Hwa asked. "You really, truly believe that some . . ." There was no proper hand gesture to communicate the enormity of what Lynch was suggesting. "Some . . . god-like AI is trying to warn you about your son's death?"

"Yes. I believe that there is a conspiracy of sentient artificial super-intelligences to kill my son."

"Like the Terminator."

Lynch's lip twitched. "No. That would be preposterous. Imagine the energy required to send physical matter backward across a line of spacetime, when we have printers right here and now that could do the job based on programming sent from any hacked satellite in low orbit. Why, the mundane AI we all depend on every day is already far too vulnerable to brainwashing. And the implants." He snorted. "The implants commercially available on today's market are, frankly, no more solid than Swiss cheese. That's why all of mine are custom coded, just like my drugs." He smiled and held up his hand, like a magician about to pull off a big trick. "Imagine: centuries from now, a post-human civilization triangulating our temporal and celestial location, and sending back retro-viruses reverse-engineered from the building blocks of their own code? How frustrating that must have been for them. Of course they finally just sent a card."

Lynch bent down a little to look her in the eye. It was obviously difficult for him to move like that. Scaffolding held up his body the way it might hold up a ruined cathedral. He was being totally sincere, she realized. He believed every word that was coming out of his mouth. He hadn't the foggiest notion that he might be completely out of his fucking mind. He smiled at her and took her hand to help her straighten up.

"Do you believe in the deep future, Miss Go?"

Her knees popped as she stood. "I never plan that far ahead."

His dry lips pulled back from his teeth. It was like a smile. Sort of. "Well, I do. And there are others like me who do, too. We've been planning for the arrival of these sapient un-consciousnesses for quite some time. Through our business developments, and through our investments, we've been trying to prove our willingness to work with these forces when they eventually arrive. It's an extension of the Roko's Basilisk idea."

Hwa decided that this was probably not the right time to remind Lynch that she was a high-school dropout, and that while she was fluent in multiple languages, her mother-tongue was cursing. She had no time for corporate lore, or fairy tales, which were apparently the same thing these days. "Did someone . . . I don't know . . . *sell* you this idea? Like maybe at a seminar, or something? Like a time-share?"

Lynch looked aghast. "Do you take me for a *rube*? Some gullible old *rube* that buys into every promise of eternity? I'm not a religious man, Miss Go. Far from it. I see things as they truly are. I'm prepared for the future. Humanity is coming to an end. Some day people like you—people who remain fully organic—will be nothing more than specimens in a museum of humanity."

"I bet you say that to all the girls," Hwa said.

"Oh, I do not mean to offend. I think yours is a very brave choice."

Choice had little to do with it. Money was the thing. When you had no money, you had no choice. But there was no use explaining that to someone like Zachariah Lynch.

"But you still have time to change your mind, Miss Go. If you choose to take this position, you will have the full benefits that come with being part of the Lynch organization. After three months' probation, you could have the latest stimplant, a chiplab, gene therapy. Whatever you like. Stay with us, and you will never have another seizure again. You will never get glaucoma. And the angioma, well . . ." She heard the soft machine whisper of his joints moving as he gestured elaborately.

Hwa swallowed. "You sure know how to make an offer."

"My youngest boy is very special to me, Miss Go. His brothers and sisters don't see it, of course. They didn't read his mother's genetic analysis. I've never bred with a finer woman, and I never will again. I've known her since she was a child, you know. I knew her parents. I introduced them."

"That's . . ." Hwa tried to think of a word that wasn't *sick*. "Cozy."

"He's everything I always wanted, and more. And he's the only one fit to take the reins when I'm gone. But he can't do that if he's not here."

Hwa set her shoulders. "And you want me to protect him?"

"*He* wants you to protect him, Miss Go. And I trust his decision. I have to. He's the future."

Lynch raised his hand. Hwa held hers up to stop him. "Wait. I have a question."

"Yes?"

"Does Joel know about these threats?"

Lynch shook his head. "No. These are more profound mysteries than he is ready for. And as his father, I don't want to frighten him. He's already lived every day with the threat of kidnapping, being my son." Lynch looked into her eyes. "If you decide to take this position, my one stipulation is that you not tell him why your presence is so very necessary."

Lynch waved. The walls fell away. Joel stood surrounded by his family, talking with Síofra. He was totally unaware of how his older siblings—his *much* older siblings—were staring at him. But Hwa knew that look. It was so plain she felt a little embarrassed for them for being so obvious, and embarrassed for the kid for not picking up on it. They were jealous. They were jealous that this skinny little brat with no discernible skills was being picked first for a job they'd been training for since they were born. Jealous that Daddy loved Joel best. Jealous that he loved fucking—or maybe just inseminating—Joel's mother, so much so that he wouldn't shut up about it. Jealous that Joel would get all of the money and power and almost none of the hassle of putting up with the media maelstrom and bottomless fountain of bullshit that was Zachariah Lynch. Just plain jealous. And it was eating them up, inside. Hwa didn't need special lenses or filters or access to one layer of reality or another to put that together. It was plain to see with the naked eye.

Lynch could worry all he wanted about killer robots or reptoids or tentacle monsters from outside of time and space. It was probably easier for the old man than facing the truth. The people who really wanted Joel out of the picture were already in the room with him.

"I have big plans for this town, Miss Go," Lynch whispered. "And I'd like my son to be a part of them. Now, do we have a deal?"

Hwa looked at Joel. He was so alone out there. Just this kid listening to all the adults. Wondering what all the fuss was. He gave her a very shy, hopeful smile.

"You." She pitched her voice at Joel, loud enough so his siblings shut up. "Come here."

Joel crossed the room to meet her. "What's wrong?" he asked.

"You really want me for this job?"

Joel smiled. He nodded emphatically. "Yes."

"It'll be hard," Hwa said. "Can you handle that?"

Again he nodded.

"I won't go easy on you just because of your family name. I don't give a shit about that. You want me to train you, then you follow my rules. You do what I say, when I say it, and how I say it. You don't whine, and you don't complain, but you do tell me if you're hurt or you're sick. Okay?"

"I don't get sick," Joel said. "And I've never really been hurt."

Hwa grinned. "We'll fix that." She glanced at Joel's father. "We have a deal."

"Good. Please give Daniel your contact information, and so on. We'll need your Social Insurance Number. Joel, come with me."

And with that, the mirrors enclosed him once more. He was gone. The others in the room seemed to take that as their cue to leave. They drifted out of the room without saying good-bye, and took Joel with them. She saw him cast a glance at her over his shoulder as the mirrors closed behind him. Soon only Síofra was left.

"So," he said. "What did *you* see in the crystal ball?"

4

Bruises

Hwa didn't tell him what she'd seen in the crystal ball. Nor did she tell anyone. She was tempted to tell Mistress Séverine, when she handed in her notice, but her union rep seemed not to care about why she was leaving. "Of course you must take this job," she had said. "It's tailor-made for you."

"I'll be back to school," Hwa said. "And there's health benefits. Better than the provincial plan."

Séverine had taken Hwa by the shoulders. "We will miss you. But opportunities are thin on the ground, in this place. You must take them as you find them."

And so they cashed out her pension, and Hwa put down first and last on a shitbox studio in Tower One. Eileen told her she should apply for something better, but even looking at places in Two or Three made her feel like a fake. It wasn't like she had a lot of stuff, anyway. And she had no plans to entertain. School started the following week, and with it came a raft of shiny new toys Hwa was supposed to wear all the time. She wasn't sure which she hated more: the specs, the bug in her ear, or the stupid tartan uniform.

"Doesn't it get distracting, like? Hearing me breathing?" Hwa asked.

"Only at first," her new boss said.

Her feet pounded the pavement. She ducked under the trees that made up the Fitzgerald Causeway Arboretum. Without the rain pattering on the hood of her jacket, she could hear the edges of Síofra's voice a little better. The implant made sure she got most of the bass tones and vowels as a rumble that trickled down her spine. Some consonants and sibilants, though, tended to fizzle out.

"You get up earlier than I do, so I've had to adjust."

Hwa rounded the corner to the Fitzgerald Hub. It swung out wide into the North Atlantic, the easternmost edge of the city, a ring of green on the flat grey sea. Here the view was best. Better even than the view from the top of Tower Five, where Síofra had his office. Here you could forget the oil rig at the city's core, the plumes of fire and smoke, the rusting honeycomb of containers that made up Tower One where Hwa lived. Here you couldn't even see the train. It screamed along the track overhead, but she heard only the tail end of its wail as the rain diminished.

"It's better to get a run in before work. Better for the metabolism."

"So I've heard."

Síofra probably had a perfect metabolism. It would be a combination of deep brain stimulation that kept him from serotonin crashes, a vagus nerve implant that regulated his insulin production, and whatever gentle genetic optimization he'd had in utero. He was a regular goddamn Übermensch.

"Look out your window," she said.

"Give me your eyes."

"I'm not wearing the specs."

"Why not?"

"They're expensive. I could slip and fall while I'm running."

"Then we would give you new ones."

"Wouldn't that come out of my pay?"

A soft laugh that went down to the base of her spine. *"Those were the last owners of this city. Lynch is different."*

She rolled her neck until it popped. All the way across town, her boss hissed in sympathy. "Look out your window," she reminded him.

"Fine, fine." An intake of breath. He was getting up. From his desk, or from his bed? *"Oh,"* he murmured.

Hwa stared into the dawn behind the veil of rain. It was a line of golden fire on a dark sea. "I time it like this, sometimes," she said. "Part of why I get up early."

"I see."

She heard thunder roll out on the waves, and in a curious stereo effect, heard the same sound reverberating through whatever room Síofra was in.

"May I join you, tomorrow?"

Hwa's mouth worked. She was glad he couldn't see her. The last person she'd had a regular running appointment with was her brother. Which meant she hadn't run with anyone in three years. Then again, maybe it would be good for Síofra to learn the city from the ground up. He spent too much time shut up behind the gleaming ceramic louvers of Tower Five. He needed to see how things were on the streets their employer had just purchased.

She grinned. "Think you can keep up with me?"

"Oh, I think I can manage."

· · ·

Of course, Síofra managed just fine. He showed up outside Tower One at four thirty in the morning bright-eyed and bushy-tailed. Like everything else about him, even his running form was annoyingly perfect. He kept his chin up and his back straight throughout the run. He breathed evenly and smoothly and carried on a conversation without any issues. At no point did he complain of a stitch in his side, or a bone spur in his heel, or tension in his quads. Nor did he suggest that they stretch their calves first, or warm up, or anything like that. He just started running.

A botfly followed them the entire way.

"Do we really need that?" Hwa asked. "We can ping for help, no problem, if something happens." She gestured at the empty causeway. "Not that anything's going to happen."

"What if you have a seizure?" her boss asked.

Hwa almost pulled up short. It took real and sustained effort not to. She kept her eyes on the pavement, instead. They had talked about her condition only once. Most people never brought it up. Maybe that was a Canadian thing. After all, her boss had worked all over the world. They were probably a lot less polite in other places.

"My condition's in my halo," she muttered.

"Pardon?"

"My halo has all my medical info," she said, a little louder this time. She shook her watch. "If my specs detect a change in my eye movement, they broadcast my status on the emergency layer. Everyone can see it. Everyone with the right eyes, anyway."

"But you don't wear your specs when you're running," he said, and pulled forward.

The route took them along the Demasduwit Causeway, around Tower Two, down the Sinclair Causeway, and back to Tower Two. New ads on new surfaces greeted them as they passed. The new city departments each had their own cuddly mascot AI that tried to remind Hwa about what she needed for her new apartment. They waved to her from pop-up carts and shop windows. They showed her sales on merchandise from brands she didn't recognize, brands Lynch had partnered with. New Arcadia was a captive audience, after all; the whole city was like one big focus group. She did her best to ignore the ads. Even if she were interested, she had no time to pay attention. It was a school day, which meant Hwa had to scope New Arcadia Secondary before Joel Lynch arrived for class. This meant showering and dressing in the locker room, which meant she had to finish at a certain time, which meant eating on schedule, too. If she ate before the run, she tended to throw up.

She was going to explain all this, when Síofra slowed down and pulled up to Hwa's favourite 24-hour cart and held up two fingers. "Two Number Sixes," he said. He stood first one one leg and then another, pulling his calf up behind him as he did. From behind the counter, old Jorge squinted at him until Hwa jogged up to join him. Then he smiled.

"You have a friend!" He made it sound like she'd just run a marathon. Which it felt like she had—keeping up with Síofra had left her legs trembling and her skin dripping.

"He's my boss." She leaned over and spat out some of the phlegm that had boiled up to her throat during the run. "What he said. And peameal." She blinked at Síofra through sweat. He was looking away, probably reading something in his lenses. One of his legs jagged up and down, seemingly without his knowledge. "You like peameal?"

"Sorry?"

"Peameal. Bacon. Do you like it? They print it special here."

"Oh. I suppose."

She glanced at Jorge. "Peameal. On the side."

Jorge handed them their coffees while the rest of the breakfast cooked. Now the city was waking up, and the riggers joining the morning shift were on their way to the platform. A few of them stood blinking at the other carts as they waited for them to open up.

"How did you know my order?" Hwa asked.

Síofra rolled his neck. It crunched. He was avoiding the answer. Hwa already suspected what he would say. Finally, he said it. "I see the purchases you make with the corporate currency."

She scowled. "I don't always have the eggs baked in avocado, you know. Sometimes I have green juice."

"Not since the cucumbers went out of season."

Hwa stared. "You're stalking me."

"I'm not stalking you. This is just how Lynch does things. We know what all our people buy in the canteen at lunch, because they use our watches to do it. It helps us know what food to buy. That way everyone can have their favourite thing. The schools here do the same thing—it informs the farm floors what to grow. This is no different."

Hwa sighed. "I miss being union."

• • •

Joel Lynch's vehicle drove him to the school's main entrance exactly fifteen minutes before the first bell. Hwa stood waiting for him outside the doors. He waved their way in—the school still did not recognize her face, years after she'd dropped out—and smirked at her.

"How are your legs?" he asked.

"Christ, does my boss tell you *everything*?"

"Daniel just said I should go easy on you, today!" Joel tried hard to look innocent. "And that maybe we didn't have to do leg day today, if you didn't really want to."

"You trying to get out of your workout?"

"Oh, no! Not at all! I was just thinking that—"

"Good, because we're still doing leg day. My job is protecting you, and how I protect you is making you better able to protect yourself. Somebody tries to take you, I need you to crush his instep with one kick and then run like hell. Both of which involve your legs."

"So, leg day."

Hwa nodded. "Leg day."

"You can crush someone's instep with one kick?"

Hwa rolled her eyes and hoped her specs caught it. "Of course I can," she subvocalized.

"I think I'd pay good money to see that."

"Well, it's a good thing I'm on the payroll, then."

The school day proceeded just like all the others. Announcements. Lectures. Worksheets. French. Past imperfect, future imperfect. Lunch. People staring at Joel, then sending each other quick messages. Hwa saw it all in the specs—the messages drifting across her vision like dandelion fairies. In her vision, the messages turned red when Joel's name came up. For the most part, it didn't. While she wore the uniform and took the classes just like the other students, they knew why she was there. They knew she was watching. They knew about her old job.

"Hwa?"

Hwa turned away from the station where Joel was attempting squats. Hanna Oleson wore last year's volleyball t-shirt and mismatched socks. She also had a wicked bruise on her left arm. And she wouldn't quite look Hwa in the eye.

"Yeah?" Hwa asked.

"Coach says you guys can have the leg press first."

"Oh, good. Thanks." She made Hanna meet her gaze. The other girl's eyes were bleary, red-rimmed. Shit. "What happened to your arm?"

"Oh, um . . . I fell?" Hanna weakly flailed the injured arm. "During practise? And someone pulled me up? Too hard?"

Hwa nodded slowly. "Right. Sure. That happens."

Hanna smiled. It came on sudden and bright. Too sudden. Too bright. "Everything's fine, now."

Hwa moved, and Hanna shuffled away to join the volleyball team. She turned back to Joel. He'd already put the weights down. She was about to say something about his slacking off, when he asked: "Do you know her?"

Hwa turned and looked at Hanna. She stood a little apart from the others, tugging a sweatshirt on over her bruised arm. She took eye drops from the pocket and applied them first to one eye, and then the other. "I know her mother," Hwa said.

• • •

Mollie Oleson looked a little rounder than Hwa remembered her. She couldn't remember their last appointment together, which meant it had probably happened months ago. After that time Angel choked her out. Mollie was more of a catch-as-catch-can kind of operator—she only listed herself as available to the USWC 314 when she felt like it. It kept her dues low and her involvement minimal. But as a member she was entitled to the same protection as a full-timer.

Hwa sidled up to her in the children's section of the Benevolent Irish Society charity shop. Mollie stood hanging little baggies of old fabtoys on a pegboard. "We close in fifteen minutes," she said, under her breath.

"Even for me?" Hwa asked.

"Hwa!" Mollie beamed, and threw her arms around Hwa. Like her daughter, she was one of those women who really only looked pretty when she was happy. Unlike her daughter, she was good at faking it.

"What are you at?"

"I got a new place," Hwa said. "Thought it was time for some new stuff."

Mollie's smile faltered. "Oh, yeah . . ." She adjusted a stuffed polar bear on a shelf so that it faced forward. "How's that going? Working for the Lynches, I mean?"

"The little one is all right," Hwa said. "Skinny little bugger. I'm training him. He's in for a trimming."

Mollie gave a terse little smile. "Well, good luck to you. About time you got out of the game, I'd say. A girl your age should be thinking about the future. You don't want to wind up . . ." She gestured around the store, rather than finishing the sentence.

"I saw Hanna at school, today. Made me think to come here."

Mollie's hands stilled their work. "Oh? How was she? I haven't seen her since this morning." She looked out the window to the autumn darkness. "Closing shift, and all."

Hwa nodded. "She's good." She licked her lips. It was worth a shot. She had to try. "Her boyfriend's a bit of a dick, though."

Mollie laughed. "Hanna doesn't have a boyfriend! She has no time, between school and volleyball and her job."

"Her job?"

"Skipper's," Mollie said. "You know, taking orders, bussing tables, the like. It's not much, but it's a job."

"Right," Hwa said. "Well, my mistake. I guess that guy was just flirting with her."

"Well, I'll give you the employee discount, just for sharing that little tidbit. Now I have something to tease her with, b'y?"

"Oh, don't do that," Hwa said. "I don't want her to know I told on her."

• • •

At home, Hwa used her Lynch employee log-in to access the Prefect city management system. Lynch installed it overnight during a presumed brownout, using a day-zero exploit to deliver the viral load that was their surveillance overlay. It was easier than doing individual installations, Síofra had explained to her. Some kids in what was once part of Russia had used a similar exploit to gain access to a Lynch reactor in Kansas. That was fifteen years ago.

Now it was a shiny interface that followed Hwa wherever she went. Or rather, wherever she let it. Her refrigerator and her washroom mirror were both too old for it. So it lived in her specs, and in the display unit Lynch insisted on outfitting her with. That made it the most expensive thing in what was a very cheap studio apartment.

"Prefect, show me Oleson, Hanna," she said.

The system shuffled through profiles until it landed on two possibilities, each fogged over. One was Hanna. The other was a woman by the name of Anna Olsen. Maybe it thought Hwa had misspoken.

"Option one." Hanna's profile became transparent as Anna's vanished. It solidified across the display, all the photos and numbers and maps hanging and shimmering in Hwa's vision. She squinted. "Dimmer."

Hanna's profile dimmed slightly, and Hwa could finally get a real look at it. Like Hwa, Hanna lived in Tower One. She'd been picked up once on a shoplifting charge, two years ago. Hwa raised her hands and gestured through all the points at which facial identification had identified Hanna in the last forty-eight hours. Deeper than that, and she'd need archival access.

"Prefect, show me this person's network."

Other faces bloomed around Hanna's. They orbited her face slowly, like satellites. Hwa scrolled through them with two fingers. She recognized most of them from school.

"Any on the hot list?"

It took a moment for Prefect's algorithms to find the likely violent offenders around Hanna. But Hanna's dad popped up immediately. That made sense. Mollie hadn't left him; she enjoyed their times together so much. They lived in different towers, now, which helped.

There was another name on the list. Jared Pullman. He was twenty-three. He'd been busted for boosters; there was also a pending assault charge at the offtrack-betting arcade where he worked.

In his photo, his eyes were very, very red. "Goddamn it," Hwa muttered.

But before pursuing him, she needed to call Skipper's. Rule them out. "Hi, is Hanna there?"

"Hanna doesn't work here anymore." Hwa heard beeping. The sounds of fryer alarms going off. Music. "Hello?"

Hwa ended the call.

There was Hanna on the Acoutsina Causeway, walking toward Tower One. The image was time-stamped after volleyball practise. Speed-trap checked her entering a ride in the driverless lane at 18:30. Five minutes later, she was gone. Wherever she was now, there were no cameras.

"Prefect, search this vehicle and this face together."

A long pause. *"Archive access required."*

For a fleeting moment, Hwa regretted the fact that Prefect was not a human being she could intimidate. "Is there a record in the archives?"

"Archive access required."

Hwa growled a little to herself. She popped up off the floor and began to pace. She walked through the projections of Hanna's face, sliding the ribbon of stills and clips until she hit the top of the list. Today was Monday. If Hanna had sustained her injury on Friday night, then Hwa was out of luck. But Mollie had said she worked all weekend. Maybe that meant—

"What are you doing?"

Hwa startled. "Jesus Christ, stop doing that!"

"Doing what?" Síofra was trying to sound innocent. It wasn't working.

"You know exactly what," she said. "Why can't you just text, like a normal person? How do you know I wasn't having a natter with somebody?"

"Your receiver would have told me," he said.

Hwa frowned. "Can you . . . ?" She wished she had an image of him she could focus her fury on. "Can you listen in on my conversations, through my receiver?"

"Only during your working hours."

"And you can just . . . tune in? All day? While I'm at school with Joel?"

"Of course I can. I thought you had some excellent points to make about Jane Eyre *in Mr. Bartel's class."*

Hwa plunged the heels of her hands into the sockets of her eyes. She had known this was possible, of course. She just assumed Síofra actually had other work to do, and wasn't constantly spying on her instead of accomplishing it.

"Are you bored?"

"I'm sorry?"

"Are you bored? At work? Is your job that boring? That you need to be tuned into my day like that?"

There was a long pause. She wondered for a moment if he'd cut out. *"You watch Joel and I watch you,"* he said. *"That is my job."*

Hwa sighed. He had her, there. It was all right there in the Lynch employee handbook. She'd signed on for this level of intrusion when she'd taken their money. He was paying, so he got to watch. She'd stood guard at enough peep shows to learn that particular lesson. Maybe she wasn't so different from her mother, after all.

"You aren't supposed to be prying into your fellow classmates' lives unless they pose a credible threat to Joel." So he'd been spying on her searches, too. Of course. *"I know what you're thinking, and—"*

"How come I can't do this to you?" Hwa blurted. "That's what I'm thinking. I'm wondering how come I can't watch you all the time the way you watch me. Why doesn't this go both ways? Why don't I get to know when you're watching me?"

Another long pause. *"Is there something about me that you would like to know?"*

Oh, just everything, she thought. The answer came unbidden, and she shut her eyes and clenched her jaw and squashed it like a bug crawling across her consciousness.

"Are you coming running tomorrow?"

"Of course I am."

. . .

Síofra had a whole route planned. He showed it to her the next morning in her specs, but she had only a moment to glance over it before heading out the door.

"Why did you stay in this tower?" Síofra asked, leaning back and craning his neck to take in the brutalist heap of former containers. "We pay you well enough to afford one of the newer ones. This one has almost no security to speak of."

"You've been watching me twenty-four/seven all this time and you still haven't figured that one out? Corporate surveillance ain't what it used to be."

"Is it because your mother lives here?"

Hwa pulled up short. "You just don't know when to quit, do you?"

"I only wondered because you never visit her." He grinned, and pushed ahead of Hwa down the causeway.

His route took them along the Acoutsina. They circled the first joint, and Síofra asked about the old parkette and the playground. This early, there were no children, and it remained littered with beer cozies and liquor pouches. She told him about the kid who had kicked her down the slide once, and how nobody let her on the swings, and he assumed it had to do with her mother and what she did for a living. His eyes were not programmed to see her true face, or the stain dripping from her left eye down her neck to her arm and her ribs and her leg. She had tested his vision several times; he never stared, never made reference to her dazzle-pattern face. And with their connection fostered by her wearables, he probably never watched her via botfly or camera. He could spend every minute of every day observing her, and never truly see her.

They ran to the second joint of the causeway and circled the memorial for those who had died in the Old Rig. "Do you want to stop?" he asked.

It was bad luck not to pay respects. She knew exactly where her brother's name was. Síofra waited for her at the base of the monument as her steps spiralled up the mound. She slapped Tae-kyung's name lightly, like tagging him in a relay run, and kept going. Síofra had already started up again by the time she made it back down. They were almost at Tower Three when he called a halt, in a parking lot full of rides.

"Cramp," he said, pulling his calf up behind him. He placed a hand up against a parked vehicle for balance. When Hwa's gaze followed his hand, she couldn't help but see the licence plate.

It was the one she'd asked Prefect to track. The one Hanna had disappeared into, last night. "I thought . . ." Hwa looked from him to the vehicle. "I thought you said—"

"I haven't the faintest idea what you're talking about, Hwa." He smirked. Then he appeared to check something in his lenses. "Goodness, look at the time. I have an early meeting. I think I'll just pick up one of these rides here and take it back to the office. Are you all right finishing the run alone?"

Hwa frowned at him. He winked at her. She smiled. "Yeah," she said. "I'm good here."

He gestured at the field of rides and snapped his fingers at one of them. It lit up. Its locks opened. She watched him get into it and leave. Now alone, Hwa peered into the vehicle. Nothing left behind on any of the seats. No dings or scratches. She looked around at the parking lot. Empty. Still dark. She pulled her hood up, and took a knee. She fussed with her shoelaces with one hand while her other fished in the pocket of her vest. The joybuzzer hummed between her fingers as she stood. And just like that, the trunk unlocked.

Hanna was inside. Bound and gagged. And completely asleep.

"Shit," Hwa muttered. Then the vehicle chirped. Startled, Hwa scanned the parking lot. Still empty. The ride was being summoned elsewhere. It rumbled to life. If Hwa let it go now, she would lose Hanna. In the trunk, Hanna blinked awake. She squinted up at Hwa. Behind her gag, she began to scream.

"It's okay, Hanna." Hwa threw the trunk door even wider, and climbed in. She pulled it shut behind her as it began to move. "You're okay. We're okay." The vehicle lurched. She heard the lock snap shut again as the ride locked itself. "We're okay," she repeated. "We're going to be okay."

. . .

Hwa busied herself untying Hanna as the ride drove itself. "Tell me where we're going," Hwa said.

"It's my fault," Hanna was saying. "He told me not to talk to Benny."

"Benny work at Skipper's?" Hwa picked the tape off Hanna's wrists.

"I told him I was just being nice." Hanna gulped for air. She coughed. "I quit, just like he told me to, but Benny and I are in the same biology class! I couldn't just ignore him. And Jared said if I really loved him, I'd do what he asked. . . ."

"Jared?" Mentally, Hwa kicked herself. She'd known he was on the hot list, but hadn't chased down the lead any further. She needed Prefect. Why hadn't she brought her specs? She could be looking at a map, right now. She could be finding out how big this guy was. If there was video attached to his assault charge. Where his weak spots were.

"Why are you here?" Hanna asked. "Did my mom send you? I thought you didn't work with us, anymore."

Beneath them, the buckles in the pavement burped along. They were still on the Acoutsina, then. It had the oldest roads with the most repairs. Hwa worked to quiet the alarm bell ringing in her head. Hanna's skin was so cold under her hands. She probably needed a hospital. But right now, she needed Hwa to be calm. She needed Hwa to be smart. She needed Hwa to think.

"With us?" Hwa asked.

"For the union," Hanna sniffed.

"Eh?"

The angle of the vehicle changed. They tipped down into something. Hwa heard hydraulics. They were in a lift. Tower Three.

They'd parked Hanna not far from where they were, then. Hwa's ears popped. She rolled up as close as possible to the opening of the trunk. She cleared her wrists and flexed her toes. She'd have one good chance when the trunk opened. If there weren't too many of them. If they didn't have crowbars. Something slammed onto the trunk. A fist. A big one, by the sound of it.

"Wakey, wakey, Hanna!"

The voice was muffled, but strong. Manic. He'd been awake for a while. Boosters? Shit. Hanna started to say something, but Hwa shushed her.

"Had enough time to think about what you did?"

Definitely boosters. That swaggering arrogance, those delusions of grandeur. Hwa listened for more voices, the sound of footsteps. She heard none. Maybe this was a solo performance.

"You know, I didn't like doing this. But you made me do it. You have to learn, Hanna."

Behind her, Hanna was crying.

"I can't have you just giving it away. It really cuts into what I'm trying to do for us."

Fingers drummed on the trunk of the ride.

"Are you ready to come out and say you're sorry?"

You're goddamn right I am, Hwa thought.

The trunk popped open. Jared's pale, scaly face registered surprise for just a moment. Then Hwa's foot snapped out and hit him square in the jaw. He stumbled back and tried to slam the trunk shut. It landed on her leg and she yelled. The door bounced up. Not her ankle. Not her knee. Thank goodness. She rolled out.

Jared was huge. A tall, lanky man in his early twenties, the kind of rigger who'd get made fun of by guys with more muscle while still being plenty strong enough to get the job done. He had bad skin and a three-day growth of patchy beard. He lunged for Hwa and she jumped back. He swung wide and she jumped again.

"Let me guess," she said. "You told Hanna you'd fix it with the union if she paid you her dues directly. Even though she's a minor and USWC doesn't allow those."

Jared's eyes were red. He spat blood. He reeked of booster sweat— acrid and bitter.

"And you had her doing what, camwork?" She grinned. "I thought her eyes were red because she'd been crying. But yours look just the same. You're both wearing the same shitty lenses."

"He made me watch the locker room." Hanna sat on her knees in the trunk of the ride. Her voice was a croak. For a moment she looked so much like her mother that Hwa's heart twisted in her chest. "He said he'd edit my team's faces out—"

"Shut up!"

Jared reached for the lid of the trunk again. He tried to slam it shut on Hanna. Hwa ran for him. He grabbed her by the shoulders. Hwa's right heel came down hard on his. The instep deflated under the pressure. He howled. She elbowed him hard under the ribs and spun halfway out of his grip. His right hand still clung to her vest. She grabbed the wrist and wedged it into the mouth of the trunk.

"Hanna! Get down!"

She slammed the lid once. Then twice. Then a third time. *He'll never work this rig again,* she thought, distantly. The trunk creaked open and Jared sank to his knees. He clutched his wrist. His hand dangled from his arm like a piece of wet kelp.

Behind her, she heard a slow, dry clap.

"Excellent work," Síofra said.

He leaned against the ride he'd summoned. Two go-cups of coffee sat on the hood. He held one out.

"You didn't want in on that?" Hwa asked, jerking her head at the whimpering mess on the floor of the parking garage.

"Genius can't be improved upon." Síofra gestured with his cup. "We should get them to a hospital. Or a police station."

"Hanna needs a hospital." Hwa sipped her coffee. "This guy,

I should report to the union. He falsified a membership and defrauded someone of dues in bad faith."

"They don't take kindly to that, in the USWC?"

Hwa swallowed hard. "Nope. Not one bit."

Síofra made a sound in his throat like purring.

. . .

During the elevator ride between the hospital and the school in Tower Two, Hwa munched a breakfast sandwich. She'd protested the presence of bread, but Síofra said the flour was mostly crickets anyway. So she'd relented. Now he stood across the elevator watching her eat.

"What?" she asked, between swallows.

"I have something to share with you."

She swiped at her mouth with the back of her hand. "Aye?"

"I don't remember anything beyond ten years ago."

Hwa blinked. "Sorry?"

"My childhood. My youth. They're . . ." He made an empty gesture. "Blank."

She frowned. "Do you mean, like . . . emotionally?"

"No. Literally. I literally don't remember. My first memory is waking up in a Lynch hospital in South Sudan, ten years ago. They had some old wells, there. They were replacing them with photo farms. I was injured. They brought me in. Patched me up. Paid for my augments. They assumed I was a fixer of some sort. They don't know for which side. Apparently I had covered my tracks a little too well. I've worked for them ever since."

Hairs rose on the back of Hwa's neck. "Wow."

"As long as I can remember, I've worked for this company. I don't know any other kind of life."

"Okay," Hwa said.

"I've never lived without their presence in my life. I've never had what you might call a private life."

Oh. "Oh."

"But you have. And that's something that's different, about our experiences."

"Yeah. You could say that."

"You don't have implants," he said. "Not permanent ones, anyway. They—we—can't gather that kind of data from you. They don't have a complete profile for you, yet. But they know everything about me. My sugars, how much I sleep, where I am, if I'm angry, my routines, even the music I listen to when I'm making dinner."

"You listen to music while you make dinner?"

"Django Reinhardt."

"Who?"

He smiled ruefully. "What I'm saying is, you're the last of a dying breed."

Hwa thought of the stain running down her body, the flaw he couldn't see. He had no idea. "Thank you?"

"You're a black swan," he said. "A wild card. Something unpredictable. Like getting into the trunk of that ride this morning."

Hwa shrugged. "Anybody could have done that. I couldn't just let Hanna go. She needed my help."

"You could have called the police. You could have called *me*. But you didn't. You took the risk yourself."

She frowned. "Are you pissed off? Is that what this is about? Because you're the one who—"

Síofra hissed. He shook his head softly. With his gaze, he brought her attention to the eyes at the corners of the elevator where the eyes probably were.

"I just want you to know something about me," he said, after a moment. "Something that isn't in my halo."

She smiled. "Well, thanks."

"Not a lot of other people know this, about me."

"Well, it is kind of weird." She stretched up, then hinged down at the waist until her vertebrae popped their stiffness loose. She pressed her fingers into the floor and looked up at him from her rag doll position. "I mean, you are only ten years old, right? You can't even drink."

He rolled his eyes. "Here it comes."

She stood. "Or vote. Or even have your own place. Does your landlord know about this?"

He pointed at the view of the city outside the elevator. "My landlord is your landlord."

The elevator doors chimed open. They were on the school floor. Hwa had fifteen minutes to shower and put on her uniform before she met Joel.

"Hey, if you're not too busy? I kind of didn't do the last question on my physics homework. So I might need some help with that. Before I hand it in."

"I think something can be arranged."

She stood in the door. It chimed insistently. She leaned on it harder. "Did you ever go to school? After you woke up, I mean? Or are you just winging it?"

"I know what a man my age needs to know," Síofra said. "Be seeing you."

5

Silent Seizure

"I hate these things," Hwa said.

"They're the latest model. And perfect for someone without other augments."

"They're . . ." Hwa wiggled her fingers in front of her specs. As she did, the device scanned the scars on her knuckles and filed them away in some silvery somewhere that was probably just a data-barge rusting off the coast of one former Eastern bloc nation or another. DAMAGED, the glasses said, and pointed helpful blinking arrows at her fingers and wrists and shins and feet and anywhere else she looked. DAMAGED. Like she didn't know that much already.

"They're loud," she said, finally.

"They're the quietest on the market." Síofra actually sounded a little hurt. Like he'd gone to the trouble of picking out something great and fucked it up instead. Which was exactly what had happened.

"Don't worry. I'll get used to it." Hwa scanned the main entrance. The specs told her where every little camera and microphone was. They lit up snitch-yellow on the map. She could pick out the angry kids (red halos), the sad ones (blue), the baselines (green), and the ones who were making out with each other (grinding columns of deep purple).

"We should have gotten them for you sooner. But for someone like you, someone who's lived for so long without . . ." He sounded uncomfortable. Like he didn't know how to finish. Hwa stared out at the uniform perfection of her fellow students. They were all mainstream: mainstream height, mainstream weight, mainstream ability, mainstream health. Technically editing skin colour or hair texture qualified as a kind of hate crime, but Hwa had her suspicions.

The world was what it was, and she knew there were parents on the rig who wanted more for their children, even if it meant putting some English on the ball.

"Without any augments," Hwa said for him. "Without any help."

"Most of these devices are designed to work alongside other services, other technologies. But you're different."

If by "different," he meant "poor," then he was onto something. It wasn't that Hwa had some moral or aesthetic commitment to living free of augmentation. But Sunny had never found money for that kind of thing. At least, not when it came to Hwa. Hwa was a bad investment. The lasers that were supposed to fix the stain running down her face had only made things worse. Why throw good money after bad? The only good thing about that was that it finally got Hwa off the hook for dance lessons. After that—after Sunny knew she'd be ugly forever—Hwa got to do tae kwon do with Tae-kyung.

"The good thing is, now I can see what you see."

Hwa snorted. "You know I'll be shutting these off when I'm in the girls' locker room, right?"

"Could you say that a little louder, please? I'm not sure the PTA heard you."

"Oh, come on," Hwa said. "You're not worried about the PTA. You work for Lynch, and Lynch pays the wages. They'd offer you a two-fer on the Lindgren twins, if they could."

She directed her gaze to a pair of blond girls wearing varsity volleyball jackets over their uniforms. They reclined against the opposite wall, chests out, knees up, all shiny hair and white teeth and laughter. They were everybody's number-one fantasy. If you didn't want to fuck them, you wanted to be them. Their parents had so liked the prediction their genetic counselor gave them, they ordered two.

"Not interested."

"Liar."

"Can we not discuss this, please? We're being recorded, you know. For quality assurance purposes."

Hwa examined the floor. Her tights had a run in them down her good leg. She inspected the damage idly, twisting her leg this way and that, but her specs had nothing to say about it.

"Much better."

"I still can't believe I let you con me into coming back to this place."

"Better late than never. We were lucky to find a candidate for this position who lacked both a diploma and a prison record."

"Yeah, that's some luck, all right."

Across town, Síofra laughed. Hwa felt it as a tickle across her skull that skittered all the way to the base of her spine as sure as if someone had run a finger down there. She twitched against the wall.

"Hwa?"

Hwa opened her eyes to see Joel standing in front of her, blazer laid neatly across one arm, school tie in a tight little knot she couldn't help but want to mess up. Christ, he was even wearing the Krakens logo tie pin. *The tie pin.* Like he didn't already look enough like the skinniest little Tory ever.

Right then and there, Hwa decided she had to get the boy in some trouble before the trouble found him first.

"Hwa? Are you okay?"

The warning bell rang. Hwa shoved herself off the wall and teetered only a little. "I'm fine," she said. "Let's get to physics."

"Were you talking to Daniel?"

"Yeah." She raised her voice slightly so her boss would be sure to hear it. "But he should be *working*, and we should be, uh . . . *learning,* I guess."

. . .

There was a basic problem on the desk when they got to class. At least, Joel said it was pretty basic: "It's Moore's Law," he said. "About exponential growth in computational ability. Didn't you cover exponents in grade eight algebra?"

Hwa tried to remember grade eight. She'd turned fourteen that year, and had a general memory of fourteen sucking worse than the other years for some reason. Oh, yeah: because her mother wouldn't shut up about how *her* first single had gone *platinum,* when *she* was fourteen. And then she'd talk about pink champagne and parties and music producers and how to fend them off, always making certain to end her stories with something like, <<Not that you'll ever have that problem, Hwa-jeon.>>

Hwa-jeon. It was a dessert in Korea. When she was little, Hwa thought her nickname being a dessert meant she was sweet and special, a nice treat at the end of a nice person's day. Then she asked Sunny to make it for her.

<<Why would I want to eat those? They're all rice flour and sugar. You know I can't eat things like that. Why would you ask me to spend money on something I can't eat?>> Her mother had taken one look at Hwa's face and rolled her eyes. <<Besides. I don't have edible flowers, much less purple ones. How can I make it look like your face, without big purple flower petals?>>

"Hwa?"

"Huh?" Hwa blinked at Mr. Branch, who was peering at her with his head cocked. In the specs, his emotions didn't register like the students' did. Maybe the faculty all had theirs screened out. Not exactly sporting. "What? Sorry. Were you talking to me?"

"Yes. I was asking you where your homework was. I was calling the roll for missed assignments. Five hundred words on one problem you'd like science to solve?"

Hwa frowned. "What?"

"Just get me the assignment," Branch said. He started calling off more names.

"You can have mine," Joel whispered to her. "I wrote two."

Of course he did. "Why would you do twice the homework?"

"I'd already written one, on faster-than-light travel," Joel said, "but then I pinged him about it, just to show off, and he shot me down. Said he wasn't taking any biology questions in physics class."

"So what'd you write about, instead?"

"How the ITER alternative reactor failed, in France."

Hwa nodded. "That'd be good for science to figure out."

"Science *has* figured it out." A smirk tugged at the edges of Joel's lips. He lowered his voice still further. "That's why we're building another one."

Hwa turned to him. "We?"

"Our company," he said. "Well, the self-assemblers our company owns. They're building another experimental thermonuclear reactor, right here. Underwater."

"Underwater." Hwa pointed at the floor. "Under *this* water?"

Joel nodded. "Under the city."

Hwa drew breath. "What the hell kind of James Bond villain bullshit—"

"You promised your father you wouldn't discuss this outside the family, Joel," Síofra said. *"Hwa signed a nondisclosure agreement, but you shouldn't make it difficult for her to adhere to it."*

"You're building a fucking *sun* under this town, and *I'm* the one you're worried—"

"Miss Go!"

Hwa's head snapped up. Branch did not look happy. Shit.

"Since you and Mr. Lynch have so many things to discuss, perhaps you'd like to discuss them in the hall. Eight bins of fetal pigs were just delivered for Miss Jarvis's biology class, and they're not getting any colder sitting out in the mail room. I'd like you to bring them from downstairs to the science lounge, and load them in the refrigerator."

"Can we have the elevator pass?" Joel asked.

Branch smiled. "No."

Hwa shrugged. She stood. "Come on."

"But—"

"It'll be good for your arms. Let's go."

· · ·

"So, are you guys gonna disconnect the whole rig and fire everybody, or just wait until your science experiment explodes and kills us all?"

"It won't explode." Joel grunted, lost control of his one bin, and set it down on the floor. "Why wouldn't they give us a dolly or a hand truck or something we could use to lift these things?" He flexed his fingers. "My hands hurt."

They were barely out of the mail room off the main entrance. They'd been walking for all of two minutes, and hadn't even cleared the lobby yet. Even if the death threats against Joel were totally bogus, and Hwa was inclined to believe they were, she'd be damned if she didn't whip him into shape. The kid could barely lift twenty pounds.

"That's because you're using your hands and not your arms. And that's because you got no arms."

Joel flapped his arms at his sides.

"No. I mean, you got no *arms*." Hwa squatted to put her two bins down and straightened up. Her spine popped as she rose to her full height. She'd been slacking off on her vinyasas, and that was clearly a mistake. She stepped close to Joel and flexed her right arm. "Feel that."

Joel poked her arm. His eyes widened. "Is that your *bicep*?"

"It's the mass of time plus discipline. That's all it is."

Sheepish, Joel shuffled back to his bin and tried to lift it in a single mighty move. Hwa winced as his back sloped forward. He was trying to carry the thing on his nonexistent belly, like a fetus. Which was ironic, given the contents of the bin.

"Okay, lesson one," Hwa said. "Put that thing down."

"We have to get back to class."

"Oh, please. Fuck that guy. Seriously. Besides, this is physics, too. Sort of. The physics of not fucking up your lumbar region."

"I think that's kinesiology."

"Whatever. Put that down. No, really, put it down. Now, watch me. See how my back is planked? It's a straight line, from the back of my head to the bottom of my spine. See?"

Joel cocked his head. "Okay."

"Now, I squat down like I'm doing a clean lift. Because that's basically what this is, is a clean lift. I'll show you one later, in the weight room. And I lift *from the knees*—"

"*THIS IS A LOCKDOWN. ALL STUDENTS MUST REPORT TO CLASSROOMS IMMEDIATELY.*"

"Is it a drill?" Joel asked.

"Keep moving." Hwa's gaze slid slowly over a series of icons in the far right of her vision. One of them was an exclamation point. It was blinking. She focused on it and blinked three times. An alert swarmed up in her vision: *THIS IS A LOCKDOWN. ALL STUDENTS MUST REPORT TO CLASSROOMS IMMEDIATELY.*

Which one was the goddamn security icon? Why weren't these things more intuitive? She blinked out of the alerts menu and roved her gaze over the others. There it was. A badge. Security. She blinked three times.

"*FIFTY SECONDS.*"

There, in her left eye, was a juddering video feed of a man in a long coat. He was carrying a shotgun. He was on the edge of the atrium at the end of the lobby. Any minute now, he could change direction and cross the atrium, where he would see them. They were boxed in.

"*THIRTY SECONDS.*"

"Is it a drill?"

Hwa focused on Joel. "No," she said. "It's not."

"*TEN SECONDS.*"

Joel bolted back to the mail room. He pounded on the door. He tried the knob. It was locked. The blinds were down. Hwa began stacking bins. If they couldn't find shelter, she would have to make one. Maybe if she stacked the bins outside the mail room, they would just look like another delivery that hadn't been processed yet. Or maybe fetal pig bodies were especially good at absorbing hollowpoints.

"Sorry, piggies," she murmured. "Joel!"

"They won't let us in!"

"Not so loud!" Hwa gestured for him to hunker down beside her in the shadow of the bins. He came over and crouched. "Here's what we're gonna do," she said, and belatedly realized that phrasing something that way meant she actually had to have a plan.

"What?"

Hwa watched the shooter in her left eye. He was moving in the other direction. Good. "We have to be really quiet," she whispered.

"Okay."

Hwa tried to remember what the school security briefing had said about lockdowns. She'd gone through lockdown drills before dropping out, but being on the other side of all that procedure was different. In the security tab, she found a subheading marked EVACUATIONS AND DRILLS, and blinked at it. It unfolded across her right eye, and as she read, her heart sank.

"All the doors are locked, now. The whole school is sealed. Main doors, fire exits, everything. It's all remote; the cops are the only ones who can open it back up."

"Daniel could open it back up," Joel said. He focused elsewhere and whispered. "Daniel? Are you there? Daniel?"

Static.

"All the communications are being jammed," Hwa said. "That's part of it. In case there's a bomb. Or in case there's a hack in the system or the augments. Or a toxin. It's a total quarantine, until the cops come in. Nothing goes in or out. No people, no information, not even the air. Nothing."

There was a terrible silence. The silence of scared kids hiding behind locked doors. The silence of fans that have stopped spinning. Dead air, closed mouths, and empty halls. Hwa had never known the school to be so quiet. It sounded like everyone was already dead.

"We're alone," Joel said, finally.

"Yeah."

"So what do we do?"

Hwa looked again at the shooter. He was far on the other side of the atrium. "We move. Now. Quietly." Hwa pointed to the left of the atrium. "We need to get to the elevator on that side. I'll force the doors open. We can use the elevator shaft to get into the ducts. Then we use the ducts to climb into the lighting booth above the auditorium."

Joel looked at her as though she had just relayed all that information in Korean. Given the situation, maybe she had. "You're crazy."

"The lighting booth is the safest place in school, Joel. It's why everybody goes there to make out. There's only one way in or out, and it's a ladder that pulls up behind you."

He didn't look any more confident.

"Joel. Come on. Your dad hired me for a reason, right?"

He nodded.

"This is that reason."

His lips firmed and he nodded again. "Okay."

Hwa poked her head out first. The shooter was peering down another hallway. This was the perfect time to move. She gestured behind herself. "Go. Now."

Joel skittered around from behind her and started running. She chased from behind, keeping herself in line behind him. Their new shoes squeaked across the floor; it was recently waxed and Joel wiped out and yelped. In her left eye, the shooter's head came up and she saw him raise his gun—

—heard the dry pops of fire—

—felt her right arm open up—

—skidded to the nearest bathroom. It was the girl's room; there was only one door and it didn't lock. Hwa pushed Joel toward the back stall and locked the door behind them.

"I thought we were going to the elevator!"

Hwa held up her arm. It was as though a mouth had yawned open across her flesh. Yellow globules of fat dangled from underneath her ragged skin. "Plan's changed."

Joel went even paler than usual. "Oh, no."

"Yeah, karma's a bitch," Hwa said. "Shouldn't have showed it off to you."

"We have to apply pressure." Joel grabbed her arm and held it.

His hands shook. He seemed entirely too focused on his hands. "Wait. I have a better idea." He put Hwa's hand over her wound and held it there. "Hold on."

Hwa watched him hop off the toilet and open the stall door. "No, don't!"

He darted out and she heard a rough scraping sound and a few grunts. Finally there was a terrible screech, and he came back into the stall with a maxi pad in each hand. "I got the extra absorbent kind."

Hwa forced her grimace into a grin. "Nice work."

Joel removed the tie pin from his tie, loosened the tie, and pulled it off without un-knotting it. He tore open the packaging around one pad and frowned at the wad of antibacterial memory foam in his hand. "That's it? That's the best they can do?"

"Hey, those were miracle Space Age fibres, back in the day."

"Wow. No wonder you're so pissed off, all the time."

Joel wrapped the pad over Hwa's wound. Then she helped him slide his tie up her arm. He tightened the loop around the pad and then wrapped the rest of the tie's length around her arm and tucked the end into the wrap.

"Can you still move your fingers?" he asked.

Hwa flexed them. "Yeah. Thanks. You're kind of a genius."

Joel shrugged. "I know. That's what my test scores say."

"Seriously?"

"Pretty much. I have a certificate and everything."

She licked her lips. The wound in her arm was now more of a dull, throbbing ache. She could work with that. But only so much. "Well, you got any genius ideas for getting us back into that elevator? I can't force the doors with this arm."

Joel pulled the tie pin from his pocket. "Actually? I do."

• • •

The elevator had two access mechanisms: a standard chip-reader, and an old-fashioned lock-and-key system for when the power went out. Hwa stood guard as Joel worked the pin into the elevator's key slot.

"This always looks easier, in the dramas," Joel said.

"Don't force it," Hwa said. "Just feel around gently until you feel something push back."

The doors chimed open. They fell inside, and Hwa slapped the "door close" button. Then she looked up at the ceiling of the elevator. There was all kinds of shit up there, wedged up between the lights and the plastic panels that were supposed to protect them. Pencils, rubber bands, dead flies both organic and robotic, even a pink assignment sheet with the word GULLIBLE written across it in green marker.

Hwa pointed. "Jump up there and take down one of those panels."

Joel reached up and jumped. It took him a couple of tries, but the panel fell open and showered him with dead flies and paper clips. "Now what?"

Hwa told him how to turn the lights off and gain access to the ceiling panel that would pop open the trapdoor on top of the elevator. She had to kneel down and let him stand on her knee to do it, but he had good hands and worked fast. Soon he had the trapdoor open, and after he climbed up through it, he helped her get up there, too.

"Hold on. Let me get into blueprint mode, here." Hwa found the blueprint icon in her vision. The school being a publicly funded building, it had to release all its plans. So she could see where all the shafts and ducts went. It took her a moment to orient herself, but the light booth was unmistakable. And as she suspected, it had a major HVAC duct sitting right up on top of it. With the stage lights, the auditorium got awfully hot during performances. The only way to control the temperature was to force the air one way or another. And the only way to do that without impeding anyone's view of the stage was to stick a big fan on top of the light booth.

Hopefully the quarantine would last long enough that none of the fans would be spinning while they were in the ducts.

She pointed at the spiny ladder leading up the shaft. "Okay. Let's go."

• • •

Climbing ladders and crawling through ducts with one arm was excruciating. There was no other word for it. Hwa smeared blood everywhere she went. The ducts were smaller and tighter than she'd expected, and the only thing that greased their way through the aluminum tunnels was anxious, frustrated sweat. It felt like being born, if your mother was an unfeeling machine with a pussy made of steel who didn't really care if you lived or died.

That was a fairly accurate description of Sunny, actually. Hwa would have to remember that for later. If there was a "later."

Finally, they made it to the light booth. The fan was still off. Hwa checked her watch. This was a long time for the cops not to enter the building. What were they waiting for?

"Let's get through before it starts up again," Joel said.

"Yeah." Hwa wriggled around until her feet faced the fan. "Turn around so your back is to mine, okay? I need you to brace me, so my kicks have more force."

"Okay." He turned around. Through his shirt, she could feel how hot and damp he was. But he didn't seem frightened. He was doing well with this whole thing. "You're doing pretty well with this whole thing."

"I have an antianxiety implant," Joel said. "It's perched right on my amygdala. It's sort of like a pacemaker, for my emotions. I don't feel high highs or low lows. I'm right in the middle, all the time. Dad had it put in right when my voice started to change."

Hwa kicked twice. The fan squealed the second time, but didn't budge. "No shit?"

"No shit."

"That's a long time to go without worrying." Hwa tried not to sound as snide as she felt.

"I'm fifteen," Joel said. "I only got it like three years ago."

Hwa focused all her surprise into her legs and kicked again. *"Fifteen?* You're a senior! You're graduating this year!"

She felt him shrug against her shoulders. "Like I said: I'm a genius."

"Wow." She kicked right at the centre of the fan. It dented around her feet. Now they were getting somewhere. She could see a rim of light around the panel. "So, that means I'm, what, seven years older than you?"

"I don't know how old you are," Joel said. "Does it matter?"

Hwa kicked hard. The fan fell in, and a couple of little kicks at its edges with her heels popped it the rest of the way. "Nope," Hwa said. And she pushed herself through.

The first thing they found was food. The light booth had an impressive array of snacks. All of it was the high-calorie contraband that the school had outlawed years ago: bright pouches and boxes of crisps and chocolate (a whole box of the cherry brandy kind), seaweed crackers, "cheddar" popcorn, "kettle" popcorn, and bottle after bottle of energy drinks. Hwa mainlined one like it was the blood of Christ.

Tossing the empty bottle into a bin, she took stock. The light booth's equipment was still all tarped over; no one had come in to use it since the summer. She plunked herself into one of the chairs and pulled the other one out for Joel.

"What's going on, out there?"

"Let's see."

Hwa opened the security tab again. More feeds had come online. Students in darkened rooms cowered under their desks. Teachers held fingers over their lips. The halls remained empty. It was standard protocol in an active shooter situation, one Hwa had drilled her self-defence students on: run, and if running is impossible, then hide.

The shooter was on the second floor, now. He was in the foreign language pod. He was standing outside Madame Clouzot's class—Hwa recognized the French flag across the door—and trying to kick it down. Hanna Oleson was in there, Hwa realized. She'd figured out Hanna's whole schedule when Jared took her. Was she as scared now as she'd been then? Had Hwa saved her just to watch her die here?

"Hwa?"

Just as she was about to explain, the bell sounded. First period was over. Christ, where were the cops? Maybe they knew something she didn't. Like maybe this asshole had chemical weapons, or there was a bomb somewhere, or he'd rigged himself to blow up. Maybe he wasn't the run-of-the-mill batshit shooter, after all.

Maybe he was the one trying to kill Joel.

Maybe he was going to kill everyone in his way until he found Joel.

"Fuck this," Hwa whispered. She stood up and started digging in the supply racks. Most of it was just extra wire and batteries and folders of gels. There was an old red toolbox that looked promising, but it had a big fat padlock on it and Hwa had no time.

"What are you looking for?"

"The emergency ladder."

Hwa fished a box cutter out of one bin. That could come in handy. She tried stuffing it down her skirt, but that didn't work so well. She dug out a tool belt, cinched it over her waist, and stuck the cutter in there, along with a couple of flat-head screwdrivers and a heavy flashlight. There was a drill, but it was a small battery-powered job without much force. She needed something bigger. Like a nail gun.

Fortunately, she knew exactly where to get one of those.

"I think I know what you're doing, and I think it's really stupid," Joel said.

"Probably is."

"You're wounded. You shouldn't even be standing up."

"Got us this far, didn't I?"

Hwa's hands lit on the emergency ladder. It was lightweight yellow nylon. Joel would have no trouble hauling it up after her.

"You're not supposed to leave me," Joel said. His voice was flat.

He wasn't afraid, but he wasn't happy, either. Hwa had a feeling this was the first time he'd seen somebody on the family payroll doing something they weren't supposed to.

Well. It was a school. Might as well make it a teachable moment. "You're safe up here. But everybody else down there is still in danger. Now you can order me to stay, or you can let me try to help. Which is it?"

Joel didn't answer at first. Instead he turned and plucked out a bunch of the gels from the lighting cabinet. On their black envelopes was an orange sticker with a campfire on it. WARNING: EX- TREMELY FLAMMABLE, it read. Then he held up a black glass tube with an electrical cord dangling from it.

"What's that?"

"It's a black light. Probably the last incandescent bulb in this whole town. It absorbs most of the visible light spectrum, so it's spec- tacularly inefficient. That makes it good for checking for lint on a red velvet curtain, which is why it's up here." He knelt down and plugged in the light. He reached for a bottle of water from the tub of snacks. Then he started unfolding the black envelopes.

"Hey! What are you doing?"

"I'm starting a fire," Joel said. "I don't want him to hear you com- ing."

The fire caught almost immediately. Joel quickly fed it more gels. A weird metallic smell arose from them. Smoke started to rise. Joel backed away. The fire leapt up about three feet. Then the alarm sounded. It was a shrill keening sound, as though the whole build- ing were shrieking in agony at being burned. Then the sprinklers came on. Together they stared up at the water. It tasted of ocean.

"Great," Hwa said. "Just great."

"I'll get the ladder."

Hwa stomped out the fire and opened the exit. Joel secured the ladder to a set of hooks hanging off the threshold. Hwa watched the ladder fall into the darkness around the nearest catwalk. If she fell, she would die. Period.

Joel's head stuck out above her. "If you kill him, I'm sure my dad's attorneys will defend you in court. They're very good. They got him out of a whole criminal negligence thing with an oil spill, before I was born. So you probably won't do any time."

Hwa winced. "That's a real comfort, Joel."

He held up both thumbs. "Good luck."

"You, too. Lock that door, and turn off all the lights when I'm gone."

Going down a nylon ladder with one arm and a heavy toolbelt wasn't easy, but it was a lot easier than the ducts. Her arm was oozing, but she felt okay. Sitting still and focusing on it would have just made the pain worse. Her feet found empty air, and she looked down. The catwalk was another two feet down. Holding the ladder with her wounded arm she quickly changed her left hand's grip on the ladder to something more like a one-armed chin-up. Then she slowly let herself dangle down off the ladder, and dropped onto the catwalk. It was slick and she slipped, gripping the railing with her whole body and getting an eyeful of auditorium. One of the screwdrivers dived out of the toolbelt and glittered as it fell into the deep dark far below.

Righting herself, Hwa looked up at Joel. She gave him a thumbs-up, and he gave her one, too. Then he started pulling up the ladder.

Twisting on the flashlight and sticking it between her wounded arm and her body, Hwa navigated across the catwalk and down a set of stairs to the backstage area. Right near the outdoor exit (locked) was a fire extinguisher. Hwa lifted it off its housing and carried it to the interior exit that led to the drama department (also locked). She lifted the fire extinguisher and bashed at the lever on the door.

Behind the door, she heard screaming.

"It's just me!" Hwa bashed at the lever. After two more tries, it fell out with a clunk. She opened the door, and a stage sword jabbed her in the belly. "Ow! Fuck!"

"A rat! A rat!" Mrs. Cressey said. She was holding on to two crying girls. She smiled. Hwa thought she had maybe gone a little crazy. "Dead for a ducat! Dead!"

Hwa pushed the stage sword away and gave the huge boy holding it a hard stare. He backed off, and she pushed into the classroom. All the other students stared at her. They were freshmen. They looked so small and formless. Like little tadpoles. She had never felt old before. Not until this moment. She was still young, and she knew that, intellectually. But staring at these kids with their jewelled eyelashes and chipped nail polish and their knees all hugged to their chests, she felt like some ancient thing that had crawled up out of a very deep and ugly pit.

She pointed behind herself. "You'll be safer up in the catwalks! Get to a higher ground!"

The students looked at each other. Then they looked at their teacher. Slowly, they got to their feet. Hwa threaded herself through them, and started bashing on the door to the hall with a fire extinguisher. As she did, other students started streaming out of the room. She watched as the last one left, and then kicked open the door and got out into the hall.

The hall was a loop that made up the vocational pod. Mr. McGarry's shop was around the bend. This time, she paused and looked through the window first before raising the fire extinguisher to the lever. No one was inside. Once the door was open, she dashed in and put the fire extinguisher down. The entire wall to her left was a pegboard of tools. The red chalk outlines for each tool's shape were all bleeding down under the sprinklers' onslaught. But the tools themselves were still in place and ready to be used. Including the big gas-powered nail gun, complete with its backpack of fuel.

Hwa wiggled her fingers. They were mostly numb. "Come to Mama."

Threading her injured arm through the straps of the backpack made the wound open up again, and she wished she'd taken that other pad from Joel. Then again, it was shop: Mr. McGarry probably had the best first aid kits in school. Hwa found one on the wall and popped it open. Right there was the syringe of puncture-filling foam. She bit the protective cover off the needle and spat it out. Hissing, she managed to peel back the padding and fill the wound with foam. It stung mightily and she howled in shock. She suddenly felt a lot more awake and alive. Endorphins were a wonderful drug.

She checked her specs. The shooter was back on the main floor, now. The same floor as she was. He'd gone up and around and down, covering the whole school. Looking for something. Or someone. She had to get him before he found the open door to the drama department. Before he found the other students. Before he found Joel.

Hwa checked the fuel gauge on the tank. It was in the green. She added a couple of cartridges of nails to the toolbelt. Then she wiped the specs dry with a chamois from Mr. McGarry's desk. In the security tab, she changed the video feed to a basic semitransparent map in the lower left of her vision: the shooter was now just a red dot on a set of lines, and she was the blue one. It would be easier to see what was in front of her this way.

Easier to aim.

She took a few deep yogic breaths to centre herself. It wasn't easy with a heavy pack on, but it was necessary. In (two, three, four), hold (two, three, four), out (two, three, four). And again. The pain dissipated. So did the endorphins. There was only her—a calm person accustomed to hurting other people—and him—an imbalanced student who probably came here with a death wish. They were probably equally frustrated by the fact that the cops hadn't shown up. One way or another, they would have to end it themselves.

Hwa entered the hall. She moved past the doors. In other classrooms, there were kids pressed up against the windows. She felt them watching as she walked to the main hall. There, way on the other side of the school, was the shooter.

Behind her, something splashed.

Hwa whirled. At first, she couldn't see it. But in the rain created by the sprinklers was a . . . shape. A human shape outlined in water trickling off its surface. Only, she could see straight through it. Without the water it would have been completely invisible. She ripped off the specs.

It moved. Glittered. Like a poltergeist caught in the act. It wasn't real. Couldn't possibly be real. She knew that. And yet. And yet. The longer she stared at it the less real everything became. The hallway. The water. The shooter. Even the pain. It was all broadcasting from somewhere else, some other channel, and she was just watching it happen. Blessed, merciful calm descended over her like a hot towel fresh from the dryer. She recognized the feeling. It was deliciously familiar, but she couldn't remember the last time she'd experienced it. Hadn't felt it in a long time. *Derealization.* That was the medical word for it. That moment when everything around you seemingly shifted to another phase of reality. It was one of the brain's many self-defence mechanisms. In Hwa, it was preparation for a seizure.

"Oh, Jesus."

All her calm vanished abruptly. She was cold and wet and wounded and alone. And she was about to seize for the first time in three years. It made sense: she'd barely eaten anything, meaning there was a dramatic change in her blood sugar, and she was under physical and emotional stress. Her brain had handled all of these challenges just fine until now, and now the sparkling aura in her vision was warning her to sit down and hold on before she hurt herself. *Scintillating scotoma.* That was the term. *Scintillating,* the doctors called it, like it was something to get excited about.

"Master control room," she said aloud. "Master control room."

She pictured the bank of buttons. Big and bright and perfectly fitted to her fingers. Imagined punching them. That satisfying click. The way each button lit up as she locked a series of doors behind her, locked herself away—

Behind her, the shotgun sounded. She turned. The shooter was running at her. Her icy fingers fumbled on the nail gun. She lifted it. It shook in her grasp. She pulled the trigger. Nothing happened. Oh, Christ, the safety, shit—

"Hwa, get down!"

Síofra. In her bones. Finally. She fell to the floor. So did the shooter. The sprinklers stopped. The siren died. Her ears rang. Her hands kept shaking. Something peeled away from the shooter's scalp. A skein of skin, with hair attached. Beneath it was a skullcap. Light danced across the shooter's skin. It slowed down, ceased, and he went limp.

"He's inoperative, now, Hwa. He can't hurt you. I'm coming. Stay there."

She tried to say something. But then there were people in Lynch uniforms, and they had bright yellow towels of absorbent foam, and they were picking her up under her arms and dragging her to the nearest wall and taking the backpack off and unbuckling the tool-belt. They were saying how sorry they were. How glad they were that she was okay.

Síofra skidded out into the hall. He nearly wiped out on the wet surface. But he just kept running until he got to her end of the hall. The others scattered and lined up against the opposite wall, chins up, shoulders back. Waiting for orders.

"Hwa?" He waved a hand in front of her face. "Are you in shock?"

"Yippee-ki-yay, motherfucker."

He laughed. He started dabbing her face with a towel. "Look at you. You must be freezing. We didn't know the sprinklers would go off. We'll change the crash protocol before the next drill."

Hwa tried hard to make her lips shape the word. "Drill?"

"Yes."

She had lost too much blood to feel proper anger. She realized that now, distantly, and without anxiety. "For . . . the school?"

"No. For you. To see how you would protect Joel." His lips thinned. He looked away. "I asked Mr. Lynch not to go through with it. But he wanted to test you, and I . . . I knew you would pass."

He smiled like his mouth hurt. "That's why we didn't use real rounds."

She really was pretty far gone, now. She couldn't even come up with something clever to say. Why was she so hot? Why was she sweating so hard? She'd barely run at all. She lifted her wounded arm. "Blanks do this?"

Síofra peeled back the tie and looked down. Blood covered his fingers instantly. Apparently she should have taped down the wound after foaming it shut. Hwa felt sticky all down her right side. She'd thought it was the sprinklers. But it was hot. It was blood. The hallway tipped over on its side.

Her boss was screaming.

"I NEED A MEDIC!"

Her vision went pure white. Then deep black. Then they were lifting her on something. A stretcher. Síofra was shaking the skullcap by the collar of his long black coat. Shaking him and slamming him against the lockers and yelling in his face about how *you fucking idiot she's bleeding out just look just look JUST FUCKING LOOK WHAT YOU DID TO HER—*

"H . . . Hey." Hwa held out her hand. It fell. She had to concentrate to bring it back up. Imagined all her muscles working like the girders on a causeway. Imagined all the tendons in her hand working her fingers into a fist. Close. Open. Close. Open. Síofra dropped the skullcap and reached out. He held her hand in both of his. They felt almost obscenely warm. She was so terribly cold.

"What is it?"

"You can . . ."

"Yes?" He bent down closer.

"You can take this job and shove it."

6

Palinopsia

The room smelled like mould. Like fungus. Like feet. Hwa suspected that she might actually be dead, and this environment—the damp dimness, the tangy air, the twitching walls alive with blue veins of bacteria—was nothing more than a vivid hallucination of her own corpse's slow decay.

"It's like a cheese cave, they says."

Even through the hospital mask, Hwa could detect her old instructor's disgust. Kripke's thick rust-coloured eyebrows knit together in a permanent scowl. He was a huge man, too big for the chair by the bed. Hwa was so glad to see him she could feel herself starting to cry. Kripke looked like he already had. His eyes were bleary and red.

"The docs had to lower your immune resistance when you came in, so your body would take the spackle. But now you have to re-populate your personal flora, or some shit. Looks like a fancy excuse not to clean the rooms, you ask me." He waved at her chart. Encased in hospital gloves, his fingers looked like sausages. "And why am I listed as the emergency contact? What about your mother?"

Hwa shrugged.

"I had to tell her, you know. Me nerves, that woman."

"Sorry." Hwa looked at the pitcher at her bedside. "Give us a bit of that?"

"Aye." Kripke poured some into a little tumbler and held it out. Hwa took it with her left hand. It tasted vaguely brackish. They hadn't had rain in a long while, and the desalinators were working overtime.

"Brain scan?" Hwa asked.

He shook his head. "Not yet. You think you . . . ?"

"Might have."

Kripke ran a slow hand over his mouth and beard. He was pissed. She had missed that, his anger. His disappointment and frustration had a certain weight and thickness. When it settled over her, like a blanket, she knew she could be doing better. She knew there was room to improve. It was a comfort.

"Some stunt you pulled, back there."

Hwa snorted. "Yes, b'y."

Kripke laid one massive palm over her right hand. Dull pain throbbed up the arm. He must have sensed it, because his grip lightened. He took gentle hold of her fingers, instead. "Remember I said you'd have to learn to kick, because with hands like these you'd never punch?"

She nodded.

"Then you gets in the ring with little Ronnie Tolliver and you ups with that knife hand strike, right to his eyes, and I hauls you out because it was an illegal hit. You almost quit right then and there because you thought you should have won the match."

"I should have. He was on his knees."

Kripke blinked glassy, wet eyes. "How're you getting on?"

Hwa reached over with her good hand and patted his. "Farbed up. But on the mend." She cleared her throat. Her accent always got thicker when she was with Kripke. The gym was the one place she didn't have to worry about her English or her Korean being wrong, and she could just talk like everyone else. "Quit the gig."

Kripke folded his arms on his belly and leaned back in his chair. He needed to lose weight. He was going to be a statistic, soon. She had a sudden desire to be back in the gym with him, lifting or running or even just having fun on the trampoline. She missed the trampoline. But the gym was different without Tae-kyung. She had tried going back, after. But it stung. His ghost was strongest there.

"You what?"

"Quit." She sipped more water. "They jerked me around. So I quit."

Kripke's furry eyebrows came together like two caterpillars checking each other out. "Jerked you around how?"

Hwa licked her lips. They were suddenly very dry. Christ, what if she'd imagined it? Imagined the weave peeling away from the skullcap's head and the flashing lights underneath. Imagined the dead look in his eyes, like a doll's. Imagined the shape in the water.

"Hey!" Kripke plucked the cup of water from her hands. "You're gonna get it all over yourself, shaking like that. You cold?"

"Aye," she heard herself say.

He was pulling the blanket up higher on her body and searching the room for something. "Goddamn hospitals. Always too hot or too cold. So. Youse quit?"

Hwa nodded emphatically. "Hell yeah, I's quit. I's done."

Kripke jerked a thumb behind him. "You tell that to your detail?"

Shit. Of course she would have to tell Joel. How was she going to explain that? "Joel? Is he out there?"

Kripke shook his head. "He left before you woke. Big tall ginger fellow came for him."

"Me boss. Ex-boss."

"Some gear, that one. Cockier than two roosters in a henhouse."

Hwa laughed. It hurt. "That's him, sure."

"Well, he raked me over the coals, asking me about you. I haven't seen a man so down in the mouth since Bellucci took the fall in the quarter-final five years ago." Kripke peered at her from under the bill of his hat. "You hearin' me, ducky?"

Hwa looked away. She didn't even have a chance to answer. A chime sounded in her room. "Jung-hwa Go? It's time for your eye test."

· · ·

"Glaucoma's pretty common in people with Sturge-Weber," the doctor said. "And you're overdue for your eye exam."

Hwa was the first patient with Sturge-Weber that he'd ever met. He said he owed it to himself to learn as much about rare diseases as he could, when they presented themselves. Rotational residents got a special hazard bonus if they agreed to do work offshore. They would be among the last to leave, in an evacuation scenario.

"Like the spackle in your arm, for instance," Dr. Hazard Pay was saying. "It's really for burn victims. We can administer it in triage situations before an evacuation. It comes out of a big extruder gun, sort of like a pastry bag."

"Nice." She tried not to imagine a huge sack bloated with pink goo attached to her arm. It didn't work.

"Glaucoma isn't so bad, in terms of symptoms," Dr. Hazard Pay said. "You've been really lucky, so far, especially given how far your angioma extends. Until now, you've been seizure-free for three years, and you made it through most of school before that. And you're still physically active, with no weakness on your right side. That's probably what helped prevent all the other symptoms, all that exercise. And your diet. It says here you eat a lot of good fats, and stay away from sugar. And the anticonvulsants, obviously."

Hwa nodded. "The angioma could be atrophying this side of my brain, though, right?"

"It's possible. The stain is bundling up the nerves and blood vessels that sit right on top of your cerebral cortex. So if you had a silent seizure, that might be a sign that the bundle is getting tighter." He squeezed a fist so she could see. "Or headaches. Have you had any bad headaches, lately?"

"Just my boss," Hwa said.

Dr. Hazard Pay laughed. He waved open the door to the optometry area. Projections of eyes woke up and winked at them as they passed. Some were blue. Some were green. Some were bloodshot. Some had cataracts. It was as though every surveillance device in the entire area had developed some special little avatar to wink and laugh at the humans in the vicinity.

"So you've had a robotic examination before, right?"

"What?"

He waved open another door to a darkened room. Inside was a tall white machine with six limbs and many eyes. As the room lit up, so did the machine. It fluttered awake, lights blinking on and limbs articulating delicately into a gesture that was most likely meant to indicate *welcome* and not *I am about to eat your eyes.*

"This is Dr. Mantis," Dr. Hazard Pay said. "He just got a new upgrade, so he's good to go. Just let him dilate your pupils first, and then he can check the pressure on your optic nerve."

"Hello," Dr. Mantis said. It held out a claw. It had a very gentle British accent. Hwa had no idea why all the robots had to be Brits. Probably the same reason Brits were always cast as Nazis.

Hwa turned to Hazard Pay. "I can't have a real doctor?"

"I am a real doctor," Dr. Mantis said.

"Mantis is fine! Better than fine! He's great! Mantis, send me that report when you finish up, okay?"

"Yes, Dr. Rockwell."

Rockwell. That was his name. The door shut behind him.

"I will take the best of care with your eyes," Dr. Mantis said. It pivoted on a giant ball in its lower thorax and hove into her vision. It was still holding out a claw. Hwa grabbed it and gave it a shake. It had a very gentle grip. It used another, lower arm to pull a chair over. "Please sit down."

Hwa sat. The lights dimmed. One of Dr. Mantis's claws came up to clutch her chin. Another held her forehead in place. "Now, I'm going to dilate your eye. Please keep it open."

"Aye."

Something squirted into her eye.

"Now I'm going to look at how much pressure there is on the optic nerve, and whether it's changed colour. If there's something abnormal, I'll map your visual field with this light."

Something on its body blinked.

"Now I'm going to come very close to you, and look deep in your eye."

The grips on her face tightened. Dr. Mantis rolled closer to her. One of its eyes came level with hers. It was a very large camera. As she looked into it, she thought she saw mirrors shifting position.

"What kind of changes have you noticed in your vision?" Dr. Mantis asked.

"I . . ." She swallowed. Her face felt numb. "I had a sense of derealization and depersonalization."

"Did you disassociate?"

"Only for a minute. And then I thought I saw a seizure aura."

"Did the aura take over your vision?"

She almost shook her head, but the claws held her fast. "No. It was localized."

"How big was the aura?"

"Big. Like, the size of a person."

"Was it black?"

"No. It was the other kind, I think. It looked like . . ." She licked her lips. Just remembering it raised the hairs on her arms. "It looked like drops of water on glass. Does that make sense?"

"Not really, but our visual fields are very different. I can see in infrared, and you can't." The mirrors shifted again in Dr. Mantis's eye. "Did you have a seizure, after seeing this aura?"

"No. Dr. Rockwell says it was probably a silent seizure—all aura, no twitching. So maybe I got off light this time."

"Have you experienced any blind spots?"

"Blind spots?"

"Holes, in your vision. Things you know must be there, but you can't quite see."

That was was one way of describing it. "Maybe?"

"Have you engaged in any accessory reality activities, lately?"

Hwa tried not to frown. "Sorry?"

"Helmets, goggles, layers, things like that. Have you put on a new pair of specs recently?"

"Uh . . . yeah. Actually. I have. And I was wearing them today. I mean yesterday. The last time I was awake."

The light switched off. A purple blur replaced its glow in Hwa's vision. The claws left her face. She felt a little dizzy without them to hold her in place. Dr. Mantis drew up to its full height.

"It might be a ghost," Dr. Mantis said.

One if its lights turned on, and a projection appeared on the opposite wall. It was an old-fashioned pencil sketch of a human eye, with a lightbulb and arrows and a pair of very old, chunky specs. As the robot spoke, the images animated across the wall.

"It's called palinopsia. It's like seeing something on a delay. You see it there, long after it's gone. It can be a side effect of seizures. Accessory visual stimuli can buffer in your perception, especially if you're not used to it. That compounds the problem, especially for patients like you. It's something to think about, if you want to keep wearing your device. You might be processing visual field information long after your eyes actually perceive it."

"So it really was a ghost," Hwa said.

"From a certain point of view." Dr. Mantis's claws clicked together. "Get it? That's an optometry joke."

"Oh. Yeah." Hwa chuckled. She gave the robot a thumbs-up. "Good delivery. Very deadpan."

All three sets of claws clasped each other. "Really? I've been prototyping my bedside manner."

Hwa suddenly felt very bad for not having called the thing a real doctor. It was just trying to run its program, like everyone else in this town. They were all perched on top of machines, after all. Even the towers were built mostly by drones. She should have shown it more respect right from the start.

"Yeah, you're doing a great job." She mustered a smile. "Thanks. How's my eye?"

"It is perfectly normal," Dr. Mantis said. "There is nothing wrong with your vision."

• • •

<<You look like shit,>> her mother said.

"I got shot," Hwa replied.

Hwa watched Sunny's gaze light on the valve on her right arm. <<Now your other side's all fucked up, too, huh?>>

"Aye."

Acknowledging her ugliness was always the right password for entry into her mother's home. It was the coin of the realm. Sunny backed away from the door and waved her into the side room. It reeked of something sweet. At first Hwa thought Sunny was trying out a new perfume, but the smell came from the floor. There was a huge pink stain in the carpet near the fridge.

"What happened?"

<<I spilled a whole tray of jelly shots. They hadn't even set up.>> Sunny sat down at the low table in front of the display. She'd gotten a bigger one, since Hwa was last there. It hung across most of the wall.

"You moved the trophies," Hwa said, and realized that was why she'd come back. Her new place wouldn't be complete without them. Sunny acted as though she hadn't heard. She kept her gaze pinned to the display. "The trophies," Hwa said, a little louder this time. "Where did they go?"

<<I'm watching this.>>

Hwa looked at the door to Tae-kyung's old room. Their old room. She could go in. Right now. She could do it.

She couldn't do it.

She moved to the refrigerator. Sunny hissed as Hwa crossed her line of sight. Hwa ducked down and squatted in front of the fridge. Not much: a jug of the iced tea Sunny swore was good for the skin, with odd bits of dried roots floating in it; a six-pack of green shakes in subscription bottles; three bottles of pink champagne; and way at the back, a jar of kimchi.

Aside from their language, it was the one piece of their heritage that Sunny had hung on to. She had grown up eating it. She credited it with her good figure and excellent constitution. It was all she ate, after every surgery and each childbirth.

<<If you're eating my food, you'd better replace it.>>

Hwa didn't answer. She wedged the fridge door open with her body and used her good arm to pull the jar out. Then, sitting against the fridge, she braced the jar between her legs and opened it with her good hand.

There was a coat of white fur across the top.

"Son of a bitch . . ."

Hwa stood up. With a pair of ice tongs left out on the counter, she removed the mouldy layer of kimchi. The stuff beneath was wet and red. Shrugging, she used the ice tongs to start eating. She'd consumed three big bites of the stuff when she noticed Sunny staring at her.

"What?"

<<Nothing.>> Sunny went back to watching her drama.

Sunny was thinner, these days. Hwa wasn't sure how that could be possible, but it was true. She had never been a big eater. Starting a modelling career at eleven years old did that to a woman. Food was the enemy. Hwa's earliest memory of actually being allowed to finish a meal was sharing a pot of ramen with her brother. He always added fun things, like eggs or hot dogs. He knew how to cut the hot dogs so they made octopus shapes. And he let her have the pot while he took the lid, so she wouldn't burn her fingers.

If there were jelly shots embedded in the carpet, there was probably vodka in the place. Hwa ditched the tongs and moved to the freezer. Inside was a mother-lode: vodka, gin, local screech, applejack, all sandwiched between fever packs and ice cubes in heart-shaped moulds.

<<I went and saw you. At the hospital.>>

Hwa pulled out a mostly finished bottle of vodka and shut the door. Sunny was still watching the screen. "When?"

<<Yesterday. You were asleep.>>

"I was in a coma."

Sunny shrugged. <<You seemed fine. So I left.>>

Hwa didn't know what to say. She had not been aware, until now, that there was a wrong way to be in a coma. "Okay . . ."

<<And you shouldn't drink that. Not if you're on drugs.>>

Hwa looked at the bottle in her hand. Sunny was right. She hated when Sunny was right. But the woman had spent more than her fair share of time in hospitals. She knew how to recover. "Yeah."

<<You shouldn't be drinking my liquor, anyway. It's expensive. Buy your own.>>

Hwa put the bottle back and went back to the kimchi. Sunny stood up. She stretched.

<<Your boss is a nice man.>>

Hwa felt the bottom drop out of her stomach. *Master control room,* she reminded herself. "He's not my boss anymore. I quit."

Sunny affixed her with a glare that was pure disdain. <<Of course you did.>>

"They almost got me killed," Hwa said, and hated herself for even feeling an urge to explain.

Sunny sighed, and before she even opened her mouth, Hwa knew which of her many girl-group stories she would tell. <<I did a show in Incheon, once, and—>>

"And your hair caught on fire, during the encore. And you didn't complain. I know."

Sunny rolled her eyes. <<Are you spending the night?>>

Not staying. Never staying. Just crashing. Always imposing. Always in the way.

"Just for tonight."

<<Good.>>

Sunny left for the professional side of the apartment. Hwa put away the kimchi and found an unopened toothbrush in the washroom. She brushed her teeth for longer than strictly necessary. Eventually, she would have to enter the room. Hwa thought of this as she stared at her face in the mirror. Sunny was right. She really did look like shit. More so than usual. Her stain was dark and her skin was dull. Her lips were too big. They looked stupid on her, like a distracted assembly-line worker had slapped someone else's mouth on her face.

She looked herself straight in her bad eye. "Stop being such a pussy."

Tae-kyung's room still smelled the same. She had known it would, but somehow it still surprised her. It was like he was still there. There was his bed, with the sheets still on it. His winter blanket still lay folded at the end of the bed. His training gloves still hung on the wall.

Sunny had moved the trophies to a cabinet at the foot of the bed, where Tae-kyung might have seen them if he were still sleeping in it. They were all out of order. Hwa put them back in place. Chronological order from left to right. Linear time. No more Singularity bullshit. No more ghosts. Everything neat and tidy and dead and gone.

Tae-kyung had a shot at going pro. Anyone could see that, looking at all the trophies and ribbons and certificates and belts. His whole history was right there, with words like "finalist" and "winner" and "champion" in big letters with sharp fonts. His future could have been there, too. He could have left home and snagged a management contract and started out on the circuit. He could have made money that way. Not a lot, but enough. He was handsome and funny and fast. He could have been a star.

Instead, he'd stayed home and gotten a job on the rig. He'd set it all aside. Said he could wait. Said he should make some money first. That he couldn't just leave Hwa with their mother. And that was why he was on the Old Rig when it blew. Because of Hwa.

She was still standing between their two beds when the ping came: *"Are you all right?"*

Joel. Her specs were gone and her earbud was out, but he still had her info. But it was odd that he'd reach out like this. They hadn't even known each other that long.

"Doing okay," she told him.

"Are you really quitting?"

Hwa had no idea how to answer that.

"Is it my fault?" Joel pressed.

"No," she said aloud, and then pinged: *"No. Not your fault. Just not cut out for the job. You were right. I was stupid. It was a stupid idea. Stupid mistake."*

The lights were out and she was almost undressed when the next ping came. It was tough going, with only one arm. She was beginning to wonder if Joel had fallen asleep. But his message came across loud and clear: *"Can we still be friends?"*

Slowly, her body folded down to the floor. She curled around her wrist, staring at the little window of light in the darkness of her childhood bedroom.

7

Murder

Because they were still friends, she met Joel for lunch the next day. It was still warm, so they ate in the Autumn Garden on Level Twenty of Tower Two, where there were trees whose leaves actually turned. The maples were planted even before the crops on the farm floors. On a plaque pounded into one tree were the logos of the tree scientists and mental health agencies that had funded the forest.

"I've never been here before," Joel said, peering up into the canopy.

"I used to come here on a lot of dates," Hwa said, eyeing the skullcap that eyed them. Joel's new bodyguard, probably. Well, a skullcap had gotten the best of her, so maybe it was for the best. "Other people's dates, I mean. Jobs."

Joel nodded. He kicked dry yellow leaves. "Are you going to go back to your old job?"

"Maybe," Hwa said. "If they'll take me."

Joel appeared to be listening to something. Síofra, probably. Hwa stopped herself from asking about it. Joel shook his head softly, and held up two tiffin boxes. "I had our chef make us lunch."

Hwa smiled. "Thanks."

"I made sure yours had the cauliflower rice," he said. "I'm still supposed to eat grains, sometimes."

"You're still growing," Hwa said. "That's okay."

Joel set things out. Hwa moved to help him, but he said something about her arm and waved her away. Evidently, he'd had the chef make something Korean: tofu stew with zucchini and shrimp. "I thought you'd want something more . . . familiar," Joel said.

"Trust me, Joel, my mom never made food like this," Hwa said. "But thanks. It's great."

"What about your dad?" Joel asked.

Hwa shrugged. "No idea. I've never met him. I don't even know if he still lives on the rig. I asked Sunny once, but she said she couldn't tell me. My bet is she doesn't know."

"So your brother was like your dad?"

Hwa felt the soup go down the wrong pipe. She coughed. "Aye. Kinda. Little bit. Maybe." She sipped hard at a thermos of iced tea. "Can you do me a favour?"

"Do you need me to get your things out of your locker? Because I already asked one of the teachers how—"

"Joel." Hwa gave him a Medusa stare. He quieted. For a moment, she focused on the sound of leaves quietly falling, and the drone of windmills outside, and the ever-present, almost unnoticeable wash of the Atlantic below. She had to do this. Had to. No other choice. Fuck the Lynches, anyway. "Turn your ears off," she said. "I need to talk to you in private."

Joel's gaze jerked like a fish on a hook. He was listening to someone else. Finally, he nodded. He tapped a complicated sequence on the skin around his ear. "Daniel says it's okay."

Hwa waited until the skullcap had drifted to the other side of the arboretum. "Joel, you know the test wasn't supposed to have live rounds, right?"

He nodded. "Yeah. It was an accident. I'm really sorry." He swallowed hard. "Hwa, I'm really sorry, it's all my fault, if you hadn't—"

"Shut up," Hwa said, and when he flinched, she added, "quit it with that shit. It wasn't your fault. You didn't know. And you didn't switch the rounds."

She took hold of his shoulder. "But someone did. And someone is after you."

Joel waited for a moment, processing, then burst out laughing. He folded in on himself, clutching his ribs and snickering. He fell back in the crunching leaves. Hwa had to quickly rescue the soup from his outstretched legs.

"What's so funny?" she asked, finally.

"Your face," he said.

Hwa recoiled. "Oh."

"No, not like that!" Joel sat up. "Not like that. I mean how serious your face was." He tried to do an impression of her, and looked like an old mask from a pantomime drama. "People threaten me all the time. Or, anyway, they threaten the family all the time. This was just a mistake! And everyone associated with it has already been fired."

The hairs on Hwa's arms rose. "Aye?"

"*Aye*," Joel said, rolling his eyes. "Come on. You got *shot*. They fired *everyone*."

Hwa doubted that had anything to do with her being shot, and more to do with Zachariah Lynch cleaning house. He knew about the death threats, and Joel didn't. "Joel, I've seen the threats."

"Of course you have. You're my bodyguard. Or you used to be."

"No, I mean, I've seen *specific* threats. Against you. Against your life. Death threats. Scary ones."

Joel frowned. He poked at his food. "But . . . that doesn't make any sense. Why . . ."

"Your dad told me not to tell you. I had to sign—"

"Why would you *leave*?" Joel looked up and stared at her with bright eyes. "If someone was really after me, why would you quit?"

Hwa's mouth opened. She hadn't counted on that question. "Because I failed. I fucked up. Not only did I leave you behind, I failed to eliminate the threat. You could have gotten really hurt. You could've *died*."

Unbidden, she saw the ghost that had followed her under the sprinklers. It hovered there for a moment in her vision, like a migraine aura. She blinked and then it was gone, but seeing it helped her remember why exactly she had to do this. *Master control room*, she reminded herself. Then she could meet Joel's eyes.

"And because, whoever's after you, whoever sent those messages . . . I don't know if I can fight them."

"But you can fight *anybody*!" His voice cracked, and they both looked away, their embarrassment as mutual as it was deep.

"Not this," Hwa said, finally. "This is something—someone—I have no idea how to handle. And whoever else your dad picks for the job will probably be better. Better equipped. You won't have to worry about me having seizures, or going blind, or any of that shit. You'll be safer without me."

Joel started packing up his lunch things. "Please excuse me," he said. "I'm not very hungry any longer."

• • •

Hwa picked up her vodka and soda. The rain had driven early drinkers into the Crow's Nest for a rib-sticking dinner. Some of them were USWC. The others were all hanging up dripping slickers and peeling off damp sweaters and shaking out their hair and ordering the first dark ale of the autumn. It was still hot out, but the damp made Hwa feel the first chill of fall breathing down her neck. Her arm ached. Outside, the pressure was changing.

"So that's why I'd like my old job back," she told Rusty. "Will you show Mistress Séverine this conversation?"

"Of course," Rusty said. Hwa looked at Nail. Nail nodded.

"Good of you." Hwa lifted her glass. "Ta."

"She regrets not being able to meet you in person. She has been in demand."

"I don't doubt it." She sipped. "Can I try apologizing again? For losing you in the crowd that day?"

"No. We have been informed that you are not allowed." He smiled. "But there is no stipulation regarding the appreciation of the gesture."

Hwa translated. "Well. Good."

Rusty looked over her shoulder. He frowned. "You're about to be attacked."

Hwa twisted in her chair just in time to get a wash of beer in the face. The cup fell to the floor and clattered harmlessly across it. New Arcadia had a rule about glasses in bars. Something about the way they could be shattered and made into a weapon.

"You selfish little *bitch*."

Andrea Davis was skinny where her wife Calliope wasn't. She was a tiny twig of a woman with a cluster of rusty red straw where hair should have been. It trembled on her head. She vibrated rage.

"Andrea—"

"*Shut up!*" Andrea directed a sharp kick at Hwa's shin. "Stand up! Stand up and face me!"

The guy on the karaoke stage now sounded a little less certain about seeing a million faces and rocking them all.

Master control room, Hwa reminded herself, as she rose to her feet. She was taller than Andrea, but not by much. She kept her hands at her sides. *Master control room. Press the big buttons. Hear the doors locking behind you.*

"What's happening, Andrea?"

Andrea slapped her in the face. She'd obviously not done it very much, if ever. Her fingernails scraped awkwardly across Hwa's nose and mouth. Hwa mentally gave her mother points for at least developing some proper technique over the past twenty-three years. Even with half her body held together with polymer and prayer, Sunny could have broken Andrea in half by now.

"I don't think there's any call for that kind of behaviour, Mrs. Davis." Rusty sidled around the table. "I'm sure there's a reasonable—"

"*She killed my wife!*"

Andrea pointed a shaking finger at Hwa. Hwa breathed through the adrenaline. Calliope? Killed? When? How?

"I was just talking to the police," Andrea whispered. "And they said *you* were supposed to be on Calliope's detail. She had a date. And she had to go out there alone. Because you quit. You *quit,* so you could work for *them.*"

Andrea pointed out the window at the rig. There was a shiny new

Lynch logo on the biggest smokestack, now. That fat L winding around a pool of black like a lazy serpent slowly choking its latest victim. Hwa turned to the other women in the bar. Half of them she'd worked with in the past. They were all looking at her very differently, right now. As though they'd suspended their visual subscriptions and were seeing her true face for the first time. As though they finally knew how ugly she really was.

"Calliope's dead?"

Andrea's knobby fingers pushed hard at Hwa's shoulders. She was stronger than she looked. Rage could do that. She kept pushing, trying to knock Hwa over. Hwa's stomach muscles lined up against her spine; she stood straight and still and let Andrea punctuate her words with her fingers. "Yes! She's! Fucking! Dead! *She's! In! Fucking! Pieces!*"

Hwa shook her head. "Andrea, I didn't know—"

"Fuck you!"

Andrea threw her bony little elbow right into Hwa's solar plexus. Pain opened a point of super-dense space behind her ribs: a wormhole of breathless, gasping panic. Hwa stumbled back onto the table. Cups rolled over and clattered to the floor. No wonder she was off her game. She wished desperately and stupidly that she could be sober. She slid off the table and onto the floor. Peanut shells poked up into the palms of her hands. Andrea kicked her hard in her side.

Hwa tried to sit up. Andrea grabbed a mostly full bottle from the next table over and swung it straight for Hwa's head. Hwa ducked and blocked, but Andrea had some crazy-fu going on and the bottle returned on the backswing to connect with her temple. It felt cold and foamy and resonant; Hwa heard the beer slosh against the plastic as it met her skin of her temple and broke it.

"Stop," she said, blocking her head tight with her outer forearms as Andrea slashed and swung. "Stop, that's my good side—"

"You don't *have* a good side, you ugly goddamn traitor."

Andrea lunged for her again, but her feet kicked uselessly in the air as Nail lifted her up, gently. He held her there above the ground as she wrestled.

"He cut her up," she whimpered. "Oh God, he cut up my baby."

. . .

Rusty and Nail made their way back to Séverine's place. "MMD," Rusty said, grabbing his coat. "Put some ice on that."

The barback at the Crow's Nest gave her a towel with some ice in it, and a measure of middling bourbon, and shooed her on her way the moment she finished it. The folk in the elevator did everything they could to avoid staring while also taking her in: the stain, the fresh blood, the slashes in her sleeves, the ragged peanut shells clinging to her tights. Her arm throbbed. She thought it might be bleeding again.

The union would be initiating its MMD protocol, short for Missing, Murdered, or Dead. It was right there in the USWC handbook: obtain and verify all facts, alert membership, stress safety, in public statements separate the incident from the work and humanize the victim (use first names, make reference to family and pets), at no point imply that the victim did anything to deserve it. It was the same everywhere, in every Canadian city, even the ones on dry land.

A sex worker hadn't been murdered in New Arcadia since before the Old Rig blew.

It came with the decriminalization, and the bodyguards, and the communication between workers. If a client was bad, everybody knew. There was a rating system. Creepiness was a metric. So was violence. So was respect for boundaries. You could take a poorly rated client, if you wanted. But you knew what you were getting into. Had Calliope? Had she read a bunch of reviews, and decided to make the date anyway? And who could be that dangerous? Hwa let the question roll around in her skull as the elevator descended to the cheaper levels. Faces tumbled up. Angel. Benny. Shit, even Moliter, a little bit. And, of course, sometimes the riggers took things to keep them awake, and some of them were on off-label mods, the kinds of things Wade was taking, and Christ, anything could happen there.

Hwa pushed herself into her apartment. It was only the one room, the kitchen things against one wall and her bed against another. What little she owned was still in boxes and piles. Only Tae-kyung's trophies had any pride of place. Now she wasn't sure she could really afford any of it.

"Prefect, show me Calliope Davis."

"Access denied," Prefect said, crisply.

Well, that was quick. Lynch had wasted no time cutting her out of their systems. Not that she could blame them. Him. Síofra. Probably his call to make. For a moment she thought about contacting him. No. Bad idea.

"Get me Belle du Jour," she said.

The client-facing side of the terminal came up. Here, too, her login was no good any longer. Still, she could call up Calliope's profile. There she was, in full makeup, sporting her tattoos, promising her specialties. She wasn't Hwa's best student, not by a long shot, but that didn't mean she was bad. Just unmotivated.

Eileen's call came just as Hwa was about to check the news.

"I heard what happened," Eileen said, and Hwa didn't know if she meant Calliope or the fight with Andrea. "It's a sin," she said thickly. "Just a sin."

"Have you looked at the news?"

"Aye, and I wish to God I hadn't." Eileen blew her nose. "Some fucking botflies took the footage. Pieces of her. Just floating out there. Just . . . shreds."

Maybe it was an accident. Maybe, somehow, in a city with a suicide barrier on every causeway, Calliope had fallen down into the water and gotten herself chopped up by a propeller. It had happened— usually if someone went down below the causeways themselves. The trolls—the people under the bridges—they died that way. But why would she go down there?

"And, of course, they're saying it's a suicide," Eileen said, as though having read Hwa's mind. "The NAPS, I mean. They said they put it through the Matchmaker and that's what it said, and so that's how they're investigating it."

Hwa found the footage. They had identified her by her tattoo. That was what had drawn the botfly's eye. A Greek cross, floating on the waves. From a distance it looked like some sort of flag. Or maybe a jersey. But it was Calliope's skin. The skin of her breasts, ragged at the edges, the cross still clear despite the bloating and damage.

"Christ," Hwa said. "Eileen, give me your log-in. Your BDJ log-in."

There was a long pause. Too long. "Hwa, I shouldn't do that . . ."

And then Hwa knew that she knew. That what Andrea had said was real. That Hwa had an appointment to look after Calliope, and it hadn't been filled when Hwa took the job with Lynch. Her lips felt hot. Her eyes burned.

"Change the log-in in an hour," Hwa said, forcing some iron into her voice. "One hour. Just give me one hour. I just need to see where she was."

"The police are looking into it—"

"The police aren't me."

8

Exit Wound

"What's your mum at?" Eileen whispered.

Hwa looked back over her shoulder at Sunny. Her mother was circulating through the narthex of St. Brigid's, making small talk and dabbing carefully at her eyes with a monogrammed handkerchief.

"Networking," Hwa said, and turned to face the altar.

It was a closed casket. Obviously. Hwa wasn't even sure why they'd bothered with a full casket, when the bits and pieces that were left of Calliope would've left extra space in a child-size model.

"Did you find anything?" Eileen asked. "I mean, with the . . ."

"No," Hwa said. "Everything's clean. Normal."

Which was the problem. She'd downloaded all of Calliope's calendars, reviews, metrics, notes, and forum posts. Nothing looked out of the ordinary. No complaints about past clients. No bad reviews from them, either. She showed up on time, always checked in, followed protocol, and filed complete reports after every encounter. A model member of the organization, really. There was nothing to indicate that she'd either had a problem with someone, or had a personal problem that would drive her to throw herself into the dark, frigid waters of the North Atlantic.

She needed more information. The hot list. Surveillance data. *Prefect's* data.

"What about the appointment?"

Hwa shook her head. "He cancelled, last week. Emergency firmware upgrade on a spinal implant. Even if he could kill someone with a slipped disc, he was at the hospital during the time slot. That's why he cancelled. He left a nice note and everything. Even sent a gift card, to say sorry for bailing. Cops cleared him straightaway."

"So she never told Andrea he cancelled?"

"I guess not." Hwa sank down further in the pew. "Maybe she didn't want her knowing she was going off-book."

"And without a bodyguard, too," Eileen said. "Why would she do something like that?"

Hwa watched as mourners streamed into the sanctuary. A host of sparkling flies hovered near the lectern. Occasionally, one would buzz past the arrangements of lilies and wreaths to scan a card. Calliope's people, whoever they were, were prepared to drop some bandwidth on a remote live stream.

"Maybe it was short notice," Hwa said. "Maybe she just couldn't find somebody in enough time."

Eileen fidgeted a little. She kept scrolling through the funeral programme, up and down, back and forth. It took her a moment to speak. She touched the valve in Hwa's arm gently. "You won't do something like that again, will you?"

"Something like what?"

Eileen's right hand landed on her left. Hwa turned to look at her. Eileen's eyes were wet. Her lips trembled. "Something really fucking stupid," Eileen said. "Like go up against a psycho with a shotgun all by yourself."

Hwa's mouth worked. She didn't know what to say. Eileen pointed up at the casket. "That could be *you,* Hwa. You could be *dead,* right now, and it's like you don't even care."

I don't, she wanted to say. Because she didn't. In the grand scheme, the loss of Go Jung-hwa from the world wouldn't be too remarkable or noteworthy. It wasn't like she provided some special service to the world. She was hired muscle. That was all. If she died, she could be replaced.

"It's not that big a deal," Hwa said. "And anyway, I quit."

Eileen looked absurdly hopeful. She wiped her eyes. "You did?"

"Yeah. They were assholes."

"Oh, thank goodness." Eileen threw her arms around Hwa. She hugged tight. A twang of pain resounded up Hwa's right arm; she yelped and some of the other mourners turned in their pews to give her a *ssh!* face.

"Sorry!" Eileen slackened her grip somewhat. She pulled back a little and held Hwa's hands. "That's great news! Are you going to come back to work with us?"

Hwa glanced around the sanctuary. Mistress Séverine was sitting in the second row back, with Rusty and Nail on either side of her. "Yeah, I'll probably try to, after the funeral." She winced. "Japrisot really wanted me to stay in school, though. She'll be pissed."

"Hwa, you got *shot*," Eileen said. "I think she'll understand if you tell her you bit off more than you could chew."

Hwa caught herself frowning. She sat up a little straighter in the pew. She smoothed the sleeve over the valve in her wounded arm. "More than I could chew?"

"Of course! They had completely unreasonable expectations of you!"

Hearing someone else make the same excuses for her that she'd made to Joel made them sound even worse, and made her sound even weaker. The real problem was the fact that they'd lied to her, that Daniel Fucking Síofra, *her boss,* had lied to her, that they were all manipulative bastards who couldn't even keep track of their own goddamn bullets.

"Well, I could do the job. If I wanted to. But I don't want to."

"Damn right you don't." Eileen crossed her legs primly. "You're much safer with us."

Hwa nodded at the coffin. "Tell that to Calliope."

Music rose. So did the congregation. Father Herlihy proceeded up the aisle swinging a censer and singing "Shall We Gather at the River?" off-key. As they watched, he circled Calliope's coffin, swinging and singing under the occasional twinkle of botflies whose lights strobed across the fragrant smoke. He turned to face the congregation, and he met Hwa's gaze and quickly looked away. Like her,

Father Herlihy was one of the last few unaugmented people on the rig, and that meant he saw her true face. He had always looked away from it, ever since she was little, when Sunny forced her to go to his Sunday school. Sunny only let Hwa stop going after her First Communion, once the chance to tease her about how stupid she looked in her dumb white dress had passed. That was the only explanation Hwa could think of for her mother's insistence on Sunday school. It wasn't like their family believed.

The song ended, and the congregation sat. The pews creaked like real wood. You could get anything fabbed, these days.

"Calliope's was a beautiful soul," Father Herlihy said. "And her relationship with this parish—and the Church itself—was a long and fruitful one. Her parents, who can only attend via telepresence—gave up everything to bring her to Canada from Greece. They escaped the Golden Dawn with a single hard drive. It had a few documents, but mostly it was just photos. Photos and video, from many generations of her family. Every birthday, every wedding, every baptism. I saw them, when she married Andrea. She brought them to their marriage workshop, after they were engaged."

Beside her, Eileen bent over and appeared to stare at her shoes. It took Hwa a minute to realize she was crying. Hwa patted her carefully on the shoulder. Looking at her hand making its awkward motions made her feel like the coach of a losing team.

"I'm sorry," Eileen whispered. "I know you don't like this kind of thing. . . ."

"Huh?" Hwa let her arm rest around Eileen's shoulders. "It's okay. You can cry. Just because I don't cry doesn't mean you can't."

Eileen looked up and wiped her eyes. "You can cry, too, Hwa. It's okay. I won't tell."

Hwa shook her head. "No, I mean I can't. I literally can't. Not out of this eye. So you have to go twice as hard for both of us."

Eileen smiled and sat up. She leaned on Hwa. "You're so tough."

"That's why they pay me the big bucks."

"Not anymore," Eileen said. She dug her head deeper into Hwa's shoulder. Hwa watched Calliope's friends queue up for Communion. They were all tattooed. Just like Calliope. Dragons. Crosses. Roses. Mecha. Kaiju. Skulls. Butterflies. Ripples of blue and black and red and pink across the flesh.

Oh, Jesus. How could she have forgotten?

•   •   •

Síofra lived on 5-15, nineteen floors down from the place where Joel and Zachariah lived. Hwa's sinuses flared up as the elevator climbed. The pain threatened to spike into a real headache.

The doors to 5-15 peeled back. Hwa stepped through. The hallway came awake as she stepped silently onto thick blue moss. On either side were more doors, each spaced a fair distance apart. Wreaths grew from their damp, thick surfaces. The walls were all indoor ivy and night-blooming jasmine. At any other time, it might have been pleasant. Pretty. Now it just smelled like failure.

How was she going to explain this? *I was wrong. I want my job back. Please give it to me, so that I can figure out who really killed my former student. I know she didn't kill herself, because she was getting a tattoo. She had plans. Permanent ones. And now she's dead.*

The door opened before she could knock.

"You know, the homeowner's association has a bylaw against loitering." Síofra leaned against the door.

"There's no such thing as a homeowner in this town," Hwa told him. "Everyone rents."

He shrugged. "Shouldn't you be in the hospital?"

"Shouldn't you be at work?" When he didn't answer, she peered around him into the unit. She glimpsed a gleaming kitchen lit like a jewelry store, and the curve of a huge window surmounting a long inset fireplace. Something bubbled in the stove. It smelled of sesame. Her empty stomach clenched like a child's grasping fist.

"Hungry?"

"What is it?"

"There is fainting imam in the oven and peanut soup on the stove."

Hwa squinted at the kitchen. "Fainting . . . ?"

"Imam. It's roasted eggplant, stuffed with tomatoes, dressed with yogurt, mint, and pine nuts." He entered the kitchen. "Are you coming in, or do I need to show you a dessert menu?"

Hwa hastened inside. She shut the door behind her and removed her shoes. She placed them with all the other shoes and slippers on a rack, under a large mirror in an ornate frame. "Where are your boots?"

"Over there." He pointed.

"Those aren't winter boots. You need something waterproof, with thicker tread, and better lining, and they should go up to here." She pointed at the place where a doctor would test the reflexes in her knee. "Do you not understand how winter works, in Newfoundland?"

"Winter's the one with all the flowers, isn't it? The trees all bud and baby animals run around?"

Hwa threw up her arms. One of them, anyway. The one that didn't hurt. Then she let it drop. "I'm just saying, you need to get fitted and put in your order soon, before the stock runs out. Otherwise you'll have soggy socks from November to March."

He rolled mint leaves into little cigars and then began slicing them into ribbons. The smell rose in the air, brightening the ambient scents of roasting garlic and cumin. "Did you really come here to criticize my choice of footwear?"

Hwa sighed. "No."

He fetched down a very small glass bottle of jewel-red syrup from a cabinet over the worktop. It looked almost like perfume. "Do you want to talk about why you really came, or should we continue avoiding the issue?"

Hwa crossed over to the bar. Laid her hands on it, flat. It was the colour of good caramel, and very cold. Hwa saw little golden flecks of mica embedded in its surface. "I want my job back."

Síofra uncorked the bottle and beaded a drop of the syrup inside on the tip of his middle finger. He sucked it off and nodded to himself. "Fine."

"Because I know that I . . ." Hwa frowned. "What? Just like that?"

"Just like that."

"Don't I have to sign something? Or interview again? Or, you know, grovel? Beg forgiveness?"

Síofra turned and picked up a wooden spoon from a rest on the worktop. It had a large, perfectly round hole in the paddle, and it looked very old. He stirred the soup slowly in lazy figure eights. He frowned at the spoon for a moment, changed his grip, and began stirring in the other direction. "Forgiveness for what?"

"I quit. I gave up. I abandoned my post."

"No, you didn't. You took a bullet for Joel, and you lost a lot of blood, and you said something you didn't mean. Now you're feeling better, and we're having a conversation about it." He returned the wooden spoon its rest and turned around. "And as part of that conversation, I should ask for your forgiveness."

Hwa blinked. "Excuse me?"

"The exercise was meant to test your response to an armed threat, and the school's response to an emergency scenario. You and Joel were never supposed to be in any real danger. But you were. And you were hurt. And I'm sorry." He stared out the window at the city for a moment. "Your job was to protect Joel, and mine was to protect you. I'm the one who failed you, Hwa. Not the other way around."

Hwa looked away. She hadn't been expecting an apology. Much less a genuine one. "G'wan, b'y," she muttered, letting her accent slip.

"I heard about your friend. You have my condolences."

"Thanks." She bounced on her toes. This was awkward. Unbelievably awkward. She'd come ready for a fight and now the fight had nowhere to go. It pooled inside her like acid in her joints, corrosive and irritating. "Can I help you? I can chop, or wash, or—"

"You can rest. Over there."

He pointed at a long leather sectional with a full view of the window. Hwa had never seen so much of the material in one place. Síofra snapped his fingers twice, and the fireplace lit up. Warily, Hwa unbuttoned the jacket of her suit and laid it across the back of the sectional. She sat down and watched out the window. Clouds hung pink over the towers, lit by the dying sun. Its light cast the other towers in dark relief. She couldn't quite see Tower Two from here; from this vantage point it looked like it was hiding behind Tower Four like an older, simpler sibling hiding behind a much smarter one.

She knew the rationale behind sticking the schools in the farm tower—all those bees, all those plants, all that science, ready and waiting—but the farm levels had far better security than the schools did. Patented seeds. Scary pesticides. Enough fertilizer to take out half the tower. For that reason alone, sniffers were posted at each major entry point: transit, causeway, the elevator court. They'd added more, after the Old Rig blew. How had anyone smuggled in live ammunition?

"Red or white?"

"Sorry?"

"The wine. Red or white?"

"Oh. Sorry. I don't drink wine. Too much sugar." She gestured at the stain he couldn't see, then dropped her hand quickly. "Abrupt changes in blood sugar are bad for . . . me."

"That's a shame. Is there anything else I can offer you?"

"Vodka, if you have it." It was the safest. But it sounded demanding, to be so specific. "Or gin. Or bourbon. Or—" She heard the sound of ice on steel. She turned, and he was shaking a martini. "Or martinis. Sure."

As he poured, he asked: "Do you eat lamb?"

Hwa shrugged. "Don't know. Never had it."

He paused. "Never? Not even once?"

Hwa gestured at the other towers. "I don't think you reckon how spendy meat is in this town."

"Do you enjoy meat?"

"Well, yeah, it's good for me, and it tastes good, and—"

He opened the door to the freezer and cut off the conversation. Out came a packet that he tossed in the sink. "We'll eat the other things first, and this for dessert. Is tartare all right with you?"

"What?"

"Raw. Would you like to try it raw?"

The moment stretched on for longer than it should have. "Sure," Hwa said, finally. "If that's how you like it. I mean, you know more about it than me, right?"

He smirked. "Indeed." He put the drinks and the shaker on a tray and carried them out to her. When she picked up hers, he held his out. "To your return."

It was a perfect martini. Literally. She'd had one once before, at the Aviation bar in Tower Four. Half sweet vermouth, half dry. Just the barest hint of sugar, the tiniest possible taste of what she wasn't supposed to have. She leaned into the moment the way she leaned into pain. Breathed through it. Inhaled deeply: leather and garlic and mint, the olive brine beading on her glass.

"I need you to tell me something," she said, opening her eyes.

Síofra was watching her closely. "Yes?"

"Can you just level with me, and tell me you had somebody following me, the day of the shooting? Somebody wearing next-gen prototype camouflage, or something? Because if that's the truth, then now's the time."

Síofra put his drink down and stared at her. "You saw it, too."

Relief flooded her. She drained her martini. "I thought I was having a seizure."

Síofra gestured at the windows, and suddenly surveillance footage was on the screen. There was the skullcap, staring at his guns. Checking and rechecking the clips. Sighting down the scopes. He bent down to tighten the laces of his boot, and there it was: a blip of pixellated white, a glitch. A glitch that looked vaguely human in shape. An invisible man, with his hands on the ammo.

Hwa pointed. "I saw this guy. In the sprinklers. The shape of him. Did you include this in the final report?"

"I did. But the live rounds left behind a trail. They were in a smart box. It looks like simple human error. And Silas wasn't interested in an alternative explanation."

A shiver ran through her. She pointed at the martini shaker. "You got any more there, b'y?"

He poured her another. "When you start back, I'll thank you to stop calling me *boy* at the end of sentences."

"It's just an expression. It's how we talk, out here. Besides, you're only ten. I can call you whatever I want."

He laughed. Hwa reminded herself stop staring at him, and pulled her focus to the footage on the screen. She was here for more than just this job. She spoke the part she'd rehearsed. "Once I get my Prefect access back, I'll start looking for who's selling camouflage in town. But I want expanded access. The premium plan, like you have."

"You mean to hunt down this phantom?"

Hwa drank. "Fucker got me shot. If he didn't want me hunting him, he should've finished the job."

PART TWO

OCTOBER

9

Acoutsina/Nakatomi/Girders/Bentham

Hwa's days began to follow a certain pattern.

At 04:30, she woke up, drank a bottle of water with vinegar, and ran for an hour. Some of the time, Síofra came with. Otherwise, she ran the Demasduwit Causeway, circled Tower Two, then ran up the Sinclair and back down again toward the school. He ran the Fitzgerald to the Sinclair, and at the end of the run they met up. They had eggs in avocado and he asked her about what was going on in the city—whether he should tweak the register of the train's announcement voice, or if the streetlights should change temperature from warm gold to cold white as the night wore on, or whether they needed more sniffers in public places. After what had happened to Calliope, he was supposed to be getting more suicide prevention measures installed. She showed him how to skip stones through the gaps in the existing motion detection. He did not ask how she knew where they were.

At 06:15, she arrived at school and visited the weight room. Weights didn't take long.

By 07:00, she was showered and changed into her uniform and scoping the school. She did a full perimeter check, and she and Prefect ran over whatever the NASS system told them was important: assemblies, games, deliveries, other changes to everyday routine.

From 08:00 to 16:00 she had classes with Joel. On Mondays, Joel had science club with Mr. Branch until 17:30. On Fridays, his father sent a special jitney to pick him up, and they did father-and-son stuff for the evening.

Weekends the family had other security in the form of skullcaps, but there was a standing invitation to Sunday dinner. It was useful for copying Joel's homework. And for reading the room. Anyway, it wasn't like she had anywhere else to go. Usually Síofra was there, too.

From 16:00 to 18:00 weekday afternoons, Hwa had Joel to train. She wanted him in the morning, originally, but it was a no-go. Joel's implants had a persnickety update schedule—they had to talk to servers all over the world, and he was simply not good to go until later.

After 18:00, she could go home. At home, she still had Prefect. And in between its other tasks, while running at very, very low background usage levels, the kind that wouldn't trigger any kind of suspicion, Prefect had put together everything she needed to know. First, she'd run facial identification.

"This woman appears a great deal," Prefect had said, the first time she showed it a picture of Calliope. *"She's also deceased."*

"I want to put together a timeline of her death."

Prefect had paused for a moment. For a moment she thought it didn't understand her command. Then it said: *"No one in your position has ever asked me to perform that task."*

"No one who's not a cop, you mean?"

"Yes."

"That mean you can't do it?"

"Not at all. But it will force me to engage in some adaptive learning. Please be patient with me."

"Sure."

"And, I will need you to sign a waiver clarifying your understanding that my powers of observation can in certain circumstances extend to the extrajudicial, and that your use of my interface does not indemnify Lynch Ltd. or make them liable to any and all resulting legal actions pursuant to your investigation."

Hwa frowned. "Eh?"

"If you use me to look at information that should in theory be covered by a warrant, and you are caught doing so, you will not hold the company responsible."

"Oh." Hwa looked at Calliope's face smiling at her from the display unit. "Where's the dotted line?"

And so they began.

This was how Calliope spent her last day:

Calliope found a recipe for dark chocolate pudding.

Calliope watched almost an entire series of *This Old Temple*.

Calliope read up on all the cast members of *This Old Temple*.

Calliope checked the dates on all the items in her fridge that might allow her to make dark chocolate pudding.

Calliope read up on food poisoning.

Calliope went down a rabbit hole of intestinal distress.

Calliope did nothing for over an hour. Probably, she slept.

Calliope received a message.

Calliope looked up some coordinates.

Calliope left the apartment.

Calliope started walking on the causeway.

Calliope disappeared.

Calliope's body surfaced on the water a day later.

"Show me those coordinates," Hwa said.

• • •

The coordinates matched a location on the Acoutsina Causeway, between the joints. Calliope had gone there sometime between 22:00 Tuesday and Wednesday afternoon of that week, when the flies found her body. Her fob logged her out of the tower at 21:48, and ambient surveillance found her at :50 and :55 looking before she crossed onto the causeway, and then again when she paused to look at a man cooking syrup sculptures. The fire under his wok picked out her features enough for the cameras to recognize her in the dimness. She smiled at him as he drizzled a butterfly shape onto a plate, carefully lifted it free, and handed it to a little girl. After that, Calliope drifted away from the crowd. And then she disappeared.

Hwa went for a night run at 22:00 the next Tuesday to see what she had seen.

At night, the pavement of the Acoutsina lit up speckled and blue, like a scattering of diamond dust had been mixed in with the asphalt. It was a pale imitation of the stars overhead. This far out to sea, the sky was still dark. It was different, on the mainland. Even St. John's had an orange sky at night. But in New Arcadia the stars were clear, so clear you could imagine how sailors had navigated by them.

The year after Tae-kyung died, Hwa had taken an off-book job guarding equipment on an observatory vessel. The biologists took their boat out at night, and during the day they wanted someone keeping an eye on all their stuff while they slept. The final night, they took her with them to watch the Perseids. The meteors kept streaking by, so many and so fast that they all lost count as the cups kept filling. Everyone was talking about how lucky they were to see it so clearly. All Hwa could think about was how even the oldest things died and became nothing, and what a comfort that was, that nothing lasted forever.

Now she slowed to a stop, near the candy drizzler and his wok. He was still there. He gave her a hopeful look, but she shook her head. He directed his shtick somewhere else.

"All right, Calliope? What did you see?"

It would be Halloween, soon, so the kiosks were selling masks and props and costumes. One guy was hawking maps to the best candy and parties in Tower Five. And there were a bunch of haunted accessory realities—you could see the whole rig populated by zombies, or vampires, or whatever. Each day the vision would change a little, until you were in full alternate-universe horror.

"Do Calliope's purchases over the past month match any of the businesses here?"

It took Prefect a minute. *"No."*

Hwa crossed to avoid a cyclist and looked out over the water. She sighed. "She was right here. I'm standing where she was standing, right before her fob started to drift. Even if she jumped, everyone would have seen her."

"Posit: she entered the water somewhere closer to the water, immediately below."

Hwa looked down. Below the low-speed pedestrian level was the high-speed level for vehicles. Lights rushed by, infrequent but blazingly fast. This late there was no speed limit. Only at peak hours did the vehicles have to watch how fast they went. If Calliope had gone down there, it was possible she'd been hit and fallen. But there was a suicide barrier at that level. She knew. She had seen Síofra's maps of the area.

Which meant she'd entered the water from somewhere below the causeway itself. Where the trolls lived.

"You have got to be shitting me."

Hwa searched for the nearest set of service stairs. The relevant logo floated up above a parkette fringed with twisted long-needle pine and a few artful boulders that suggested human shapes huddled against the wind. Set in among the trees was a set of rusting steel doors. The rust had all but eroded the New Arcadia logo that burned high above in Hwa's vision.

"Here goes. Open her up."

It took a moment, but Hwa heard the bolt squeal to one side. She pushed down on the doors, but they wouldn't budge. They'd rusted together. Hwa looked around at the people crowding the causeway. No one was really paying attention to the woman in the trees. The trees themselves reeked of piss—probably everyone had gotten used to ignoring whoever stood there.

Hwa gave the door a nudge. Then a shove. Then a full body check. The doors fell open and Hwa stumbled down into cold, stale darkness. She found herself in a tight tunnel that reverberated with the roar of passing vehicles. The stairs went almost straight down. Their edges glowed, dimly. She felt around for a switch, but there was none.

"Lights," she said, but none came. She waved her hands. Nothing. Even if there were lights, their circuits might have burned out years ago. "Who used to manage this part of the causeway?" Hwa asked.

"*The last manager on file is listed as Nakatomi & Sons,*" Prefect said.

"Aye? How long ago did that contract wrap up?"

"Five years ago."

"Great. Lovely. Beautiful." Hwa gripped the rail tighter. "Well, give it to RoFo, okay?"

RoFo was a sub-persona deployed by the Urban Tactics office to create an evolving portfolio of tasks based on residents' complaints. You just pinged RoFo, and complained about any damn thing you could think of. A crack in the wall. A clogged drain. The way your doors kept opening and shutting, opening and shutting, all night long, because the motion detector was tuned so fucking high the food moths set it off. It didn't mean the problem would get fixed right away, but it did mean you'd been listened to. It was an easy way to feel like someone cared. Even if no one really did.

As her feet found another step, she heard a creak and then a clang. Then complete darkness. The doors had closed.

"Are they supposed to do that?" Hwa asked.

"All the service doors leading to high-speed causeways have an automatic locking protocol."

Hwa slowly let the breath out of her body. She closed her eyes. Her own personal darkness was warmer and safer than the howling blackness of the tunnel around her.

"Prefect, are you able to open the door? Down here, on the high-speed level?"

Silence.

Hwa swallowed. *Master control room*, she reminded herself. *Just picture the master control room. Picture all the buttons and screens. Picture all your problems on those screens. They're far away. Remote.*

"Prefect?"

A blip in her ears. A pop. Bad audio. A voice that sounded like it was underwater.

"Prefect!"

"—Apologies. Another process briefly borrowed my cycles."

Down below, another bolt screeched to one side. A door yawned slowly open. Violet light and noise from the high-speed causeway followed. The light exposed the little landing three steps below where Hwa stood.

Blood.

Everywhere.

Old. Rusty. Like the doors.

Handprints. A puddle. A dark blossom on one wall.

Calliope had died here.

. . .

For about five seconds, she thought about calling the police. Then she thought better of it. She could send an anonymous tip, later. For now, there were the trolls.

They lived under the causeways. Hence the name. Hwa had only visited them once before. Someone stole her backpack and put it there. Probably Missy Thompson, the grade five class bitch, though Hwa never found out exactly who it was. Which was probably for the best.

Then as now, she'd found the secret entrance that took her below the vehicle level and into the girders. It was a runoff channel, meant for slurping down melted ice and snow and whatever else the pavement didn't want, and dumping it out to sea. She was still just small enough to fit through, once she found a square of grate that was rusted enough to pry up. Back in grade five, she'd had to bring her own crowbar. Stealing the crowbar was half the job.

In October, the runoff was low. Not too much had washed down there. But if someone had killed Calliope—and someone had fucking butchered her—they had to drop her from somewhere. Somewhere close to the water. Somewhere under the causeway itself. In the girders. In the lowest place you could go.

She walked on in darkness. Ahead of her, something skittered. She paused. "I'm friendly," she said, although it sounded stupid. "I'm not police."

Nothing. Silence. Just the occasional rush of a ride overhead, and the dry whine of the wind in the channel.

"My friend died," she said. "She was killed. Here. Close to here. And I want to know who dumped her body."

A grunt. A rustling. Multiple trolls were in the channel with her. She heard something crunch behind her, softly, and she held up her hands. Who knew what edits they'd done to their eyes. Her own specs told her nothing. There were no maps for this place. No one had bothered to make them.

"I swear I won't tell anyone how I got down here," she added. "I won't bring anybody else into it. I just want to know, for me own self."

Clicking. A wet clicking, like many tongues striking many roofs of many mouths. Some of the trolls were all networked together, brain to brain, via early skullcap prototypes. Or so she'd heard. That was part of why they were down in the girders. The bleedthrough was too intense. Addictive. It was the only real social network.

Something poked her in the back. It pushed her forward. Together they advanced through the channel. Hwa kept her hands up. Eventually the quiet lessened, and she heard a steely shrieking, and they pushed her out into the light.

In the sudden bright glare of light was another city altogether. Unlike the city topside, it had not changed much. It was still paved with particle board and threading plastic. Its buildings were old disaster pop-ups, some of them still silver. Others were grown, mushroom-like, riven with green veins of mould, bigger now than when she remembered them. She had expected tarps, the first time, but didn't know why. They wouldn't hold through the winter. And these people had been here longer than most. Wind whistled through the other city. Hwa heard a cat. She smelled cooking.

"I'm down here," a gravelly voice said, a few balloons away.

Hwa walked. She kept her hands out, her wrists loose. She tried to avoid looking at any one particular tent or balloon.

"Warmer," the voice said.

Hwa paused in front of one balloon that was actually two of them stitched together. Someone had painted an evil eye sigil across it. Outside stood a huge mask of bone and antler, so large it needed stilts to stand on. It loomed over Hwa. The wind rose up and she heard something inside it rattle.

"Hot," said the voice inside.

Hwa went inside. The woman waiting for her sat in a wheelchair. She was Inuit. Her hair hung lank and gleaming with grease. The balloon smelled of her unwashed scalp. She was blind. Or rather, her eyes no longer saw. Hwa didn't know if they were out of warranty, or what. But the machines where the old woman's eyes were had gone pearly. Nonetheless, she motioned for Hwa to sit down on an old can of cooking oil. The whole place was cans. Corn. Peas. Tomatoes. Hwa only knew them from the pictures on the labels. The languages, she couldn't read.

"I'm sorry," Hwa said.

"For what?"

"Not bringing anything. I didn't know I'd be coming here. I was looking for my friend—"

"Your friend isn't here. She's dead."

Hwa nodded. "I know. What I don't know is what happened."

"She died."

Again, Hwa nodded. She listened to the ocean below. "I want to know how she died."

"She was murdered."

Hwa sat forward. "Did you see it?"

A huge, rotten laugh exploded wetly from the old woman's throat. Hwa wiped her face with the back of her hand. Now the tent smelled of tobacco and teeth and sickness, all at once.

"Blood, first," the woman said. "Yours is clean."

Hwa swallowed. "Organic." She wasn't sure if she should mention the anticonvulsants. Knowing whether to mention it would mean having some inkling of what the woman wanted with her blood, and she very much didn't want to have that. "No machines," she added, just in case. How had this woman known?

"I see things," the old woman said, as though she'd heard Hwa's thoughts. "Through other eyes."

Outside, Hwa heard the synchronized clicking of tongues.

"You control them?" Hwa licked her lips. "You hacked them? Through the skullcap?"

"Did you know that the root of the word *cybernetics* comes from the ancient Greek for *pilot*? Of course they can be piloted. Give me your hand." The woman reached into the folds of her flesh and tugged. An oyster knife appeared, the shiniest thing in the place, bright and hard as the edge of a fresh moon. She reached for Hwa's hand.

"No, my arm," Hwa said. "I'm already wounded, there. Take that."

The woman shrugged elaborately. Smell rolled off her as her shoulders shifted. Hwa peeled up her sleeve and exposed the pink flesh of her bullet wound. The woman leaned forward and Hwa's eyes burned and the knife rode up, up, up, gently, until it hit scar tissue.

The old woman inhaled deeply. "That's the stuff."

"What will you work with it?"

Again, the woman laughed. It was a thick, awful sound. "Work? Nothing. People here need transfusions. They got bad implants. Hep C."

The knife slid in under the scar. Hwa expected it to hurt more than it did. But the knife was extremely sharp, and barely tugged the skin.

"He'll cut you places you don't know about, yet." Phlegm gurgled in the old woman's throat. "He's been coming for you for a while. Him and all his brothers. He has a lot of souls. You just have the one. Be careful you don't lose it."

Hwa thought about asking where her other souls had run off to, but she wasn't sure she'd like the answer. "Did he dump her from here? My friend? She was in pieces."

The old woman nodded. "He was here. But he's everywhere. Behind you. In front of you. Almost touching but not quite."

Hwa frowned. "A shadowboxer?"

"Aye."

"How do you know?"

The woman tapped the ruined lenses of her machine eyes with one brown, mouldy fingernail. Then she pointed out of the hut. Again the mouths outside clicked. "My eyes see things most can't."

"Ghosts?"

The woman's hand left her face and stroked Hwa's. She pushed the hair back from Hwa's face. The skin of her hand was surprisingly soft and warm. It occurred to her that Sunny had never touched her this way. This gently. This carefully.

"Oh, my little one," the witch murmured. "Wish t'were that simple."

. . .

"This had better be good," Kripke said, when she found him. "I was just about to lock up."

Hwa rolled her eyes. She nodded at the people still in the gym. They looked tired, and most of them clustered around two women leaning into each other and learning the finer points of a kidney punch, but they were still around. "Aye. I can see that, b'y."

He sighed. "Fine. What is it?"

"Can we have your office?"

His eyebrows lifted. Then he shrugged and led her back into the office. From behind a glass door, he could watch all the fights as they proceeded. It was still just as much of a disaster as she remembered: posters peeling off the walls, empty canisters of protein, dead aloe plants, greasy boxes of takeout.

"So." He dropped into a chair held together almost entirely with duct tape. It screeched terribly and he had to adjust himself in it in order to sit normally. It continued squeaking as he leaned back and crossed one ankle over his knee. "What is this about?"

"Say I needed my blood looked at," Hwa said.

"Then I'd say this fine country of ours has universal healthcare, and you can visit any doctor you want and ask for a test."

Hwa rocked on her heels. She jammed her hands in her pockets. "Say I wanted something a bit more specialized."

He crossed his thick, hairy arms over his belly. He was still getting bigger. Hwa blamed the takeout. And the shitty printed protein. The man needed a produce subscription. Come to think of it, so did she. She could afford it, now. It was weird, being able to spend money. She'd spent hours deciding which new pair of shoes to get, before deciding on the ones she always wore. It just seemed safer. Like getting anything better would just be asking for trouble.

"Are you pregnant?" he asked.

"*What?*" Hwa backed away. "No! That's insane! Like, completely, certifiably insane. I'm not pregnant, and I'm not going to get pregnant. And even if I were, that wouldn't be any of your business."

"Sturge-Weber isn't hereditary, you know. You could have a perfectly healthy baby, if that's what you wanted to do."

"Good Christ, please stop talking." Hwa found a poster to look at. It was a detailed explanation of the major muscle groups. *Latissimus. Pectoralis. Soleus.* She found the Latin names for things very calming. "I can't even look at you, right now. That's how fucking awkward this conversation is."

He heaved a deep sigh and leaned forward in his chair. "Okay. Fine. None of my business. I'm sorry."

Hwa met his gaze. "I'm fine. I just want to know where I can go to get a blood sample looked at."

"To look for what?"

"Anything. Everything." She stepped a little closer to him. "Quietly."

Kripke sucked his teeth. He set his jaw. Then he snapped his fingers at his desk, and the display lit up. It was old and flickery and uneven, but it still worked. He cleared a bunch of things away from it, before lighting on a single list.

"This is a list of people I banned from the gym," he said. "Most of them were trying to sell my customers on freelance regimens. If you buy into the open-source ones, that's your choice. But these guys had no approval *and* they refused to give up the code, or show any testimonials. But their prices were great, and boxing makes you stupid."

He pointed at one name on the list. "This guy was selling blood-dopers. I kicked him out when he gave one of my guys the bends. I went to his place personally."

Hwa whistled low. "Damn."

"Yeah. That's what he said, after his new jaw went in." Kripke leaned back in his chair. "Anyway. He had a lot of equipment. And I think he still lives in the same place. In fact, I'm pretty sure he does."

"Oh aye?" Hwa smiled.

Kripke smiled back. "Aye. You pays him a visit; you tells him I say hello."

. . .

His name was Dixon Sandro, and his address was 4-31-24. Tower Four featured two concentric rings of units—the outer, even-numbered ring had windows out to sea, and the inner, odd-numbered units had extra space to compensate for the lack. You could choose storage, or aesthetics. Every day, the inner and outer rings rotated around each other like at a country dance, so that you had a different set of neighbours every day. Each wall in the residential units was modular. You could turn the walls on to get some privacy. Or you could leave all the walls off, and share a bunch of space with friends for a few hours, or all day, or all night.

Hwa used to do a lot of work in Tower Four. It was a party tower.

Dixon Sandro was entertaining. Both his door and his neighbours' were wide open and completely transparent. Before she entered, Hwa changed the defaults on her halo. Now no one who peeped her would know she worked for Lynch.

Smoke hazed over both units. The people inside were mostly cuddled around pillows that cuddled them back. Their faces were blank. Occasionally they would all giggle at the same moment. They each had the same "huh-huh-huh" stoner laugh. Hwa stepped in and around them, but they didn't notice. Their cushions inched out of her way as she walked, parting like some soft velour sea.

"Dixon?" Hwa looked around. Nobody perked up. "Dixon here?"

Above her, an arrow in the ceiling came to light. It was a soft, minty green, and it pointed back and to the right, around a corner wall that Hwa guessed was the washroom. The washrooms were generally all in the same spot, in these places. Otherwise the pipes wouldn't line up. It was the same with the central air ducts. It was part of what made Tower Four so easy to build—you just printed the same unit, over and over, without any need for customization. Hwa followed the green arrow past the people on cushions. To the right was a nook with a window. A man sat watching the feeds in his eyes. He'd cracked the window, a little.

"You nervous about that shit getting in your lungs?" Hwa asked.

He jolted. His legs and arms flailed for a moment and he struggled to stand. Dixon Sandro was a tiny man, bald, with a head too big for his body, with Liefeld muscle definition on a frame two sizes too small. That was the actual brand name for the regimen: Liefeld. Hwa knew other guys who had taken it. Like Dixon, all of them had the worst acne imaginable. You had to, if you were fucking around with your testosterone like that. Dixon's acne was everywhere: his face, his shoulders, in the creases of his neck, in the cuts across his muscles. Awful, cystic, painful pustules. For a moment, Hwa almost felt sorry for him.

"What the fuck happened to your face?"

The moment passed.

"Kripke sent me," Hwa lied.

Under his acne, Dixon went pale. It made the red spots seem redder, like little eyes embedded in his skin slowly going bloodshot. "What does he want?"

"He wants you to do something for me." Hwa slung her pack down from her shoulder and opened it. Out came her old shoes, in a vacuum-sealed bag. "He wants you to take a sample from the blood on these shoes, and tell me about it. Now."

"Now? Like right now?"

"Yes, like now. Like right fucking now."

Now he got petulant. "Why should I? What's in it for me?"

"What's in it for you is you don't need your jaw reprinted. Again." Hwa looked at the shoes, and then at him. He really did have a lot of equipment. And he was surprisingly neat about it. The scanners weren't at all dusty, and the big live-cell imager was still gleaming, no dents. He was probably the real deal, once. Maybe even had some education, and a real degree, until he did his version of the thing everyone did that brought them to New Arcadia. "You do this, we leave you alone. You can't come back to the gym, but we don't come around anymore."

"For real? You swear?"

Hwa made a show of examining the room and its inhabitants. "I think there's enough business for you in this tower, don't you? Don't think you need to go looking for work."

"Yeah." He licked his lips. They were peeling. Blood seeped out from the cracks. "Okay. Got it. Just . . . run the sample?"

"Aye."

"Am I checking for anything specific?"

"Whatever you can find." Hwa waved her hand over a cushion and plucked the air with her fingers. The cushion inched over to her. "I have time."

Dixon got right to work. He took a scraping from the soles of her shoes, activated it in vital serum, and ran it through the imager.

"Been dead a while," he said, looking at the screen.

"Aye." Hwa stood up. "She has."

"You know the sample?"

"I'm the one asking the questions," Hwa said.

"How long was she sick for?"

"Sick?"

"Yeah. Her white count was through the roof."

Hwa thought of the last time she'd seen Calliope's face. If she was seriously ill, that might explain a suicide attempt. But the witch under the bridge had said it was murder. And the bloodstains in the stairwell didn't look like a gunshot wound. They looked like an explosion. Someone had popped Calliope's body like an over-full balloon.

"She wasn't sick."

"Fine. Just making conversation. Not like I'm an expert, or anything. Come look." He gestured for Hwa to lean down and look at the image. On the display were a series of schooling machines. As she watched, the machines trembled for a moment and then divided. Each looked just like the other. They swam off in different directions. After a moment, they divided again.

"That's . . ."

"Illegal." Dixon leaned back in his seat. He picked his jawline, squeezing a cyst that seemed unready to burst. He continued anyway, digging at it with his fingernails. "Really, really illegal. And I know from illegal. This is it. Bio-nano is strictly subscription-only in Canada. No replication. No copying."

"Um . . ." Hwa scratched the back of her neck. "I don't have any . . . You know, implants, or augments, edits, or whatever. So, I'm kinda in the dark, here."

He groaned, like he was explaining something to his dotty old grandmother. "The *copyright*," he said. "You want the augment, the subscription, you gotta pay the licensing fee. Or your provider does, if you're covered."

"So? You can't bootleg a copy?"

"Sure. But your devices will report you. The toilets. The specs. Everything. There's random scans everywhere. And then, boom, a C-and-D and a big fine." He leaned back in his chair. "Besides, it's bad for you. Serial replication error. A copy of a copy of a copy. You want a shitty knockoff unclogging your arteries from the inside? I don't think so."

Hwa chose not to comment on the irony of Dixon Sandro making this particular argument. "Well, do you recognize them?"

"The machines? No. I can try running a match, though. It would take a while." Sandro kept squeezing. Blood bubbled up between his fingers. He didn't notice. "Could I try building with them? I'd know more if I got my hands dirty."

"Aye." Hwa frowned. It had not occurred to her until now to ask this question, but it made sense to, here. "Do you know where I could find some good camouflage? Like real poltergeist shit. Army grade."

"Lázló," Sandro said, without hesitation. "He lives in this tower. Moves around, though, unit to unit. Paranoid." Sandro spun a finger beside is temple.

"You know for sure he has a suit? Or a line on one?"

Sandro nodded. "I've bumped into him, wearing it."

"Bumped into? Like you walked into him?"

Again, Sandro nodded. "He wears it all the time, see? Says he feels better with it on."

"So how do you know he's there?"

"You don't."

The hairs on Hwa's arms rose. "What if I wanted to talk to him?"

"Then you go to the elevator in the nine o'clock position, with a bunch of fresh chips and vinegar," Sandro said. "And you wait."

. . .

In the elevator court, she ran into Eileen. She was with Sabrina and two other women whose names Hwa couldn't remember. By the looks of things they were just getting started: the four men they were with were laughing and wrestling each other and making bets about who could flip who fastest.

They had no bodyguard.

Hwa missed her elevator and jogged over to the party. The men ignored her—filters, probably, or maybe they were just high—and Hwa sidled up to Eileen as casually as she could. "Everything okay here?"

Eileen startled. She started to smile, and then it fell from her face. She put it away like a summer dress after the first fall rain. "What do you care?"

Hwa frowned. "Excuse me?"

"Don't you have another job to get back to? One that pays better?"

Hwa's mouth worked. "What?"

"You said you were quitting," Eileen hissed. "You told me, at Calliope's funeral, that you were quitting."

"Well, yeah, but . . ." Hwa didn't know how to explain. She watched the elevator's display. It would be there soon, to take Eileen and her party away. "It's complicated."

"No, it's not. It's not complicated at all. You've always wanted to leave this town, and now you're going to. Congratulations."

"It's not like that," Hwa said. "Really. It's not. I'm doing something important."

"Oh, yeah, going to homeroom with Richie Rich. That's real important."

Hwa looked down at the floor. The carpet had an odd pattern that ripped in her vision the longer she stared at it. Orange and pink and brown. It was astoundingly ugly, now that she really looked at it. "I'm sorry."

"Don't be. You're doing what's best for you."

Hwa swallowed. Her lips felt hot. Her eyes felt hot. "Youse don't have an escort."

"Short notice. No other bodyguards on shift."

Hwa nodded. "Yeah. Okay."

The elevator continued its journey downward. The guys in front of it—the clients, Hwa reminded herself—were doing leg-wrestling moves on the floor. Lifting their legs straight up in the air and entwining them and trying to flip each other over and insisting that they had no interest in fucking each other.

"We have to take what work we can get," Eileen said. "They shut down another one of the pumps today. The riggers are leaving. We're losing clients."

"The reactor will have workers," Hwa said.

"Scientists. With families. Lunch-time Larrys. Not all-nighters."

Fewer hours. Less pay. Less service. Lower fees. Eileen didn't have to say it. Hwa heard it just fine. The elevator chimed, and Sabrina jumped in to hold it open while the guys on the floor struggled to stand. Eileen adjusted her hair. Smoothed her dress. Inspected her nails.

"Anyway. It looks like you made the smart decision."

And with that, she walked away. She was the last in the elevator, and one of the men looped his arm around her waist. She smiled at him, and kept her smile up when she turned back to Hwa. It was still plastered on her face when the elevator doors slid shut.

10

Viridian/*Angel from Montgomery/* Nine o'Clock Elevator

"Again," Hwa said. "Harder."

Joel began another round of awkward kicks to the dummy. His range was improving; he couldn't get into the splits yet, but a daily practise of single-leg circles (clockwise and then anti-clockwise, breathing in as the foot swung away and out as it returned) was getting him to where he could do a respectable standing split and his legs could make a good ninety-degree angle with his body for about seven breaths at twelve beats each. His kicks would improve once he developed more muscle in the core and the legs, but his posture was still a problem. The kid's navel just didn't want to meet his spine.

"Your muscles are like a rubber band," Hwa said, for what felt like the hundredth time. "Right now, they're fine. You got by this long without working them because they're young. But you have to work them, tighten them up—"

"Wouldn't working a rubber band *diminish* its elasticity?" Joel asked, as his kicks grew weaker. His leg was flopping around everywhere. Dumb kid was about to throw out his hip flexor and IT band. Again.

"Other leg. And yes. But I'm the one who knows this stuff, not you."

He snorted, and sweat flew up into his hairline. "That's not much of an explanation."

Hwa mimed playing a violin.

"I'm doing the Armstrong regimen when I'm done growing," Joel huffed. His leg hammered the dummy. He held his breath tight inside his chest. She watched his shoulders begin their slow climb up to his ears. It was like his body could only do one thing at a time:

breathe or kick. The air whooshed out of him in a single frustrated stream. "You know that, right? Once my muscles are done—"

"You have to *have* muscles, first, for the Armstrong regimen to work," Hwa said. "Get into Pigeon."

His leg fell. "What? Again?"

"Your hip flexor is still too tight."

Joel looked around the rest of the gym. "It'll look really weird, in front of all these people."

"Oh, yeah, because you were really a paragon of catlike grace right there." Hwa nodded at the mat. "Do it."

Joel muttered something and knelt down. He tucked one knee under himself, and stretched the other leg behind him. He was still too tight to stretch his ribs over his knees, or even rest his forearms on the floor.

"Shouldn't I be lifting weights, to gain muscle?"

"You can lift weights after you build your core. You need something to hold your spine in place before you start doing power-cleans. You're only fifteen. This is a building year, for you. Next year, you can start to sculpt."

Next year. If he had a next year.

"Hey, Hwa!" From the other side of the gym, Coach Brandvold waved her over. Hwa jogged over, and stiffened when Brandvold greeted her with a hug. Brandvold was always giving hugs. It was weird. "How are you doing?"

Hwa was never sure what people really meant when they asked this question. It could mean any number of things: *How's the gunshot wound? Had any seizures lately? How are you getting along now that your brother's dead? What's your whore mother up to, these days?*

"I'm good," Hwa said. "I got a new apartment."

"Oh, neat! Where?"

"1-07."

"1-07?" Coach Alexander snorted. "Do they not pay you enough? Shit, *I* live on 1-13."

Hwa shrugged. "I'm just trying to save money."

Coach Alexander *hmm*'d in her throat, which was the noise she made when someone turned in an assignment late in Social Studies.

"You going to the game? Homecoming's . . . coming, I guess."

"Nope. Sorry."

Coach Brandvold elbowed her. "What about the dance?"

"I don't go to those things."

"Won't you have to, if Joel goes?"

Hwa shuddered. Trapped with her detail on the community floor of Tower Two, constantly swatting away fairy-lights and standing in line for the washroom behind giggling girls whispering blowjob tips to each other was one of her visions of Hell.

"Let's hope it doesn't come to that."

"How is Joel?" Coach Brandvold looked over her shoulder at him. Joel winced and gave Hwa a dirty look. "He's looking more flexible, lately."

"He's making progress." Hwa shrugged. "Anyway. I should get back to him."

She made to leave, but Coach Alexander leaned over and whispered something at her. "Hey, Hwa. Is it true one of the other teachers here has a type?"

Hwa frowned. "A type?"

"You know," Coach Brandvold said. "That someone else on staff would rather keep relationships . . . professional."

Moliter. Someone had seen Moliter with Eileen. On a date. And now it was all over the school. Whoever was doing Hwa's old job was doing a shitty job of it.

"Couldn't say," Hwa said, scratching the place on her face where Moliter's scar would be, and winked.

Both women laughed. Coach Alexander tapped her temple with two fingers and then pointed them at Hwa's specs. Instantly, her personal contact information popped up in Hwa's vision. "Let me know if you want someone to run with in the mornings," she said. "We might as well, living so close."

"Hey, don't leave me out!" Coach Brandvold shared her information with Hwa, too. Her profile fluttered in on little bird wings. "You should have a housewarming! I want to see your new place!"

Hwa ducked her head and began backing away toward Joel. "Okay. Thanks. I'll think about it."

"You might actually have to buy furniture, if you have a house-warming," Síofra said, in her bones. *"Maybe even invest in some plates."*

"I have plates," she muttered.

"You have one set of dishes that you picked up from the Benevolent Irish Society shop. Those don't count, just like those farmshare crates you stacked up against the wall don't really count as shelves."

"I didn't realize you were an interior decorator," Hwa said. "Not all of us have been earning Lynch wages for the past ten years."

"True."

"Besides, why should I invest in anything when it might be vaporized by this time next year?"

"It's an experimental reactor, Hwa, not the apocalypse. You can buy furniture. You're allowed to be comfortable."

Ads for sofas blossomed up in her specs. Most of them were too big: apparently Síofra was only looking at furniture that fit his apartment, not her studio.

"You're shopping for your place, not mine."

"Not at all," he said. *"I just want a chair that actually fits me when I come by."*

"You plan to come by a lot?"

Silence.

From the mat, Joel huffed air up at his curls. "Can I *please* get up, now?"

Hwa waved away the ads with a swipe of her hand. She focused on Joel. By now, he'd worked himself down on his forearms. "Yeah. Sure. You should—"

Another message popped up in her vision. Oh, boy.

"Hey. Síofra."

"You can call me by my name, you know."

"I can train Joel any way I want, right?"

"Within limits, yes. His father doesn't want him passing out or hurting himself, obviously."

"But we don't have to work out in this gym?"

"No. In fact, I've told you numerous times that you should feel comfortable to use the company gym, in Tower Five."

"The company gym is full of augmented assholes from Security," Hwa said. "And they all have a staring problem."

"All I ask is that you go to places where I can see you."

"Okay. There's a boat that just pulled up. An old fishing trawler called the *Angel from Montgomery*. That's where we're going. And it's just about the safest place I know."

. . .

Hwa marched them down a rusting flight of stairs and onto the pier. With the *Angel from Montgomery* had come the birds. They wheeled and squawked overhead. Hwa peered down into the pontoons. She hadn't been this close to the water in a long time. Not unless she counted going under the girders.

"Nobody's going to take me for ransom or something, are they?" Joel asked, glaring down at the sailors on the *Angel*'s main deck.

Hwa smiled, but shook her head. "I've seen how these guys tip. Money's not a problem. And they like this town. This is a favourite stop, for them. They won't do anything that'll get 'em blacklisted."

It took her a moment to find Rivaudais, but being as he was the best-dressed man for miles, it wasn't difficult. Today he wore a plum-coloured suit with a gold silk tie. It strained across his shoulders as he checked his shoes for what must have been the tenth time in the last two minutes. He toted his tartan umbrella a little higher.

"If you were worried about birdshit, you should have worn different shoes."

Rivaudais turned and gave her a big smile and a Montréal-style kiss, one for each cheek. But when he spoke, he was still from New Orleans. "You looking healthy."

"And you keep on not aging. It's weird."

"Black don't crack, baby girl. You know."

Hwa sucked her teeth. "Joel Lynch, meet Étienne Rivaudais, owner and proprietor of the Aviation bar on 4-30."

Rivaudais's eyebrows jumped up into his bald forehead. "Joel Lynch? As in *père* Zachariah Lynch?"

"*Oui.*" Joel held out his hand and Rivaudais shook it. He looked a little confused. Probably because Joel was still wearing his gym clothes and wasn't surrounded by skullcaps.

"I'm Joel's bodyguard," Hwa said. "And part of my job is physical training. So I thought I'd bring him along."

Rivaudais glanced at Joel. "And you're all good with this plan?"

"I'm still not entirely sure what's involved."

Rivaudais laughed. He had a big laugh, one that rocked him back on his heels and caused his umbrella to tip back a little.

"And the rest?" Rivaudais gestured at his skull and looked at Hwa. "Good?"

Hwa shrugged. "Mostly."

"*Et votre mère?*"

"*Encore une chatte.*"

Rivaudais grinned and slapped her on the back. "All right. Let's get it done."

Together, they crossed the dock to the *Angel.* She had new turrets, each mounted to a sizeable generator with a gyroscope icon on the side. The turrets awakened and tracked them as they mounted the stairs to the main deck. An insistent chirping sounded. Rivaudais swiped an invite at the camera posted at the top of the stairs, but the chirping continued. A team of guys in sweaters and orange waders jogged their way. Hwa didn't recognize them. They seemed not to recognize her, either. How many times did she have to do this gig before the crew just wrote themselves a fucking note?

"What's going on with your face?" one of the crew asked. He had a fuzzy beard the colour of weak tea, and a huge mop of hair to match.

"What's going on with your attitude?" Hwa hawked back and spat on the deck. "I have a rare seizure disorder. Thanks for drawing attention to it."

The asshole in question stared at the glistening wad of phlegm she'd just horked up, and then at her face. His face registered no emotion whatsoever. "Your face fucks up our cameras," he said. "Is that on purpose?"

Master control room, she reminded herself. *Push the buttons. Lock the doors.*

"Je reste intéressé," Rivaudais said, *"si ce connard s'excuse."*

"You heard the gentleman." A blond man wearing vintage, unconnected aviators and a Peruvian wool sweater over a bare chest and loose surfing shorts padded over to them on browned, callused feet. "Apologize to the lady."

"Sorry." Moptop turned. "Sorry, Captain."

Matthews held out one tattooed arm. This year it was pixies emerging from lotuses. As his skin moved, the glowing pigments activated and the fairies danced up to his shoulder and across his chest. "Mr. Rivaudais. It's good to see you."

The two men shook hands. Matthews turned to Hwa. "You look good. Healthy."

Hwa frowned. "Why do people keep saying that? Did I look sick, before?"

Matthews didn't answer. He gestured for them to follow, and began leading them belowdecks. Lights flickered on as they went down past the bottling floor toward the hold. The two guys standing on either side of the massive, rusting door threw their shoulders back and pointed their chins when Matthews came down the spiral staircase.

"Guys, guys, it's cool. Calm down. I'm just introducing Mr. Rivaudais here to this year's product."

The guys looked pointedly at Joel.

"And me," Joel said. "I'd like to, uh, sample some of what's on offer."

Matthews clapped his hands and pointed. "See? This is good. This young man knows what he wants. And I like a man who knows what he wants. It just cuts through all the bullshit."

The door spun open and they stepped into a cold, dark place. Hwa held out her hand for Joel. "Watch your step," she said, as the lights blinked on.

Joel's mouth opened. "Wow . . ."

It was vast. To their left, a set of gleaming steel tanks three metres across and two metres deep sprouted pipes that disappeared into the rafters and reappeared on the other side of the room, near tall stacks of barrels. They bore insignia Hwa didn't recognize from her previous trips to this room.

"Those are new."

Matthews nodded. "Whiskey barrels. Got 'em in Hokkaido. We're doing a weiss bier in there, with yuzu peel and shiso decoction."

Hwa whistled. "Nice."

"You want? I'll tap it for you right now."

Hwa shook her head. "I don't drink beer. Beer makes you fat."

Matthews clicked his tongue. He led them toward the bourbon barrels. "You need a little extra fat, for this climate! Otherwise how can you handle the winters?"

"Are you . . . aging the alcohol on the ship?" Joel asked.

"Oh, my Lord. *The alcohol.* This one's just adorable." Matthews turned around and walked backward, so he could address Joel. "Why yes, son. We do age *the alcohol* onboard this ship. The *Angel from Montgomery* used to be a fishing vessel that contributed to the mass-murder of ocean wildlife, and I'm helping that wildlife take revenge by ruining the livers of every human I come across."

Joel blinked. "Seriously?"

Matthews gave him a shit-eating grin. "No. Booze is good business, that's all. It's a good business in bad times, and even better business in better times." He gestured at the barrels. "As we circumnavigate the globe, the temperature in this room changes and so does the humidity. The barrels expand and contract, and that has an impact on the flavour of my product. The aging process that takes some punk-ass in Okanagan a whole year takes me four months."

Joel nodded. He glanced at Rivaudais and then back at Matthews. He trailed one hand over a barrel. "So you can sell it faster, and pick up more raw materials as you travel. The wheat, or grapes, or whatever it is you need."

Matthews nodded. "Exactly right."

"And even blend stuff from other countries, at different stages of production."

"Yes, indeedy."

"And create different collections, as you go. Limited editions."

"*Very* limited." Matthews beamed. He snapped his fingers and pointed one at Joel. "You got your daddy's business mind, son. I'll give you that."

Joel looked at all the barrels. It didn't seem to faze him that a stranger might know who he was. Then again, Matthews had probably already picked it out of his halo. Or maybe he was just used to it. "Do you follow the harvests?"

"Mostly. It's October, so I'm about to go collect some Alberta wheat from the east coast. Montréal is our next port of call."

Rivaudais cleared his throat. "That reminds me." Rivaudais nodded at Hwa. "I have a message I'd like Captain Matthews to relay to a mutual associate of ours."

Hwa nodded. She steered Joel down the aisle toward the sampling barrels. "Come on. Let's go."

"This is really interesting." Joel's gaze remained on the barrels stacked high into the darkness. "Thank you for bringing me."

"You think it's interesting now, wait 'til you taste it," Hwa said.

"I thought you said you didn't drink."

"I don't drink *beer*. The average serving of beer has as many calories as a candy bar."

"Do you like drinking?"

Hwa had never heard it put quite that way before. "I guess. I like having been drinking."

"Is it really all that fun? Because it seems like it just makes people stupid."

"Being stupid is fun, sometimes."

"Is it like sex? Because everyone acts like it's really important, but it just seems . . ." He wrinkled his nose. "Messy. And possibly painful."

Hwa swallowed in a dry throat. She reminded herself that she was a grown-ass woman much older than Joel. She was the adult. She could handle this. Hwa spotted the tap kit and picked up her pace. "If we're going to keep talking about this, we're going to have to start drinking."

She picked a bourbon aged in cherrywood casks that promised a medium-bodied drink with notes of heather, vanilla, clove, and leather. At that particular moment, she would have taken hull cleaner. She opened the tap and poured off two measures into tiny sampling glasses.

"These glasses look funny," Joel said.

"They're antique insulators." Hwa peered at the glasses to make sure they were equal. "Like on old transformers."

"Cool." Joel took down all his bourbon in one drink. There was one terrible moment when he looked like he'd swallowed a bunch of broken glass. His eyes watered. His lips puckered. Then he coughed so hard he had to bend over. *What the hell is that?*

Hwa took a more delicate—ladylike, even—sip of hers. "It's a medium-bodied bourbon, with notes of heather, vanilla, clove, and leather."

"It tastes like licking my dad's desk chair."

"Your tongue ages along with the rest of your body, you know. So you taste different stuff as you get older." Hwa checked the PO for Rivaudais's bar. "Huh. You lucked out. We're not moving too many cases."

Joel goggled at her. "*That's* what we're here for? To move product?"

"Aye. Rivaudais owns a bar. This is a place that distills alcohol and sells it wholesale. What did you think we were at?"

Joel pointed at the two insulator caps in her hands. "Sampling!"

It was hard to make a *pshaw* motion when both her hands were full of pricey artisanal bourbon. "Come on. You wanted to lift weights? These are the weights."

Joel now looked significantly less impressed with the whole operation. "Don't they have people for that?"

"Yes. Us. We're the people." Hwa had a feeling this second sample would taste a bit better with some ice. It needed more time to open up. Where it was once sharp and grassy and green, it now tasted more heady and floral. She took a picture of the barrels with her specs. She wanted to remember this one.

"You've got good taste," Captain Matthews said, from down the aisle. "That one's special to me. We used rainwater from Ireland."

Hwa gave him what she knew to be a very skeptical look.

"No, really! We have catchment clients. My water taster said it really made a difference."

"Your water taster is robbing you blind," Hwa said.

"So it's not a great batch?"

"Of course it's a great batch. But the water makes no difference. It's all the barrels." She stuck her tongue out. "I'm a hundred percent organic. I know these things. I taste better than other people."

Matthews leaned against some barrels. Dimples appeared in his smile. "Well, now. That's quite the claim."

Joel's hand landed heavily on her shoulder and curled into it. "My bodyguard and I have some cases to lift," he said, suddenly all seriousness.

They had to fetch the cases of bourbon from the retail area and bring them to be weighed, then take them all via hand truck and jitney to the Aviation and load them into the barback's area. Why Rivaudais never had the barback himself do the job, Hwa didn't know. She suspected he simply didn't trust him not to pocket something on the way. That was why she did a lot of small jobs like this, she explained to Joel, as they wheeled all the cases of liquor to the weigh station. People trusted her.

"I think it's 'cause I don't have any augments. I have an *honest face*."

"I can't believe I let you talk me into this." Joel tugged on a pair of gloves one of the men had given him, and lifted a case. He began walking it to the weigh station.

"Hold on!" Hwa darted around from her cart. "We have to zero it out, first. Keep lifting that. It's good for you."

"Am I lifting it right?"

"Yes." She smiled. "You are. You lifted from your knees. That was the right way to do it."

He huffed his bangs. "Well, get to it. My arms won't hold out."

Hwa jumped on the weigh station. It was nothing more than a black platform set away from the racks of barrels. Two flats of barrels stood beside it. Each barrel had a weight-by-liquid-volume stamped on it, and then a secondary stamp indicating whether it met the acceptable minimum. They'd all met the right weight. Captain Matthews, for all his shirtless, barefoot lassitude, ran a tight ship.

"Shame you can't pick up some more from us," she heard him say.

"*Les loyers,*" Rivaudais said. Hwa turned. Rivaudais was jerking his thumb up in the air. The rents were going up. No wonder Rivaudais couldn't afford more merchandise. Joel watched her, oblivious. Of course they wouldn't say this in front of him. His dad was the one raising the rent.

"I'm getting another cart," Joel said.

"What? Okay. Hold on." Hwa tapped the panel on the weigh station. She tilted her head and took off her specs. Maybe she was looking a little healthier, but she hadn't tripled in size since her last weigh-in. "Get off the platform, Joel."

The numbers danced in the panel. Fell. Back to her normal weight. Then they rose again. Like lottery numbers, rolling up and up and up. How was he doing that? It was like he was bouncing high in the air over the platform and then silently crashing back down onto it. Maybe he had some special high-tech Lynch Ltd. toy that made it all possible. She'd dragged him here and now he was punishing her for it. She put her specs back on.

"I mean it, Joel. Quit it."

He was right behind her. She could feel him—the glee at his stupid teenage boy prank radiating off him as heat. She turned to face him. "Seriously, quit—"

No one was there.

"Quit what?" Joel was hunched over another cart of cases. He frowned and moved to join her on the platform. "Who are you talking to?"

Behind her, there was a long, yawning creak. An audible sloshing. The sound of something snapping. Wood. Something cold and hard solidified in her stomach. Time seemed to stretch out, as though adrenaline itself could somehow pull the fibres of space and time just a little bit more taut.

"Joel! Run!"

But he just stood there, staring, and he kept staring even when she stumbled off the platform and rushed him. She grabbed him around the waist and snapped him up like she was doing a lift in a match. Then she veered to the left and carried him into the retail room and shut the door.

From behind reinforced glass, they watched the whole flat of barrels nearest the weigh station roll down from their perch and spill across the floor.

"Oh, no," Joel said. "All that product . . ."

Hwa whirled. "Are you shitting me? You're worried about the *bourbon*?" She bent down and rested her hands on her knees. "We almost got pancaked there, you know."

"Yeah." Joel looked at himself, and then at her. To her surprise, he grinned. His smile stretched wider than she'd ever seen it. "You know, you could have thrown your back out, lifting me like that. It wasn't exactly the correct technique."

Hwa reached over and tousled his hair. "Very funny."

. . .

In a ride on the way back to school, Joel asked her not to tell anyone what had happened. "Because *nothing* happened," he said. "It was just an accident. And besides, you'll get in trouble. I don't think moving crates of bourbon was what my dad had in mind when he hired a physical trainer."

"You're right," Hwa said. "But lying will make things worse."

"I didn't get hurt," Joel insisted. "Isn't that what matters? I'm less sore now than I would be after a day of training. And I learned something about the city! Isn't that what I'm supposed to be doing? I'm the one who's going to take over here, someday. I should start learning everything I need to know."

Hwa shrugged. "If you say so."

"*He* didn't tell *me* about the death threats. So *I* don't have to tell *him* everything, either."

Oh. That explained some things.

"Have you talked to him about that?"

Joel shook his head. "He's been sick. More sick than usual." He stretched. Hwa heard something pop in his spine. "I guess that's the other reason I don't want him to know. I don't think it would help."

Hwa settled back in her seat. She reclined it. Closed her eyes. "Okay. Fine."

It wasn't okay, and it wasn't fine. Eventually—probably very soon—Joel's dad or one of his brothers would find out, and freak out. On the other hand, she had told Síofra where they were going, and he hadn't objected. They had some cover, at least.

And, she figured, the whole story would go over a lot better if she had more details on the invisible man who had attacked them today.

"Why don't you come over for dinner?" Joel asked, when the ride stopped.

"Thanks, but maybe Sunday," Hwa said. "Right now I'm craving something from the chip truck."

. . .

It was very difficult, not eating the chips from the chip truck. She'd ordered the largest size they had, with extra vinegar and extra salt. The smell was so good, so heady, that the other people in the elevator that stood at the nine o'clock position in Tower Four had no choice but to stare. That, or they knew exactly whom she was summoning.

It wasn't until she hit the seventeenth floor that she suspected Lázló might have joined her. The lift doors hung open for just a hair longer than they should have. She felt nothing, no bounce in the lift, just that little pause in which the machine seemed to decide something on its own.

"Is that you?" Hwa asked. "'Cause the chip oil's burning me fingers."

After a moment, she felt the paper packet of potatoes lift out of her hands. They hovered for a moment, and then seemed to vanish in a wrinkle of something or someone whose outlines became just visible if she stared hard enough.

"I want to ask about your suit," Hwa said. "How you use it. Who can use it. If anyone else has ever asked to use it. Where it can be bought."

A muffled voice told her that she was not the first to ask this.

"I don't want to buy it myself, understand," Hwa said. "It's your suit. You can have it. I just want to know more about how they work."

The voice said they worked just fine.

Hwa let her accent thicken. Let him know she was for real. That she was town, through and through. "I'm not trying to hire you for a job, or anything. I's not asking you to steal something, or hurt somebody. That's not why I's here."

The tension in the elevator lessened, fractionally but measurably.

"All I wants to know is where you were on a certain day."

And just like that, it was back. Hwa's hand strayed to the pocket of her jacket. As quietly as she could, she flipped back the cap on a canister of spray paint.

"I want to ask—"

The first blow caught her completely by surprise. It was a solid right cross to her jaw, and it was strong enough to knock her into the other side of the elevator. Only the dropped packet of chips alerted her to where he would be. Hwa lashed out and up with her feet. The first kick landed glancingly on what felt like an inner thigh. It was more luck than anything else. The second went nowhere.

Not wanting to waste time, she dug out the bottle of spray paint and started hosing the room. The paint came out a ridiculous electric purple. He knocked it out of her hands. It clattered against one wall of the elevator and rolled across the floor, out of her reach.

She launched herself forward at the moving streak of purple and hit legs. He hammered her shoulders, then her back, then her kidneys. The suit was slippery, silken, tough to grip. No balls to be found. He grabbed her by the hair and threw her up against one wall. Brought her head back. Smashed it into the wall. And again. She saw stars. She curled her fingers around the handrail for balance. Her foot shot out behind her. It connected soundly. She heard the air leave him. He gagged. She threw herself at him, tumbling into the illusion of ugly patterned carpet, and started hitting. Blood from her mouth and forehead dripped onto the suit; she targeted her fists there. He reached for her throat but she didn't stop, just swung harder, her fist arcing through the air like she was pounding a crooked nail into stubborn wood.

Slowly, the hood of the suit began to slip away. She grabbed with both hands and yanked. It peeled away from him. He screamed. And screamed. And screamed.

Beneath the hood, he had no face.

There were eyes. A slit for a mouth. Something that might have been a nose, once. But he'd been burned. Horrifically. Tufts of hair threaded away from the back of his gleaming purple skull. The skin under his eyes was bubbled and melted. He howled and covered his face with his suited arms, but the illusion wavered. Now she could see more than just the edges of it. This was why he lived this way, she realized. A simple filter hid her true face from most eyes, but this man, whoever he was, couldn't bear even that attenuated amount of scrutiny.

"Please don't kill me," he whimpered. "You found me. That's enough."

"Didn't *you* try to kill *me*?" Hwa asked.

"No." He spoke from behind his hands. His ruined face peeked out from behind glimmering fingers. "It all went so wrong. So wrong."

"Why? Because the wrong person wound up hurt?"

He shook his head. It was a motion of his whole body. His neck, she realized, was so thick with scar tissue that it would no longer move. "They said no one would be there."

Hwa frowned. "During the lockdown?"

"During the shift. They said it was a dead shift. Maintenance day. So fewer people would be there. They just wanted the apparatus destroyed. But they got the schedule wrong."

Something very hard and very cold began to form in the pit of Hwa's stomach. Her voice came out quiet. "What?"

"They said it would be fine. *He* said it would be fine. He said *I'll find you something you want, and give it to you.* But it all went so wrong."

Hwa's vision swam. "How long have you been like this?"

"Three years." He sounded exhausted. "I change my mind. Kill me. Kill me now. I'm so tired. Maybe you know what it's like. You have some sense of it. I can tell. I can see it on your face. Your real face."

Hwa wiped blood from her eyes. Most of it was blood, anyway. She had thought of this moment so many times. What she would do. How she would do it. Fast or slow. Painful or painless. Here was the face on every heavy bag, the spirit inside every training dummy.

She had not expected it to be this wounded, already. This much like her own.

"You killed my brother."

He brought his hands away. "I killed all of them. Or I helped. I'm the only one left alive. The rest of us didn't make it. I got all the money. There was a lot of money. They wanted this city. Badly."

She needed to know more. And desperately hoped he wouldn't tell her.

"But you know that." He was wheezing, now. "You're on the payroll, too. Just like this whole town."

11

Emergent

When she entered Daniel Síofra's apartment, the freezer was the first place she went. She had the passcode from one of their running meetings. A Saturday. He was late that day thanks to a group call, and he said she should just take the train and meet him upstairs. How long ago was that? A week? Two weeks? Three? Was it normal, the way they'd fallen into step with each other? No. He'd pushed boundaries from the start. She should have put a stop to it. But it was good, having a friend like him. Someone for whom she could be new, someone who didn't know her—that poor sick girl with the terrible mother. Someone who didn't pity her like she knew Eileen and Mistress Séverine and even Kripke did. And now she knew why he'd become her friend. Why he'd followed her so very closely. She thought she might be sick.

It didn't matter. Not anymore. She folded the ice up in a towel and took a seat facing the door and waited. At the hospital, Dr. Mantis had said she would need ice. She knew all that already, but the anti-concussion machines were worth the lecture.

It was very late when Síofra arrived. He came through the door carrying a bottle of chilled vodka. The frost on it retreated from his flesh where his fingers curled around the neck of the bottle. She saw as much when he set it down on the coffee table. He'd bought it quite recently, then. On his way home. Some remote part of her noticed these things and filed them away someplace where they couldn't hurt her.

"Hwa," he said, smiling. He came closer. She had only the fire on, and kept it low. Lights hurt. "Hwa?"

Then his face changed, and he was on his knees in front of her.

"What happened?" His hands came up to her face and she flinched and he pulled them away. He kept his hands in her line of sight. "Who did this? Hwa? Oh, my God. Tell me who did this."

To her disgust, a single tear rolled down from her good eye. Síofra's hands struggled on the arms of the sectional, fingers twisting the fibres of the blanket that shrouded her. He wanted to hold her. She wanted to let him. It would be so easy. She could lie and say there was just another fight, Andrea maybe, or maybe someone at the school, and he would bundle her up in martinis and pity and tell her he'd never let anyone hurt her, not ever again.

I'll find something you want, he had said. *And then I'll give it to you.*

"We should go to the clinic, upstairs," Síofra said, almost more to himself than to her. "Zachariah has women doctors, too. They're on call. Remote, but on call. Completely private and secure."

Jesus Christ. He thought she'd been raped. A sound left her mouth. She wasn't sure if it was a laugh or a moan or just indignation and grief. She bent double in her seat. The sound poured out between her knees.

"Just tell me where it hurts." He was at her ear, now. Urgent. Whispering. Pleading. "You were so right to come here, Hwa, I'm so glad you did, but you have to let me help, now, you have to talk to me—"

"Did you feel bad for me?" It was not the question she thought she would lead with. But it came out all the same.

"What?"

Now she could face him. She brought her head up and watched him searching her eyes and then her wounds. "Did you feel guilty? Is that why you hired me?"

He frowned. "For what happened with the saucer? A little. But that's not why I hired you. Why are you asking this, now?"

"Why *did* you hire me? Why did you hire me back? Why do you . . . ?" She didn't know how to ask the next part. *Why are we friends? Are we really friends?* "Why do you try so hard?"

His hands stilled beside her. He caught her eye. "Is now the time for this conversation?"

Hwa blinked hard. "Did you know? Did you know that my brother died there? On the Old Rig?" Her throat hurt. She wanted to scream. "Did you know that, when you hired me? Is *that* why you did it? Because you *felt bad*?"

Síofra rocked back on his heels. "What on earth are you talking about?"

"Don't." Hwa stood up. He stood with her. In front of her. She tried to move and he moved with her. "Just don't. I know what you did. So stop lying."

"What are you saying—"

"Stop. Lying. To. Me."

"I'm not!" His hands fluttered. They settled on her shoulders. "Hwa—"

"Don't touch me." She broke his grip instantly. "Did you *know*?"

His hands hovered in the air. Almost near her face. But not quite. "Know what?"

Hwa swallowed. Her throat hurt so much. Her brother's murderer had tried to choke her out, just hours ago. It seemed like days ago. Like years. Like he'd wrung the life out of one version of her, and another version had left the elevator.

"How long have the Lynches wanted this town?"

Síofra glanced quickly out the window at the city's elder towers glittering in the dark. Far away, a train wailed over the water. From here it was a banshee sound. As though the dead beneath the waves were calling to the living above the surface. "I have no idea. That's another branch, that's acquisitions, that's not me—"

"Where were you, three years ago?"

A quiet understanding settled over him. He looked at her out of the corner of his eye. "What are you accusing me of, Hwa?"

"The day the Old Rig blew. Where were you?"

"I don't know. It was years ago."

Hwa shook her head slowly. "Not good enough."

"You want me to dig back in my records? Because I will. But you won't believe me, will you? No matter what I say." He gestured at the apartment. "Hwa, these people took me in when I had nothing, and gave me all this. You can't just ask me to believe they would do something like that. They're like my family. I don't have anyone else."

"Neither do I!" She shut her eyes. It was easier than looking at him. He looked so hurt. So shocked. She wanted to believe him. Terribly. "The person I loved the most went up in that blast. It killed almost a hundred people. And I just met the sole survivor."

Her eyes opened. Her voice came out low. Lower than she'd ever heard it. As though she were speaking from deep inside a pit. "I was hunting the phantom. And I found one."

Síofra's eyes widened considerably. "Hwa." He swallowed. Licked his lips. "Assuming everything you say is true, assuming this person, whoever they are, wasn't lying to you, I need to ask one thing." He took a deep breath. "Is he still alive?"

Hwa made herself smile. It pulled taut across her face until it became a snarl. "You'll never find him. I can promise you that."

Síofra's hands rose to cover his mouth. He squeezed his eyes shut tight. "Oh, Hwa. Oh, God."

She made to leave. She had thought she might hit him. Kick him. Draw more blood. Fight him again. Finish what she'd started up on the catwalks, that first day. If he pushed her. If he touched her one more time. But he hadn't. And somehow that was worse.

"What will you do?" he asked. "Will you quit? Again? Tell the world? Tell Joel?"

Joel. She remembered his weight on her shoulders. His back to her back, in the ventilation shaft. The way he could laugh away what was happening around him, claiming that it was *just an accident* or *just a mistake,* because he'd never truly been hurt. Never lost anything. Not yet. His family of murderers had kindly insulated him from tragedy. And it was very likely, Hwa realized now, that one of them was trying to take him out. It was one of the first things she had taught Calliope and the others in her self-defence class: *The people most likely to hurt you are the ones closest to you.* The stats bore it out—marital rape, child abduction, domestic violence. Murder, too. And if the Lynches were willing to blow up an oil rig full of workers to score a deal on a ruined city, what was one more life?

"There is someone after him," Hwa said. "Someone wearing invisible armour attacked us, today. The same person on the footage from the school. Joel won't tell you about it. But someone means to kill him. And I mean to stop it."

. . .

By the next Sunday dinner, most of her bruising had faded. Síofra was not there. "He had a conference in Toronto," Joel told her, when she arrived. "Sorry. Now you'll be bored."

There might have been a message to this effect in Hwa's account. There was something with Síofra's name on it. She had not allowed herself to look at it. If she read it, she would have to start taking his pings, and then she would have to hear his voice.

"I won't be bored. You're here."

Joel grinned. He led her in. There had been some sort of brand strategy meeting, so much of his immediate family was there: his father Zachariah, his brother Silas, his sister Katherine, and a set of fraternal twins named Paris and London.

"Paris is my brother," Joel reminded her quietly. "His husband is over there. And that's London. Her wife and their girlfriend are by the champagne bucket. Paris and London share that girlfriend, actually. She's really nice. And you know Silas. His wife left him last year. I think he's with my cousin's ex-girlfriend now, but she's not here. Then Katherine, from Dad's third marriage. She doesn't see anyone seriously. Then me."

"How come they're all white?" Hwa asked.

Joel shrugged. "Dad only married white women, up until my mom. She's Eurasian? I guess? Sort of like you! She still lives in Singapore. And he wouldn't marry her."

Zachariah had given up on marriage by the time he'd conceived

Joel. Or had him conceived. "Too expensive," the old man had said, once.

Whatever the reason, it meant there was a wide gap in the ages of his children. Hwa had never really considered the gap between her and Tae-kyung—she had certainly never talked about it with Sunny—but realizing that Joel's cousins had children who were still older than he was threw her for a loop. Part of it was Zachariah's age: the old man acted like he was going to live forever, and so far none of the women in his life had cared to disagree. In practise, it meant that Joel's middle-aged brothers and sisters looked at him like he was a new puppy their father had adopted in his dotage. Cute, but bound to make a mess.

No wonder they wanted him gone.

"I like your suit," Joel said.

"Thanks. I forgot how much I liked it, until recently."

"I'm sorry about your friend." Joel grimaced. "Do they know what happened to her, yet?"

Hwa felt a prickle of pain in her arm, thinking of that night under the Acoutsina. She needed to pay Dixon Sandro a visit, and see what he'd built with the machines pulled from Calliope's sample. "No. Not yet."

The chime rang for dinner. The dining table was a huge slab of pink salt supported by two whalebones. It sat under a chandelier of bleached antlers. Unless they were eating soup, or some form of dessert (which Hwa always shoved over to Joel), they ate without plates, scraping food directly off the salt.

"It's very healthy," Zachariah had insisted, the first time she joined the family dinner. "Healthier than plates. Bacteria gets in there, you know. In the micro-fissures made by knives and forks. This is much more sanitary. Nothing can grow in all that salt."

"Sure," Hwa had said, and he laughed and laughed, and Katherine poured more wine for everyone.

Now they sat down to an amuse-bouche of oysters on the half-shell. It should have bothered her, breaking bread with the architects of New Arcadia's destruction, her brother's murderers. Maybe she should have found a way to poison them all. Maybe if they let her keep coming to dinner, she would. She contemplated the dinner knife at her place setting. Like everything else at the table, it was well-made, blade and handle fashioned from a single piece of steel. It was certainly sharp enough to do some damage. She could probably jam it in Zachariah's neck before anyone wrestled her to the ground.

"Don't you like oysters?" Joel asked.

"What?" Hwa blinked and put her knife down. "Oh. Sorry. I was just admiring the cutlery."

"We'll get you a set," Joel said. "Dad, Hwa needs some more knives and forks at her new place."

"Then she shall have them." Zachariah drew a circle around his place setting with one finger, splayed all ten fingers at the setting, and made a pinch-and-throw motion in Hwa's direction. Her watch purred, and there it was, an alert about the gift. The old man smiled. "Ten place settings. No plates, though."

"I think I can manage the plates," Hwa said. "And thanks."

"Do you do a lot of entertaining, in Tower One?" Katherine asked.

Had anyone but Sunny raised Hwa, she might not have recognized the shade for what it was. But Sunny had accustomed her daughter to being despised. "Not as much as I'd like," she said. "My friends work unpredictable hours."

"Still keeping in touch, as it were?" Silas asked. Paris and London tittered.

"Oh, aye," Hwa said. "On Fridays we have sleepovers. Pillow fights and practise-kissing. Then we sell the footage to the highest bidder."

The table was silent. Hwa slurped her oyster. She dabbed her mouth with her napkin. "That was a joke."

Zachariah guffawed. It was a surprisingly resonant sound, coming from such a fragile body. The old man did a good job of pretending not to be sick. He raised a flute of champagne in Hwa's direction. "I do wish you would come to dinner more often, Miss Go. The one thing I forgot to engineer in my children was a sense of humour."

"Nobody's perfect," Hwa said, and Zachariah laughed even harder.

They moved on through the soup course (pumpkin-coconut bisque, served in small gourds), and the salad (shaved fennel and blood orange, laced with olive oil and pink peppercorn), and the entrée (pork loin on whipped celeriac, with a black garlic *gastrique*).

"Let us talk about the future," Zachariah said, after the soup was served. "Joel, tell your brothers and sisters about your science club project."

"I'm designing a generation ship," Joel said. "In the library immersion unit. It has the highest level of processing power we're allowed for intramural competition."

"Using the lessons gleaned from your experience here, no doubt," his brother Paris said. "This city is a closed system, too, of sorts."

"Of sorts," Joel said. "It would be better if it were closed off entirely. That's what Mr. Branch says. It would be better to be self-sufficient."

"We thought the same, on the commune." Zachariah slurped his soup noisily. "We grew our own food. Barrelled our own rainwater. What rainwater there was. It was too late, of course, for California. But California has always been a place where dreams go to live or die."

"A dream is a wish the heart makes," London Lynch said, and they all raised their glasses and drank, except Hwa, who was still nursing her gin and soda.

"Generation ships are a good thing to put your mind to, Joel," Zachariah said, when they were done toasting. "Someday we'll leave this whole planet behind, and we'll need that kind of thinking."

"And we'll need the Lynch brand out there, too," Silas added.

"You and your little friends have any idea how to shrink the reactor we're building, down there?" Silas stamped on the dining room floor to indicate the one several hundred miles below, in the Flemish Pass Basin. "Because that's what you'd need, to power one of those ships you're talking about."

"I know," Joel said. "But the spectral analysis probes are showing us rocky surfaces out there in the Kuiper. That means thorium. We just need to get to it first."

Silas looked nonplussed. It didn't translate to Hwa, either. But it made Joel happy to work on it, so she didn't mind. Mostly all she cared about was that Mr. Branch wasn't touching on him in a weird way, and that none of the other kids in the club locked him in a supply cabinet. She'd have felt the same no matter what he was working on, even if he randomly decided to take up knitting, or breeding rare iguanas, or chain-saw sculpture. That last one would actually be pretty good for his upper body strength.

"Of course, humanity will never make it to the stars," Zachariah said. "Not as we are. We must change. Become more durable. Wouldn't you agree, Miss Go?"

Hwa pretended to carefully examine the dripping red segment of blood orange trembling on the tines of her fork. "I don't really feel any need to go to space."

"You don't want to ascend into the heavens, and be seated at the right hand of evolution?" Katherine asked. "Why ever not?"

Hwa lifted her drink. "I doubt they have gin there. So there's no reason for me to leave."

Again, Zachariah laughed, and then they all laughed, for as long as seemed required. "But of course you, Miss Go, must feel the need to transform," Zachariah said, when the laughter died down. "You have a number of conditions which could be easily corrected. You could live on indefinitely, with the proper treatment. Why sentence yourself to a short, unhappy life?"

Hwa drank deeply from her gin and club soda. "This is the thing

I've always wondered about vampires," she said, after a moment. "Every vampire story is about how sad they are. You'd think it would be great, eh? But no. And after I got me first job, I understood. If you want to *live* forever, you have to *work* forever. Unless you're rich. To be a vampire, you have to be rich." She finished her drink and rattled the ice cubes in the empty glass. She stared around the table at all the Lynch siblings in turn. "And I got no taste for blood, me."

Flatware clinked onto the salt table. Gazes flicked from Hwa to Zachariah and back again. Zachariah himself was staring at her, and she didn't know if he was profoundly amused or deeply offended.

"But you *have to* live a long time, Hwa," Joel said, plowing through his salad as though nothing had happened. "Because *I'm* going to live a long time. Even longer than Dad. So you have to get the treatment. Implants or machines or editing. Even a whole new body. Whatever's the best, you have to get it. I'm going to run things one day, and I won't trust anyone else to protect me."

Hwa reached over and squeezed his shoulder. She smiled at the other Lynches. She again thought about how quickly she could kill them. "You got me there, Joel. You got me there."

• • •

Later, she wheeled an overnight invitation out of Joel. It was after the sorbet and cheeses, when the older siblings and their partners were all doing cognac and coffee, and Hwa was checking her homework against Joel's, and it was getting on toward 22:00.

"It's silly for me to go all the way back to One," she said carefully. Joel was trying to juggle, as he paced the length of his room. The juggling wasn't going well. The pacing he was fine at. "We're just going to school in the morning anyway. And Síofra isn't in town for me to run with. I have a spare uniform at school, so that's not a problem."

"You should just come live here," Joel said, watching the balls in the air. "I know you're still technically on probation, but I think it would be better if you lived here."

Hwa frowned. "Better how?"

"Well, more efficient. We have the same schedule. And it would be safer."

Until now, Hwa hadn't noticed any sign that Joel might be nervous about the death threats. But that didn't mean he wasn't. "Are you worried about stuff like that?"

Joel gave her a completely disdainful look that, for once, made him look fifteen and not fifty. "I didn't mean safer for *me*," he said. "I meant safer for *you*. Daniel says that the Tower One security isn't nearly good enough."

Hwa snorted. "You want me to be a Fiver like you guys, eh?"

"Would that be so bad?"

Hwa didn't answer. She couldn't imagine living this way. The moment she finally got used to it, it would all be taken away for one reason or another. And she would be afraid of that eventuality, all the time, and so she'd never be used to it, would always be waiting for the other shoe to drop. So it was better to stay where she was. But she couldn't possibly explain all that to Joel.

After Joel was in bed, Hwa relaxed somewhat. She listened for the other Lynches to leave, until it was just Zachariah and the softbot that followed him around. Hwa wasn't even sure the old man slept normal hours. Then she heard the steady rhythm of his machine, and knew he was down for the count.

Even so, she waited another hour just in case. By then both Joel and his father were sleeping soundly. They breathed in synchronicity, the old man and the boy, even across the flat. Joel must have grown up hearing the sound of his dad's iron lung. Maybe by now it was a comfort. Better than the alternative. For the first time, Hwa wondered what would happen to Joel if the old man died soon. Which of the assholes at the salt table would be his legal guardian? It seemed like a reasonable concern, and yet no one had brought it up to her. Did the old man really think he was going to live forever?

Hwa rolled herself off the smart cushion beside Joel's bed, took the boy's watch, and made for the old man's study.

The door opened for Joel. As she entered, his content shimmered down from the ceiling. The room itself was blank, aside from a vintage lucite desk, a white tulip chair, and something on a white marble pedestal, shrouded with a square of blue velvet. The crystal ball. For a terrible moment, Hwa had the urge to look into it again. See how it worked. Figure out the trick to it. Because it had to be a trick. A special effect. A prop. It could not be real.

Her hand dropped. No. Not again. She had things to do.

She took a seat at the desk. In a groove inset into the top of the desk was a single stylus. It was very light, and etched with the image of a serpent with a crown on its head hatching from a large egg. It was made of bone.

DANIEL SÍOFRA, she wrote on the desk.

Síofra's profile effervesced into the air. It was far more detailed than anything Hwa had access to. Performance reviews. (*"Mr. Síofra seems very concerned with learning proper procedure in all things; he prides himself on knowing the best way to accomplish any task."*) Pictures of him at every Lynch event with highlights of who he'd spoken to and for how long. Long logs of bio-data: heart rate, brainwaves, temperature, sleeping patterns, calories in, calories out.

Brain scans.

X-rays.

Images of a burned body.

Hwa covered her mouth to keep the moan inside.

"We did our best with him." Hwa whirled. There in the door stood Zachariah's softbot. It glided in, buoyant, deflated arms trailing at its sides. "Yes," it added, after a pause for breath in the other room. "I can direct this device from my ventilator."

Hwa looked around the room. Shit. "I was just—"

"You were curious about Daniel. That's natural. A young woman like you. He's very attractive."

"It's not like that," Hwa said.

"He keeps a close eye on you, too. A little mutual surveillance is," another pause for breath, "only fair."

Hwa swallowed. There was nothing for it. Short of asking the old man if he'd blown up the Old Rig, she would never find the answers she was looking for this way.

"Sorry about this. It was stupid. I shouldn't have done it. I don't know what I was thinking."

She stood up from the desk, put the bone stylus back, and made for the door. The softbot swerved in front of her. She wondered what it would take to puncture it. She'd played with a hugbot, once, during the process of diagnostic therapy for her seizures. It was a tough old thing, built to take a beating, and this looked much the same. It regarded her with soft blue eyes. They spun independently of each other.

"What did you think you would find here, Miss Go?"

Without meaning to, Hwa glanced at the images hanging and twisting in the air above the desk. The specs of machinery. Two deep brain implants. Neural mesh along his spinal column. Labs on chips synthesizing custom drugs on demand. As she watched, the implants and the mesh and the chips faded away, replaced by the original scans of his injuries. Then they assembled themselves. The machines inside him built themselves up, then rebuilt him from within. She watched his metamorphosis over and over. It was total, and it was magnificent. Whoever Síofra was before, Lynch had put him back together piece by piece, including large segments of his brain. And they'd built him better than he was before.

"I was just thinking," she said carefully, "how much we could have used this kind of technology when the Old Rig blew up."

"Yes, that was tragic," Zachariah said, with the softbot's gentle voice.

Hwa swung her gaze back to him. "My brother died that day."

"I know," Zachariah said. "And I am sorry."

Hwa's lips felt hot. Her throat began to close. "What are you sorry for?"

The softbot's limp arms filled slightly and rose in an approximation of a shrug. "At my age, the list of my regrets is much too long."

"Do you regret not buying this town sooner?"

Both the softbot's eyes brightened and dilated. She was being focused on. She stared hard into the blue light.

"Did you want to buy it, sooner?" she heard herself ask. "*Before the Old Rig blew up?*"

From the other room, she heard a rough, awful sound. Laughter. Dry and dying and slow. Zachariah could barely breathe. But he could still be amused. The softbot's head manifested a giant happy face.

"Pay no mind to gossip, Miss Go," Zachariah said. "This city was already dead long before that day. Now it is resurrected. Much as our friend was," a wet, sucking breath, "ten years ago."

"Ten years ago? Not . . ." She forced the words out. "Not three?"

"Oh, my dear Miss Go." One of the softbot's arms filled and rose and gestured at Síofra's profile. "Mr. Síofra is very special to me. My hopes for him are quite high. I would never allow him to risk his life in any meaningful way. Not after I invested so much in building it."

One of the arms slithered over her shoulders. "My hopes for you are similarly high." He breathed, and the tubing of the softbot's arms curled around her neck. The pressure was very gentle but very real. Her neck and throat were still sore enough to magnify it. "You are two of a kind, you and he. A man without a past and a woman without a future. You want to have a future, don't you, Miss Go?"

Mute, Hwa nodded.

The coil around her neck squeezed softly. Right where the sole survivor of the Old Rig had squeezed. "You want to share our future with us, don't you? With Joel? And Daniel?"

She shut her eyes. "Yes."

Now the pressure was definite. She fought to take deep breaths. "We've invited you deep into our world. Deeper than we've allowed outsiders. This is a family business, Miss Go, and you are not family."

"I know that."

"But you are valuable, in your own way. Unique. Rare. I like rare things. I like having the best. Are you the best?"

He could squeeze the life out of her, right here and right now. "Goddamn right I am," she choked out.

The tubing slipped away from her neck. Air rushed into her lungs. "Then I think you should go back to Joel's room, don't you?"

She was out of the room before she could agree. When she entered, Joel rolled over and his eyes blinked open. He sat up. "Where's all the blood?" he asked.

"Eh?"

"He shot you. There should be blood."

Hwa frowned. She waved a hand in front of Joel's face. His eyes didn't track the movement. They leaked sudden tears. Hwa wiped them away carefully. She felt something inside realign itself, like a joint popping back into place. "You're still asleep," she said gently. "Lie back down."

Joel did so, but his body remained stiff and his eyes stayed open. Hwa tested his forehead with the backs of her fingers. No fever. She sat beside him on the bed. "Close your eyes."

"He shot you. I saw it."

"You're dreaming, Joel. I'm right here. I'm fine." She reached over and pushed a hand through his hair. Joel's eyes closed. His body went slack. She scratched her fingers across his scalp. Under her nails, she felt the scars where his implants had gone in. "I'm alive. And I'm not going anywhere. I'm not leaving you."

12

Aviation/Metabolist

"So," Hwa said. "You've done some succubus play, right?"

The Aviation was alive with jazz. Violet light streamed across the black-and-white chequered floor. In the centre of the room, the bar rotated slowly. One revolution an hour. Hwa had counted three revolutions. She had lost track of how many bourbons that meant. Or which of the very specialized types she'd been drinking. Probably all of them.

Layne sipped her drink. "Sure, like once or twice. It's super rare, though. Like it's a thing they try once and don't really go back to, unless they *some* like it. What are you at?"

"Where did you get the suit?" Hwa gestured at herself. "For being invisible."

"Oh, my God. You don't need to be *invisible*, Hwa. Get over yourself."

"No, it's not like that," Hwa said, for the second time in as many days. "I don't . . ." *I don't want to be invisible,* she should have said, but the words were harder to get out than she expected.

"Besides, it's fucking tough to rent that shit," Layne said. "Like, it's super regulated. Like worse than guns. Which is kind of sad. Background checks and everything. They're woven with smart sensors; if you rent one, the person you rented it from knows where the suit is every minute."

"Could you buy one?"

"Yeah, a shitty one. Not the good stuff. The military stuff costs."

"But if I wanted to buy the military stuff."

Layne looked at Hwa as though she were extremely stupid. "Then go to the Lynches! They have a whole Security branch, right? Don't you work for them?"

"I'm in another department," Hwa said. "I file reports to Security, but I'm a . . ." She struggled to find the right phrase. "Discretionary hire."

"Well, if anybody has that stuff, it's them. I even heard them joking about it. Or Eileen did. I think she's the one what told me about it."

Hwa said nothing. She'd tried to ping Eileen, just to talk, and had even tried to explain why she'd gone back to working for the Lynches, but nothing came of it. Eileen had written her off. Completely. And Layne knew it. Everyone knew it. And it was awkward and awful as hell.

"What else is going on at work?"

Oh, not much, they just blew up this town so they could build a star in the ruins.

"They're making me go to Homecoming," Hwa said. "With Joel. They're sponsoring it."

"Don't look so sad! You can handle it. It's just a dance."

Layne looked sleepy. It was late. Her flapper costume was fading. She'd rented the look for only a few hours, and now her pearls flickered in Hwa's specs.

"It's the whole principle of the thing," Hwa said. "I don't dance. Sunny dances. I don't dance."

"Who is Sunny?"

"Never mind."

"Do you mean your mom? Wasn't your mom a dancer?"

"*No.* She was in a girl group, and the *group* danced, in videos. But she wasn't, like, a *dancer.* She wasn't an artist, or something. She was just following orders."

Layne brushed her pink hair aside and stared at Hwa hard through the veil of way too many brandy Alexanders. "Go Junghwa." She pointed. "You hate your mother."

Hwa shrugged. "So? The feeling's mutual."

"What did she do when you moved out?"

"Nothing," Hwa said. "I mostly moved out three years ago, anyway. She was probably just glad to get the last little bit over with. She'll have another closet, now. That's why I had to share a room, growing up. Because she needed a whole other bedroom just for all her sexy shit."

Layne nodded to herself knowingly, like she'd just solved some big mystery. She wagged a finger. "I get it."

"Get what?"

"No, I get it. I finally get it. You're worried that if you let any part of yourself be pretty, you'll turn into your mom."

Hwa drained her bourbon. As she did, she felt the world turn gently on its axis. This was the moment she had been waiting for. The perfect and complete awareness of her own fucked-up-ness. The moment at which her body finally hinted that maybe, just maybe, she should have a drink of water.

She rapped the bar with her knuckles, and turned to Layne. "No," she said. "I don't try because trying would be stupid. I have the kind of face that people edit out of their vision. It's not going to look any better with makeup, or a subscription, or augments, or whatever. So I don't bother."

Layne frowned. Because she was drunk, it looked as though she were trying to thread her whole face through the eye of a needle. Hwa frowned. "Are you okay?"

Layne was not okay. She was clutching her throat. She was turning blue. She was falling off her bar stool.

"Layne!"

Hwa fell with her. Layne slid down her body to the floor. Hwa felt the music thrumming up through the tile and slicing through the air. Drums and trumpets and sharp, shimmering piano. Layne wriggled on the floor. Was this how Hwa looked when she had a seizure? All around her, people were laughing. People laughed when she seized, too. It had happened at school once, when she was in grade four. She peed herself and Sunny didn't come and so she had to wear clothes from the Lost & Found and everyone called her Diaper Baby and Retard after that.

Funny, the things you remembered, as your friend lay dying in your arms.

It happened faster than Hwa thought possible. A couple of minutes at most. But those minutes stretched out, became unbearable, like a note held too long or a terrible, damning silence. One minute Layne's eyes were roving around the room, as if she were trying to remember every detail all at once, and her heels were driving into the floor, squeaking and leaving black streaks. And the next minute she was gone. Not still, but absent. Vanished. Like someone had done a magic trick with her body, and replaced the real Layne with a warm, limp dummy.

"Oh, shit," Hwa heard herself say. "Oh, Jesus. Layne. I'm sorry."

The music had stopped. Layne stared straight ahead. Pink foam dribbled from one corner of her mouth.

"Come on, baby." Someone's arms were around her. Lifting her up under her shoulders. Rivaudais. She knew his cologne. The rings on his hands. "Come on, now. Up you get."

"She's dead." Hwa's knees went out from under her, and Rivaudais pulled her up. "She's dead."

"I know, baby girl. You just come on back."

"We should cover her up—"

"Someone else can do that. Let's get you some coffee, right now."

Hwa untangled herself from his grasp. She stood herself up. "We were just talking." She pointed. "We were just talking, just a minute ago."

· · ·

The police took her statement at the bar. Rivaudais's coffee helped. He made it light and sweet with a lot of sugar and real cream. It tasted like a headache. Hwa felt that headache spiking somewhere deep in her skull as she drank it, but she drank it anyway, and then had some more, a fresh cup every time she told the story of the evening. The cops asked her about Layne. How they knew each other.

What Layne did for a living. If she'd been sick. If she'd caught anything. If she and Hwa had an arrangement. If this was off-book.

Then Hwa said the words *bodyguard*, and *Joel Lynch*, and they focused on something in their eyes, and suddenly they were very nice and said that of course she could leave, this was just a statement, and if she thought of anything else she could contact them any time, day or night, no problem.

It was drizzling by the time she made it to the train platform. More wind than rain. Colder than she remembered. Her shirt stuck to her skin where Layne's bloody foam had soaked it. It would look a sight on the train, she realized. But there was nothing for it. She pushed forward.

In a pool of orange exit light, Síofra sat waiting for her on a bench outside the station. His hair was soaked black. Even his eyelashes were wet.

"Where is your coat?" he asked.

Of course. She'd forgotten it upstairs. That was why she was suddenly so cold. Hwa examined him. Wherever he'd come from, he'd left in a hurry. "Where are your socks?"

He stood and pulled his coat off and draped it over her shoulders. Hwa watched his fingers doing up the toggles. She didn't recognize his pants. They were too loose for running, too casual for work. Just a t-shirt on top.

"You were sleeping," she said.

"Yes." He folded down the collar of the coat and gently pulled her hair free of it. "Prefect woke me. You were in close proximity to officers of the law, and your heart rate spiked, and you weren't answering Prefect's pings. Those are the criteria for that particular alert."

"But you didn't come upstairs."

"I spoke with a Mr. Rivaudais, who assured me you weren't being detained." Síofra hugged his bare arms. "He told me what happened. Hwa, I'm so—"

Hwa held up a hand. He silenced. She shut her eyes. She clenched her fists. She made herself hold it all in until the wave passed, until all she could feel was the rain trickling down her scalp, and then she made for the train. Síofra followed.

. . .

He followed her all the way home. At her door, she thought about warning him about the state of the place. Then she decided it was his problem if he didn't like it—not everybody had spent the past ten years filling their wallets with Lynch's blood money. But when they pushed through, he just stared at the heavy bag, and the reflex bag, and the trophies with Tae-kyung's name on them.

"Where are yours?" he asked, finally.

"I kept getting disqualified," Hwa said. "Illegal moves."

"If I stay, will you kill me?"

Hwa opened and closed her fists. Tested their strength. One was already weaker than the other. She couldn't hurt him even if she wanted to. "Not tonight." She thought of the profile in Zachariah Lynch's office. Dates and times and locations and heartbeats. His miraculous transformation, like that of some martyred saint, from broken to fixed, vulnerable to invulnerable, all on the Lynch dime. And why? Just because they felt like being generous? No wonder he was so loyal. "If you stay, they'll know."

"Yes," he said. "I'm well aware of that."

She showered and changed. When she finished, Síofra was shutting off the kettle. He fetched down two mugs and started digging in the tea cabinet.

"How's your stomach?" he asked, without turning.

"Not great." Hwa pulled a pillow off the bed and sat on it in front of her display. She hunched forward. "Prefect."

"Ready."

"Gather all available surveillance from the Aviation bar in Tower Four, over the past three hours. Find Layne Mackenzie, female identified, twenty-five, white, pink hair. Show me every appearance."

"Visual, audio, data, bio—"

"Everything."

Síofra set down a mug of something steaming in front of her. Turmeric-ginger-chamomile. The same hangover cure she herself would have chosen. "You don't have to do this," he said. "Not right now."

"Yeah," she said. "I kinda do."

Síofra nodded. He stretched out on the floor beside her, propped on his elbows. As he crossed his ankles, his trousers rode up a little. The freckles on his inner left ankle formed a perfect circle, like a fairy ring.

To stop staring, she focused on the display. "Is there a camera behind the bar?"

"Several. The clearest feed is the one from the bartender's right eye."

"So it was live while Layne and I were there?"

A pause. *"According to the end user licence agreement, recording during work hours appears to be a condition of employment."*

"Show me."

The bartender switched between filters of vision as he worked. Thermal vision was pretty handy for knowing exactly when a martini was icy enough. The shaker always turned a special shade of purple before he poured out its contents. Layne and Hwa weren't always directly in his line of sight, but he did keep glancing at Hwa, toggling between filters as he tried and failed to focus on her face.

It was odd, seeing herself the way augmented people saw her. The bartender couldn't turn his eye off, so he always got an adulterated version of her. First there was the Stop Staring version, where her face was a real-time render of what it would have been had Sunny made different decisions as a mother. Then there was the thermal version, where her left side was just slightly brighter than her right, on account of all the tangled nerves and blood vessels. But he spent the most time in the iContact filter, as the focus-detection algorithm in his eye found everyone in the crowd around the bar who was trying to catch his eye, and ordered their faces into a queue for service. Hwa's face didn't show up in that filter. She was just a dark, empty blur, like a shadow. Like a ghost.

No wonder he'd kept offering Layne another round first.

Hwa kept her attention on the bartender's hands as he mixed the drinks. He kept his hands in full view, focusing on them in a way that seemed intentional. Maybe that was part of his contract, too. Hwa watched him pour the last two drinks for her and Layne. Nothing amiss. Then the bartender retrieved the next face in the queue, and began mixing a martini. He switched to thermal vision. He focused on the shaker.

Something flashed bright white in his vision.

It was there, and then it was gone; the bartender flipped over to focus-detection and the flash vanished, like he was trying to rid himself of a common glitch. Hwa was just a shadow Layne was talking to. Then Layne fell. Then Hwa moved. The other faces in the room scattered away from them, focused on them and not the bartender, depopulating his vision. Hwa twitched back along the reel. She landed on the right moment. There in the centre, frozen in that single second, the blazing white shape loomed.

"It's him."

Hwa nodded. "Aye. But what would he want with Layne?"

Síofra watched her carefully. "Do you not see it?"

"See what?"

Síofra logged in. He had a whole folder to show her. He twitched back along footage until he found the place he wanted. Hwa recognized the weigh station within the *Angel from Montgomery* almost immediately. Once more, she saw herself in thermal vision.

And there, behind her, that blinding white heat in the shape of a man.

"But . . ." She couldn't look away from the image. "Joel's the one with the death threats."

"And you're the one with a stalker."

"But . . ." Hwa frowned. "That would mean that whoever switched the rounds during the drill . . . killed Layne."

"Perhaps your friend picked up the wrong drink, Hwa." He looked toward the air mattress. "May I have one of those pillows, please? Dawn isn't for a few hours."

. . .

Hwa didn't hear him leave. She didn't properly remember falling asleep, either. They'd been discussing next steps, and then for some reason he started telling a very long story about a job he'd done at a reactor in Vladivostok, and it involved an explanation of Russian baths, and talk of hot steam and cold pools, and how you had to be careful not to go to sleep in the sauna, and she thought it would be fine to close her eyes, just for a minute. After that, she slept until the door buzzed her awake.

"I didn't order this," Hwa said, squinting outside at the delivery man holding tiffins of food.

"T'were a gentleman's name on the order, Miss. Said your head were right logy."

Hwa pinched the bridge of her nose. "Aye. He's not wrong."

She brought the tiffins in and opened them. The kitchen looked different. Cleaner. Neater. Good Christ, he'd done the dishes. His performance reviews weren't kidding about that quest for perfection.

"You didn't have to do the dishes," she said, when she called.

"Good morning to you, too."

"And thank you for breakfast."

"I thought it might help. Do you plan to go to school with Joel?"

"Aye."

"And after that?"

She had stuffed the shirt with Layne's blood into a self-sealing pouch. Hopefully its time on her floor hadn't contaminated it. "Have to see a man about a blood sample."

"And where is he, now?"

Hwa shook her head, then remembered he couldn't see. "You're not coming."

"Hwa—"

"It's not your kind of place," she said quickly. "You're too . . ." *Pretty,* she wanted to say. "You're too fancy."

"You would feel the need to protect me."

Hwa rolled her smile inside her mouth. "Aye, and I already have one bodyguarding job. Which reminds me, I want you to call Joel and take him out somewhere, when my shift ends."

"Where?"

"Anywhere. Just get him out of the flat." Hwa cleared her throat, thinking of Zachariah's softbot coiling one of its many arms around her neck. "He asked me to come live there with him. Joel did."

"That's sudden. Are you sure the two of you aren't moving too fast?"

"Very funny." She contemplated the air mattress and the boxes. Síofra had slept on a yoga mat with a blanket spread over it. "I'd be in Tower Five a lot."

"That would make things easier." He coughed. *"Running, for example."*

"Aye. Running."

• • •

School was fine, but Mr. Branch was sick for the day, so science club didn't meet. Hwa suggested they do a full circuit, just to burn off the day, but Joel wanted to keep working on his project in the library. At least, that was what he said in order to get her into the library. His story changed the moment they were inside.

"What do you have here that's about serial killers?" Joel asked.

Mrs. Gardener's tattooed eyebrows rose only slightly. Her forehead would not permit any further wrinkling than that. "Quite a bit, as a matter of fact," she said. "It's a very popular presentation topic in Mr. Harris's Introduction to Psychology elective."

"Could I please see what you've got?"

"Certainly. Are you looking for books, periodicals, media, threads, or immersion?"

Joel brightened. "You have immersions for that kind of thing? Really?"

Mrs. Gardener lowered her voice to a delighted whisper. "You

have *no* idea. If you want, I can let you walk through Whitechapel.
Or Leimert Park. Or Jones Beach. Even the Manson houses! Every
scene of every crime in the catalogue."

Hwa blinked. "Seriously?"

Mrs. Gardener nodded. "The more recent cases sometimes have
their faces changed—when the victims' next of kin wouldn't li-
cense their likenesses—but all the other details are the same. Some
of the nudity is fogged over, naturally." She snapped her fingers.
"Not for you, though, Hwa! You're not a minor, any longer."

Hwa grimaced. "That's fine, thanks. Had my fill of it."

"We're interested," Joel said, as though he hadn't heard her.

"No, we're not," Hwa said.

Joel held up a finger. "Just a moment, please."

He walked a little ways away from the immersion booth. "What
are you at?" Hwa asked. "I thought you wanted to work on your generation ship thing—"

"I think your friends are being hunted by a serial killer," Joel said.

Hwa blinked. "Eh?"

"Well, Dad took me on a trip to D.C., because he had to talk to
Congress? Or a subcommittee? Or a hearing? Something like that.
Anyway, I went to the FBI's Museum of Behavior. It used to be called
the Evil Minds Research Museum. I don't know why they changed
it; I think Evil Minds would have looked better on the t-shirts in
the gift shop. But they had a whole exhibit about serial killers. It
was next to the Wall Street exhibit."

"Serial killers."

"Yeah. They're pretty rare. And they don't happen as much,
anymore, because of the birthrate and data collection and stuff.
Also now that the *DSM* says you can diagnose psychopathy in
children—"

"Why would you think someone like that killed Calliope and
Layne?" She shook her head. "Sorry. My friends."

"Because they were prostitutes," Joel said. "That's who they kill.
Mostly. Prostitutes."

Hwa closed her eyes. "The correct term is *sex worker,* Joel. I belonged to the *sex workers'* union. Okay, b'y?"

"Okay. I'm sorry." He sounded genuinely apologetic. It was hard to tell for real. But he was the kind of kid who liked to know the right words for things. "But, if you've been looking into it at all, I mean, if you had some data to make sense of, you could put it into the immersion unit. There's a lot of processing power. You could even ask the AI inside some questions! It's been really helpful, with the ship design."

"If I'd been looking into it."

Joel looked at the floor. "You know, investigating it." His voice cracked. "It would be private. Outside the Prefect system."

She let the full weight of her gaze fall on him. "Joel? Is there something you want to tell me?"

"You might want to change your privacy settings," Joel mumbled.

Hwa rolled her neck back to look at the ceiling. *Master control room,* she reminded herself. She waited for the overhead lights to beam some patience into her eyes. "I'm going to make you very sorry, during tomorrow's workout."

He sighed. "I know. But . . ." He gestured at the booth. "This is better, isn't it? Better than going out there on your own."

She didn't know how to tell him that his instincts were better than he knew. That in all likelihood, the person killing her friends was probably after her, too. On the other hand, an offsite storage facility for all the data, all the footage, was probably a good idea. If she stored it somewhere else, maybe the people peeping her Prefect account would think she'd given up.

"You don't get to go in there, with me," Hwa said. "I don't want you looking at that shit. Any of it."

"I won't see anything! I'm a minor!"

"Aye, exactly me point. You're too—"

"I thought you were trying to toughen me up," Joel said. "And not just physically. It's going to be my town, someday, Hwa. I have to take care of it. I have to learn how to take care of it."

Mrs. Gardener walked them to the booth. It was fashioned entirely of glass, or something like glass that wouldn't break and wouldn't transmit sound. You could wear the helmet in perfect silence, and no one would be annoyed or distracted by your commands. As Hwa watched, Mrs. Gardener waved her way into the booth with her right hand. The doors clicked open, unfolding as though to embrace the booth's next visitor. Mrs. Gardener pointed at a couple of X's on the floor marked out in tape.

"Stand on those," she said. "You have to hit your mark so it can calibrate. Now, where would you like to start?"

Hwa shrugged. "The beginning, I guess."

Mrs. Gardener smiled. "Whitechapel, then. Oh, before I forget." She dashed behind the help desk and came back with a towel. "Tuck this into your collar, would you? The booth is just so tough to clean. There's a special cleanser and everything, and it's unbelievably expensive. I tried vinegar and water once, and the damn thing reported me to the company!"

Hwa plucked at the towel. "Um . . . Why exactly do I need a towel?"

"For when you throw up, of course!" Mrs. Gardener shut the doors to the booth. She started programming something into a panel only she could see. "Good luck!"

Hwa waited until Mrs. Gardener was gone, then she untucked the towel and left it in a heap on the floor. She reached for the helmet and wiggled it down across her head. It smelled terrible: bad breath and cheap pomade. Her skin would probably break out tomorrow. As if standing in a glass booth talking to yourself in front of the whole library weren't embarrassing enough.

PLEASE FOCUS, she read in large white letters on a black ground.

Hwa focused.

LOOK LEFT.

She looked left.

LOOK RIGHT.

She looked right.

LOOK UP.

She looked up.

LOOK DOWN.

And as she looked down, Helmut the Assistant Librarian walked up to her and introduced himself. He was a tall white guy in grey trousers with a black turtleneck sweater. He seemed excited to see her. He held out his hand. Hwa shook it.

"Welcome back, Hwa! It's been a while!"

"Three years," Hwa said.

"Wow! Time flies! So, you want to go to Whitechapel?"

"Yeah."

"Well, can you just sign this waiver, for me? The manufacturer needs to know that you don't hold us responsible for any adverse effects you might experience."

"Sure," Hwa said.

Instantly, her eyes filled with boilerplate. She sped to the end, and signed her name with one finger. When she'd finished, the boilerplate dissipated into fog. The fog was grey and dim, lit only by spots of orange glow that might have been flame. Hwa heard horses and something rattling. She looked around—a big team of black horses was about to run her over. She jumped out of the way and straight into a puddle. The horses pulled a carriage full of laughing women in corsets and tiny hats. When it pulled away, a man stood across the street and looked at Hwa. He hadn't been there before. He had an impressive brownish beard streaked with white, and his top hat perched above a head of the same. He brandished a cane, and it tapped on the wet cobbles of the street as he crossed it to meet her. When he ascended the sidewalk, he held out one elbow. There was an awkward moment where they both stared at his protruding joint, and then at each other. Maybe these people didn't believe in shaking hands. Hwa stuck out her own elbow, and touched it to his.

"You're supposed to take it in your hand, and let me lead you," he said in a very deep, rough voice.

"I don't really like being led," Hwa said.

He nodded. "As you wish."

"Who are you?" Hwa asked.

"You may call me Mr. Moore," he said. "Welcome to White-chapel."

. . .

"Could I put this data into an immersion unit?" Hwa asked Sandro, once her time in Whitechapel was over.

"Sure," he said. "What, you want an AI to work on it? 'Cause I've got one here. Not, you know, top of the line or anything, but not bad. Fan-crafted. Kind of a DIY thing."

"That's cool," Hwa said. "But I've got some elsewhere."

"Your call," Sandro said. "What's in the bag?"

"'Nother sample." Hwa tossed it to him.

He peeled it open. "Your shirt? Your blood?"

"My money. My questions."

Sandro shrugged. He plucked the shirt out with a pair of long chopsticks, then threw it into the scanner. He pressed the green button with one big toe. He chewed his thumbnail as it ran. Then he pressed another button with his toe and leaned back in his chair.

"Got cold tea, if you want," he said. "In the cooler."

Hwa pulled two bottles free from a brick of foam, and tossed one to him. She watched him drink, decided it was safe, and took a long pull from her own bottle.

"How's she gettin' on?" Sandro asked.

"I'm on nish ice with this job."

Sandro's lips twitched. He nodded to himself. He leaned forward in his chair, and spun to face her. "I've been getting me hands dirty with the other sample you showed me. Wicked stuff. Evil. I don't want it, no more. I want it gone, whatever it is."

"And what is that?"

Sandro stood. He stretched. He gestured for her to stand, too. "Come on, then. Let's have a peek."

He made a pulling motion in the air, and a frosty pane of glass slid aside, exposing another room. They strode through. Inside the new room was a set of five terrariums.

Inside the terrariums were different clots of decaying flesh.

Sandro waved some buzzing flies—real ones, not botflies—away from the glass boxes of rot. As Hwa looked closer, she saw that two of them appeared to still be alive. They pulsed. Their terrariums fogged. Hwa tried to breathe through her mouth. Not that doing it that way was much better. The scent stuck to her tongue like rancid fat.

"The fuck *is* that shit?"

"It's tissue," Sandro said. "Programmable tissue."

Hwa thought of Síofra's broken nose, and how quickly it had healed. "What, like a regimen?"

"Like fucking cancer, more like. Fucking uncontrollable. I keep hiving it off and trying to kill it."

"Aye? Any luck?"

He shrugged his massive, oozing shoulders. "It's cancer. It hates radiation."

"What, you've got like random isotopes just lying about?"

"Nah. I had a friend take a sample under her shirt, during treatment in St. John's." He drew a line across his throat with one finger. "Killed it right dead."

Hwa pulled up a stool and watched the samples. They seemed to breathe. Each of them were hooked up to various bags of fluid. One of them looked like beer. How had Calliope gotten something like this in her system? All the USWC members were extremely cautious about health. Testing for all types of cancer was regular. Having unprotected sex was verboten. Unless you went off-book. And Calliope had.

"Could you give this to someone else?"

"Who else you want to be looking at this shit?"

"No, I mean, could one person pass it to another? Sly like?"

Sandro frowned at the samples. He squeezed a pustule on his arm. "Maybe. I heard the CIA tried giving Putin cancer, way back when, with the early programmables. You could program these tissues to make a tumour, I guess."

"So you could get someone sick, and then hold their health for ransom?"

Sandro's eyes widened. He crouched on his knees. "Gonna pretend you didn't just say that. I don't even want that thought in my head."

The timer dinged. They went back into Sandro's "office," and he slid the glass wall back into place. Then he threw images up on it. Hwa recognized the dates. He was comparing the two samples, Calliope's and Layne's.

They were identical.

"You know a lot of sick people," he said.

"I know a lot of dead people."

Sandro reached over to a shelf above the scanner, dug in behind some beakers and flasks, and pulled out a necklace. A rabbit's foot dangled at the end of it. He slung it over his head. "You're an ill wind, you."

"You should meet me mum."

"Think I have, once or twice," Sandro said, and winked.

Hwa snorted. "Is there enough here to do a search?"

"Now there is. Now we got more of the original."

He expanded the image, capped it, and threw it onto another screen. Rapidly, similar images overlaid it, like cards being shuffled together. Finally, another image popped up.

It was the Lynch logo. A press release. About the experimental reactor they were building deep in the Flemish Pass Basin, right under New Arcadia.

"Project Krebs will allow Lynch to build Canada's energy future from the ground up, with less risk and fewer errors. We are confident in the capability of the Krebs self-assembling devices to assist in construction of the reactor . . ."

And there, at the bottom of the release, was a render of the self-assembler machines. It wasn't a perfect match—the matching function straight-up said it wasn't—but it was close. Damn close. Almost like looking at the difference between a prototype and the finished product. Only one was made of protein, and the other wasn't.

"Why would industrial construction devices be in your friend's blood?"

"I don't know," Hwa said. "She had a lab on a chip to keep an eye on her hormones, but I don't think she was on any other regimen. Especially not anything this shiny and new. The union couldn't afford it. But keep digging. I'll be out of town for a bit."

"Lucky you."

"Not really." Hwa winced. "I can't stand the woods."

13

Terra Nova

"I won't be coming with you to Terra Nova," Síofra told her, as she zipped up her pack the morning of the trip. *"Sorry. I've been asked to refocus myself here in town."*

"Refocus yourself?"

"There's some concern . . ." He cleared his throat. *"Katherine and Zachariah wonder if perhaps my attention is a bit divided, lately."*

Hwa scowled. "Divided how? What do they mean? You're great at your job. You—"

"It's all right, Hwa." He chuckled softly. *"Don't worry about me. It was always a little strange for me to be going on the trip. The panels and talks are only at the very fringes of my subject area. I put in for it because I wanted to go, not because I needed to go."*

"They're punishing you," Hwa realized. "You stayed the night, after Layne died, and they know where you are all the time, and now you're being punished."

"I suppose you could read it that way, but—"

"This is bullshit," Hwa said. "Nothing happened!"

"I know." He sounded very tired. He'd probably woken up early just to tell her this. It was 03:45.

"You were just being nice. My friend died, for shit's sake. You were just being helpful."

"I suppose you could read it that way," he repeated, after a long moment. *"In any case, I wanted to let you know myself. And tell you to be careful."*

"I'll try and avoid the Big Bad Wolf, b'y."

He laughed. *"Please do. Wolves are a threatened-enough species as it is. My heart bleeds for the wolf who meets you on the road."*

. . .

Naturally, her period came the night before they were supposed to travel. She was regular as clockwork, but had secretly hoped that just this one time, she might be a little late. Because very few things sounded less appealing than taking a seaplane—a beer can with wings—all the way up Newman Sound while bleeding like a stuck pig. The water taxi to the seaplane jetty did nothing to help. It bucked across the waves so hard her teeth clicked.

"Rough one out there, today," the taxi driver said. "Real cunt of a current."

"How come nobody ever says it's a real *dick* of a current, b'y? What's with that?"

The driver said nothing more.

Being on the water meant getting a better view of the rig and the site of the future reactor. The rig looked sadder, these days. Only a couple of the pumps were still working. Just enough to claim some tax credits. But the signs proclaiming progress on the reactor were brightly lit, even at this hour.

FUTURE SITE OF FLEMISH PASS BASIN EXPERIMENTAL REACTOR, the signs read. Diagrams of the reactor awakened and projected as the taxi bobbed past. It looked sort of like a Chinese steam bun with a big egg yolk inside. Only the egg yolk was really a wad of experimental matter, and the pastry was several layers of bio-crete. It would have been more impressive if one of the projectors hadn't been hacked to play old footage of Chernobyl and Fukushima and Three Mile Island to the tune of "Where or When."

The rough currents on the North Atlantic were matched only by the turbulence of the skies above it. And in the seaplane, they felt every peak and valley in the pressure. After the third time Hwa bounced out of her seat, she started to wonder if her cup would manage to stay in place the whole trip.

The turbulence did nothing to reassure her. It did give her an opportunity to learn more about the team Security had sent to watch over them at the event. Apparently, Silas Lynch had picked them himself. He'd only sent their profiles over the night before—his assistant had apologized profusely, of course—and Hwa spent a good portion of the night going over their histories with Prefect. Their names were Theodore, Christiansen, McGuire, and Beaudry. Most of them were athletic white guys who hadn't scored hockey scholarships or, for that matter, any other kind of scholarships. Not that Hwa had any room to judge. They were all about Hwa's age, and good-looking. In the file, Silas had said something about finding "camera-ready security" and "putting an attractive face on protesters' concerns." Beaudry had applied to the Mounties, but he washed out of the basic psych exam. He was the one Hwa worried about.

The four of them spent the whole flight texting and laughing about the goings-on at a party they'd all been to on the weekend. Hwa made her status invisible, and used Prefect to peep their channel. She watched the conversation flow across her specs as Joel went over his notes for the next day's meeting.

B: then we spitroasted her

T: fuck I missed that

B: I know u poor bastard

C: u missed out

M: more for us

T: shit

B: it will happen again tho no worries

C: Silas likes to reward loyalty

M: parties > bonuses

B: f'real

M: bonuses > parties

B: wrong—nowhere to spend that money in that shithole

T: point

C: we should get hazard pay, not hookers

M: you won't say that if the rig blows up again

M: you'll wish you got your dick sucked more

B: me I just want more anal

B: that firecrotch threw down without batting an eye like a real pro

M: oh yeah Eileen

M: cum on Eileen

B: shit we sang that song so many times

C: I think I got tennis elbow that night, playing that game

T: it's a shithole, for sure, but it's also like the perfect island of pussy

B: yeah no wonder the riggers won't leave

T: "i can't leave all this p00n!"

M: soon none of them will be able to afford it

M: it'll just be us and the other lynch guys

B: THE LYNCH MOB

M: holy fuck

M: that's hilarious

"Are you all right?"

Hwa startled. She ripped her specs off and looked at Joel. "Eh?"

"Your knuckles are white."

Hwa looked at her hands. She licked her lips. "Oh, aye. Turbulence, b'y. Just turbulence."

. . .

The resort had designated a guide to take them through the forest to the estuary. They were supposed to spend time looking at rare birds, and then have a PechaKucha—whatever the hell that was—about how young people could shape the future of Newfoundland and Labrador's environmental conservation efforts. But really, the meeting was about the reactor. Joel was supposed to be the face of the company that appealed to younger people. That meant he had to allay their concerns, even though he was technically a lot younger than all of the people he was trying to persuade and, historically, Hwa suspected that fifteen-year-olds had a hell of a time convincing people in their early twenties of anything at all. After that, they'd have a press conference about how the meeting had gone.

A swarm of flies followed them into the forest. Hwa relaxed a little when she noticed them. Anyone who tried making trouble for her or Joel would be caught on camera. As long as she stuck close to Joel, they'd be fine. And that was good, because being in the woods creeped her out. She couldn't see anything. Sure, there were maps in her specs and bright orange t-shirts and it would take a solar flare for her to be physically capable of being truly lost to GPS. But everything was alive out here. And not in a good way. Not in a "doors opening for you because they know you're there" kind of way. In a "things eating you" kind of way. Every step she took, she felt bugs under her clothes.

Eventually, the guide led them to a fork in the path that led to a split-rail boardwalk. It stretched out over green marshland dotted with lilies and dragonflies, and ended in a tiny piece of marsh that sprouted like an island among the washes of bright, shallow water. In the centre were two concentric circles of logs. This was where they would have their meeting. Even Hwa had to admit it was sort of pretty, mostly because it was out in the middle of the water under an open sky, and not in the long shadows cast by trees that creaked and groaned and whispered every time a wind came up.

And this was why, when a soft chime sounded in her ear, Hwa asked to be excused. It was doubtful that anyone would try to get to Joel while he was surrounded by a bunch of white scholarship kids talking about which variety of coconut oil was the most ethical. She would be basically defenceless. Vulnerable. The perfect target. If someone on Silas's team was trying to get rid of her, this would be the perfect opportunity.

Hwa followed the trail a little further up until she heard water. She'd decided that this creek would be the best place, when she first mapped the trail in preparation for the trip. It was ideal. Someone could drown her there. Just sneak right up behind her and shove her face under the water. They'd be fools to pass up an opportunity like that. She stepped off the path and climbed down a little ways to the water. She paused to raise her arms and stretch. She bent and touched her toes. Twisted her spine, first to the right and then to the left. She rolled her neck. Cleared her wrists of any tension. Then she settled on her haunches, to wait.

"Prefect," she whispered, "show me Joel."

A feed unfolded across her vision. The whole group was still sitting there on the circle of logs, but now they were doing some sort of dance. No, it was a game. It looked like charades. Probably some sort of alternative communications thing. Hwa counted all four of Security's guys at the fringes of the gathering. None of them was watching Joel. All of them were watching two girls mirroring each other with their hands. As the exercise continued, Beaudry elbowed Christiansen and got him to pay closer attention to the girls.

Hwa refocused. Beaudry nodded at Theodore, and then he headed back to the trail. He drifted out of the fly's vision, and Hwa switched back to her own vision. She tabbed over to infrared. The battery icon warned her about not using it for too long. She winked it away. In infrared, the trees turned from green to grey. They looked like tall, silent ghosts judging her for a long-forgotten crime. She did a quick check of her blind spots. Nothing. She turned her earbud up. Calmed her breathing. Waited.

Nothing.

Birds. A twig. The rush of water. Something crawled under her shirt. She tried not to think about it.

Something rustled in the brush across the creek. In her specs, it registered as a big white blur hunkered down on all fours. It trundled along through a break of ferns and stopped at the water. Only when it stretched out its head to drink did she understand what she was looking at.

A bear.

Hwa didn't breathe. She had really only skimmed the safety warnings about the wildlife. The real danger, the guide had assured them, was the fact that it was moose season, and there were hunters in other areas of the park. Thus those terrible orange t-shirts. They were so nobody got shot by accident.

A hand closed over her mouth. She reacted: reached up and grabbed the little finger on her attacker's hand and yanked it down and away. Heard the snap when the bone broke free of his hand. Bounced up to her feet, slamming her head back. Felt it connect with bone. Whirled around, other hand already cupped and outstretched to box his ear. It was Beaudry. She cuffed him upside the head. When she advanced on him, he scuttled away up through the brush toward the trail.

"What the fuck is wrong with you?" he hoarsed, cradling his hand. "I was protecting you from that fucking bear!"

Hwa turned. The bear was long gone. Ferns wavered in its wake. Apparently that whole thing in the brochure about animals being more scared of you than you should be of them was actually true.

"What bear?" Hwa asked.

"Oh, come on." Beaudry stood up He hawked back and spat blood. It glowed white for a moment in the infrared, and then cooled to grey. "That thing was staring straight at you. You're lucky I came along."

"Oh yeah. I'm real lucky you snuck up on me." Something sparked in her mind. An idea. A gamble. "That's just your M.O., right?"

Beaudry wiped his nose. "What?"

"And at the school. I saw you. Under the sprinklers. Your shiny new invisibility suits ain't shit under the water."

His eyes narrowed. "How do you know about those?"

"It doesn't matter. What matters is that I'm on to you."

His face closed. She watched him take a deep, calming breath. The kind of one you took before you told a big lie. He swallowed. "I don't know what you're talking about."

"Yeah, you do. You think I don't know how your boss feels about his baby brother? Of course I know. It's fucking obvious. But if you think you're gonna scare me off this job, you better think again."

Hwa snatched his hurt hand. Squeezed the fingers together. Watched tears rise up in his eyes. Smelled his chicken soup-y fear sweat mingling with black earth and pine resin. She lowered her voice to keep it from shaking. "And if I find out that you or any of your fucking *Lynch Mob* over there had something to do with my friend Layne dying, your finger won't be the only thing of yours that gets broken. Do you understand me?"

He pushed her away, hard. She stumbled back. Almost fell. Corrected herself. "No," Beaudry said, "I don't. You're a crazy bitch. I shouldn't have helped you."

Hwa watched him making his way back to the trail. When he was a good three paces ahead, the adrenaline trickled in. It had been a long time since anybody put hands on her like that. She forced the air from her lungs. Made fists. Pictured the master control room. All the buttons. All the switches. Big convex screens with her problem on them, walking away, getting smaller, turning into mere pixels.

She'd given the whole game away. She'd let their whole theory slip right past her lips. But there was nothing for it. It was done, now. And it was time to attend Joel's press conference.

· · ·

The press conference was more like a briefing. Only a couple of local journalists came, and the rest was done by telepresence. The questions—or at least, their focus and tone—had all been approved by stratcomm the day before. That was how each telepresence journalist earned the right to their log-in. They'd tag in to the conversation as it unfolded, their avatars briefly lighting up the same spot of floor positioned so that Joel and the folks who'd handed out the scholarships could talk. Hwa spent most of her time just scanning the crowd and not really listening. The pain that she'd managed to keep at bay had redoubled its efforts, and now it felt like someone was excavating her uterus with a rusty garden trowel. It was hard to stand up straight. She had to pretend that her chin was balanced on a shelf in order to maintain her posture. She kept her hands behind her back so she could knuckle it once in a while, when she thought no one was looking.

"Joel, your father's company has come under fire for using self-replicating nano-scale machines to build this new reactor, and not human crews."

Hwa snapped to attention. She focused on the reporter asking the question. She was a round-faced blonde from the PST. Her avatar moved its lips at a slight lag behind her voice. It made her look like an old cartoon. The extra eyelashes she'd tattooed onto her cheekbones didn't help matters, either.

"My father believes in the power of innovative technology to accomplish large-scale projects that help people."

The reporter smiled winningly. Dimples appeared in her cheeks. "And do you share those beliefs?"

"Yes," Joel said. "I think mankind has always used tools to improve basic standards of living. In this case, we're using these machines to do dangerous work that would put human crews at serious risk."

"Do you share your father's beliefs about the Singularity?"

Joel blinked, the way he did when he heard something he couldn't quite comprehend. "Pardon me?"

"Your father has gone on record stating that he believes super-advanced artificial intelligence will eventually take over our planet. Is that why he trusted the reactor to the Krebs machines? Because he believes that only so-called strong AI can do the job?"

Joel's mouth opened. Nothing came out. Hwa cleared her throat. Instantly, Joel stood up straight. "My father . . ." His voice cracked. Hwa couldn't keep the wince off her face. "My father almost died of neo-polio," Joel said, finally. "He was born on an anti-science commune in Northern California, and it was the site of a major outbreak. Until he got his augments, he was in constant pain. He had to relearn how to walk, how to type, all of those things. But even so, he's always told me that he felt luckier than the other kids. Because he didn't get measles, and that's the reason he's still alive today."

Joel licked his lips. "My father's beliefs about the future aren't the reason I'm here. I'm here so that I can talk to my peers about *our* future. And I don't think that's what you're interested in. So I think I'm done talking to you. All of you."

A cacophony of questions and a sparkling array of flies rose up as he descended the podium. Hwa got between them and him as he went through the doors. "Nice work," she said, as the doors closed behind them.

"I think I'm going to throw up." Joel bolted for the fire stairs. He charged up the first flight so fast Hwa almost had to chase him. "I want to go to my room."

"Hey, slow down!" Hwa put a hand on his shoulder and he whirled on her, eyes dilated, sweat dotting his hairline. "Calm down," she said. "It's just adrenaline. It's not real."

"I think I need a new implant," Joel said. "I'm not supposed to get stage fright. I'm not supposed to get frightened at all."

Hwa snorted. "You did *not* look frightened up there. You looked great. You *did* great." She grabbed him by the shoulders and shook him a little. "That feeling that you're feeling? That's not fear. That's exhilaration. You're excited, because you totally nailed it back there, and that's okay. Okay?"

One corner of his mouth curled up. "Okay."

Then he threw his arms around her. For a minute, Hwa didn't know where to put her arms. When she did, she felt both firm new muscle stretching across his back and shoulders, and sprig of pride blooming up in her. The boy was already stronger. It was time to level up his training.

"Is this weird?" Joel asked.

"Only a little," Hwa said. "People don't really hug me."

"I can't hug my dad." Joel backed away. A pink blush blossomed in his cheeks. "Sorry."

"No, it's cool. We should, uh . . . feel the love. Or something."

Joel's head tilted. "Just so you know, I don't want to have sex with you."

"That's okay. People don't. Generally. Want to have sex with me."

Joel smiled. "It's too bad Daniel isn't here. We should buy him a present. Let's go to the gift shop."

. . .

Finally they were allowed to leave the state dinner, and Hwa could go back to her room check up on any news about Layne's death. To her surprise, the NAPS had rushed Layne's toxicology report. Maybe Rivaudais had pulled some strings—he wanted to clear that food safety inspection, after all. Prove that it wasn't his liquor that had killed an innocent member of USWC 314's tech support. That it was an allergy, or an accident, something he could fire somebody over and be done with it. And that's exactly what the report ruled: Layne's throat had closed suddenly due probably to an anaphylactic reaction, and she'd asphyxiated. There was no explanation for the foam in her mouth.

Hwa flopped back on the bed. The images followed her gaze, strobing across the ceiling. Calliope. The Aviation. Layne. Layne on the floor of the Aviation, pink oozing out of her mouth and onto her hair, her eyes wide.

"Go Jung-hwa."

Layne was talking. Her eyes didn't move, but her mouth did. She spoke through the bloody foam, but it sounded like she had no trouble. Like she was just chewing on some gum, or some candy. Like the bubbles in her mouth were sweet.

"You should get your eyes checked, Hwa."

"I just had them checked," Hwa told her. "Dr. Mantis checked them."

"Check them again."

"I'm fine. My eyes are fine. My brain is fine."

"You're not fine. You're really fucked up."

"Yeah. Well. I'm not dead. That's something."

"You have a blind spot. A big one."

"No, I don't. Dr. Mantis said I don't."

"It's a big black hole in your vision, Go Jung-hwa. And you're going

to fall into it." Layne's mouth opened. Hwa saw down inside it. It wasn't pink, or even red. It was black and huge and deep and cold. Like the ocean. *"You're going to fall into it, just like the rest of us, Hwa. Hwa. Hwa. HWA!"*

She sat up. Joel had both his arms up, forearms out, blocking the sweeping blade of her arm. Sweat rolled down her neck. Slowly, stiffly, she lowered her arm.

"Your lights were still on," Joel said. "And you were shouting."

The adjoining rooms were to help her protect him, not the other way around. So much for that idea. She ran a hand over her face. "Sorry."

"Are you okay?"

"I had a bad dream. That's all."

Joel turned around. The images from Layne's and Calliope's files were still projected up on the ceiling. "Well, no wonder."

"Oh. Shit. Sorry." She raised her arm to wave the pictures away, but again Joel blocked her movement.

"Are those your friends?"

"Aye." Hwa nodded. "They are. Were. They *were* my friends."

Joel sat down on the bed. He tucked one leg under him and leaned back. "Two USWC 314 members, both with Krebs machines in their bodies, a month apart." He raised his voice slightly. "Prefect, does time of death for each of these women match the same phase of the moon?"

"No."

Joel shrugged. "Just a guess. Sometimes these things are lunar."

"These things?"

"Serial killers."

Hwa shook her head. "No. It's not that. Layne died when she was at the bar with me. Not like Calliope."

Joel turned to look at her. "Your friend died right in front of you?"

Hwa's lips went hot. She looked at her knees. It occurred to her that her arms and legs were bare—she was just in a singlet and her underwear—and Joel hadn't even mentioned her stain. Jesus, the kid was so good. Great, even. Zachariah Lynch was right. His youngest really was the best of the line.

"Yeah," she said. "She died right in front of me. I couldn't . . ." She clamped her lips shut for a moment. "It happened really fast."

Joel grabbed another pillow and placed it behind his head. Then he lay down perpendicular to her along the foot of the bed. "Prefect?"

"Ready."

"Confirm Joel Lynch."

A pause. *"Confirmed."*

"Execute override code Juliett Lima Oscar, 080378."

Slowly, the mosaics over the redacted forensics reports dissolved away to reveal complete documents. More images appeared. So did other documents—and they looked to be internal memos, with the Lynch letterhead over all of them.

"What did you just do?"

"I have a backdoor to the Prefect system." Hwa watched Joel pull up Calliope's and Layne's reports. He blew past all the personal data and opened up the designs of the Krebs machines. "Requesting profile data on all team members related to Krebs development, including classified material." A series of folders with headshots and employee ID numbers appeared. Joel turned to her. "Anything in particular you think we should look for?"

Hwa stretched out alongside him to stare at the ceiling. "Filter out all developers not living in New Arcadia."

A significant number of employees faded from view.

"Fifteen men and five women," Joel said. "We really have to work on that ratio."

Hwa checked her watch. "Prefect, if I gave you my old password to the Belle de Jour system, could you try to match these names against client and appointment data? They'll be encrypted."

Another long pause. *"That will not be a problem."*

"User G-O space J-U-N-G hyphen H-W-A; password G-zero-F-C-K-Y-R-dollar sign-L-F."

"Nice," Joel said. "Subtle."

Prefect showed them four files: three men, and one woman. The woman and one of the men were a married couple. Two weeks ago, they'd visited a nice Russian girl named Maria together. It wasn't their first meeting with her; they'd met earlier in September, and from Maria's review of the encounter, it looked like it was going to be a regular thing. Maria mentioned no feelings of doubt or weirdness about the arrangement—they had not asked her to do anything that wasn't previously outlined in their initial conversation, and had not tried to overstay their time or undercharge for fees. They paid on time and made new appointments the same day. In other words, perfect clients. Hwa screened them out.

The two profiles that were left looked eerily similar. Two white guys with programmer tans and the same deer-in-the-headlights expression that everyone wore while being issued an ID badge. Their names were Smith and Mueller. Mueller was a relatively new hire from Arizona. He'd written his dissertation on sustainable methods of extracting energy from experimental matter. Before that, he'd served in the JROTC. Technically, he was still a member of the National Guard, even if he was working in Canada on a visa. By contrast, Smith was Canadian. His doctorate came from Waterloo. He had been with the company for fifteen years.

His profile was covered in redactions.

Hwa pointed at the profile. "What are all those logos, at the top of the page? Above all the black parts, I mean."

"Those are project logos. They're so you can see at a glance what people have worked on. See, there's the logo for Project Poseidon." He pointed. Hwa recognized the image from the sign indicating the experimental reactor. But there were others: a single drop of blue on a white ground, a red dragon rampant, a circle of white dots on a green square. That last one reminded her of something, but she couldn't remember what.

"Prefect, what other projects beside Poseidon has Smith worked on?"

"Project Clearwater, Project Blake, Project Changeling."

Changeling. How did that image and that word match up? How were fairy babies switched with human ones at all reminiscent of a ring of white on grass green? She'd read the Irish folk tales in Mrs. Cavanaugh's class, just like everyone else in New Arcadia. And changelings were switched in the cradle. They didn't come from fairy rings.

And just like that, she knew. She knew exactly where she'd seen that image before.

"Hwa? Is something wrong?"

For a kid with an anti-feeling chip, he was still pretty damn good at reading her. She turned to Joel. She forced some sheepishness. Faked embarrassment. "Just realizing I forgot to report to Síofra," she said.

Joel beamed. "I'll bet you could ping him now. He doesn't sleep very much." Hwa didn't ask how the boy knew that. "Do you think he'll like our present?" Joel continued.

"Aye," Hwa said. "I reckon he will."

14

Metabolist/Subspace/LynchLabs/ Tower Three

The trip back to New Arcadia was smoother than the trip out. Joel slept most of the way. Hwa used the time to look at some more employee profiles. By the time they arrived, it was early afternoon and Joel was talking about meeting some friends from science club to discuss next steps.

"Do you have your outfit for Homecoming, yet?" Joel asked.

Hwa turned and gave him the finger. "Don't ruin my day. I'm going home."

"Don't forget the Falstaff paper!" Joel yelled.

The train back was mostly empty, for a Sunday. Maybe people really were leaving. The crowds were a little thicker on the Demasduwit. It was one of those crisp autumn Sundays that made her happy to be out on the Atlantic, where the air was clean and the sky was clear. She let herself be overcharged for a big mess of dandelion greens, yams, and eggs, and she took the stairs up to her place without once encountering the tobacco dealers who made it their usual Sunday afternoon meeting place or the anti-reactor kids with their chittering ads and radiation spam.

The door to her apartment hung ajar. Plastic splintered and threaded away from the jamb. When she touched them, the locks fell through the door. She heard them clunk heavily on the square of carpet remnant she'd scavenged in lieu of a welcome mat. After all, she hadn't planned to welcome anybody. Why was she focusing on that one detail? Why did her mind seem to get smaller, at moments like this?

Every time she told other women about this kind of moment, she told them to walk away.

Don't even stop, she told the people in her self-defence classes. *If there's something wrong with your door, and you think there's been a break-in, just keep walking. Don't go in. Just go somewhere safe and call for help. You don't know who's in there, waiting for you. You don't know what they're on, or how crazy they are, or what they plan on doing to you. Don't go in. Whatever you do, do not open that door.*

Hwa put her groceries down. And her backpack. She rolled her neck. Flexed her feet. Cleared her wrists.

She kicked the door in so hard it bounced off the opposite wall.

No one came running out. No guns started blazing. There was only the echo of the door hitting the wall and the flutter of seagulls from the stairwell and the chaos that was her apartment. She could . see it from here: shelves shoved over, display cracked on the floor, bed and pillows cut up with their stuffing spilling like guts in a combat drama.

Her oven was on.

She could see straight into the kitchen from the door, and in the dimness the oven light was the only real illumination. It was for this reason that she went in, and only this reason, even though she knew the invader could be hiding in the washroom. It was the only other room in the place, and the only space large enough for another human being. She didn't even have a proper closet, or proper cabinet, just an old luggage cart with clothes hanging on it. So if someone were still there, they were in that room.

She stepped through the door. One step. Two. Three. Turned right. The washroom door was shut.

She pretended the room belonged to Joel, and checked all the corners and behind the door. No one. She crossed into the kitchen and found her good vegetable knife out on the counter. It was under the shattered remains of an antique lacquered bento box Rusty had given her. Odd, that no one had taken the knife. She gripped it hard, blade facing up, so the muscles engaged in the stabbing would be her stronger underhand ones, not her overhand ones.

She kicked in the door of the washroom.

A reek of shit and piss hit her in a slow, awful wave. The room smelled like hot roadkill. They'd shit in her sink. In the shower. Piss was everywhere, dried and yellow. Her garbage was strewn across it. They'd pissed on that, too. Her toothbrush was in the toilet, stuck in a pile of her tights and rash guards. There was cum on her hairbrush. At least, that's what it looked like. Hwa dropped that in the toilet, too, and then realized she'd just have to fish it out again and walked away.

LOOKING FORWARD TO RAPING YOU, her mirror said, in dried toothpaste.

In the oven were two baking sheets. Both were full of melted plastic and fibreglass. A thin film of gold and silver coated each thick puddle of goo.

They'd melted her brother's trophies.

She turned the oven off. Sank to the floor. Felt its heat on her back. Smelled the molten metal and alloy and whatever else it was that they made those things out of. It was probably toxic. It was probably giving her cancer, right this very minute. Somewhere in her body the assembly line was going all wrong and the cells were dividing toward her doom.

She didn't care.

Outside, someone shuffled past her door, and then shuffled back. The old homeless guy. He was a skinny white man who wore a tattered yellow slicker and boots with no socks. "Are you all right, Miss?"

Hwa wiped her eyes with the ball of her hand. "Not really, no."

"You had a break-in?"

She nodded.

"You gonna call the cops?"

It occurred to her that she didn't really have to call them. Not if she didn't want to. That was the other thing she always told other women: *Call the police. Start a paper trail. Establish a pattern.* Now she understood why some of them never did. Because it felt so useless. So stupid. What would she tell them? *I broke some guy's finger and he called his buddies and they fucked up my place and they say they're going to rape me. Yeah, you're right, Officer. I probably shouldn't have broken his finger. This is all my fault. Sorry for bothering you.*

It wasn't like those trophies would ever come back together. It wasn't like the cops would help her clean up. It wasn't like she'd ever really feel safe here, ever again.

"You know, if you don't call them, and the super finds damage later, you lose the deposit," the old man said.

"That so?"

He nodded. "Happened to me, once."

Hwa stood up. She grabbed some clothes off the rack. "You know what? You stay here tonight. I'll be back later. Maybe."

. . .

Nail led her down to the subspace alone, which meant she didn't hear about her backpack or her groceries until she was inside the door, where Rusty stood waiting to take her coat.

"My goodness," he said. "Look at all that."

"Sorry." Hwa set her things down in a pile. "Rusty. I'm really sorry."

"Whatever for, Miss Go?"

Hwa swallowed hard. "Just dropping in like this. I haven't been around much, and I know that, and I couldn't make it to Layne's funeral, and . . . I've been a bad friend."

Rusty frowned. On him, it looked like just a gentle pinch of his lips and a quirk of his pale eyebrows. Like a curious Corgi, almost. "I believe you can tell my mistress that yourself, Miss Go."

"Aye." Hwa smoothed her hair and tugged her shirt into place. "Is she in?"

"Yes. Let me show you through."

Mistress Séverine sat in her office, contemplating a massive display of spreadsheets. It looked like a register of complaints. "Hello, Hwa," she said, without turning around.

"Hi."

"How's the new job?"

Hwa found herself standing taller. "I'm sorry I didn't make it to Layne's funeral."

Séverine shook her head softly. Her white hair swept back and forth, back and forth, against the lace back of her dress. "No one blames you for that. You were there when it happened. Attending the service would be too much to ask." She waved away a document and another bloomed up to replace it. "You didn't answer my question, my dear."

"About the job?" Hwa licked her lips. "It kinda sucks, actually. They're making me go to Homecoming."

Séverine twisted. "Oh, that's not such a bad . . ." Her manicured hand met her lips. "Why, Hwa, what's happened?"

It was useless, trying to keep secrets from her. Mistress Séverine had a sixth sense. Maybe even a seventh one. She just knew when you were vulnerable. It was her trade.

"My place got broken into."

The Mistress crossed to her and clasped her gently by the shoulders. She took Hwa's chin in her hands and turned it to the left first, and then the right. "Well, are you hurt?"

"No. They were gone by the time I got there. They did a number on the place, though. There's shit—sorry—everywhere. And they melted my brother's trophies."

"Animals." Séverine smoothed her hair. "Just *animals.*"

"They left a threat on my mirror. They said they were going to come back, and, uh . . ." Hwa let the other woman see her eyes. "Finish the job."

"You don't even have to say it. Not if you don't want to."

Hwa nodded. "Thanks."

Séverine moved to her desk and opened the top left drawer. She fished out a bottle and shook it. A smile crossed her face. "Do you know who did it?"

"Aye. Got a pretty good idea."

"Mmm." Séverine shook out a pill from the bottle and offered it to Hwa. "You take that. You've had a scare, and you need to rest."

Hwa blinked at the pill in her hand. "Will I sleep?"

"Later, you will. It's very slow, this one. We'll feed you, to help it along. I'll have Rusty make a big cioppino. And bread! We'll eat bread. As much bread as you want. And a big olive oil cake for dessert, with honey. And Manhattans to start. Then an old vine zin I've got kicking around. Oh, darling, don't cry."

Naturally, Hwa started sobbing right that second. Séverine patted her hair. "It's all right, dear. It happens to all of us. It's happened to me, once or twice."

Hwa only sobbed harder. Her throat hurt. Her eyes hurt. It was much worse to think of this happening to the people she knew. To think of all the women this had happened to, before her. All the women who had read those same words in some other place, at some other time. Maybe not for the same reasons, but the reasons didn't matter. What mattered were the words. The threats. The people who made them. And their hate.

"It's a sign of success, actually. If they're trying to intimidate you, you must be doing something right." Séverine handed her a glass of water. "You should tell your employers that you might not be available for the next little while."

Hwa nodded. It was the last call she wanted to make, but the Mistress was right. There was no way around it. She wiped her eyes again. "Thanks. Thanks for everything."

Séverine reached out and stroked Hwa's face with just her fingertips. The bad side. The stained side. She was the only one who would ever touch it. "You are so much bigger than this bullshit. Remember that."

Hwa squeezed the tears out of her eyes. "Yes, ma'am."

When the door closed behind Séverine, Hwa pinged Síofra.

"How's the laundry going?"

"Not great. My place got, uh, tossed. Probably some guys from Security. You know. In retaliation."

A long, long pause. Dead air. "Did you hear—"

"I heard you." His voice was iron. *"Where are you? I'll hire a boat."*

Hwa shook her head, then remembered he couldn't see it. She mastered her breathing. Thought of the master control room. The buttons and switches. The screens, with her apartment on them. Her first real place. Tae-kyung's trophies. Christ.

"I have a place to stay."

"You have a place to stay right here. You know that."

Hwa squeezed her eyes shut. She had considered it. Wanted it. Just show up in Tower Five, at his door, the smell of jasmine and honeysuckle, the mossy dimness of his hallway. Just fob herself in and tell him everything and damn the consequences.

"That would go badly for you, wouldn't it?" Hwa asked. "They'd know, I mean. If I stayed the night. You'd get in trouble."

"Stop protecting me. I'm not the one who needs protecting."

"We . . ." Hwa didn't know how to finish the sentence. She decided on another truth, instead. "I just wanted to stay with a woman, eh? I needed some, er, girl time. Someone who gets it."

A long pause. A defeated sigh. *"Of course. I'll run by your place and set up some flies on the wall, just in case."*

"Okay. Thank you. But, you should know, this homeless guy is in there. Watching the place."

"I'll try not to scare him."

"Thanks."

Another pause. Why was she letting this continue? Why was she just waiting for him to talk? They had nothing to say to each other, really.

"They miscalculated, Hwa. We're going to use this against Silas. We are going to show this to the board and get him demoted."

Demoted. That had a nice ring to it. It was something, anyway. "Well, you'd better take some sample kits, if that's your plan," Hwa said. "There's enough DNA there to convict most of Silas's division. Maybe not Beaudry or the others who came with us to Terra Nova, but all the other lackeys."

"DNA?"

"You'll see when you get there. I apologize in advance. Bring some, uh, gloves. And maybe an allergy mask."

She was talking just to prolong the conversation. She knew that. The drug was in her, now. Its progress spread easy warmth all through her limbs. It made him easier to talk to. Made her less nervous.

"I'll call you when I'm finished there," he said, as if having read her mind. *"We'll talk again. Tonight."*

"We always talk again." Why was she saying this? Why make this admission? What good could it possibly do? "You're like the last person I talk to at night and the first person I talk to in the morning."

Silence.

She'd overstepped. Said the wrong thing. Or maybe just said too much. Made too sharp an observation. Pointed out one of those things that was so obvious that nobody ever mentioned it, because they didn't really want to.

"Sorry," she started to say. "I took a pill, and it's kicking in, and—"

"I'll call you before you go to sleep," he said. *"I can see it, when your heart slows down. That's how I know when to call. I keep your heart— the icon of your heart—in one corner of my vision. All the time."*

Her stomach flipped over and tried to exit through her fingertips. Adrenaline jangled down her arms like music. Her mouth went dry and all she could taste was the burn of the drug in her throat.

"See, there? It skipped."

• • •

Hwa slept through the ping. The pill and the wine and the food were too much for her, and she passed out halfway through a film named, ironically enough, *The Big Sleep.* Rusty insisted she hadn't really missed anything—the story was secondary to the flirting.

"And the fashion," Séverine said, over breakfast. "Speaking of which. You mentioned Homecoming?"

"Oh, fuck." Hwa covered her face with her hands. "Sorry. Yeah. Yes. I have to go."

"Do you have anything to wear?"

Hwa shook her head.

"I thought as much. But! I have just the thing. Nail, please fetch me my pearls."

This conversation was uncomfortably similar to the one she'd had with Layne, the night she died. It didn't bode well for Séverine. Hwa was about to tell her so, when she got a ping from Joel.

"We have lunchtime appointments set up with those two Krebs developers," he said. "They're back to back this afternoon, before my science club meeting. I still have to make it to that, because Mr. Branch has this movie he wants to show us. It's supposed to help us with our ship design. So Diane scheduled our other meetings during school hours, but that's okay because Daniel said we weren't going in today, anyway."

Technically, she could have gone. Her uniform was right where she'd left it, in her locker. She could go and get it at any time. But Síofra probably didn't know that. "Okay."

"Daniel said your place got broken into. He's very angry about that."

"Well, I'm not too pleased about it, either."

"No, I mean, he's furious," Joel said. "Dad and I were having break-fast, and Daniel walked right in and told me we weren't going to school because of what happened to your place, and then he asked to see Dad in his office right away. He wouldn't even take any coffee."

Well. That was saying something. "And then what happened?"

"He shut the door, and Daniel started yelling, and my dad told him to calm down, and then things got really quiet, and Daniel said something about Silas."

"Silas. He told your dad about Silas."

"Yeah. I know they don't like each other, but . . . do you know what's going on?"

Hwa wondered how much to tell him. It seemed wrong to share her suspicions of Silas and his goons without any proof. Sure, Silas was an asshole, but he was also Joel's brother, and their father was dying. The kid would need his whole family around him, soon enough. Best not to alienate him from them any further.

"Yeah," she said. "I have a pretty good idea what's going on. Stay where you're at, and I'll come to where you're to. I'm in Three, but I can be at Five soon."

"Hwa, are you and Daniel in trouble?"

"Me and Daniel? No. No more so than usual. I guess."

"You slipped. You called him by his first name."

Hwa rolled her eyes. "Just wait for me. I'll be there soon."

• • •

The meetings meant going all the way out to the reactor lab. It floated above the Old Rig. That was part of what made it such an ideal location, Joel explained as they made their way across the waves. There were already multiple concrete slugs that could contain a leak. If the reactor overloaded, the town would still need to evacuate, but there would be time. This way, they could sink the tritium into the reactor and draw seawater in directly from below, all in a contained space purpose-built by machines. It was because of the Old Rig that they had purchased New Arcadia. If it had not blown, they would never have come.

"I'm sorry," Joel said, when Hwa said nothing. "I forgot."

"It was three years ago," Hwa said. "It's okay."

"I saw some of his matches, when I looked you up. He was really great."

Hwa smiled. "Thanks."

The first interview was with Smith, the man with the redacted profile who'd worked on all the projects. He was big, and bald, and he seemed genuinely interested in helping Joel with his project. He offered them coffee, then took them on a tour of the lab. It was what one might expect: basically a lot of displays for watching the Old Rig and the progress of the machines, and a lab for repairing the larger robots tasked with doing excavation and major building.

"But the really interesting part is the control room," Smith said. "It's going to completely change how we do energy security. Every time I walk in there, it just blows my mind."

Joel gave his best *I'm thrilled to discuss my company's many assets* face. "Can we see?"

Smith led them past several cubicles to a special room unlocked by a hand wave. The door was marked EMERGENCY CONTROL PROTOTYPE, and past it was nothing but white.

"I've been here, before," Hwa said. "This is like the NAPS holding cells."

Smith and Joel both laughed. The laughter trailed off when Hwa gave them a look that said she wasn't joking. Smith cleared his throat and summoned three chairs out of the matter in the floor.

"It's completely customizable, as long as you have the right implants, and the implants have high-enough authorization," he said. "Even down to the interfaces. I imagine an interface, and boom—there it is." He closed his eyes, and a slender wooden table spiralled up out of the floor. It trembled, and out of its surface bloomed an old-fashioned rotary telephone. "It requires an implant, of course, but . . . it's all ready to go."

"And there's one of these down in the reactor?" Joel asked.

"There will be. Once the Krebs dig out enough space, we'll pressurize this room and move it down there. The straw's big enough to handle the transport—this room isn't actually that big. It just looks that way."

"So . . ." Hwa frowned. "So how is this a security measure?"

"It's highly personalized," Smith said. "There's no system to learn but your system. So if, say, I'm down there watching the reactor, and some guys burst in and put a gun to my head, they won't know how to work the system. The room locks in on the design from the highest clearance in the room, and it bakes in for the length of that day's shift."

"Doesn't that mean that if somebody passes out at the switch, their system is still live?"

"Nope. The room also watches for change in the beta/theta ratio. It sees you when you're sleeping. It knows when you're awake."

"Could you fake up one of the implants?" Hwa asked, thinking of Sandro. "You know, implant a knock-off, or something?"

Smith shook his head. "The system relies on self-replicating implants. They're not even implants, really. Implantation is really invasive. These are more like the Krebs devices: living machines that go where they're needed and talk to the ambient technology. But they can only live in a really specific growth medium. If you wanted to steal mine, you'd have to steal my blood."

He smiled. "Speaking of which, you wanted to talk about the Krebs machines?"

"Yes," Joel said. "I know that the Krebs are used for primarily industrial work, but have you ever considered biological or medical applications?"

Smith grinned. "Sure! But that's not my division. I'm an engineer. I'm a doctor, but not that kind of doctor."

Hwa leaned forward in her seat. The seat shifted subtly underneath her to bring her that much closer to Smith. "But it is possible?"

"In theory, yes. They can work at the nano-scale doing just about anything. Ours are down there sealing pipes and helping the bots, but we've had them do things that are like working in biological systems."

"Such as?"

Smith shrugged. "Well, one example is the filtration web. It's an easier way to preserve ions in water, and so we tell the Krebs to weave a web. And that web looks an awful lot like an old dialysis membrane, which is to say that it can do the same job as a kidney. And, basically, we could extend that to multiple systems in the body."

Hwa thought of Síofra's broken nose. "Like programmable tissues? Like this room, but in the body?"

"Well, yeah. But it would still require a subscription model. These machines have really short telomeres. They're, uh, two-pump chumps. They do one job and then they die. Like mayflies."

Joel frowned. "Is that why we didn't develop it?"

Smith held his hands up. "Not to put too fine a point on it, but that's something you'd have to ask your father. I know they had the opportunity, but they decided to go full industrial instead."

Joel shook his head. "I've never heard that. When was this?"

"It might have been before you were born, I guess. But the people you should really be talking to, if you're interested in the bio applications, are the people from Project Changeling."

Hwa felt herself go very still. "Changeling?"

Smith nodded. "Yeah. Lynch has a whole charitable division that does work all over the world. Changeling was part of it. It was sort of like an incubator for medical technologies to benefit people from, well . . . you know."

"The places where the oil used to come from," Joel said.

Smith turned a shade of red that Hwa had previously only seen on men whose dates ran late. "Well, you didn't hear it from me, but from a PR perspective . . . it didn't hurt. The students got to keep their tech, as long as they kept it open source, and Lynch got to fund some new ideas while being friendly with the natives. That was the idea."

"What was the focus of the research?"

Both Joel and Smith frowned at her. Smith leaned back and crossed a leg. "I told you. Medical."

"That's a pretty broad description, from someone who used to work on it." When Smith's mouth fell open and he held up his hands as though to argue, Hwa leaned forward. "Don't bother. I've seen your file. Now tell us about the project."

Smith winced. "It's company policy—"

"Dr. Smith, I *am* this company," Joel said. "Now please tell this woman everything she wants to know."

Smith drew breath to speak, then let it out in a rush. "Fine. Okay. You win." He turned his seat a little to face Joel. "Now, keep in mind, I never saw this as a stated goal. It wasn't in the abstracts, or any of the grant applications, or the official literature. It was just what some of us thought might be going on, based on the work that was coming out of the labs in Russia and South Sudan."

Joel wrinkled his nose. He pointed at Hwa. "Shouldn't you be talking to her? She's the one who asked you the question."

Smith shook his head. "No. You see, the answer concerns you." He edged forward in his seat. He spoke in a whisper. "It's life-extension technology, for the creation of human bodies. You know. Sleeving. Avatars. Body-jumping. That's why your father was so interested. He's been interested since he received his polio diagnosis."

Joel looked profoundly impatient with the man in front of him. Hwa had never really seen this side to him before. "Sleeving is a myth, Dr. Smith. The science has been settled on that for years. Machines? Yes. Flesh? No. The nervous system is too complex to just copy and paste. It requires years of learned response to be any good. There is no such thing as immortality. There is only good medicine."

"I agree with you," Smith said. "But the rest of the business world hasn't quite gotten that particular memo. Especially those who believe in life after a Singularity, or a life in deep space. Your father and his associates—"

Hwa's watch pinged her. They all jumped. In the small room, it sounded extra loud and absurdly chirpy. "Sorry about that." She pulled back her sleeve to look at her wrist, and Sabrina's face was there.

HELP ME, it read.

. . .

"You should wait until the NAPS get there," Joel said. "I just called them. They'll be at Tower Three soon. That's where she called from, isn't it? You can wait until then."

Hwa shook her head. She hopped into the boat. "No. I can't."

Joel sighed. He jumped into the boat beside her. "Okay. Then I'm going with you."

"What?"

"Think about it, Hwa." Joel started cinching on a life vest. "First your apartment gets ransacked, and the next day your friend calls for help with a single text? This is a trap. And I'm not letting you walk into it alone." He fired up the boat. It was his own, a gift from his father, and he'd adhered a bronzed mecha toy to the prow where angels and mermaids and logos usually went. "Now, you can stand there arguing with me, or we can go check it out. But I'd rather go with you than think about my dad trying to upload himself into a custom-made *übermensch*."

Hwa snorted and began untying the boat from its mooring. She joined him at the controls. "You know, you're really getting into this whole crime-fighting thing. You sure you still want to take over the family business, when you grow up?"

Joel smiled at her. He gunned the engine. "You know, Hwa, I think you're the first person in my life who's ever seriously asked me that question."

And with that, they raced across the water. Tower Three wasn't far from the Old Rig, but every second that passed made the water seem like ice. Joel handed his keys to a valet, and they made for the elevators. In the gym, nothing seemed amiss. No screaming. No blood. They checked the separate studios, and the massage room, and the women's locker room, but Sabrina wasn't there.

"Prefect?"

"Ready."

"Can you tell me if Sabrina Kimball checked in, here? Did she come to the gym today?"

A pause. *"Yes."*

"Did she check out?"

"No."

Hwa's gaze lit on the men's locker room. There was a wet floor logo projected on the floor and a cleaning cart in the doorway. "Okay." She turned to Joel. Suddenly all she could see was the puddle of dried blood where Calliope's body used to be. "Stay close to me. And if I tell you not to look, don't look."

He nodded. "Let's go."

The men's locker room was empty. No one at the urinals. No one in the stalls. No steam from the showers. But one of the shower cabinets had a closed curtain.

"You don't have to open that, Hwa," Joel whispered. "I don't think you should open that."

Her fingers brushed the curtain. The room was silent. No cries for help. No whimpers of terror. No frustrated wriggling of a person who might be bound and gagged.

"Don't open it," Joel said. "Please don't open it. We can wait. We can wait until the NAPS come."

Hwa gathered the curtain in her fist. "Don't look."

She yanked the fabric off its rings. Sabrina sat folded up in one corner of the shower. Her clothes had puddled around her. At first Hwa thought that they had somehow grown larger, but in fact, Sabrina had grown smaller. Dramatically smaller. Thinner. She looked skeletal. Sucked dry. All hollowed out. Like a mummy. When Hwa reached out, Sabrina's hair came away in her fingers.

And her eyes opened.

And she screamed.

The scream was a dry, awful whistling from a collapsing throat. Her hands had no strength. They flailed weakly. "Hwa . . . ?"

Hwa spoke around the hand she'd clamped to her own mouth. "I'm here, Sabrina. I came. I showed up."

"He said . . ." Sabrina's eyes rolled around wildly in her head. "He said he was . . . going to make me pretty. . . . Off-book . . ."

Hwa's vision blurred. "You're already pretty. You're already so pretty."

"He said . . . he could make me . . . different . . ."

"You didn't need to be different, Sabrina." Hwa wiped her eyes. "You were fine, just the way you were."

Sabrina tried to shake her head. As she did, more hair came off on the tile walls of the shower. Behind her, Hwa heard a small sound. Joel was crouched on the floor. And somehow that made it worse, made it real, and Hwa felt her self-control start to slip.

"Sabrina," she said. "I'm so sorry." Gently, she took Sabrina's hand. It was dry, papery, like the outer skin of an onion. "You're not alone. I'm right here."

"Hwa . . . Why . . . ?"

"I don't know, Sabrina. But I'll figure it out. I will. I promise."

Again, she tried to shake her head. It became a wave of her entire body, like a dead flower trembling in a light breeze. "Why did you leave us?"

The locker room door squealed open. Hwa turned. A whole squad of NAPS officers poured through the doors. The crowd opened up, and a medical unit jogged in. Someone's hands landed on her shoulders. She heard medical speak. Cursing. Someone tugged her away from Sabrina. Separated their hands.

"More . . ." Sabrina wheezed. Her eyes locked with Hwa's. "He. Said. There. Will. Be. More."

15

Whitechapel/Viridian/Autumn

"Welcome back to Whitechapel," said Mr. Moore. "What brings you back here?"

In the thick fog of the simulation, it was easier for Hwa to say exactly what was on her mind. "I need to know how he's choosing them."

"There are many theories. Your essay—"

"I'm not writing an essay." Hwa tugged at the gloves the simulation had given her. They were little lace things, and way too pretty for her. The whole outfit was far too pretty for someone like her: a default in-world monstrosity of corsetry and bustling in purple silk. She could barely see around the puffs in her sleeves. It was ridiculous. Like putting lipstick on a pig. "I'm catching a killer."

"*We're* catching a killer," Joel added. "A serial killer. Someone who's hunting down women."

"Oh." Moore stroked his beard. "Well, then. That's very different." His furry brows knit together. "You understand I am not liable for the answers I provide. My projections are only admissible in certain courts."

"But you're an expert, right?" Joel gestured at the cobblestones and fog and the great black carriage with its open doors. "You know this whole story better than anybody."

"Yes. I represent the sum total of expert knowledge on the subject. I know more about it than any individual can know, and am constantly updating that knowledge from reputable sources on the subject. But I am still a secondary source, not a primary one. Do you understand the difference between primary and secondary historical sources?"

A little question mark icon appeared next to Mr. Moore's top hat. Hwa waved it away. "Aye, we get it. Just walk us through all the reasons somebody would have for doing this."

"The motives?"

"Aye. The motives."

"Ah." Moore tapped his walking stick against the cobbles and gestured at the open carriage door. "For that, we will need to take a ride."

Joel made a big show of helping Hwa into the carriage—it was hard not to trip on her dress, even if it was a simulation—and soon they were off. Just like Hwa's previous tour through Whitechapel, Moore showed them the canonical five murders from 1888. Joel couldn't see all the details the same way Hwa could, but Hwa thought that was probably for the best. He'd seen enough already. And this way, instead of cringing, he hopped out of the carriage at each site and asked the questions Hwa didn't think of, like *Why did no one suspect a doctor* and *What about a midwife* and *Is there any truth to the Freemason connection?*

So he didn't see, really, how the murders got worse each time. How much more vicious they became. How the Ripper took more and more, each time, until the faceless, sexless body of Mary Kelly lay before them shrouded in censoring mosaic. Her lips gone. Her breasts gone. Her uterus and clitoris removed.

"They do seem like ritual killings, yes," Moore was saying. "But it's very rare for cults to kill people outside of their own membership."

"What about the Santa Muerte cults?" Joel asked. "I saw a whole exhibit about them at the Museum of Behavior."

"There was no Santa Muerte cult," Moore answered. "There was only a ritualistic response to the chaos of *narcocultura* in Mexico. That's all any ritual is. An attempt to pilot a rudderless world." Moore used the ball of his walking stick to point out the street around them and the people walking it. "In fact, I think that's the only reason anyone does anything at all. The cult that raised your father, for example. And the one he belongs to, now."

Hwa caught Joel's eye. "Excuse me?"

"This is Joel Lynch. His father is Zachariah Lynch." Again, Moore pointed with his walking stick. "Zachariah Lynch was born into an anti-science commune led by Gaia Opal Abramson. At first it was all basket-weaving and free love—"

"Until kids got the measles," Joel said. "And polio. But my dad isn't a member of that group, anymore. Or any other group, much less a cult."

"Is the Lynch company not a cult?" Moore asked. "Is it not a novel organization fanatically devoted to making possible the wishes and dreams of a single figure, based on his view of reality?"

"That's not a cult, it's just a family business," Joel said. "And it doesn't have anything to do with murders like these. Murders that people attribute to organizations like the Freemasons."

Moore smirked. "The Gull theory—Stephen Knight's theory about the killings as a Masonic coverup of Prince Albert Victor's illegitimate child—is implausible for a number of reasons. Not least because the threat posed by an illegitimate child of Albert's would have been negligible, especially if the child were Catholic, as Knight claims the child would have been. The Settlement Act of 1701 excludes Catholics from succession. And even if Albert Victor had married, his marriage would have been invalid without consent from the sovereign under the Royal Marriages Act of 1772."

"So what you're saying is, there was no real reason for these women to die." Hwa watched police officers mill around the body making notes and lighting pipes. One ran away to be sick down an alley.

"No," Moore said. "Someone killed these women for a reason. But that reason was entirely personal. Only the killer can explain it. And even then, the explanation would be inherently limited by the killer's own self-awareness."

"Forgive me, Mr. Moore, but you're leaving something out," said a little man in a dapper blue suit from the wrong century. He was very pretty and apparently from the American South—his voice sounded like a higher, crisper version of Rivaudais's. He melted out of the space between two police officers and held out his hand. It wasn't until Hwa shook it that she realized he had extraordinarily long pinkies.

Moore tapped his walking stick. "And what would that be, Mr. Capote?"

"Just one very simple thing. One very tiny, simple, basic fact." Capote did a double take as he passed Joel. "Aren't you a picture."

"I'm fifteen," Joel said.

"And worth waiting for, I'm sure," Capote said. He turned to Hwa. "Oh, I *am* sorry. They don't let me out, much. Not my adult alter, anyway. Everyone loves Dill, and stories about Christmas, and Harper, but try to be yourself all by yourself and suddenly everybody has to sign a waiver."

"Do you know about serial killers?" Hwa asked.

"He was wrong about Manson," Moore said, into the sleeve of his coat.

"Oh, never you mind that, *everyone* was wrong about Manson. If you read a novel about a greasy-haired little starfucker like him seducing dumb suburban girls into helping him jump-start a *race war*, and therefore *the apocalypse*, you wouldn't believe it. It's simply not plausible, until it actually happens." Capote looked imploringly into Hwa's face. "That's the thing, my dear. There's really only one explanation for all this that actually matters."

"They hate women," Moore said. "Serial killers are the zenith of misogyny."

"No, Mr. Moore, that would be the invention of the corset," Capote said. He took Hwa's hands in his own. "Besides, there are plenty of serial killers who kill men. Randy Kraft, for example. And plenty of female serial killers, for that matter. You know what they say about the female of the species. But what people forget about these killers, what they always miss, is so simple. So human."

Around them, the walls began to flicker and die. The cobblestones pixelated. The fog turned pale. In Capote's face, Hwa saw wire frame. "What is it?" she asked quickly. "What am I forgetting? Why is he doing this?"

"Why does anyone do anything they do?" Capote asked.

Beside her, Joel vanished. Under her feet, the cobbles fell away. The fog thinned away into bright white.

"I don't know!" Hwa broke his grip and took hold of his shoulders. "Please just tell me."

"*He wants to,*" Capote whispered. "That's why he does it. Because he wants to. Because he—"

The simulation ended. Nausea boiled up to Hwa's throat from her gut. She ripped off the helmet so as to avoid puking in it. Mrs. Gardener stood outside the booth with Joel, who was looking sheepishly at the floor. Mrs. Gardener said nothing. One of her hands rose to pluck at the elaborate knot of the pink scarf at her neck, as though doing so might free the words that kept failing to escape her throat. But she had no time to answer, because the door to the library swung open and there was Hwa's boss.

And he was covered in blood.

. . .

"Daniel!"

"I'm fine, Joel," Síofra said.

He wasn't fine. At least, he didn't look like it. He looked like shit. As much as a man who looked like him could look like shit, anyway. There were purple hollows under both his eyes, and the knuckles of his hands were raw and bloody, like chewed-up meat. Blood stained his collar and his jacket. His shirt was untucked on one side. He looked tired. Very tired.

"Please excuse my appearance, Joel. I've come to brief Hwa on some changes to your security protocols. Then I have an appointment with your father and Katherine and Silas. I thought I'd take the two of you home, on my way."

"What were you even doing in this tower?" Joel asked.

But Hwa already had an idea. Beaudry lived in Tower Two. She'd looked it up when she ran his profile, because he lived the closest to the school and therefore the closest to Joel. Most of the others working for Silas in Security lived in Three or Four, but Beaudry was cheap. It was why he'd said bonuses were better than parties. And Beaudry was the one whose finger she'd broken. And he had a face Síofra would know.

"It doesn't matter," Hwa said. "Let's just go."

She let Joel walk a little bit ahead of her as they moved toward the exit for the high-speed causeway. Síofra fell into step beside her, and she waited as long as she could before asking the question. "Did you—"

"Don't ask me," Síofra said. "It's better for both of us if you don't know."

Hwa swallowed. "Right." She caught herself staring at his hands. "You should heal those up, though."

"I don't know." Síofra held his hands out in front of him. They shook slightly. Not a full-on palsied tremor, but just the smallest quiver. He clenched them, and blood beaded up in the cuts across his knuckles. Defensive wounds, they were called, in police reports. They were the reason you wore gloves in a boxing match. Because real fights did just as as much damage to you, most of the time, as they did to your opponent. "Sometimes it feels better not to let something heal."

"That's true," Hwa said, before realizing just how true it really was.

They were within sight of the exit doors, now. Joel was waiting. Síofra slowed his pace without completely stopping. He lowered his voice. "Why didn't you tell me?"

"Tell you what?"

"What they wrote. On your mirror."

It seemed like such a long time ago. And so trite. So amateur. Beaudry and the others had had some buddies wreck her place while she wasn't even there. It was intimidation, but nothing like what she and Joel had just witnessed in Whitechapel. Only maybe they were really all part of the same thing. Maybe that was how murders like that started. One day you were telling some woman how you were going to rape her and a few years later you were cutting her tits off and eating her kidneys.

Judging by the look on his face, Síofra already believed this to be true.

"Didn't seem important," Hwa said.

Now Síofra did pull up short. It took Hwa a step or two to realize this, and when she turned around to face him, his face looked unbearably sad. "Not important?" he asked. "Not *important*?"

"Aye. Not really. Not in the grand scheme."

"The grand scheme."

Hwa shrugged. She looked at the floor. "Aye."

On the floor, she saw his shoes come closer to hers. His had blood on them. So did hers. "Look at me."

She looked. It was hard. She didn't know why it was so hard, only that meeting his gaze felt like keeping her eyes open in a snowstorm. It stung.

"Who was it," he asked, "that taught you that something like that, that *a threat to your life*, wasn't important?"

And just as though she were staring unblinking into the winter wind, Hwa's good eye filled with tears. She blinked them away. Shook her head. Pulled her lips back into a grin. "What're you at, eh? You gonna do this dance again, if I tell you?"

"No." Síofra took another step forward. When Hwa tensed up, he paused and backed away a little. He pitched his voice even lower. "No. I wouldn't do that. I don't hit women."

Unbidden, Sabrina's face rose in her vision. And Layne's. And Calliope's. Was her mother next? Hwa squeezed her eyes shut. *Master control room,* she reminded herself. *Press the buttons. Flip the switches.*

"New security protocols?" she heard herself ask.

"Oh, that." He cleared his throat. "I brought Joel's suggestion to his father's attention. You'll be living with them from now on. And we have a brief you need to read, about the Homecoming dance."

. . .

The dance took place on a viewpoint level of Tower Four. Each hour, the whole floor would make a single revolution, so couples at tables could see both the city and the ocean. This was by far its lowest-tech feature. The Synth-Bio Club had engineered all manner of plants and animals just for the occasion: grabby little tentacular vines that climbed up the walls, twirling maple keys that danced and spun in the air like pixies and spiralled up from whatever surface they touched, butterflies that dampened signal by flapping their Faraday wings.

None of the students really noticed. They were too busy miming anal on the dance floor.

"A Homecoming at New Arcadia Secondary." Hwa stood on a balcony overlooking the action. She waved expansively at the crowd. "You may never find a more wretched hive of—"

"Yeah, yeah, I get it." Joel smirked. "We agreed to hate this equally, remember? Let's go upstairs."

Upstairs was the corporate event. The music was quieter, and it came from instruments played by human hands. The guests weren't really dancing so much as clustering as far away as possible from the dance floor. Partners and investors and developers of interest to the Lynch family had all been invited to see how this whole experiment in urbanism was getting along. When Hwa toggled over to one layer of vision, all she saw were brand identities communing with each other over tiny egg tarts sprinkled with chives.

Zachariah had a big announcement planned. Hwa had no idea what it was. When Joel had asked, his father only replied with the coy "That would be telling." Most likely it had to do with Project Poseidon. Why else would Zachariah have invited so many people, and many media presences?

"Zachariah's really done something special, here," Hwa heard a woman say to a group of robots who looked like Dr. Mantis, as they entered the other party. Emerald green feathers appeared to grow from her scalp. Hwa had no idea if they were real or not. "Shame he won't be around to see it all come to fruition."

Hwa steered Joel away from the conversation. "Whose flesh do you have to press?" Hwa asked.

"Well, the designer of my implants is here," Joel said. "I should probably say hello."

"Fine. Let's do that. Where is he?"

Joel nodded over to their right. "He's standing next to that woman with the red hair."

Hwa didn't need to look. She looked anyway. Eileen stood beside a short man in a tux, listening attentively and smiling. She looked a little rounder than usual. Tired. Like she didn't have the time or inclination for proper food. When she saw Hwa, her smile fell a little. Oblivious, Joel pushed forward across the dance floor with his hand outstretched.

"Hi, Dr. Carlino," he said.

The doctor lit up when he recognized Joel. Literally. Something in his eyes flashed a bright gold. They reminded Hwa of Dr. Mantis's eyes, and she wondered if he'd gone all the way—cameras in both eyes, not just the one. When he focused on her and she saw his pupils dilate sideways, she knew he had.

"Hello, Joel! I was hoping to see you this evening. And this is the bodyguard, yes? The organic one?"

Hwa squeezed his warm, damp, fleshy hand. "That's me. Go Junghwa. Nice to meet you."

"What a wonderful specimen you are, my dear." Dr. Carlino refused to let go of her hand until Hwa forcibly removed it. The blush spreading up into his vanishing hairline was going absolutely nowhere, though. He gestured at her. "You must be so proud of all this."

Hwa didn't know if he was talking about her outfit or the body it covered. She wasn't particularly proud of either. They were both temporary. "I work out," she said, finally.

"Oh, no, my dear, I meant your genome." Dr. Carlino plucked the air around her like a faith healer doing a cold read. "It's so . . . pristine. Intact. No edits. No augments. Pure and simple and austere. Almost, dare I say it, *zen*."

Whatever part of Eileen that still thought of Hwa as a friend must have activated on autopilot, because she quickly put her hand on Dr. Carlino's arm before Hwa could give him a piece of her mind. "I'm a little thirsty. Can we get you two some drinks?"

"Sure," Hwa said. Eileen was one of the few people in the room she'd trust to pour her anything. "Club soda for both of us."

Eileen pointed to the dance floor. "Just so you know—"

"Is that your mom?" Joel asked. "Dancing with Daniel?"

"There. Now you know," Eileen said, and followed Dr. Carlino.

Hwa was dreaming, and this was a nightmare. She was derealizing, and this was a seizure. She was dead, and this was Hell. A Hell of perfunctory jazz standards and crudités and an eternity spent watching her mother grinning at her from over her boss's shoulder as she ran one gem-studded hand up and down his back.

"I want to go downstairs," Hwa said.

"She looks nice," Joel said. "That gold colour really suits you both. Of course, hers is the whole dress, and yours are just the pearl buttons on that catsuit, but—"

"*Hwa-jeon!*"

Some in the crowd paused to glance at Sunny. Sunny ignored them. She lifted her hand from Daniel's shoulder and gestured for Hwa to come forward. Hwa's feet had no desire to move. None whatsoever. And yet they were moving, perhaps steered toward her mother by Joel. Abruptly they came to a stop, and Joel offered his hand to Sunny.

"Hi. I'm Joel Lynch. Hwa is my protection. I'm very happy to meet you."

Her mother shook Joel's hand. "How nice to meet you, Joel! I'm Go Sun-hwa. Most people call me Sunny."

Customers, Hwa added silently. *Punters. Marks. Not friends.*

"Are you having a good time?" Joel asked.

"Oh, it's just a *beautiful* party," Sunny gushed. "You've just out-*done* yourselves."

The creeping nausea that always assailed Hwa each time her mother opened her mouth climbed up from her belly to her throat and began tightening its grip. Why did she have to be here, with him? The payday from events like these was never small. She didn't need to bother Síofra. She could find some other sorry sap to cling to without any issue. She had chosen Síofra because she knew he worked with Hwa.

"May I please cut in?" Joel asked.

"Eh?" Hwa and her mother said, in unison.

"You don't mind, do you, Daniel? I just want to learn more about Hwa straight from the horse's mouth, as it were. You'll dance with her, won't you?"

"Naturally," Síofra said, and took Hwa's hand before she could protest. And then Joel and her mother were drifting away, her mother scowling at her from across an ever-widening gulf of marble floor and good breeding. And Síofra was gently trying to lead her. "Re-lax," he kept saying. "They'll be fine. I'm keeping an eye on him, too."

Hwa kept her eyes pinned to his chest. "I'm sorry. I haven't really danced since I was, like, ten. People don't really get in my space unless I'm sparring them, or fighting them."

"Is that what it is?" He seemed to be adding something up in his mind, like calculating his share of a long, awful, complicated bill. His fingers played absently with the stays at Hwa's back. They were what really held the whole suit together, Séverine had told her. The pearl buttons—real golden South Seas sewn directly into the dark leather—were just for show. "Nobody's ever come this close with-out hurting you first? That's why you flinch?"

Mute, Hwa nodded.

"You're not flinching now."

She shook her head.

"Well. That's something." He did something with their hands that made their fingers enlace, and his other arm tighten around her. "They're playing our song."

It took her a few bars to identify "Ain't That a Kick in the Head," and she laughed despite herself. He spun her out, and then spun her in, closer this time. Surprising, how easy that was.

"See, that wasn't so hard," he said, as though having read her mind. "All you have to do is trust me."

Hwa had nothing to say to that. But his grip stayed tight.

"Your mother nicknamed you after a dessert I've always wanted to try," he said. "Hwa-jeon, I mean. I was in Pyeongyang in the winter, and my hosts told me the fresh flowers were what made the pancakes best. That I should wait until they bloomed."

Hwa peered up at him. Odd, how his face could open and close like that. How she could climb right into the soft warmth of that gaze and make a nest in there, if she wanted. "Who are you, really?"

He smiled. "She speaks. You know who I am. I'm Daniel Síofra. Pleased to meet you. Who are you?" He spun her out. Spun her close.

"Tell me what you saw in Lynch's crystal ball." It was worth a shot. And he had asked her, once. Somehow she wished she'd told him when she had the chance.

His head tilted. "Have you been looking at my file?"

"Your file is redacted," Hwa said. "Completely. Why is that?"

That same look of defeat crossed his face that she'd seen when he watched the glitch at the shooting for the first time. His mouth worked. "Hwa . . ."

"Are you vulnerable? Hackable? Like a skullcap?"

"Hwa." He bent double. Hwa caught him. Held him. "Hwa. Something's wrong."

"What's wrong? Headache?"

He straightened. Smiled. "No. Not at all, Miss Go."

Ice ran down her spine. He didn't sound like himself. What

had the old witch under the bridge said, about piloting a skullcap?

"Hey," Hwa whispered. "Say me name, b'y."

"Go." His head shook. His fingers curled around her shoulders. Like he was holding tight to the tiller on a roiling sea. "Go Jung-hwa. *Jung-hwa-sshi.*"

"That's it," she said. "There we go."

"Hwa, there's something very wrong with me," Síofra whispered. "Oh, Christ, Hwa, I'm—"

Something light and wet glanced off her left shoulder. Hwa smelled something sweet. A champagne flute shattered near her. Gasps followed. Whispers. Tittering laughter. Hwa turned. She almost didn't recognize the figure at first. Her mind was on Síofra. But in the centre of the dance floor was Mr. Moliter, and he was very, very drunk. Drunk enough to throw a champagne flute at her head and miss badly, anyway. How had he gotten up to this level? Did they let the Homecoming chaperones drink?

Silently, she put herself between Síofra and Moliter.

"You." Her old teacher pointed at her. "You don't got anything worth selling on the open market, so you take it out on everyone else." Moliter shuffled around the dance floor like a rolling sack of rotten potatoes. His pointing finger wagged at her. He grinned his big, drunk, shit-eating grin, the same one he sometimes wore when Hwa dropped Eileen off at his place. "Girl with a face like that in a town like this, with so much pussy for sale, doesn't stand a chance—"

Hwa's fist snapped out so fast she almost didn't register it as movement. One minute Moliter was standing, and the next minute he was on the floor. He writhed helplessly, a potato bug curling in on itself, struggling to talk through the bloody gurgling in his throat.

"You little fucking *bitch*," he said. "With your big fucking mouth."

Coach Alexander. Coach Brandvold. *Is it true that one of the teachers here has a type?* "What, did Administration finally fire your ass? They finally find out how you were spending your lunch period?" She mimed him jerking himself off.

Moliter spat blood at her. It spattered dark red across the creamy marble floor.

"You're pathetic," Hwa turned to the assembled crowd. "This guy, right here, he used to be my teacher. If you can believe that. And senior year, right after my brother died—" She choked on the words. Took a breath. Forced them out. "He said it was a shame about my face, because if I could make money the way my mother did, my brother wouldn't have died working on the Old Rig."

Hwa toed one of his ankles. "You're lucky I don't have time for you."

She turned back to Síofra. He was clutching his head. He looked miserable. Hwa reached over and held him. The crowd gave them room. She ushered him to a banquette along the wall. He slid down and folded into himself. She stroked his hair. His face. His breath came light and fast and shallow. Like he was bleeding out.

"Oh, God, I'd forgotten how much things could hurt, Hwa, it hurts—"

"It's probably just a migraine, eh?" Hwa tried to sound breezy. "I'll find Joel, and then I'll get you home, and get you sorted. Joel?"

Silence.

"Joel." She swallowed hard. She made fists in Síofra's suit jacket to keep her hands from shaking. This was just too much for one night. "Joel, goddamn it, you answer me right this fucking minute, or I swear to Christ—"

"Joel, you simply must understand." Zachariah's voice sounded in her ear. Joel had opened a live feed, rather than answering her. That meant he couldn't answer. Or wasn't at liberty to do so. Hwa scanned the room for him. He was nowhere she could see. *"I plan to live a very long time. And your friend Daniel is a part of that plan."*

Hwa's stomach turned over. *I have great plans for Daniel,* the old man had said. Oh, Jesus. Oh, Christ. Oh, fuck.

"Joel, where are you?" Hwa whispered. She toggled her vision. She found Joel. He was on the floor above her. She pressed her forehead to Síofra's. "Hold on," she said. "Hold on, Daniel."

"My name." He cracked a smile that was also a rictus of pain. He spoke through chattering teeth. "You know my name."

"Goddamn right I do," Hwa said. She ran.

· · ·

The Lynch family stood gathered in a small meeting room above the forest. The floor was a one-way mirror looking down onto the red and gold of the trees below. The walls of the room were glass. Through it, Hwa could witness the aurora borealis rippling overhead, green and purple against the stars, a tingling in Hwa's teeth, an itch across her muscles.

She hunkered close to the floor.

"The time has come," Zachariah Lynch said. "Joel, you will inherit this company. That has been my plan since long before you were even alive. Even before you were but a blastema in your mother's uterus. But I never intended for you to do it alone."

She heard it in an odd stereo effect. Joel had opened his ears to her, and so now she heard it in both sets, organic and mechanical. Briefly, she wondered where her mother was down in that forest. Where Eileen was. Where everyone was. How she had reached this dark, hushed place herself. How it had come this far.

"I don't believe in death." Zachariah paused for breath. "I think death is a myth. A fairy tale, to keep humanity in line. Something to make us fear our own decision-making power. Something to make us tremble before the capacity of our own agency."

A murmuring among the Lynches. A habitual agreement. Like an *amen* or a *praise God*. Like a hymn they'd been singing their whole lives.

"I have devoted my life to this company," Zachariah said. He was leading Joel around the perimeter of the room, gesturing at the stars outside the glass. "I have tried to have what might be called a fulfilling existence. Tried to have it all. Work. Family. Space for art and culture. Some dreams."

The old man turned to face Joel. In the dark, the buttons and switches on his breathing cuirass glowed and pulsed. "What I've learned is that no one can have it all." His smile stretched wide and pale in the dark. "You can have it all, but not all at once."

Joel frowned. "I'm not sure what you're saying."

"I'm saying that I'm retiring," Zachariah told him. "I'm saying that the time has come. The future I envisioned has taken too long to arrive. It's time I made a transfer. Never enter a position without first designing your own exit strategy, Joel. Once you have it in place, you can run things the way you want without fearing the consequences. That's the only way to innovate, in this world."

"Exit strategy?" Joel cast his gaze to his brothers and sisters. They all looked elsewhere. Each of them held a picture in a frame. The images in the frames flickered: Zachariah old, then Zachariah young. Zachariah sick, then Zachariah healed. His whole history was told in those icons carried by his older, more devoted children. "Transfer?"

"Don't look at them, look at me," Zachariah murmured. "I'm the one who has put you in this position. You're my heir! You're the future of this company!"

"But, Dad . . ." Joel looked at his father, and then at the iron lung in the centre of the room, under the massive skylight. "Dad . . ."

"I'll still be your father," Zachariah said. His rubbery lips pulled back into a gleeful smile. His prefab teeth gleamed unnaturally white. "If anything, I'll be an even better father. I'll be able-bodied. I'll be prepared to travel with you, to help you make decisions, to help you chart a course for this company. But I'll also finally be able to have my own life. I'll have a fresh start. And some day, so will you."

"You mean a hundred years from now," Joel said, flatly. "You mean after that?"

"We've all made sacrifices," his sister Katherine said. The icon of her father glowed in her hands. "It would have been easier to take the company public. But we wanted—we needed—something different. And now it's your turn to give something up."

"This is the future," Paris said.

"It's not like Daniel was a real person," London added. "Not really. We *made* him, Joel. We had him built. Like a doll."

"An action figure," Silas rumbled. And they all laughed. Hwa's stomach flipped over. Dr. Smith had tried to tell them. Project Changeling. An avatar. A sleeve. They had built him to their specifications, raised him up and made him comfortable, like a sacrificial lamb. And now it was time for slaughter.

"We must not laugh at Daniel," Zachariah said, gently. "He's been very obedient, until now. Quite the model employee. It's just this young woman that's turned his head."

Hwa shut her eyes. It was her fault. If she had only wanted him less. Needed him less. She forced her head back into the game. Joel had asked her up here for a reason. And it was with Joel, she realized now, that her loyalty lay. The rest of the Lynches could go fuck themselves.

Joel stared at his siblings. He looked at his father. He reached over and brushed something from the old man's collar. Then he leaned over and hugged him. The two of them stood together for some time.

"Hwa," Joel said, in a clear voice.

"She revealed the truth to me," Zachariah said, patting Joel on the back. "She showed me what I needed to do. Why I needed to move now, and not later. To strike while the iron was hot."

"Hwa, save Daniel." Joel was still embracing his father. He held tight. "Hwa, save him. Save him now."

"Yes, b'y," Hwa muttered.

She charged the two of them. She pulled Joel off his father, and pushed him behind her with one arm while her other reached out and clocked Zachariah right in the face. Let him try to transfer his consciousness when he wasn't even conscious. See how well that worked out, for the old man.

Zachariah Lynch wove on his feet. Only his cuirass held him upright, standing on his knees like a puppet whose strings weren't entirely cut. "Joel . . ." he murmured through blood. "You can't see the future that's coming . . ."

"You didn't see me coming, either," Hwa said, and levelled a devastating kick to his ancient body. He fell like a sack of autumn leaves. She turned to Joel. The boy stared at the old man. Then he looked at his siblings. As one, they rose from their seats. The other Lynches stared at Hwa and Joel. For the first time all night, it occurred to Hwa to wonder about prison. She knelt. Zachariah still had a pulse. "He's alive."

"Shame," Katherine whispered. "Fucking megalomaniacal prick. Roko's Basilisk. Honestly. It's like he never left the cult."

"He was crazy," Silas said. "I loved him, but he was fucking nuts."

"Well said," Paris Lynch said, pulling his jacket straight. "I must say, Joel, for a first official executive decision, you're doing extremely well. We won't forget this, anytime soon. Naturally we'll be helping you with the transition, now that Father's health has taken such a rapid decline." He winked at Hwa.

His twin, London, tossed the icon toward the centre of the room. The others quickly joined it. She shook her head as though to clear it. The other Lynches pricked up their ears, identical in their mannerism of listening. "Oh dear. Is that screaming? From downstairs?"

"Happy Halloween," Silas said, and raised his glass.

Joel ran. Hwa followed.

· · ·

"Joel!"

He was running much faster, these days. She had only a moment to be pleased about that before the crowd crushed her against one wall. She ran against the current of crying teenagers heading upstairs. They sobbed and tripped on their trains and tails as Hwa moved downstairs. She watched Joel weaving through them, getting further ahead of her, his footwork quicker and more graceful after only a few weeks of training. Prefect tried to tell her something but it was so loud, on the stairwell, echoing with feet and cursing and frantic pings. Her specs flooded with information on each student and she ripped them off, jammed them down her collar. She rode the handrail the last few steps, dashing out onto the dance floor.

Joel was there, with Dr. Carlino. He looked like he was asleep. The older man cradled him in his arms.

"Get away from him!"

Hwa shoved the doctor out of the way with a body check. She picked up Joel and felt his skin. Still warm. Pulse still good. Breathing even. "Joel. Joel, come on, b'y. What's happened?"

"I have a killswitch," Dr. Carlino was saying. He looked at her with dead eyes. The cameras were off. Black. Empty.

"Fuck you." Hwa blinked hard. She threaded her arms under Joel's shoulders. She had carried him once. She could carry him again. She knelt. Prepared herself for a fireman's carry. Looked up.

A drop of blood splashed on her upturned face.

"For moments like these," Dr. Carlino said, "a killswitch is the best thing."

Eileen hung from the ceiling in ribbons. Her skin was a parody of crepe paper, stretched and curled like old-fashioned party decorations along the rafters. Her eyes were gone. Her lips were a rose. Not a real rose, but one made of flesh, as though her face had suddenly decided to bloom instead of smiling or laughing or crying or screaming, which she must have done.

She must have screamed so much. So hard. In so much pain.

Like Hwa was doing, now.

More blood dripped down. It fell warm on Hwa's cheeks like tears. Some pattered across Joel's face and she wiped it off, frantically covering his face with her hand and his limp body with her coiled one. *He shouldn't be stained,* she thought. *Not like me.*

How had he done it?

Where had he found the time?

Daniel had been dancing with her. From the moment Eileen left the room. Her eyes had never left him.

"Daniel," she heard herself say. "Daniel. Daniel. DanielDaniel-Daniel."

"I'm coming," he said, in her bones. *"Just stay where you are. Don't move. I'll be right there, Hwa. Hwa?"*

Her body started to shake. It whispered up her right side first, a slackening, a sudden lack of control, the terrible awareness of not being able to stop it, of not being able to stop anything, of not being able to do anything, of all the things she could not and would never do. How time stretched out in that moment, the moment between consciousness and arrest, between tragic event and brain event. Was that how it was for Eileen? For Sabrina? For Layne? For Calliope? Had the final moment stretched out into an infinite agony?

Was that Hell?

Warm darkness covered her eyes. Warm arms wrapped her and Joel up. Warm lips in her hair.

Daniel.

"I'm here," he said.

The seizure ripped through her.

PART THREE

NOVEMBER

16

Daughter

"Would this fit you?"

Sunny held up a sheer black wrap dress. "It's see-through," Hwa said. "I don't want it."

Sunny clicked her tongue. She tossed the dress on the *leave* pile. The *leave* pile was a hell of a lot smaller than the *take* pile and the *maybe* pile. Hwa looked at the closet. They weren't even close to done. She suspected that her mother's closet might actually be connected to a subspace pocket the universe had labelled COLD WATER WASH; LIKE COLOURS.

"The people from the Benevolent Irish Society are going to be here in two hours to collect stuff," Hwa reminded her. "Why can't I help you?"

"You don't know where anything is," Sunny said. "I can't ask you to find anything, because you don't know where I put things. I have a system."

An avalanche of mesh and velour and feathers poured out of the closet. "Some system."

Sunny stood up straight. She pointed at Hwa. "Don't fucking start. Don't even fucking start. If the Lynches were actually able to *catch* this crazy motherfucker, I wouldn't even be in this position."

Hwa looked at the piles of clothes. The boxes of dishes. Why was Sunny even packing dishes? She barely ate anything, anymore.

"If you'd voted for the Lysistrata strategy—"

"I didn't join a union so I could strike. I joined for the fucking pension." Sunny wadded up a pile of pink lace and threw it on the *maybe* pile. "I work like everybody else in this town. As hard as I can for as long as I can."

"I know."

Sunny turned up the drama as she pawed through more piles of stuff. There appeared to be no organization whatsoever. Storage devices on top of clothes on top of old tax records on top of rolls of towels. Over twenty years of total chaos strewn across the floor of the living room. Hwa couldn't even see the coffee table, anymore. She wasn't sure that what she was perched on was even a chair, under all the clothes.

"I hate moving," Sunny said.

"Yeah." Hwa spotted a Christmas card she'd made in pre-kindergarten sandwiched between the pages of an artisanal blown glass dildo catalogue. She decided not to mention it. "Moving sucks."

"Is that why you're staying? Or is it your *boss*?" Sunny arched an eyebrow. "Is he making it worth your while to stay?"

"Mom!" Hwa buried her face in her hands. "We haven't . . . We don't . . . He's my boss."

"Never stopped me and Tae-kyung's father," Sunny said. "He was my manager. It's the same thing."

Time to change the subject. "Will your place in Calgary even have enough room for all this stuff?"

"Of course it will. It's Alberta. Big sky country."

"That's Montana."

"Whatever. It's the mainland." Sunny stood up and stretched. She bent at the waist and Hwa heard all the pops in her spine as the muscles finally relaxed and the vertebrae found alignment. Sunny's hands traced through the wreckage, pushing aside old cookbooks until her hands lit on a box. Before she even opened her mouth, Hwa knew Sunny was about to switch tongues.

<<Do you want these?>>

"What are they?"

<<Photos.>>

"Of me?" Hwa asked. "And Tae-kyung?"

Sunny shook her head. It was a tiny movement, like the jerk of a fish on a line. "No. They're of me. Do you want them?"

"What, they're like your publicity shots? Because I can go online and see those. And besides, I thought you sold all of them already." She gestured at the clothes. "You should be selling all this shit, too. You've still got fans. I'm sure someone, somewhere, wants your old underwear."

Sunny sucked her teeth. <<Are you done?>>

Hwa shrugged.

<<They're of me. When I was a little girl.>>

Hwa stared at the box. "Before you started working? Before you signed your first contract?"

Sunny nodded. <<Before my surgeries.>> She held the box tight to her sternum, like if she let it go for one second it might run away from her. <<Do you want them?>>

Hwa nodded. "Fine."

Slowly, Sunny handed over the box. It was a movement of her whole body. Like something in the box would die if she ever let it leave human hands. When Hwa opened it, Sunny hissed. But inside there was just an envelope secured with an elastic. The years were written on the envelope in script Hwa didn't recognize. Her grandmother's, maybe. Hwa had never met her. Hwa tucked the envelope down into her vest.

Sunny let out a deep sigh. She looked at the piles. "Take that one down," she said, pointing to the *leave* pile.

So Hwa packed up two giant garbage bags full of clothes and started down the hall. The garbage chutes were all full. Who thought it was a good idea to stuff a whole diaper bag down one of those things? Or a whole dressmaker's dummy? Everyone really was leaving town, after all. Though the end of the month was always such a disaster in Tower One. She'd have to go down a floor or two. She found the nearest set of elevators and wiped her eyes. Everyone dragging their castoffs out must have stirred up extra dust. Her eyes burned. Her sinuses burned. Something smelled awful. The clogged garbage? No. Too acrid. Not sweet enough. Almost like . . . fertilizer.

There aren't even any sniffers. Daniel had said that, about Tower One. It was why he was happy she'd moved.

A song came over the emergency intercom. An old jazz standard. Sweet. Slow. She'd heard it before. On the water. In the taxi. "Where or When"? That was the title. It autoplayed every time you passed the protest signs about the experimental reactor.

Oh, Jesus.

<<MOM!>> Maybe she would hear her. Through the doors. Over the drama. Over the song. <<MOM!>>

The contents of the garbage chute exploded. Heat washed over Hwa's face. She fell to her knees. No alarm sounded. No sprinklers came. They'd hacked the building. Must have. Fire everywhere. Tae-kyung had died this way. Just like this. Flame licked the ceiling.

Beside her, the elevators chimed open. She bolted. Too late, she saw the darkness below. The empty shaft.

She fell.

. . .

Her mouth was full of blood.

Her ears rang.

Her leg throbbed.

Her head ached.

All in all, it was like the outcome of most of her early matches.

The elevator beneath her had major cracks in it. It looked . . . crumpled. She felt like the egg in one of Mr. Branch's physics experiments. From what height did Hwa need to fall before she broke?

How much of her was broken?

She couldn't move. Couldn't breathe. Not comfortably, anyway. Was that smoke inhalation, or a collapsed lung? Did it matter?

"Prefect?"

Nothing.

"Daniel?"

Nothing.

"Joel?"

Nothing.

She was in a giant Faraday cage. Communication with the outside world was impossible. She had two options. The first was to crawl up out of the shaft, somehow. The second was to open the trapdoor on the elevator she'd landed on, and hope that something inside still worked.

It took hours. Her fingers were bloody by the time it was done.

Weakly, she pressed the emergency intercom button. Static. "Worth a try," she muttered.

Even her watch was broken. Sometimes light flitted across its spider-cracked surface, but nothing coherent or intelligible. Just blurs. And her specs hadn't lasted two minutes. All she had to her name were the clothes that had helped break her fall, and the photos Sunny had given her.

She was going to die here, probably. She had one working hand and one working leg. Every time she tried to sit up, she puked. She searched her vomit for blood, but it was hard to focus. And there wasn't much light. Just one single fluorescent coil.

This was the way she would have always gone out, she decided. She used to climb those elevator shafts like they were playground equipment. It was a dumb thing to do. Arrogant. She'd thought that just because she'd never had a bad fall that she never would. But now it was her turn. Her number had come up. She'd rolled snake eyes. Aces and eights. There was really no end to the list of appropriate metaphors, except there was no metaphor for falling down an elevator shaft during a terrorist attack and dying alone surrounded by your mom's old clothes.

She made a nest for herself.

She slept.

Sleeping was good.

It preserved oxygen.

. . .

She kept pressing the emergency call button. Nothing.

She kicked with her good leg at the walls of the elevator. Miners did that, when they were trapped in a cave-in. They had to read passages from a book on the subject in French class. *Germinal.* That was the name. At one point the men started eating pieces of leather belt and shoe to feel full. Hwa wondered if it would get that far, with her. She hoped not.

She kept kicking.

. . .

The light started to die. Whatever source it had been attached to, it was no longer attached. So she had to do the thing she'd been avoiding. Because doing it meant that things were well and truly over. That her days were numbered.

She pulled out the envelope Sunny had given her.

It was hard with one hand. But she pulled down the elastic and out spilled all the old pictures. None of them were very good. The person taking the pictures didn't really know how to take pictures. Most were blurry. Ill-composed. Taken at things like parties, without much context.

The little girl in them was profoundly plain.

Not cute.

Not magnetic.

Not remarkable.

Not in any way noteworthy.

<<Sun-hwa, 4,>> read one of them.

She'd looked just like Hwa. Like Jung-hwa, Just Hwa, Miss Go, Squirt, the miserable little bitch with the big fucking mouth. The girl without a future. Sunny had looked just like her. Before all the surgeries. Unstained, yes. But still plain. Plain and basic and not very special at all. Certainly not like a girl who would sing in a girl group. Not like a woman anyone would pay attention to, much less pay for.

No wonder Sunny hated her. She'd spent thousands of dollars doing everything she could to avoid seeing that face in the mirror every day, and then it came out of her body anyway. Only worse. Defective. Of course Sunny couldn't love her.

It wasn't an apology. But it was an explanation. And that was a damn sight more than she'd offered in the past twenty-three years.

Hwa tucked the pictures back under her collar, against her chest, and closed her eyes.

• • •

Light.
   Cold.
   Air.
   A crack in the room.

17

Lover

Snow.

Quiet and white and thick. It covered everything. She buried her face in it. Drank. Licked. Nibbled until her teeth sang with pain.

How had she gotten out of the elevator? Maybe she'd blacked out.

She swung her legs through the snow as best she could. Pulled herself along by one snowy railing that remained unbent by the blast. It felt cold and hard and good under her bare hand. She hugged it as she pulled along. Felt it wedge up under her ribs. Let it hold her up. The rail ran up the incline of the jetty and alongside the stairs as they wound up to the low-speed level of the Demasduwit Causeway. Multiple flights of them, all switching back against each other, each surface hung with a long white beard of icicles.

So many.

No boats on this side of the tower. Probably they were all on the other side, the ruined side, putting out fires. (Were there still fires?) Or rescuing people. (Were people still alive? She was still alive. But she did not feel like a person.) This far out the water had a skin of ice on it, and it was accumulating snow. Without the railing, she might have stepped onto it at any time.

"It's good there's this railing," Hwa heard herself say. "Otherwise I'd just walk out on the ice and drown."

Drowning didn't seem so bad. She'd heard it was the good way to go. You asphyxiated, and then there was nothing. Layne had asphyxiated. Drowned in her own lungs. That didn't look like a good death—the bloody pink foam oozing up out of her throat and onto the electric pink of her hair.

He'll cut you in places you don't know about, yet. The witch had said that. Under the causeway. In what Hwa had thought was the lowest place she could go.

Hwa had to physically lift her bad knee with her good hand in order to get up the stairs. Eventually she just sat down on the stairs gingerly—the ice—and started pushing backward on her good knee. It was probably for the best. She was already seeing stars. Probably being completely upright was a bad idea anyway.

"I could probably just go to sleep, right here," she said, after the second flight of stairs. "That'd be a thing to do."

When her eyes opened, she was further up the stairs.

"Ping RoFo." She pushed up another slick stair. "Prefect, get RoFo on this shit."

Prefect said nothing. Probably the system was trying to reach her in its own way. Hwa looked around for cameras. There was an ancient-looking dome, black and smooth like a shark's eye, and she waved at it. She doubted it would help. Half those things were dummies anyway. She twisted around—pain searing up her sciatic nerve from her ankle to her shoulder like someone had replaced her tendons with twisted wire hangers—to look at the rest of the stairs. Far up above was a rectangle of white light. What time was it? How long had she been in the shaft? What if everyone had evacuated?

What if she was the last one in town?

She started crab-walking as fast as she could. Her breath left little clouds of steam as it hissed between her teeth. Her knee felt fuzzy. Like someone had replaced the joints with steel wool. She started reciting "My Bonny Lies over the Ocean" to herself. Not singing it so much as breathing it, using it to keep pace.

"Bring *back*," she muttered, pushing herself up stair by stair, "bring *back*, oh bring back my bonny to *me*, to *me* . . ."

Her knee throbbed. Her tailbone ached. Her hands froze into claws. Sweat trickled down her back and pooled at the base of her spine. Then it cooled on her body and she shivered. Her teeth chattered. Without her earbud and her watch she was alone. No augments. Just meat. Just flesh and bone and blood and breath. A solitary figure crawling up the leg of the city, like a bedbug or a flea.

She pushed.

At the top of the stairwell, she rested. The gate to the stairwell formed a natural break from the wind, and she sat there for a while watching the snow whisper down. She could just barely make out Tower Three, and if she turned—oh, Christ, that hurt—she could see Tower Two only a little bit better. That was good—if it got too cold to snow, then she really could die of exposure.

Up ahead, there stood a set of blinking roadway blocks. They were yellow and black where they weren't covered in snow. And beyond them stood two columns of tents, also that special shade of caution yellow, with a snowy aisle in the middle. In the special quiet made by the snow, Hwa heard radios coughing to each other.

She was almost there before someone in a bubble coat came jogging out to meet her. He wore massive mirrorshade goggles. Both were flecked with snow.

"Where you to?" he asked. She thought she recognized his voice. "Holy shit, Hwa!"

He ripped the mirrorshades off. Underneath, Wade still had the face she'd almost broken. He hadn't left the city after all. Her vision tilted. Went sideways. At first she thought she'd fallen down. But Wade was carrying her. And running. "FATHER!"

Her vision bounced along as they cleared the roadblock. Then they were in a tent city. It smelled of instant food: oatmeal and coffee and freeze-dried orange juice. Someone cut through the crowd. Father Herlihy. The priest ushered them through the tents. The white sky turned to yellow tarp, orange cable, and dolly tracks. Someone brushed past her foot and her knee twinged and she yelped.

"Is your ankle broken?" Wade asked.

"I think my everything is broken."

He lay her down on something. It felt like a dentist's chair. Then he put a blanket on her that looked like foil. It was immediately, stunningly, blissfully warm.

"I rode an elevator in free fall," she said. "Twenty floors. Twenty floors? I don't know. Do you know in France, they don't even count the first floor?"

"DR. MANTIS! DR. MANTIS, WE NEED YOU OVER HERE RIGHT NOW!"

Dr. Mantis swooped down from the dollies. His thorax clung to the network of steel tracking rods above, but his many eyes and claws swung low to look at her.

"Miss Go!" he chirped. "Hello. What seems to be the trouble?"

"I think I have a concussion. And my knee hurts."

"She's hypothermic," Wade said.

"Oh, dear. That's not very nice, is it?"

"My mom died," Hwa said. "I think."

Dr. Mantis strobed its vision into her eyes. "You are concussed. Your knee has also sustained some damage. I am going to inject your leg with freezing to bring down the swelling. There's also a joint filler to help the cap start to seal."

A sharp pain in her knee that dulled as she breathed. She imagined the needle as the hardest thing in the wad of jelly that was her joint. Would she ever kick again? She used that leg to pivot.

"And you need to rehydrate. This is saline."

Something in her arm. A pinprick. Angel's eyes seemed so big. Father Herlihy's, too. Father Herlihy was crying. No, not crying. More like weeping. Tears streaming down his face, silently. He'd probably seen so much already. Maybe this was it for him. Maybe he was hitting the wall.

"Does she need blood?" Father Herlihy asked. "Because I could . . . I'm . . . I . . ." His hands opened and closed, as though he were already pumping his blood into her. What a strange thing to offer. How would he even know they matched?

"It's really not that bad." Hwa tried hard to focus on the father's face. Make sure he heard her. Maybe then he'd feel less bad. "I've had concussions before."

"Too many, according to your records," Dr. Mantis said. "From tae kwon do?"

"And me mum," Hwa added.

Father Herlihy ran from the tent.

She looked at Wade. "Did I say something bad?"

Dr. Mantis turned her head gently in its claws. "Look at me, please."

Outside, someone was raising his voice. Wade's huge shape rose and blocked the tent flap. The standard bouncer pose. Then a burst of illumination. A flash-pass. Credentials. Wade stood aside.

Daniel stood in the door.

"Hello, Mr. Síofra." Hwa wondered how Dr. Mantis knew. Then again, he was a robot doctor. He probably really did have eyes in the back of his head. "How are your hands?"

Daniel had his hands behind his back. "They're healing nicely. Thank you."

He came to stand beside the bed. Ducked around the sack of saline hanging from the ceiling. Took one of Hwa's hands in both of his. He said nothing. Just pressed her hand between his and blew on it, slowly, putting the warmth back in.

"You're like a bad penny," he said, after drawing another breath.

"What's a penny?"

His face cracked into a smile. He wiped one eye with the heel of his hand. "Do you want to stay here after this is done, or come back with me?"

The fireplace. That bathtub. All that vodka. The things that made it nice to have a body that bled and burnt and died. Compensation for being meat.

"That second one."

• • •

"I think I need a shower," Hwa said, when he offered to draw her a bath. "It sounds like heaven, but I don't think I can manage the tub right now. Getting in and out, I mean. I'm a little dizzy."

"Of course." Daniel reached into the shower and played with the knobs, testing the heat on his own arm. When it satisfied him, he turned back to her and looked carefully at her torn clothes. "Do you need help with those?" he asked quietly.

Hwa moved her shoulder experimentally. Pain shivered down her spine and along her sciatic nerve. "Yeah," she admitted.

Daniel knelt. He started with her socks, lifting her foot by the ankle and placing it on his knee as he unrolled them. First one, then the other. He looked up at her from the floor.

"Turn your filters up," Hwa said.

He frowned. "What filters?"

"In your eyes. The filters. So you won't see . . . me."

He stood. "Why would I not want to see you?"

She swallowed. "People edit me out," she said. "I'm ugly to look at. And I'm twice as ugly to look at, naked. I'm doing you a favour, here."

"Do you not want me to see you?"

Her mouth worked. She had been invisible—or blurred, or filtered, or hidden—for so long that whether or not she wanted to be seen rarely came up. "I don't know. But you've gone this long without seeing it—me—and you're probably better off."

"I don't know about that." Daniel looked genuinely confused. "The augments in my eyes are to help me see *more*, Hwa. Not less. I don't know what you think I see, but I have *never* edited you out."

Hwa crossed her arms across her chest. She wanted to hide. Desperately. Her hands climbed up to cover her face.

"No, don't." Daniel sounded alarmed. "Please don't do that. Don't hide. Not from me."

She started to curl in on herself. It would be better, now, to be smaller. To disappear. Daniel's hands took gentle command of her shoulders. He kept her from falling.

"I saw you the moment you collapsed, that first day," he said. "After the pain ray hit you, I cut off the camera feeds in my eyes. And I took your pulse, and I picked you up and carried you down all those stupid gangplanks. And I watched your face, and your halo, and I read everything I could about you, and I wanted them to get a doctor for you, but they wouldn't, and so I *waited,* for *hours,* and, Christ, I'm so sorry I offered you this job, Hwa. Look what it's done to you. What *I've* done to you."

His voice was thick and wet. She splayed her fingers and looked up. Tears had slipped down his face. For once, he looked exhausted. No, not exhausted. Human.

"It was selfish of me," he continued. "Selfish and arrogant and stupid. You'd have been better off if we'd never spoken to each other, after that day. If I had just left you alone. You were happy. And your friends were alive. And . . ."

Hwa let her hands fall. "You sound like you've been thinking about this a lot."

He wiped his eyes with the heel of one hand. She could just barely see the faint red tracery of wounds across the knuckles. "Yes. A lot. Over the past few days."

Hwa looked at the broken mirror hanging above the sinks. "Oh."

"I'll close my eyes," he said, and shut them. He helped her step the rest of the way out of her clothes. She stepped into the shower and hissed at the hot water on the open wounds. She twisted it down to a softer, trickling volume, and turned around. Daniel stood with his back against the cube, idly twisting a towel in his hands. Now she could ask. Now that the water was quieter and he couldn't see her.

"You . . . *wanted* to see me?"

"Yes," he said, a little too quickly.

"*All* of me?"

After a long pause, he nodded, as though to himself. "Yes," he whispered.

Maybe she just had no adrenaline left. Maybe that was how she could be so calm. Maybe shock had its benefits. "People don't really look at me that way."

The laughter pushed out of him in a rush. He aimed it at the ceiling. She watched him shake his head through the glass. "That is *completely* false. You may not have glaucoma, but you have an *enormous* blind spot."

A blind spot. Layne had said something about that, in the dream. Was this what she'd meant? Was this what one stray fragment of her subconscious had been trying to tell her?

"It's just hard to believe, is all. Name one other person."

He shrugged. "I don't know their names. I just see them looking at you. And then they see me looking at them, and they stop looking at you." He cracked his knuckles.

"Those people are staring at my face. That happens all the time. All they see is—"

"Your mouth." The back of his head thudded against the glass. Like he was trying to knock the thoughts clear of his mind. "Your mouth and your hands and your legs and your neck and how you move. How you walk. How you talk. How you fight. How you dance."

Hwa picked at the smallest point. It was easier than taking him at his word. "I don't really dance."

"You danced with me." His voice was small. "Wearing that . . . I don't know what to call it. All those buttons. I wanted to take you home with me. I *should have* taken you home with me. I should have kept you here all night."

Hwa leaned against the glass, behind him, her hands on the foggy place where his shoulders were. "And done what?"

His head turned fractionally. "Anything you wanted." She watched his throat working. "Even if it was nothing at all."

"I wouldn't . . ." She looked down at her stained leg and her scarred arm, her bland body that was only good for causing pain. "I wouldn't really be any good for that, though," she said. "It's not exactly my area of expertise."

"You think I don't know that?" He sank to the floor. "You think I didn't think about that? About how wrong this is? I wanted to *wait*. I wasn't going to tell you until after you left the company. You could make your own choice, then."

That explained some things. And it was good of him. He was right: anything further would have been wrong, even if they had been riding a razor's edge from day one. Lynch had so few boundaries, but Daniel had tried to keep this one, to hold the one line he most wanted to fall.

"So you're just a company man through and through, eh?"

"Not lately," he muttered. "I thought I owed these people something. I thought they had *saved* me. And all this time I was just their backup plan."

"So . . ." Hwa let her fingers make clear streaks in the steamed glass. "You don't really owe them anything, do you? You don't have to play by their rules, anymore. Not if you don't want."

His hands stilled. The towel was tight between them. Taut and white and trembling. "Let me look at you. Please."

Hwa stepped back under the water. She opened the shower door all the way. He scrambled to his feet, all elegance gone, and pushed in, eyes red, clothes on.

"God, Hwa," he muttered, and his mouth was on hers, on the stain, on her closed eyes, her neck, the palms of her hands when they came up, tentatively, to hold on to his shoulders. The two of them fell back against the wall of the shower and she yelped. He pulled back instantly.

"Am I hurting you?" He held her face in his hands. He looked scared. She couldn't remember the last time anyone had been afraid of hurting her. Of her actually being hurt.

"I don't know how much longer I can stand up."

His smile was so open and genuine she didn't quite recognize it. "Should we lie down?"

Hwa nodded. "I can't fall asleep, though. The doctor said."

He reached around her and shut the water off. This close, through soaking wet cotton, she could feel every inch of him. Solid but springy, like a good mat. And warmer than her own skin, warmer than the water dripping from it, almost unbearably warm. A solid wall of heat that made all of her aches but one seem very distant and unimportant. He smoothed wet hair away from her face.

"I will not let that become a problem."

. . .

She did well, for someone on the injured roster.

He went slow. Torturously slow. Drying her off, laying her down, oiling her skin, inspecting all the hurts and scars and rough patches with gentle fingers and a gentler mouth. The time she fell through a glass coffee table. The time a chain cut open her hand. The time Sunny pressed her arm to a hot oven. Belts and medals and trophies. The bullet wound, still pink and glossy. He looked so reverent, so transported, she had to shut her eyes. He let her lie still and quiet and then asked, quietly, if things would feel fairer if he were naked too. She nodded into the pillows and heard him kicking things away. When he was done she felt his weight dip the mattress behind her. He reached for her tentatively and waited until she said it was okay for him to come closer. And even then he just held her, skin to skin, speaking softly into her neck only when he thought she might be falling asleep.

"I'm sorry," Hwa said. "I'm sorry I'm not . . . doing more."

"I don't need to be seduced, Hwa. I just need you to be here, and alive, and safe, with me." He paused, and nestled a little closer. He stroked down the length of her spine, his touch reminding her of the way his voice would shiver down her nerves when he spoke to her from across town. This was better. Much better. "Although if there's anything in particular you feel that you need, please tell me."

Hwa rolled over to face him. It was more difficult than she had imagined it would be. Her body didn't want to move. And her eyes didn't want to meet his. "I just . . ." She swallowed. "I just don't know how to do this."

He gathered himself around her carefully. "You don't have to do anything. You've had a shock. You've had three months of shock.

It's all right if you want to process that. It's probably healthy. But it's also all right if you want to forget about it, for a little while."

She deliberated on that for a while with her eye in the hollow of his collarbone and her ear tuned to his breathing. If he noticed the tears on his skin from her good eye, he said nothing about it. Just kept up that light but insistent stroking down her back until she felt boneless.

He flinched when she finally reached for him. Gasped and shuddered like she was made of fire. It felt like triumph, like finding an opening in an opponent's defenses. "All you ever had to do was this," he whispered. "I made that rule for myself. That if you started it, I'd finish it."

"Like a fight." Hwa's mind drifted with her hands. She wished it were a fight. Then she would know the moves. She would know how to read him. She froze, and he froze with her, a question on his face. "That night. You came back here with vodka. Chilled vodka. Because you knew I was here waiting."

"Yes." He smiled and buried his face in her neck. "I hoped that night might end differently."

"Like this one?"

"Like this one. If you want."

She did want. She wanted powerfully.

It didn't hurt as much as she thought it would. It did hurt. But after all the other pains she'd endured, the vague knee-scraping sensation between her legs wasn't all that bad. Stranger was the sense of her muscles accommodating something new. It felt like things had shifted around in there. That was weird, until it wasn't. But it was still better than *not* having the sensation—by the time he was inside her, he'd cranked her past the point of words. So she didn't ask for what she wanted and simply flipped him over and climbed on top.

She thought that would have done a number on her back, but she felt fine. Better than fine, actually. A little bowlegged, but even her knee felt better. Apparently a bunch of dopamine rushes were good for the body's healing process. They certainly left her sleepy. And this time, he let her close her eyes.

But when she woke, Daniel was gone.

Hwa put on his shirt and moved out into the living room. There was a martini shaker and two glasses out, but Daniel wasn't there. She went back to the washroom. Maybe the bathtub. But no. Gone. And no note.

Maybe he was getting food. But they had plenty of stuff in the fridge. *They.* That was weird. They were a *them* now. Bizarre. And yet also not. Since meeting, they'd spent almost every day together in one way or the other. This was just another way of being together. The bizarre thing was him wanting her.

"Prefect?"

"Ready."

"Prefect, where is Daniel?"

A long pause.

"He is with Joel, on the top floor of this tower."

"Is Joel all right?"

"He is with Calliope and Layne and Sabrina and Eileen."

Adrenaline poured ice water over her dopamine haze. Fear replaced buzz. Her afterglow flickered out and went dark.

"What?"

"We are all here, Hwa. Waiting."

18

Killer

Enter the Dragon.

That was the first thought Hwa had, when she saw this room for the first time. How many times had she and Tae-kyung watched that movie? Sure, it was jeet kun do and not tae kwon do, but Bruce Lee was a classic. Hell, they'd even watched *Game of Death* a few times.

"Joel?" She wandered through the halls of mirror and crystal. "Daniel?"

Why hadn't Joel been evacuated? Surely the city as a whole wasn't safe any longer. Who knew what other explosives might be lurking in the Slocum spheres? Ridiculous to think it was all over.

"Joel?" She made her voice bigger. "Joel!"

Her voice echoed back to her across the crystals. Hwa watched multiple versions of herself advance slowly across the room. "Daniel?"

And as though the room had heard her command, one of the facets opened and out spilled Daniel, with Joel in tow. Daniel was holding a gun. He was pointing it at Mr. Branch.

"He's gone insane!" Branch held his arms a little higher and splayed his fingers a little wider. "His switch has flipped!"

Cold adrenaline washed over Hwa's nerves. "What?"

"Don't listen to him, Hwa. It's him. It's Branch. *He's the one.*"

"Daniel, why are you doing this?" Joel looked scared. His eyes were red. He'd been crying. "Just put the gun down. You don't have to hurt anybody."

"Joel, he wants to kill you," Daniel said. "He's the one who sent the death threats."

"No, Joel! It's Daniel!" Branch pointed. His eyes were wild. He was panicked. "It's *Daniel* who wants to hurt you. Daniel's been skullcapped. From the inside. Your brothers and sisters sent him to eliminate you. That's why they needed you to get your father out of the way. He was the only one protecting you. They were hoping all along you'd get Hwa to kill him. Luckily she had plenty of good motivation."

Joel turned the colour of the modelling clay they used in art class. Not just pale, but grey. Ashen. Those were real words for real colours, Hwa realized. People actually looked that way when they were afraid. And Joel was terrified.

Joel turned slowly to face Hwa. His voice cracked. "What . . . What is he talking about?"

Hwa shook her head. She kept her hands open. She moved very slowly toward him. "It's nothing. He doesn't know what he's talking about."

"She believes in conspiracy theories," Branch said. "About your family. About the company. She thinks the company blew the rig, three years ago."

How would Branch know that? She had told exactly one person about her suspicions. Bile rose in her throat. She turned to Daniel. Daniel was shaking his head. "It wasn't me," he whispered. "Hwa, please believe me, I promise you, I didn't tell any of them anything, I—"

"What is he saying?" Joel asked.

"It was never about you, Joel. She came back to work just so she could get revenge for her brother. Why else would she return, after being shot?"

And just like that, Hwa remembered who had sent her out in the hallway that day.

Is it true one of the other teachers here has a type? She had thought Coach Brandvold and Coach Alexander meant Moliter. But they hadn't. They were talking about Branch.

Branch had cancelled science club the day they found Sabrina. She'd been alive, when they found her. Her only available timeslot was in the afternoon. After school.

"Oh, my God," Hwa murmured. "It was you. You son of a bitch, it was you."

She ran at him. Joel threw himself at her. He body-checked her and she stumbled back on her bad knees. From the floor, she watched as Joel raised his fists and assumed the standing position. The fighting stance. The one Angel had tried so hard to drill into him, when the summer was freshly dead and snow was just a distant hope.

"No." She shook her head. "No, Joel. I won't do that. I won't fight you."

"Are we really friends?" Joel asked. "Or are you just using me?"

Why are we friends? Are we really friends? Why do you try so hard?

She stood up. "Yes, Joel," she said. "We're friends. I am really your friend. I would still be your friend, even if there was no money."

"No. *I'm* your friend. Your *only* friend. She's just the woman who's paid to spend time with you and make you feel like she's your friend. Just like her mother, the whore."

"Fuck you," Daniel said, and fired the gun. Hwa hit the floor. Joel hit the floor. Branch wove on his feet for a moment. Then he, too, hit the floor. Only Daniel remained standing. Hwa started crawling toward Joel, who had covered his head with his hands.

"Joel," Hwa said. The boy whimpered. She kept crawling. "Come on over here, b'y. Come on, now."

On the floor, Branch began to twitch. Hwa smelled something terrible. Something like the smell of Sandro's lab. She watched Branch sit up and shake off the wound that had sheared off half his face.

"That's why Daniel hired her," Branch continued, as though nothing had happened. His voice was a thick burble of blood and rot. "Didn't you ever find it a little strange that you had a full-time bodyguard when Security was right there?"

"Daniel," Hwa murmured. "Daniel, run, now."

He fired, instead. He kept firing. And Branch kept moving.

"Joel. Listen to me. Get up. Come over here. Right now."

Joel said nothing. He looked confused. Terrified. Frustrated. This was too much for him, Hwa realized. Too much for his implant. He was overloading. He hid his face, but Hwa saw it in all his other reflections. The way his face crumpled. The way he stared at the floor. He was shutting down.

"Joel." Hwa reached out for him desperately. "Come here. It's going to be okay."

"No, Joel." Branch walked over, reached down, and put a hand on his shoulder. "It's not."

And then he picked up the boy by his collar and threw him against one wall. The crystal crunched and cracked where his body hit it. Shards went everywhere. Hwa ran. Daniel ran. Daniel got there first. She watched as Branch picked him up and threw him to the floor. Blood pooled under him.

Hwa skidded to a stop. She stood between them, facing Branch. "Which one will it be, Miss Go?" Branch asked. "The boy, or the man? The leader, or the follower? The meal ticket, or the pity lay?"

Hwa heard herself panting. She had never wanted to kill someone so much in her whole life. Not even Lázló, in that elevator. The desire to hurt Branch was so strong it made her shake. She felt it from the roots of her hair to the tips of her fingers. She made herself walk to Joel's prone body. Made herself kneel down. Made herself feel for a pulse. Made it look calm.

"Get up," she kept saying. Like she were coaching him out of a particularly bad fall on the mat. "Get up, b'y, come on, get up. . . ."

"When he wakes up, I'm going to tell him that *you* did all this," Branch said. "I'm going to be that one special teacher that changes his life. The one who shapes him and moulds him into who he's supposed to be."

Hwa felt a pulse. Joel wasn't conscious, but he also wasn't bleeding too heavily. That was good. She assessed: her comms were out. Her watch was gone. But the doors were still opening for her.

"You always think you're going to change him," Branch said. "Every single time, you think you're the one who's going to make him see how the other half lives. But in the end, he always makes the right choice. My brothers and I, we inspire him to become the person he's meant to be."

He's right behind you. Him and all his brothers.

"I don't know what you're on about," Hwa said.

"Of course you don't. You never do. Not until it's too late."

She had to play for time. Get him to go all supervillain on her and waste some time while she figured out a plan. Get to Daniel. Get to the gun. See if there were more rounds. "Brothers?" she asked. "What brothers?"

Branch waved a hand. He looked like a lord of the manor gesturing for quiet. As he gestured, the crystal walls of the room began to flicker. Some brightened. Some dimmed. In all of them was another version of Branch. In some he was a man. In others he was a woman. In still others, he was a machine: all glowing eyes and gleaming skin. In another he had six arms, each of which floated around him on delicate monofilament, twisting this way and that.

"These are my brothers," he said. "And all of my brothers share the corporate mission. To extend the Lynch brand into the stars."

Hwa sat back on her haunches. Beside her, the Branch brother in the crystal gave her a little wave, and pulled back a smile that revealed row upon row of long, black teeth.

"The science club project," Hwa said. "The generation ship."

"Precisely." Branch smiled. He steepled his fingers. As he did, the fingers themselves appeared to blur. Like parts of his body were winking out of existence. "I'm going to inspire him. Mould him. Shape him. Send his mind spinning on that sense of wonder that you're all so very vulnerable to. It's so absurdly easy to exploit. All you need are some images of nebulae and some swelling violins and suddenly everyone believes in manifest destiny again."

He—if it was a he, if he was a person, and not a thing, not some otherworldly awfulness that could send death threats from between layers of time, oh Jesus, oh Christ, oh Sacred Heart of Mary—had a point.

"You want to teach Joel? Great. But this"—she waved a hand at the broken crystal and blood—"this isn't teaching."

"Oh, I don't want to simply *teach* Joel," Branch said. "I want to change the course of his life. And the history of this company." He smiled thinly. "And that's much easier to do when you're not in the picture."

"I don't get it."

Branch moved his hand again, and the crystals flickered once more. Only now they showed Hwa. Many versions of Hwa. All of them younger. All of them stained. All of them dead. Some were burnt. Some were beaten. Some rotted in the girders underneath New Arcadia, their eyes plucked by gulls. Some floated down past barnacles and sharks to the bloodworms down below. Some had never been born at all. Hwa knew this because those crystals showed Tae-kyung in them. An adult Tae-kyung. With medals and a championship belt and a pretty girl who even looked Korean and cute babies, and her mother was there, Sunny was there, too, and she was fat and grey and her eyes wrinkled when she smiled and she didn't seem to give a damn. They were all so much happier. So much better off without her.

"Have you ever wondered why, deep down, you hate yourself and you want to die?" Branch asked. "It's because you're supposed to be dead."

Hwa blinked tears away from her eyes. It was Lynch's crystal ball all over again. She'd come back to right where she'd started: on her knees, weeping, seeing things that weren't real. Couldn't be real.

"Time is a panopticon, to me and my brothers," Branch said. "Like this tower. We stand in the centre, and we open the doors we need. But this door, the door to New Arcadia, is the most important one."

"Oh yeah?" Hwa made herself stand. All her sisters stared at her from their crystals. Maybe this same moment, this same fight, was playing out somewhere else, in some other time, forever. "How's that?"

"Everything that shapes the vision, mission, and strategic plan of the Lynch corporation for the next two hundred years happens here. And it starts when your influence on Joel ends. When you leave the company."

Hwa frowned. She started circling the room. Examining all her corpses. When her body was swollen or broken or burnt, her stain didn't seem like such a big deal. It mattered a whole lot less when she was dead. Why had Lynch's crystal ball shown her a face that was unstained? Whose future was that?

"But I would never leave Joel."

The crystals abruptly turned black. Branch grinned widely. His hands clapped together. "I know! You don't! You never do! You stick it out, right until the very end! That was the mistake my brothers all made. They tried *killing* you. But that was worse! He loves you even more after you die!" His eyes glowed. "But I knew, if I could only *discredit* you, *weaken* you, *make* you leave Joel behind . . ."

"You wanted me to quit." Her hands became fists. "That's why you killed my friends. You wanted me to quit."

"I thought you would, you know. You did, after Calliope. And then you came back. Too bad, really. The others would be alive now, if you hadn't."

Hwa wanted to throw up. She didn't. She took a deep breath. Thought of the master control room. All the buttons. All the switches. The big glassy screens with Branch on them, shrinking and shrinking to a single bright point and fading to black.

The master control room. Of course.

"You're very hard to predict, though. No implants. So little data to work with. We have trouble modelling your simulation."

Hwa couldn't look at Daniel's neck. She reached for his hand, instead. It was limp. Lifeless. She began feeling around for the gun. "What happens if I quit?"

"The human race, if you can still call it that, leaves this planet thanks to Joel's corporate policy. He makes long-haul space travel a priority after his father's death. Everything he learns in this town about long-term habitation in an isolated, closed system informs his intentions as a CEO. He finds the right people and makes the right investments. He becomes a captain of industry like his father before him. He doubles his father's lifespan, creating a dynasty that lives in the stars for thousands of years after his passing. And all because he doesn't get stuck *here,* in the *mud,* on the *Earth,* imprisoned by gravity and lack of vision. Your lack of vision."

Hwa's fingers clasped around the gun. She had never fired one before. It felt heavy. Cold.

"And if I don't quit?"

Branch's mouth formed a thin line. "The company fails. Joel disbands it. The Lynch name dies on this planet."

"So you're just here to protect an investment?"

Branch smiled. In the crystal walls, his brothers wavered into being and smiled right along with him. Insects. Beasts. Ghosts. Monsters. All with the same huge, hungry smile. A salesman smile.

"Don't you understand?" Branch asked. "We *are* the Lynches. We are Joel's descendants. We are Tactics, just like you. We carry out Strategy's plans for the company by making targeted investments in the past. We have expanded our holdings, embraced the true potential of our technologies, and travelled the stars. It was there that we began to prototype long-haul travel solutions. And that was how we developed the doorways into a viable infrastructure. And once we realized how far we could go, the influence we could have . . ." Branch held his arms wide. "We may not be human anymore, but we still have a family business to maintain."

The laugh erupted from her throat before she could stop it. Her shoulders shook. Her body trembled. She laughed until it became tears. She couldn't stop.

"What's so funny?"

"You." She fought to get control of her breathing. "You're what's funny. You fucking idiot." She looked at Joel. "Joel *chose* to help me.

He *chose* to, after you started killing my friends. He *wanted* to. Because he's *that good*. He's *that kind*. And the harder you tried to pull us apart, the closer he stuck to me."

Hwa picked up the gun with both hands. She reached down into Daniel's waistband and felt more ammo tucked into his belt. She held the gun steady between her knees, in the shelter of Daniel's body. "You poor dumb sack of ones and zeroes." She raised the gun, loaded now. "You watched the data so close, you forgot there was a fucking *person* underneath."

She fired once at him, and ran for him. She aimed a kick squarely at his head. Suddenly she was in the air. Swinging in a circle like a child's toy. He was so strong. Unbelievably so. His hand was around her ankle, and his hand felt like this room: made of diamond. Branch was just like this awful place, a hollow creature of silicon and hate, hard and brilliant and cold. Not sapient. Not necessarily. Not even conscious, maybe. Just running a program. Just living the brand identity to the fullest. The future Zachariah Lynch had longed for was here, and it was this monstrous inhuman thing, this venture capital pitch made flesh.

"Did you think that would work?"

"Worth a shot."

"You—"

One side of his face ripped away. It bubbled and twisted and stretched, trying to repair itself. Suddenly he wore another face— Daniel's. Then Joel's. Then Zachariah's. Then her mother's. And Sabrina's. And Layne's. And Calliope's. And Eileen's. He stumbled back. He let Hwa go. She smelled rot. Cancer. It oozed out of him. Inside he was meat, the same as she. All his power was just appearance.

A muffled voice told her to leave.

It said to go now.

It said it had not lifted her out of perdition in that elevator shaft just to see her die here.

It said it would hold this monster, as long as it could.

It said it was sorry.

For her brother.

For the city.

It said to keep running.

So she did.

. . .

Hwa barely felt anything in her knee or her shoulder as she bounced along the waves to the reactor lab. The ice was soft and slushy out here, offering no real resistance to the boat she'd commandeered.

It was snowing again. It came down fast and hard and sideways, meaning she couldn't drive as quickly as she wanted. She only noticed the other boat following her because of the tiny orange flag waving through the storm in her wake. Branch. Cold wind whistled along her teeth, her gums. It should have hurt. It didn't.

She pulled up alongside the reactor and jumped from the boat to the dock without slipping on the thick coating of ice that sheeted it. Ice overhung all the lights, dispersing their violet glow in a weak and watery way. She wasn't even conscious of the cold.

There was a padlock on the lab. Hwa shot it off. She yanked the door open. Left it yawning open behind her. Let him know where she was. Let him follow. The lab doors all opened for her. All she had to do was wave them open. And when she snapped her fingers, the emergency klaxon shut off.

It was like having the keys to the city. Like being a new person. A person with status. All the doors that should have remained closed now opened. Finally, the school doors would open for her, if she only tried.

She had no time to try.

It was also like being back on in the ring. A series of decisions, each calculated to inflict maximum damage in the shortest amount of time available. Everything else just faded into a dull noise. There was only this moment, this choice. It was so simple. So blessedly, mercifully simple. She had missed it.

"Prefect."

"*Ready.*"

"Prefect, I need a Bullet."

The minisub burbled up to the surface like a bout of bad tacos; Hwa spun its hatch open with ease. It should have been heavy. Difficult. It wasn't. She was like one of those mothers who could lift a car off her baby. It felt like being drunk. That special slick easiness that came with not feeling the full extent of her extremities. Maybe that was what came with knowing some extra-dimensional asshole was after you. You just stopped caring.

Hwa watched the boat as it came closer. Then she turned to look at the city. She wished for a moment that the towers were not shrouded in snow, that ice was not clinging to every surface. She tried to think of it in sunlight, under a blue sky, on a calm sea. And with that, she jumped into the submersible.

Inside the minisub, the winch worked just as easily. She spun it shut until a little green light came on in the shape of a happy face. She gave it the thumbs-up. The sub's controls were simple: an accelerator, a joystick, and a brake. It was tethered to the big milkshake straw, so it couldn't go very far. The other instruments on the panel were for lights and cameras, and Hwa had no need of those.

Down.

Down.

Down.

The reactor loomed large in the sub's bubble. She initiated a docking program, and watched as an animation in the instrument panel told her how close she was to making contact. It all looked vaguely obscene. But finally the connection was made, the airlock threaded, and she could emerge.

The interior of the reactor control room looked exactly as its designers had promised. An empty tube led to a blank-walled room. The room had a few displays hanging in it. They showed the reactor's progress and the safety of the core. It was already up and running in a small state; to increase gain you'd have to draw more ions from the seawater and layer in more tritium. But from here, you could vent the whole thing, or seal it off entirely.

The door clanged open. Right on schedule.

"This room." Branch looked for the door that had just been behind him a minute ago. Now it was a smooth expanse of blank white wall. "What room is this?"

"It's *my* room." Hwa closed her eyes. Raised her hands. Hoped it would work. Hoped that her instinct was right. And began to draw.

Master control room. All the buttons. All the switches. The door locking behind you. The door no one can open but you. A perfectly secure room where you are in complete and total control. Where you have all the power. It will respond entirely to your commands, and only your commands. It will behave exactly as you need, because this is an emergency. Because no one should be down here. If someone is down here, it's because the city of New Arcadia and everyone who lives there is in profound danger.

When she opened her eyes it was there. The master control room. The one she and Tae-kyung had always talked about. It hummed. It peeped. It sang. The displays showed the reactor in ancient pixellated fonts, pale green on black. It was big and clunky and the buttons were so bright they were hot to the touch. And right there, right under her thumb, was a big fat red one. The Button. The one in every doomsday scenario. The one you weren't supposed to push. Ever.

"Your problem is, you got no imagination," Hwa said, and pushed it.

INITIATING OVERLOAD, the displays read.

Branch looked at the displays. He looked at her. "You'll die."

Hwa shook her head. She swept away all the buttons. Now all the arrays were nothing but grey plastic. "No. *We* will die. Here. In the mud. Together."

Branch made a noise unlike any Hwa had ever heard before. It was a long, resonant screech of frustration. He threw himself at the walls. He kicked and punched and launched himself at their smooth white surfaces. Nothing opened for him.

"You have to be organic," Hwa said. "Sorry."

He vaulted over a rack of useless arrays and grabbed her by the shoulders. He shook her. "End it! End it now!"

Hwa started to laugh. It was the strangest thing. She should have been scared. Terrified. Anxious. Worried, a little, about all her skin falling off and her eyes melting out of her skull. But there was something so delightful about Branch's frustration. He wore the same expression as a cat trying to fight itself in a mirror. Vicious and angry, but still profoundly stupid. The longer she thought about it, the longer she laughed. Slowly, he let her go. She started hiccuping, and he slapped her.

"Aye." Hwa rolled her neck. The slap barely hurt at all. "Aye, b'y. Really? That's the best you've got?"

He punched her in the stomach. It hurt, but not as badly as it might have. Maybe he was already weakening, somehow. If anything could do that to him, it was probably fusion radiation. At least, she hoped so.

"You poor dumb fuck." She spat at him. "You really fucked this one up, b'y. No gold watch for you. They can just take your Murder Drone of the Month plaque right off the wall."

Branch wiped the blood and bile away from his mouth. "You're just as spiteful and stupid and small as your sisters," he said. "You have no vision. No sense of what you're doing."

Hwa grinned through the blood. She let her accent go just as thick. "Aye? The way I reckon, a chain of murders, a major explosion, and a reactor leak t'ain't so great for business. So youse tell me: how's Joel supposed to make all the right investments, when he's busy cleaning up this mess? Won't all that capital be lining the pockets of all yourn attorneys? Because I think the people of this town have grounds for a lawsuit. I think the Lynches might have to sell some assets. Maybe do a wee reshuffling."

Branch backed away. He turned to the countdown clock on the display. Sat down on a swivel chair. Watched the numbers. Watched the levels of radiation climb up to the red zone on the meter.

"I've failed," Branch said. "I'm a failure."

"You get used to it. Eventually. In my experience."

"I failed to close the loop," he murmured. "The strange loop."

"Eh?"

"You are the strange loop," he said. "The disorder. In the litera-ture, in the modules, when we train for this job, that is how you are called. The Disorder. Our job is to order you."

Hwa still had a chuckle in her bruised stomach. "Cute. I'll tell me mum about that one. When I see her in Hell." She watched the levels climbing up and up and up. She didn't feel so good. She felt hot. Feverish. Slow. Branch flickered like a candle. Like he was hav-ing trouble keeping himself together. She had to ask him now. "Why the birthday cards?"

"What?"

"The threats," Hwa said. "Why did you send the death threats if you knew they'd hire me to protect Joel?"

Branch gave her his last condescending sneer. "We didn't."

The room filled with light.

19

Human

A sonorous voice. Beautiful. Rich and deep and perfect.

"I have of late, (but wherefore I know not) lost all my mirth, forgone all custom of exercises; and indeed, it goes so heavily with my disposition; that this goodly frame the earth, seems to me a sterile promontory; this most excellent canopy the air, look you, this brave o'er hanging firmament, this majestical roof, fretted with golden fire: why, it appeareth no other thing to me, than a foul and pestilent congregation of vapours. What a piece of work is a man! How noble in reason, how infinite in faculty! In form and moving how express and admirable! In action how like an Angel! In apprehension how like a god! The beauty of the world! The paragon of animals! And yet to me, what is this quintessence of dust?"

Her eyes opened.

Nail sat beside her, reading from a compact. His hair was a little longer than she remembered, but otherwise he looked exactly the same. Pale and handsome and well-dressed. Like nothing in the world had changed.

"Oh. You're awake. The Mistress will be pleased."

Her mouth worked.

"Yes. This is my speaking voice. I gave it to her as part of our contract. But she is lending it to you, during your convalescence. We are allowed to converse. Would you like some water?"

She was alive.

That was impossible.

She nodded.

Hwa had only the vaguest notion of how radiation poisoning was supposed to work, but she knew she wasn't supposed to still have skin. Or eyes. Or a working set of lungs. She was supposed to be a puddle of melted human cheese. That was how it worked. Right?

The water tasted wonderful.

"Thank . . . you. . . ."

"It is quite all right. I live to serve."

Hwa stretched her feet experimentally. Wiggled her toes. Tapped her fingers on the sheet. She was in the Lynch clinic. Had to be. There was an orchid on the table beside her bed, and a cut-crystal tumbler full of water. The lighting was soft. She waited for the turn of a windmill blade. None came. Five, then. She wrapped her left hand around the glass and brought the glass to her lips.

Her hand was wrong.

Clean.

Pure.

Unstained.

The tumbler trembled in her hand.

"Yes." Nail retrieved the tumbler. He set it down on the tray beside her bed. "About that."

"How . . . ?"

"They're not sure. I've heard them talking, and they seem to think you're augmented. With augments they've never seen before."

A white room story. That was the term. Mr. Bartel used it for one of the clichés they were supposed to avoid during the creative writing unit. A woman wakes up alone in a white room, unsure of how she got there or even who she is. He was really excited about just getting to teach one of those creative writing units at all. He promised he would edit an anthology of their stories. Share it with other schools. Put the whole thing in the library system where other students in the province could read it. Hwa realized she had never turned in her assignment on time. Never even turned it in at all. Just shrugged and turned the other way and focused on the killings. She probably had so much homework to make up. She was never going to graduate.

She held out her left arm.

Still clean.

She swung her legs off the bed. Stretched them out.

Her left leg was just as pale as her right one.

"Shall I fetch someone?" Nail asked.

"I guess." He stood, and Hwa grabbed awkwardly for his elbow. He turned. "Thanks," she said. "Thanks for sharing your voice with me."

He beamed. "Rusty will be glad to know you are well. All the Mistress has asked for since you've been here is pasta and bread and cake. It was as though she were trying to eat your weight in comfort food."

He left. The floor was soft under her feet. Moss. The longer she stood there, the more moss grew around her feet, blue and springy and pleasantly alkaline smelling. She dug her toes into it. Flexed her feet. Her ankles had no pop. Her joints felt flexible and loose.

It was her eyes, she decided. Her eyes were probably so damaged that she had needed new ones. Or contacts. Some ocular prosthesis that would replace her melted eyes and also allow the installation of a filtered perspective. So of course her stain was filtered out. She ran her right hand over her left arm. It didn't feel any different. One long smooth line of skin. No change in density. Just skin. Just like the other arm.

She pinched it. Scratched it. Watched her fingernails drag down the skin, leaving little white lines in their wake. Studiously avoided the mirror near the door.

Branch couldn't be right.

She wouldn't allow him to be right.

Why would I edit it out?

A sound bubbled up to her mouth. A whimper.

"It's your eyes," she whispered. "It's just your eyes. You're still you."

Her mother's face would *not* be waiting for her in the mirror.

"Stop being such a pussy."

She walked over to the mirror with eyes closed. Trailed her fingers along the wall. Stopped when they hit the frame. Entered walking position. Her muscles still felt the same. Light. Ready.

"Ready."

In the mirror stood the woman she had seen in the crystal ball. Behind her stood Daniel.

. . .

"A beard?" Hwa asked. "Really?"

He stroked his chin. "You don't like it? I sort of like it. I stopped shaving once you were in here. There wasn't much point."

"I thought you were dead. I *saw* you . . ." Her voice shook. It was suddenly much deeper and rougher than it should have been. She reached out and touched the beard gingerly. "I watched you *break*. . . ."

"I know." He kissed the tips of her fingers. "I watched the footage."

She spoke in a whisper. "How is this possible? How is *any* of this possible?"

Daniel snapped his fingers at the mirror. She turned to look, and a swarm of machines appeared in the glass. They swam along in schools, occasionally pausing to wriggle their hairs at something before continuing along their merry way. As she watched, one of them divided in two.

"Those look like . . ." Her head tilted. "The Krebs. But different." She enlarged the image. They were so delicate. So fluid. Like animals. Like cells. Like something alive.

"That's your blood," he said. "Our blood."

She looked up at him. "What?"

He pushed the Krebs to one side and opened another file. This one had his name on it. The same machines were gathering in thick clusters. When he zoomed out, he revealed his rib cage and collarbone. The pattern of broken bones. The machines were literally scabbing over his bones to mend them.

"If you'd just waited," he said. "Just a minute a longer."

Hwa shut her eyes. "Please don't make me look at that."

"All right." She felt him move behind her. "It's all right. You can look."

When her eyes opened, the Krebs were back. But he zoomed the image out, and there was her name on top of the file. The Krebs danced across her whole body. But they were most densely concentrated in the place where her stain used to be. They were there, under her skin, a second stain of proteins and circuits.

Hwa swallowed. "How? When?" She turned to him. "Did you let them do this? Why would you let them do this?"

She didn't bother waiting for an answer. She left the mirror. Found the water glass. Drained it. Contemplated the orchid in its slender vase. It looked like something Séverine would have chosen.

"It's not that simple," he was saying. "But if you want to blame me, you can. You should. It is my fault. If you want to think of it as a fault. As a bad thing."

He laced their hands together. "I didn't mean to give this to you. I didn't think it could . . . spread. I've been careful. Every single time. Until now. But with you, with us . . ."

Heat flooded her. The memory was still fresh, as though it had happened the night before and not months ago. "Are you saying what I think you're saying?"

He nodded. "I didn't donate my regimen to you. The Krebs were already working on you, when we found your body. As far as the doctors can tell, they entered you when we . . ." He pursed his lips. "Probably through a tear in your tissues. You did bleed. A little. That's all it takes, apparently."

"You *spread it* to me?"

He nodded. "You're a changeling, now. Like me."

Just like Branch. Just like how he'd spread his devices to Calliope and Sabrina and Eileen. What had killed them had saved her. It wasn't fair. It wasn't fucking fair at all. She didn't deserve to be alive, any more than they deserved to be dead. And if she had chosen differently, if she had just held out, they would still be alive. For the first time since their deaths, she allowed herself to miss them. She would never hear Eileen's gossip. She would never nag Layne about a BDJ question. She would never see the delighted triumph in Sabrina's eyes as she landed a solid punch on the heavybag. They were gone and it was her fault. Both her eyes filled with tears. Daniel reached for her and she scrubbed the tears away before he could say anything.

Hwa sighed. "So you're saying my whole body is full of proprietary technology? You're saying I went from pure organic to . . ." She opened her stainless hands. They felt stronger than before. The skin was more even than she remembered. Softer. More elastic. The nails smooth. Almost buffed. No calcium deposits. No scars. No swollen knuckles. No evidence that she'd ever been a fighter. No evidence she'd ever been the person she knew herself to be. "To whatever the fuck this is."

He shook his head. "Don't. Don't do this." He leaned his forehead against hers. "Please don't do this."

"Everything that made me who I am is gone."

"Is that what you think?" He kissed her very gently, over her left eye. "That all you are is a disorder?"

"Branch said I was."

Hwa sank down to the bed. Looked at the orchid in its glass. The order of the room. Everything clean. Nothing out of place. She *was* disorder. That was Branch's whole point. She was the disorder that needed to be ordered. The one hair out of place. The one thing set askew in the plan. That was what set her apart. What made her, in some incredibly fucked-up way, special in their cosmic simulation. A wild card. A black swan. Lightning in a bottle. And for a moment, just knowing that had been enough. Even if it wasn't meant to last. Even if her life was about to end. All the seizures. All the bullshit. It was all worth it. Just to be the one who stuck it to that bastard. It was the kind of death that deep down she'd always wanted. And now she was alive.

"He said, I'm the only one to make it. That I'm not even supposed to be here. All the others . . ."

"The others?"

"The other versions of me. In other times, I guess. Other branches of possibility. He said I'm the only one who's ever made it."

Daniel reached up. He held her face in his hands. "Then clearly, this is the best of all possible worlds." He kissed her forehead.

She was about to tease him for being such a sap, but as she drew breath to do so, the door opened. Joel stood there, flanked by Silas, Katherine, and members of his staff. He wore a suit. He looked taller. Broader. How long had it been? What else had changed?

"Miss Go," he said in measured tones. Hwa's heart sank. A few weeks without her and he'd become the vessel his father had always wanted. Perhaps Branch really had won. "I think we can continue this conversation later," he told his siblings. "Silas, can you please tell your people to put that order through?"

"Sure thing," Silas said.

"Katherine, I want to go over the infrastructure tour, on the Iceland trip," Joel said. "I need to know who is who. Can we go over that, later, please?"

"Of course," Katherine told him.

Joel nodded. He smiled pleasantly. "Thank you. You've both been a big help lately. I really appreciate it."

His older siblings shared a look. He was trying so hard. But they weren't giving him the same stares they had when Hwa first met them. Maybe that had changed, too. After all, he had done them a great favour, unburdening them of their father. The door closed behind Joel, and then it was just the three of them.

His corporate face broke into a huge smile.

Then he ran to Hwa's bedside. Threw his arms around her. He almost knocked her over. It took her a moment to understand why he was trembling. Joel, the boy who never cried, the boy who had witnessed school shootings and serial murders without tears or frustration, was weeping. Loudly. Hotly. Right into her neck.

"Hush, now, don't cry, b'y," she muttered, through her own tears. Her lips found his hair. It very much needed a wash; he'd started using some sort of awful product in it. She kept kissing it anyway. Inhaling the scent of his scalp. His living flesh. She had promised to protect every single hair on his head, and he was healthy and safe; he was the best of his line; he was the first of her students to surpass her, in his own way.

"I thought you might never wake up," he said.

"Makes two of us," Hwa said.

"I've never been that scared, ever."

"I know, b'y, I know."

"You can't get hurt. Not ever again. I won't allow it."

Hwa set her chin on his shoulder. She tested her new smile on the boy's skin. It was rougher than she remembered. Just the faintest traces of beard were coming in. "Aye. We'll see about that." She stroked his back. "Iceland, eh?"

Joel pulled back. He was beaming. "You'll love it. There are barely any trees."

"And baths everywhere," Daniel added.

"If you stay with Lynch, that is," Joel said. "You are staying with us, right? Hwa? With the company?"

Hwa tilted her head. "And if I said no?"

Joel's mouth worked. She watched him struggle to put a good face on things. "Then I'd still ask you as my friend," he said. "Because I think you'd like it. And because I don't want to be—to travel, I mean—alone."

Hwa smiled. It was not the best of all possible worlds. Not by a long shot. But it was hers. And she could make it better.

ACKNOWLEDGMENTS

This book belongs to a lot of people. First, there is David Nickle, who listened as I talked about it at length, and somehow still wanted to marry me when it was finished. Then there is my agent, Monica Pacheco, who believed in the concept. Then there is Charlie Stross, who first introduced this book to my editors, Patrick Nielsen Hayden and Miriam Weinberg. And naturally there are Patrick and Miriam, who worked hard to make this book as special as we knew it could be.

I also want to thank Cory Doctorow and Kathryn Cramer for their timely career advice (and their patience doling it out), and Jessica Langer, the Atlantic Council, Nesta, Data & Society, and Kate Heartfield for giving me work to do while I worked on this book. Thanks are also due to Neil Clarke and Dave Maass, both of whom allowed me to publish stories from this universe in their anthologies.

Also I want to thank Anthony Townsend, Melissa Gira Grant, Terri-Jean Bedford, Morgan M. Page, Mistress Matisse, Tina Horn, Andrew Nikiforuk, and many others whose writing and advocacy helped me to understand the reality (and the future) of urban planning, sex work, and energy.